18/16

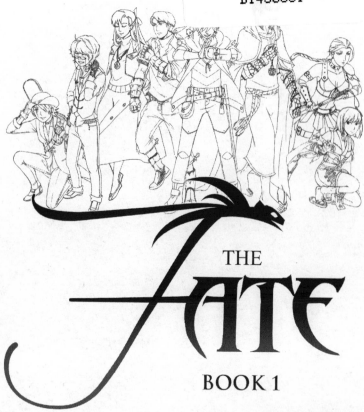

THE

Fate

BOOK 1

J O H N   K O

The Fate: Book 1
TOURNAMENT WYSTERIA

by John Ko

Published by IDealSoul Stories

Copyright © 2015 by John Ko

ISBN-10: 0997341718
ISBN-13: 978-0-9973417-1-3

First Edition (Print)

Character Illustrations © Rizky Viyanriri & John Ko
Cover Graphic © John Ko
The Fate Logo © John Ko
Crests and Graphics © John Ko

Feedback on this book is welcome at:
TheFate@idealsoul.com

PRINTED IN THE UNITED STATES OF AMERICA

Always in my thoughts
My Mother, Myung Ja Ko
Evan, Rockwell & Elise Ko

IN MEMORY OF:
Gregory Alcendor

SPECIAL THANKS TO:
Hyung Ko | Jenny & Giorgio Ko | Jeffrey & Pelin Wolak | Ahn Ly
Chris & Yoonhee Chang | Timmy & Hanh Nguyen | Brian & Ragni Walker
Jamal Anthony Sally & Louis Lee Jr. | Tony & David Pujals
Grove Printing (Tommy, Steve & Gina) | Beth Balmanno | V.T.

CHAPTER 1

THE FATE

[THE VILLAGE OF THE SLATE CLAN]

The boy stares at the path before him, waiting ...

It comes as a whisper—a sigh of the sun, the sea, and all that lies beyond. It caresses the back of his neck and traces swirls down his arms. It rustles for a moment and then the wind roars.

The trees of the mountain bend low. Leaf and limb begin to sway, grasping at one another. And as the wind rushes overhead, a sky full of leaves begins to dance, casting shadows that race up the mountainside. And just behind, the boy gives chase—leaping, scrambling, even scurrying where he must. Each step screams his intention. Each stride tells no lie. *I will not lose.*

The young man moves as he is, and he is nothing but truth ... unless, a smile can tell a lie. That's the one thing you'll find he's never without, a grin so practiced it's almost sincere. It's simply the way Terrantius Slate, the first Fate in a hundred years, is and always will be.

Not that anyone would care ... well, at least that he's a Fate, anyway. These days you'd be hard-pressed to find anyone in the Three Kingdoms of Wysteria who's ever even heard of one. But that's what he is and that's what he calls himself—the Fate.

And at this very moment, the Fate has the wind's shadow at his fingertips. So he dives. Extended to his fullest, he dips his hand into the shimmering lights.

For the briefest of moments, they dance across the palm of his hand before he shuts his fingers tight.

As if offended, the wind gives a final push before gusting upwards and away, but not without leaving one last gift. Leaves, newly freed, rain down upon the trail ahead. Whatever it is he may've caught is already forgotten as he releases his grasp and grips the stick at his side. Rather long and ever so slightly curved, its enamel gleams darkly, begging to be drawn.

He complies, lunging like lightning's kiss upon a tree too lofty. The Fate stutters in mid-step, from a blur to a flash— too fast for the untrained eye to follow—his form materializes impossibly far ahead.

Without so much as a look back, he swings his weapon sharply, clearing it of skewered leaves. In his wake, the trail remains clear. He picks the speckled red one that almost got away from his thick, black hair and flicks it to the side.

Before the leaf can reach its final resting place, the chase has already moved on. Though, it isn't until halfway up the mountain trail that he manages to tuck the unwilling switch back into one of his low-hanging belts. The pair of loose leather straps doesn't actually help much in holding up his pants, but they do manage to hold other things. Lined with tiny compartments, pockets, pouches and even a slot for his Stick—the belts make for good storage.

Fortunately, his pants, along with the rest of his outfit, are well-fitted, with the exception of his hood, which hangs loosely from the back of his short, sleeveless coat.

The Fate has run this trail countless times, but today … *something is just not right,* he thinks, finding himself stroking the back of his head. *My Warrior's Braid …*

It used to just get in the way, but he wore it with pride anyway. After all, he is the youngest of the Slate Clan to have earned one. But when he awoke this morning, his Warrior's Braid was gone.

"Stupid Princess Rules," the Fate mutters, remembering the note left in explanation.

Tracking the sun, the Fate knows he should make it just in time. It'd be a shame to miss the sunset at his spot. *Well, it is hers, too,* he supposes.

Even though he was the one to discover the way up the cliff, it's Ieiri who spends the most time up there. Wondering if that's where she's been hiding all day, a sudden "Squeak," disturbs his thoughts. It's not an unfamiliar sound in the forest, but this particular one feels out of place. Thinking not much of it, he heads deeper into the thick brush.

Leaves blackened by dusk swallow him whole. Twilight streams through tiny gaps in the canopy like so many stars. But there's only one speck of light that will lead him out of here. He finds the twinkle easily enough and follows it until it turns into the sky.

The trees part to reveal the sun hanging just above the ocean's grasp. But from much closer on the little overhang comes a, "Squeak, Squeak, Squeak!"

There, standing right on his favorite rock is ... *a chipmunk?* It continues to chatter away, only growing more incessant as he approaches.

"Eh?" responds the Fate in unexpected dismay. "Excuse me, Mister Chipmunk, but that is my rock you are standing on." His hopes of it simply darting away are dashed when the little creature glares back at him, unflinching.

"There are plenty of other nice rocks all around, but that one is mine. I watch the sunset from it every day and tomorrow ... well, tomorrow, I will be going away."

The little fellow doesn't seem to care one bit.

With a sigh, the Fate lowers himself eye-to-eye with the chipmunk and adamantly declares, "My rock!" Having wasted enough precious time, the boy attempts to ever so gently sweep the troublesome creature off of his rock. Which ends with ...

"Ouch, ow, ow!" The Fate hops around waving a barely bleeding finger. "You bit me! With those vicious spikes!" He sticks his pricked pinky into his mouth.

The chipmunk lets out a string of squeaks, all the while refusing to budge. After an unusually thoughtful moment, the Fate whispers to himself, "Well, if the wind cannot blow the man's coat off ..."

He figures a warmer approach may be in order. The young man bows his head and apologizes in Han. "Mian Hae," he says. They say the animals of the forest are more apt to understand Han. After all, it was the language most heard in these lands for over a thousand years.

"That was wrong of me," he admits, holding up empty hands as a sign of peace. His right, the bitten one, is covered by a fingerless, wool glove that looks innocent enough, but the heavily armored, left one—not so much. He quickly lowers his hands to his sides.

"Hmm ..." the Fate wonders aloud, tilting his head and scrunching his brow in examination of the small, striped creature. The chipmunk is full-grown with a thick, shiny coat ready for the coming cold. A rather ordinary chipmunk, nothing unusual, at all, except for that it's on his rock. In the end, he decides, *a chipmunk is just a chipmunk. And they are all bound to like the same sort of things.*

He removes a roughly woven pouch from his belt and begins to work it open. "Do you know what this is?" he asks, pulling out a small, round object.

"Yes, it is a nut, but it is no ordinary nut. This one has a Tear Shard embedded in it, and I know the Technique to make it grow. Would you like to see?"

The chipmunk edges closer. The Fate scoops up a chunk of soft earth and places the seed into the ground. He intones loudly, "Seed Craft: Bloom Hodo Nut."

A small stalk pushes through the dirt, which quickly

straightens and sends smaller stems branching outward. Tiny leaves sprout as the stems harden and brown. The barely visible dots between its leaves grow into compact buds, which open and fall to the ground. In a matter of moments, a small, nut-bearing bush stands there, soaking up the last of the sunlight.

The Fate leaves the chipmunk to its inspection of a particularly large nut and climbs, triumphant, onto his favorite rock. And he's just in time.

The ocean looks particularly blue today, accented by bleeding ribbons of crimson stretching from either side of the blinding sun. High above, the vibrant sky holds a scattering of clouds that fly directly towards the sinking golden light. He reaches out with his hand and watches the colors stream through his fingers.

The Fate's ready to leave it all behind, but he had to see it one more time, the sunset at his—their favorite spot.

"Did you know that when the red and yellow of the sun kisses the blue of the ocean, it makes every color imaginable?" he asks no one in particular. He's quite fond of the sight and nowhere is it as magnificent as here. "Things like this matter too—I will have to remember that," he says, surprising himself. Watching sunsets has never been part of the plan, but perhaps when he's finished ...

Always the believer, he closes his eyes without losing sight of that dream. "I suppose, I will have to return here someday," he declares. "So, look forward to that day, the day I have captained a team to one hundred victories on the Tournament. To this, I swear."

The conjured bush has already begun to wither. Its shriveled leaves fall and swirl away with evening's first breeze.

Leaning over, supported by his armored left hand, the Fate begins to sift through the dirt. Absorbed in his search for the original nut, he doesn't notice the chipmunk poking around his bracer and gauntlet.

Tiny flecks of dust lift off the ground and fly towards the iron gauntlet. Constructed of solid plates, the armored glove looms gigantic against the boy's slim form. But it's the bracer and the tear-shaped stone set within that draws the chipmunk's interest.

Abruptly, the Fate's Tearstone flashes brightly. And for an instant, he glimpses the inconceivable—the chipmunk stands there surrounded in glowing armor.

"That is what happened," the Fate explains to the tiny wrinkled man sitting cross-legged across from him. When the Head of the Slate Clan fails to respond, the boy wonders if the Elder is just mulling the story over or if he's really fallen asleep.

Since the Elder's eyes are closed anyway, the Fate leans in for a closer look.

Just as he gets close enough to be mesmerized by how the hair growing from the Elder's nose sways in and out with his slow breathing, the Head of the Village snorts loudly. The Fate scampers back to his floor mat.

The Elder raises an eyebrow without opening his eyes. The Fate knows that it's his patience which is in question—as always. The young man smiles innocently, his eyes darting back and forth in search of something, anything of interest. But there's nothing he hasn't seen a hundred times before.

The one-room home of the Elder is large. He'll give it that much, but otherwise, it's no different from the dozen others of the village. All of them constructed of wood, lacquered dark with bean oil and tiled in thin-cut stone. Each home built directly onto one of the many granite terraces lining the cliffs of the beach.

He looks up and begins counting the thick wooden beams. There are nine of them, just as there was the day before. *But something is different today,* he realizes. *Where is everybody?* The Elder's House should be bustling during the late meal hour.

The Fate twists to and fro looking for a clue before realizing they're all outside, preparing for the feast—his Farewell Feast.

"What happened after you saw the chipmunk glow?" the Elder asks him, snapping him from his thoughts.

"He climbed up my back and into my hood. I think he did something very bad in there. It stinks now. When I tried to grab him, he bit me with his vicious, spiky teeth a second time." The Fate imitates menacingly with his fingers.

"I see, and he is still in there?" asks the amused Elder, pointing at the pile of cloth in the young man's lap.

"Yes, sir." The Fate nods. "He has been quiet ever since. I believe that he may be sleeping."

The Elder goes silent again. With his tally of the beams already complete, the Fate begins counting the veins running through the warm, stone floor.

Finally, the Elder opens his eyes and asks, "Are you absolutely sure that there was no one else present?"

"I am sure," the Fate says. "There was no one else."

"Then, it can only be one thing, really—you have somehow bound that chipmunk as your Tear Companion. There are no other reasonable explanations for what you have seen. The glow must have been his Spectral Armor," the Elder tells him. "Unfortunately, an answer like that just leads to more questions. Can you feel the beast's presence?"

"No ... maybe. I know he is in there," answers the Fate, gesturing to the dark jumble of cloth. *Could that really have been Spectral Armor?* he wonders.

"I realize you might have had other plans, but still, you should be more excited. Having a Tear Companion is a wonderful thing. Even after all these years my greatest joy is watching—

no, *feeling*—Cheo soar, wind between her teeth and the sun at her back. And it's all thanks to this," the Elder says, patting the amber-colored, tear-shaped stone hanging from his neck.

"But does it not require training with a properly matched and newly born beast to make it your Tear Companion? This chipmunk looks somewhat old and I am far from sure that we are properly matched," the Fate says.

"True, that is how it's done today. With the abundance of Master Level Trainers and all of our domesticated breeds, gaining a Tear Companion is usually quite a simple task," the Elder says. "But, before it became so convenient, the most reliable method for acquiring a Tear Pet was to perform a ritual *Calling*."

"A Calling?" the Fate asks. "I have never performed one of those."

"It is what it is. I've never heard of it being accomplished in recent times, but the old stories make mention of the ritual. From what I understand, a Calling is a truly unique Technique, one in which a Tear-User applies thought and desire to attract a kindred spirit. The ritual would be performed daily until attracting a compatible soul. This could take years to complete and even then many a Calling went unfulfilled. Which is of course why it fell out of favor generations ago," the Elder explains. "Boy, you say he found you on the cliff. That is a place you go to daily, is it not?"

"Yes, Ieiri and I go up there when we are done training for the day."

"What do you and Ieiri do up there?" asks the Elder. "Daily?"

"Sit?" The Fate shrugs. "It is quiet and big up there. We go together, but we do not really speak much once we are up there. I feel alone, small, but if I hold up my hand, I can block out the whole sun. Then there is only one voice, my voice, and I listen to it for awhile."

The Elder looks at him with sad eyes. "Perhaps you have been meditating on the whereabouts of Old Claw? Has your usual unwavering confidence blinded me of a troubled heart?"

"No, Elder, I do not worry over my Old Man. I know he is fine," the Fate tries to explain. "It is just that ... he should be here for this. At least, I always thought he would be. But I cannot wait any longer."

"It was thoughtful of you to try, but really you should have reported months ago for the Tournaments with the others who turn seventeen this year. Instead, you've been going to the same spot at the same time every day and wishing for the return of Old Claw. Perhaps the chipmunk mistook this for a Calling."

"But I never called for a pet or even wanted one. Especially, something so useless ..."

"Squeeeeeak!" The pile of cloth comes to life revealing an angrily chattering chipmunk.

The Elder chuckles. "I think you've upset him."

"He has been like this since we first met," says the Fate, covering his ears.

A few moments later, the old man says in surprise, "Oh my, this is not just some random chattering. He is performing a ritual vow."

"What ..." The Fate starts to say before the Elder waves him off. The chipmunk scurries back and forth, continuing his shrill squeaking.

"This is serious, boy. He is performing a Death Vow," the Master Level Trainer says. The chipmunk stops and stares at the Fate. He uncurls a tiny claw and points it first at the Fate, then at himself. The chipmunk squeaks loudly once and is quiet.

"I do not think he likes me very much."

"It's much more than just that," says the Elder. "You have to be more careful with your words. Now, you're stuck with a pet that just took a Death Vow to never fight by your side. Although, I'm not quite sure what the single claw meant."

"A Death Vow? But why?"

"Your guess is as good as mine, but it is almost as if he did it in response to our conversation."

"So you think he understands what we say?" asks the Fate.

"I wouldn't go that far; the most intelligent within my herd may learn up to a hundred commands. It is a rare animal indeed that can follow a conversation," the Elder replies. "He has obviously received some sort of training. Even more so than that, good fortune seems to shine down upon him."

"Why do you say that?"

"If he had shown up even a day later, you would have already departed for the Tournaments. Speaking of which, we better get going. You can't very well be late to your own Farewell Feast."

"I am sorry for not understanding you," the Fate says to the chipmunk. "It is just that I have been preparing a very long time for tomorrow and you are not part of the plan. But I am thankful that you answered my Calling and you are welcome to accompany me, even if you will be of no use."

The chipmunk takes a deep breath as if to unleash another slew of squeaks, but instead, holds his tiny tongue and disappears back into the bundle of cloth.

"Are you fine with this?" the Elder asks.

"It changes nothing," the Fate says.

"But you will not be able to bind another. Were you not planning on someday making Nalda your Tear Companion?"

"I was, but that was for Nalda, not for me. I was not going to bind her until I returned from the Tournaments," the Fate says. "I am sorry, Elder. I was planning on leaving Nalda behind. I have left 1,460 molasses drops individually wrapped in wax paper in a wooden box at the stables. If you would be so kind as to give her one each morning, I would be most grateful."

"Nalda's a special filly, but I always knew that she was not special enough for you. I'm sure she'll miss you greatly, but the molasses will be sure to make it easier on her." The Elder's eyes twinkle at the thought before another comes to mind. "Is that why you built the fish pond?"

"No, I do not think horses like fish. Perhaps, she could use it to swim, but ..."

"No, no, boy. Did you build the pond to honor your Old Man's promise? The one he made when you two joined the Clan?"

"My Old Man brings fish to those who cannot get their own, so I do so when he cannot. But who will when I cannot?"

The teary-eyed Elder laughs loudly. "I should have known the most unusual boy that I have ever met would become a truly remarkable man."

"I just wanted to ensure you old folks kept getting your fish."

"You can leave us all the fish in the ocean, but I promise you this; it won't keep us from missing you. The world is in for a quite a treat ..."

"That is good; everyone likes treats."

The Elder laughs again before remembering one final thing. "There is one more thing you should know; have you heard of Natural Kindred?"

The Fate shakes his head.

"It is a theory that everyone has a perfect, complimentary soul, a Natural Kindred. It is said when Natural Kindred fight together that they have no weakness. Each of the three Beast Tamers to have sat upon the Conqueror's Throne, including the Three Kingdom's own Lady Seo, are said to be Natural Kindred. And it's believed that a Calling would often produce this type of match."

"Natural Kindred ..." says the Fate. "Is it because we both like the same type of rocks?" He reaches over to pet the pile of cloth the chipmunk is hiding in, only to quickly pull his hand away.

"Did you see that? He tried to bite me, again!"

The Elder wipes away a tear and asks, "Who will make me laugh when you are gone? I know how much you hate it, but may I give you a hug, boy?"

"If you must," the Fate says with no joy in his voice.

"I must."

CHAPTER 2
RISER
[THE ROAD TO GREENWOOD]

Flanked by silvery fields, a girl with ill intentions blocks the path. It's the one day a year these pale wildflowers bloom, blanketing the hills as far as the eye can see. *It's like being surrounded in storm clouds,* she thinks, watching the blossoms whip back and forth. *A perfect day for a revolution!*

Esperanza Enyo double-checks her bindings, ensuring that each section of her leather armor fits skintight. Although, today it seems that her armor is just not fitting as well it should be. And she knows just who to blame: Ieiri Skyshadow.

Her stomach growls. "Nuts and berries are not a proper meal," she grumbles, recalling last night's dinner *and* today's breakfast. "I'm a warrior in training. I need a real meal, a hot meal. How about a little meat? A fish, a hen, some pork chops even! Can't a growing girl at least get some eggs? I should have walked right past her yesterday."

Upon seeing the slight figure on the road the day before, Esperanza actually thought her youngest teammate had come to welcome her. She should've known better. Just like she should've known better than to accept that girl's innocent-sounding challenge. *Unforgivable!*

But that was yesterday and today she would be using the very same trick on the Captain. Giggling uncontrollably at the thought of it, she fails to hear the approaching footsteps.

"Riser, is that you?" calls out the Fate, his head cresting the low hill ahead. Silhouetted by the early morning sun, he rumbles closer, pulling a handcart packed past its brim.

Off guard, she wonders aloud, "Oppa?" The Daughters are the oldest clan, and he is the only person in the whole world she would call Oppa, or big brother. As for what he calls her, Esperanza has always been honored by her goddess-given name, but she doesn't mind being called Riser by her teammates. After all, it does describe her quite well.

"I did not know if that was you laughing or some devilish fiend," the Fate says, making an impish face. "What are you doing out here? Why did you not come to the village as you were supposed to?"

"I was catching up with Ieiri, but that doesn't matter. You know why I'm here," says the green-eyed warrior as she tightens the straps of her gauntlet. "I, Riser, Esperanza, current First Daughter of Enyo, Wind Dancer of Ehecthal challenge you, The Fate, Terrantius of the Slate, for leadership of the Team."

The Fate drops the handles of his small wagon and scans the area. "Going up and down all these hills sure is hard work. They were getting rather boring, however, since I already knew what would be on the other side. At least, up until that last one ..."

"Fate," growls Riser, cutting him off before he can prattle on anymore.

"Riser, you do not turn seventeen for another week. You cannot challenge me, yet," he says, trying to knead a kink out his shoulder. "It is easy for me to remember; we have the same birthday, after all."

"Just because you were born a year earlier is no excuse. Today, a couple days from now, what does it matter? Stop avoiding the inevitable, Fate. We're going to fight for the right to be Captain, right here, right now."

"If you insist, I will fight you. It seems I already have my

Terra Boots on," the Fate answers, tapping his metal plated Battle Boots. "Please try not to hit the cart, all my things are in there. Esperanza, current First Daughter of Enyo, I accept your challenge."

She pounds fist to palm and grins. "Count it off."

The Fate begins to raise his hood, showering himself with cracked shells, nuts, berries, and an angry chipmunk.

"What is that?" she asks, annoyed at the delay.

"A chipmunk."

"And just why do you have a chipmunk in your hood?"

The Fate shrugs. "Because, sometimes he glows."

"Are you telling me, you bound that thing?"

"I did not do anything. He did," he says, pointing at the chipmunk scurrying through his hair.

Unbelievable, she thinks, wondering just how she let the fool boy become her Captain. *At least, that's about to change.* "Just be careful with him. A Tournament is no place for a creature like that."

"I will see to it that he comes to no harm," he says.

She almost feels sorry for him. It takes many years of training with the right pet for it to be worth sharing your Spectral Armor with. At least, he doesn't have to use the chipmunk in battle.

"Enough stalling." She grips the sheath hanging from her skirt of blades. A Light Blue stone glimmers between her fingers like a piece of sky paled by cloudy whites.

"Very well, *three,*" he says, brushing the remaining debris from his hair.

"*Two.*"

He pulls out his Stick. The switch trembles in anticipation.

Riser grabs the handle of her best friend, Ehecthal. A centuries-old katana, he is one of the Fabled Five Instruments of the Champion of the Fight, Enyo, the Delighter of Discord.

"*One.*" The Fate closes his eyes, and his ever-present smile widens into something else.

He presses the Earth Aspect Tearstone on his wrist activating a golden glow. A brilliant yellow line shoots straight out of the spreading light and splits in two. The glimmering lines climb up his arm and past his shoulders.

As the faint golden light grows to envelop his entire body, the gleaming yellow line continues to multiply until fully tracing out his Spectral Armor.

Now, she can hit the fool boy as much as she wants. The glowing armor surrounding him represents his Life and will absorb attacks by another Crier. He'll still feel it, but at least, his flesh will know no harm. *Pain will do just fine.*

At her touch, the Light Blue Tear on her sheath blooms. An azure glow encases the Daughter in her own ethereal armor.

When she opens her eyes, she sees a whole new world, *The Color World.* Between her and her opponent, flow beams of light of every color. They're known as Prismatic Lines; streaking lights that connect all things living. Ranging from blue, yellow to red and every color in between, they fly past her at incredible speeds, so fast that she can barely distinguish one from another. Except for the Light Blue ones: those she can pick out with her eyes closed. After all, she is a Tear Fighter—or Crier, as they like to say—with an affinity for Air, and Light Blue is more than just her Color, it is her birthright.

"Go!" The Fate snaps his eyes open. The way he leans forward makes it seem as if he's looking up at her. But it feels more like he's looking through her. It takes all her will to meet his stare—eyes so sharp they cut away everything but the moment. The past is forgotten; the future unwritten; all that matters is now. Her hairs stand on end and the blood rushes through her. It feels good.

"Thank you," he whispers, just as he does before every match.

"Rise," she grunts in response. Wind gusts from her boots and she is lifted off the ground. A few inches are all the Wind Dancer needs to execute her first form.

From twenty paces, he charges. Riser closes her eyes in

concentration and spins down into a crouch. The blades of her skirt slice outward before quieting like chimes after the wind. Kneeling in midair with her back toward her charging opponent, she waits.

The faintest of breezes flickers through her hair signaling the exact moment for the performance to begin. Without hesitation, she picks the proper Prismatic Line and begins her assault. The Daughter unwinds, launching herself toward her opponent with the momentum of a hundred winds.

"Earth Leap," he answers, activating his boots. The road shakes as he dives straight for her.

"Sing, Flying Serpent Ehecthal," Riser screams, drawing her sword so clean it rings silent against her scabbard.

A moment before contact, the Fate says ever so softly, "Iron Blood Block." The enamel covering his Stick darkens to a pitch-black before absorbing the attack. With a flick of his wrist he strikes a glancing counter blow. She jumps clear before he can land another.

His weapon returns to its natural shade with a tiny new addition. A small sprout has sprung from its bloodthirsty tip.

The Wind Dancer rises once again. "So you can block the first verse, now? No matter, I have some new Techniques, too," she says, clenching her gauntleted offhand. Like the Fate, she only wears one, and like his, there is a circular emblem inscribed on its back. But that is where the similarities end. Where his is dark and solid, hers is sleek and constructed of light blue-steel. As she lowers her hand, the wind hisses through the many small vents covering her Air Gauntlet.

Riser knows better than to expect a response. If she's learned anything in the last couple years she's been on his team, it's that the Fate doesn't talk during a fight. He'll name his Techs—he has to—but that's not really talking. The only conversation he's interested in during a fight begins with his Stick and ends with aching spots all over his opponent.

Quick as a shiver, he's upon her. The Daughter reaches out and squeezes the Air itself. "Air Block," she says, pulling her hand back and leaving a chunk of condensed Air behind that is solid to the touch.

The Fate studies the oncoming Block of Air carefully. He's never seen one before. It's a new Tech, one Esperanza dedicated a good portion of the past months mastering. But still, it's too much to expect for him to simply crash into it.

A moment before impact, he thrusts his hand down and says, "Earth Repel." The road around him is a cloud of dust, but at his command, the cloud shrinks around his gauntlet, only to explode against the ground, sending him hurdling safely away.

Riser responds with a twirl. This time she stands tall with her katana fully extended. The flat of her outstretched blade strikes the Block of Air, sending it flying towards her adversary.

"Earth Leap," the boy shouts in response. Still in mid-leap, he lowers a foot close enough to the ground for his boot to just graze the dirt road's surface. The road trembles and in a blink he is almost behind her. *Not bad, but not good enough.*

"Air Block," Riser commands, noting just how close to the edge of the road the Fate has circled to.

This is too easy, she thinks, sending the block of solidified Air flying towards him.

The Fate's forced to swerve off the path, directly into the field of wildflowers. He lands with a plop, boots sinking deep into the mud.

Her captured prey thrashes about, but only manages to immerse himself deeper into the thick muck.

"Ha!" rejoices Riser. "You're best off not flailing about like that. It's only going to make it harder to get you out later."

"Earth Leap" is his answer, which does nothing more than shake the surrounding flowers of their silvery petals. Riser's triumphant grin grows as she watches the Fate's knees disappear into the mud.

Undeterred, he takes a swing at the mud ... only to create more of a mess.

"You still don't get it, do you? You're trapped, it's over," she tries to explain.

He pays her no attention. Instead, her soon to be ex-Captain begins unbuckling his pants.

"No, no, what are you doing? That's not going to work. That's no ordinary mud you're stuck in," Riser says in horrified amusement. Despite his ridiculousness, she forces her attention back to the task at hand. *So far, so good; he's trapped. But I still have to finish him off. He won't be able to dodge, but he can still block and parry. Regular attacks won't be enough, and now he can even block my first Technique with that Iron Blood Tech.*

But a Move like that needs a good amount of recovery time. Its cooldown won't be up in time, and even if he is able to use it again, there's no chance it could block 'that.'

"Enough, this ends here," the Daughter proclaims. She sheathes her katana and coils up in preparation for the finale. It's time to show the Captain just what she's been up to these last couple months.

"Sing, flying serpent Ehecthal!" Riser screams, flying forward with the force of a tempest behind her. As the world blurs past she pulls her sword free of its scabbard with all her might.

Just as she knew he would, the Fate answers, "Iron Blood Block."

Their weapons clash. Riser recoils, flying back and away. Flipping once, she kicks her feet high into the air behind her. The Daughter straightens herself in midair, her sword pointed directly at Fate's heart, her body rigid and deadly as an arrow she shrieks, "Verse Two." Her boots sputter once and then twice before gusting viciously, flinging her forward as if freed from a bow.

Now, it's over. The second verse of Ehecthal's Song is twice as hard to master as the first, and much more than twofold as devastating.

"Squeak, Squeak," answers the ball of fur that emerges from the Captain's hood. The unassuming little creature is just in time to witness the end of the one he's bound to. He holds up a single claw for the boy to see before leaping from his shoulder—directly at the oncoming Daughter.

With a shrug, the tiny chipmunk deflects Riser's mightiest attack.

He falls back onto the boy's shoulder. The chipmunk looks up at the Fate, his gaze piercing through the boy's battle frenzy. With his statement made the chipmunk disappears into the boy's hood.

More than shocked, Riser picks herself off the road and blinks twice. The Fate reaches over and presses the tip of his Stick to her chest.

"Fluttering Blade," he says. The sprout that appeared earlier has grown into a single leaf. The petal begins to dance wildly as if caught in a squall. As it twists and turns, its razor sharp edges shred the Daughter's Armor. The blade-like leaf slashes away faster than her eyes can follow. In a blink, the vibrant blue surrounding her fades until disappearing altogether.

Her Tearstone rings loudly and she is encircled in a giant, glowing sphere. The duel is over. The Loser's Ball, as the impenetrable orb surrounding her is popularly referred to, is a safeguard designed to protect the defeated from overzealous attacks after the fact.

When the protective sphere splits in two and vanishes, Riser is greeted with her Captain's familiar smile. Instinctively, she manages to sheath Ehecthal. But her mind still races, attempting to comprehend just how assured victory was just stolen from her grasp.

"That was close, too close," says the Fate, grinning sheepishly. "Are you injured, Riser? Why is your mouth hanging open like that?"

"Umm ... Umm," she repeats in pure shock.

"You almost had me there. I had no clue Spikey would do something like that. But I guess that is what the one claw meant from earlier."

"What the hail are you talking about?" she screams. "You're a filthy, failing cheater! You and Ieiri! I'm First Daughter! I don't lose matches, and now I've lost two, back-to-back." *Unbelievable!*

Esperanza sinks to her knees. *Unforgivable!*

Tears of rage fill the Daughter's eyes as she looks for something to strike out at. She slams her fist into the ground, over and over again. Her knuckles begin to ache, and blood drips up and then down the side of her hand turning muddy as it meets the dust of the road.

It's a stupid, pointless thing to do, but she can't help it. The one thing she hates most in the world is losing. Even though, when all's said and done—a loss is her ultimate goal.

Only another Daughter of Enyo could possibly understand. And there is no one that understands what it meant to be First Daughter but her.

Esperanza has more than just a legacy to uphold. Long before the existence of the Three Kingdoms, before the discovery of Tearstones and Tournaments, there was the first kingdom, the kingdom of Silla.

Since as far back as the First Age, the Age of Beasts, the fighters of Silla have been famed for their skills in the art of war. During the Second Age, the Age of Champions, Enyo herself was born to Silla. And from that point onward, her Daughters have become legendary for their strength in combat; not only in this part of the world, but all parts of the world. *And I'm supposed to be the best of us now.*

To the rest of the world the Pilgrimage of Enyo is nothing but a joke. But to a Daughter it is everything. The tradition of the journey was one of blood, but Tears changed all that. *If these were the old days, this would've ended in bloodshed.* She looks down at her muddied, red knuckles and laughs.

At the rate she's going, she doubts she'll even make it out of Wysteria. What would her Sisters think of her then, especially the younger ones? *Unacceptable!*

"Riser, do not be like that." the Fate says. "How about helping me out of here, instead? It stinks down here. And just where did all this mud come from? I passed by here two weeks ago and it was all solid then."

"Fail you, Fate ... and your chipmunk too," mutters Riser. "How can you be our Captain? You can't even figure us out, let alone those we'll have to face."

The Captain smiles back with no understanding in his eyes.

"Think about it for just a moment. You were with Ieiri when you last passed by here, right? She must have brought you here on purpose to make sure you thought it was solid.

"I bet she started flooding this hollow the very next day. She probably diverted a stream or something. That girl arranged it all for you, but for some reason she ended up using it against me."

"Ieiri did all that?" he says, growing quiet until admitting, "I hope that she is fine. I have not seen her in two whole days. She did not even come to say goodbye ... and why would she challenge you?"

"Nothing of your concern. Just one of her silly promises," she says, for the first time taking a long look at the boy she's now stuck following.

"Nice haircut, by the way." She begins to caress her own long braid.

"Thank you," the Fate says, rubbing the back of his head. "Ieiri cut it while I was sleeping. She can be pretty sneaky when she wants to. I only know it was her because of the note she left behind. She also said goodbye in it, but it does not feel right not saying it face-to-face."

He won't even take teasing properly. What use is he? she thinks. "What else did the note say?"

"Just that she had to cut it off for my protection. Princess Rule #53," he says, "And to remember to keep my promises."

"For as strong as that girl is getting, she makes no sense whatsoever. And please, buckle up your pants." Riser snorts at the state of her Captain.

"You should not make light of the Princess Rules. Countless heroes have fallen to their Dark Arts," the Fate says, straightening his pants the best he can.

"I don't think I have to worry about that," she says flatly.

"I, for one, am glad to have her looking out for us." He holds out his Stick. "Grab on and brace yourself."

Riser grasps a hold of the other end and braces herself for all that's to come.

The wind has calmed and now the flowers stretch forever, pale and still as fluffy clouds.

The pair lay sprawled on their backs with nothing to stare at but the sun. For a day that's just begun, they're already sweaty, muddy, and in Esperanza's case, starving. Her stomach grumbles loudly, which earns itself a swift punch from its owner, who in turn collapses with a moan.

"Riser, is something wrong?" asks the Fate. He receives a second moan for a reply.

"Hungry? I have leftovers from last night in the cart." The Fate gestures behind him. "Wrapped in a white handkerchief ... should be near the top."

She bolts for the bed of the small wagon. Wide-eyed, she spots the precious lunch wrap and grabs it greedily. A bone is already sticking out of her mouth as she flops back down onto the ground next to her Captain. The food-laden plate lands safely in her lap.

"There should be enough for both of us," the Fate says.

Riser emits a low growl in response.

"Very well, then. I suppose I should clean myself up," he says, pulling mud out of his pockets. "You have until I am finished changing and then we are off. We have forty or so miles to cover today."

Riser's growl turns into a groan.

Freshly renewed, the teammates embark on their quest to do the impossible—the hard way. Their grandiose plans to win it all start here on the road to their first Tear Tournament. Still a ways away from the host town of Greenwood, they'll need to make good time to arrive by nightfall. The road has flattened out; without hills it seems to go on with no end.

The Fate sets off at a quick pace, cart and Riser in tow. He's always been like this, Riser thinks, trying to keep up. *Get out the way or get dragged along. Like he's some sort of freaking force of nature or something.*

"You haven't changed much in the past year," she grunts, finally hitting her stride.

"I am taller, now," he says. "My hair is shorter, as well."

"That's not what I meant."

"Oh, I suppose I am always me, then. That will never change," he says with a grin. "Same with you, Riser, you will always be you—we are the same that way."

"Enough with the babo talk," she grumbles, tiring of his foolish nonsense. "It may impress Ieiri, but that won't work on me."

They continue on in silence until he quietly asks, "Did you notice how much Ieiri has grown? She is on a whole different level now."

"Enough about her, too. She wouldn't have beaten me in a fair fight. And I know she hasn't passed you yet, either," Riser mutters in disgust. "What I really don't get is how she's already internationally ranked and we're not? It's a stupid system. She wasn't even born in the Three Kingdoms."

"Those are things that do not matter, Riser. I am looking forward to the World Circuit as much as you, but for now, we have to focus on the task at hand: Wysteria's Tournament." he tells her. "Besides, we should be proud of her. We are all on the same Team."

"Yeah, I know. Don't get me wrong, we're sisters sworn and I can't wait until next year when she'll be old enough to join us," she explains. "It's just ... do you know what it means for a Daughter of Enyo to be defeated?"

"I thought all Daughters dreamed of 'Glorious Defeat.'"

"Not by another woman," she replies flatly. "Also, I'm done challenging you for leadership of the team, but I'm warning you, if you mess up ..."

"Daebak!" the Fate says, using the Han word to celebrate good fortune. "But why? That's not like you. I do not understand."

"What's new, Oppa?" She snickers, wondering if it's really true, that he's a direct descendant of the only man to have conquered Silla. *It must be*, she decides.

The Venerable, including her own mother, ordered everyone to consider the boy a brother to all Daughters. Esperanza never really understood what that meant or why it was even necessary to declare. The boys over at Gregory's House, where the sons of Daughters would often end up, have never warranted such a label. Which reminds her ...

"Fate?"

"Yes, Riser?"

"I heard about the Old Man," she says watching him closely. "I'm sure he'll be back any day now. Knowing him, he's probably just cozying up with some new lady friend."

"No, I do not think so," he says, "I think he is doing something important—something that matters."

"Yeah, either way, I'm sure he's fine," Riser says, remembering what Ieiri told her—that the whole reason plans had changed was in hope that the Old Man would return soon. Now, they will be entering the Tournament at the very end of the season. It's a pretty dumb thing to do, to say the least. But she's not too worried about it.

"I also believe he is fine," he says too easily. She glances over at him, but there is no sign of worry. *It's not like Old Claw to be this late. What could be keeping someone like him away?*

"I have been worrying over something, however," the Fate says. "I hope you have been faring well in your studies."

"Studying, yes ... my studies have gone well. I only took one subject over the summer, Advanced Defensive Tactical Maneuvers," she tells him. "I came in first in class, of course."

"That is great, Riser," the Fate says, turning to look directly at her. "But that is not what I meant. I want to know how you fare concerning your studies for the pre-exam."

"Oh, yes, of course," she says already knowing that. *But what am I supposed to say. That my studies are going unbelievably bad—that I haven't been able to pass even a single practice exam?*

"Riser, you have been studying, correct?"

"Yes, of course I have" she says, "I've read the required material over and over, but ... but it's just not sticking."

"I see," the Fate says to a miserable-looking Riser. "Then, perhaps we should review together. Please start from the beginning; the very beginning."

"Do I have to?" Riser asks in annoyance. She looks over at her Captain. His hair just covers his eyes but she can tell he is looking straight ahead. And that smile; it's dumb-looking and scary at the same time. Not that she'd ever admit feeling the latter.

"Captain's orders," he says. "It was the first question they asked when I took the pre-exam."

"Okay, okay ... Before the beginning there was nonexistence; formless and without color," Riser recites.

"First came Light and with it White filled the spaces in between, becoming the Pale Aspect and all that is incorporeal. Where there was something, the Light cast a shadow of Black, the Deep Aspect, and all that would become physical.

"So that Light could contrast Light and Darkness itself vary, the first colors came to be, the primary colors: Yellow, Blue, and Red.

"That we would have a place to set our feet when we walk and lay our head when we sleep, we were given the *Deep Yellow Aspect—Earth.* So we may always have the life and warmth of another to look forward to, we were given the *Pale Yellow Aspect—Sun.*

"That we would always seek fulfillment, we were given the *Deep Blue Aspect—Water.* So that we would forever be connected to the world around us, we were given the *Pale Blue Aspect—Air.*

"That we may pass something of ourselves onto another, we were given the *Deep Red Aspect—Blood.* So that we may have the power to create as well as destroy, we were given the *Pale Red Aspect—Fire.*

"And from those Three Primary Colors; Yellow, Blue and Red, every other color was born and from those the world was created," Riser finishes.

"That was very good, Riser! You have been studying," the Fate says. "But reciting another's words is one thing, and understanding them another. Can you explain the basics of Tear Theory? How exactly do Tearstones work?"

"Why don't we go over major battles or strategy or something?" the Daughter complains.

"Because you like those things," he answers. Riser steals a glance to make sure he isn't looking and makes a face. He turns slightly and sticks his tongue out in return. *How'd he see that?*

"Do not spare any details. You will be asked to elaborate on everything."

She knows there's no use arguing with him. With a sigh she begins. "Tearstones start off clear and colorless, once bound they attune to one's innate color. I'm naturally Light Blue, so that means I'm aligned to the Aspect of Air, which is probably the most common, but I'm fine with that."

"Air is pretty good," the Fate says.

"It's the best. Anyway, binding a Tearstone is just the first step. The next is learning to activate your Tear and forming your Spectral Armor. Once activated you gain access to the Color World."

"What does it look like to you?" the Fate asks.

"Why do you always ask that? It looks the same to me as it does everybody else. It's just a bunch of glowing lines and traces of color on top of the real world. I see a lot of Blue Spectrum Lines, but auras and other effects all look the same to everybody. You're Yellow, so you see mostly Yellow Lines, right? Sounds kind of boring to me."

"It is what it is," he replies with a shrug. "Go on ..."

"Once you can see the Color World, you can use it to affect the real world. I guess it's easiest to think of the Color World as being like a shadow or reflection of the real world. Either way, when something changes in the real world, it's reflected in the Color World. And it goes the other way, too. Altering a Line in the Color World has a direct effect on the real world. That's the basis of Tear Physics and how Criers perform their Techniques."

"Do not forget sound," he says.

"I was going to get to that," she says. "Sound remains the same in both worlds—it's what ties them together. That's why Techniques require a verbal component. Naming your Techs pulls the worlds together, even tighter, making it so even complex actions are more easily repeatable."

"Impressive, Riser!" her Captain cheers. "It really is amazing if you think about it."

"Yeah, it's like we found out how to move someone's shadow and the person has to move along with it or break the Laws of Reality," she says.

"That is what they say, but sometimes, I wonder."

"What do you mean?"

"You never really know what might happen. What if I really was able to move your shadow right now? Maybe you would stay still and the sun would move instead, or the whole world would move and you and the sun would stay still, or maybe the world would just break right here and now. Who knows what would actually happen."

"Is that going to be on the test, cause you're beginning to hurt my head?"

"No, not really," says the Fate. "I am just saying that there is still a lot we do not know."

"I already know that, babo.

CHAPTER 3
RACHEL

The first rays of dawn push back the remnants of night still lurking through the streets of Greenwood. Against the coming light, the darkness retreats into the long shadows cast by the industrious few beginning to fill the main street of the small town.

Delivery boys scurry among the merchants who prepare their stalls for another long and fruitful day. Already customers are gathering around the old lady known for her pies. The Tour is in town and it's about to get busy.

Tall and fair, Rachel Avenoy picks her way through the growing crowds trying not to think of how delicious those pies smell, especially the strawberry—not so much the herring. *Who would even want a fish pie?* she wonders before noticing the chorus of meows coming from the alley next to the bakery.

What a nice lady. She must bake, at least, some of those for them. I'll definitely have to stop by on my way back for a strawberry-cream. Oh, and I'll pick up that bread with roasted peaches and peppers that Wake likes so much. Maybe even a fishy one for the kitties, she thinks to herself.

But for now, she has a task to complete. With her eyes shut tight in concentration, Rachel continues down the street. Even with freshly baked pie on her mind, she is able to notice the small child in time to avoid a collision.

With a gentle pat on the head and a warning to be more careful, she sends the little boy scurrying back to his friends, all without ever opening her eyes. The last thing she wants is to frighten the little boy. And by the sounds of the kid's whispering behind her, she decides she made the right choice.

This sort of thing happens often on Tour. Many of the smaller towns have never seen a blind person before and the fact that she 'sees' without seeing is always a curiosity. Sometimes, this annoys her brother, but she never minds.

Why would she? The chill of autumn is in the air. It tastes of fallen leaves and grasses crisping yellow. The sun is a caress across her face, a touch of brightness in a world gone dark. Light is a feeling. People are auras, and the world a black canvas that stretches on forever. Rachel lives in the Color World and she is grateful for it.

She's also thankful that unlike the last town on Tour, most of Greenwood's signs are Tear-brushed. Meaning, even Rachel can read the markings clearly. Other than that small luxury, Greenwood is a fairly typical stop on the Tour, with the all too familiar layout of a main street lined with shops, a village square to act as the Lobby, and of course the Tourney Grounds on one end.

You'd have to be pretty foolish to get lost in a town like this, she thinks, quickening her steps. If she hurries, she just might be done before the streets get really packed.

Just as she begins to wonder if she may've missed a turn, she hears the familiar sounds of a guitar that assures her the Lobby is nearby. The guitar's song is quite lovely, but the bard that plays it, played only it, a fact that usually got the young boy chased away well before noon.

The Lobby is already beginning to fill with those trying to set up practice matches or hoping to get picked up by a team. *Not that any decent team would be recruiting this time of the year*, Rachel thinks sadly.

Which only serves to remind her of her current predicament. *How could Kearney Dim cut us so close to the end of the season? And why? Just because I said I wasn't interested in him?*

It all started off well enough. Kearney seemed so nice and thoughtful at first. But as the months slowly changed, so did he. And in Ravenwood, their last stop on Tour, he changed altogether.

She shouldn't have laughed when he told her he liked her. But it just came out. She couldn't help it. It's just how she is. Ever since she was a little girl, it was just what came out. Stub a toe, she'd cry and laugh. Embarrass herself and she'd laugh awkwardly. Scare her and she'd jump in fright and laugh. It wasn't just her too, but her brother also—at least, when they were younger.

Her little brother, Wake, had long ago grown into a serious young man. Still though, every once in a while, when no one else was around and something set them off, they'd share an uncontrollable fit of laughter. Those are the best. But more times than not, she holds it in—at least, when she can. No one wants to be known as a tittering fool.

But her laughing out of nervousness had cost her and her brother their best chance of qualifying for school. When they arrived in Greenwood, Kearney told her she was going to be replaced.

A charity case, he called me, like I didn't bring anything to the team. As if half our points didn't come from the Relay, she remembers almost angrily. *And poor Wake, he could've stayed. He should've stayed—he's so close to qualifying.*

I should've just played along for his sake.

Rachel shudders at the thought. It isn't just that Kearney turned out not to be a very nice boy. It's just that, he ... is a boy. At the very least, he's far too young for her. Even though the majority of competitors are true crybabies, first-timers on Wysteria's National Tour, Rachel's a veteran.

She failed to qualify before turning of age and already served her two years. Unlike most, she's here strictly for the admission into Criers College that comes with placing high enough in the Tournaments rather than the excusal from Service.

In truth, she barely tried her first time on Tour. It was just all too much for her back then. And as with all those who did not qualify for school, she reported for Service. The two years of mandatory duty did her well, though. She even stayed a third and fourth year to fully master her appointed trade skill, *The Long Brush.*

This time around was different, however. Rachel worked so very hard, put up with so much. And now, she's so close she can taste it. *After all we've gone through is this really how it's going to end?* Her mind's so wrapped around the thought that this time she fails to notice the young man in her way. That is until she crashes headfirst into him. Her fair hair flies free from her cowl and for an instant become indistinguishable from day's early light.

"Ouch, ow, ow, that really hurt," says the boy, grabbing his ear and hopping in pain.

Rachel sits there in the middle of the road, wincing between laughs.

After wincing a few times himself, the boy asks, "Are you hurt?" Which is somewhat unexpected. She was sure he would be asking why she was laughing, instead. Looking up, she notices his aura for the first time. It is abnormally rigid, dominated by a deep yellow with flecks of dirty red and streaks of blues bleeding into murky greens. The colors are heavy and dark. It is quite possibly the most repulsive aura she's ever seen.

"I'm sorry ..." they both begin. The young man is quiet for a moment and then his aura shifts strangely. "Are you not Rochelle Avery, the Light Tripper?"

Taken aback, she answers, "If you mean *Rachel Avenoy.* Yes, that is me."

"Forgive me, I am not very good with names," he explains. "But it really is an honor to meet you. I am a huge admirer. I have watched the Memory of your race at the Hallows, at least, a hundred times—your other ones, as well. And the tutorial you made is simply the best."

"Really?" She wonders. *That's flattering, I suppose ... but more than a little strange.* The Light Course is by far the least popular event on Tour. Up until this very moment, she wasn't even sure if the tutorial she had the Reminiscer record was ever viewed by anyone.

"No one can ride the Lines like you. I try to copy your form exactly."

"It's just a small part of one event," she says.

"It is much more than that ..." he begins before asking again, "Are you sure that you are fine?"

"Yes, I'm fine, thank you; just a little bruised and dusty."

"Please let me help you up," he says. When she reaches forward to grab his hand, she finds herself grasping the end of a stick instead. With a gentle pull, she's up on her feet, dusting herself off.

"I am glad you are uninjured. I should not have stopped in the middle of a busy road, but I thought I saw a sign for the Office of the Registrar. I am having difficulty in locating it."

Figures he's lost, she thinks before remembering her own first day on Tour. Fresh out of Ice Ridge, she was just as lost her first time away from home.

Ice Ridge was a fine place to grow up, but the northern city far from the heart of the Wysteria did little to prepare her for the outside world. As much as the icy caverns that her hometown were built into, sheltered and protected the little town, they also isolated the townsfolk. *That's probably why Mother chose to raise us there in the first place,* she thinks, remembering her loving, but always cautious mother.

"Look, I'm heading over there myself, so if you want ..." she offers.

"Really? That would be most wonderful," he says. "By the way, I am Fate. It is a pleasure to meet you."

"Nice to meet you, too ... Fate?" she says.

"That is what they call me. Also, I am supposed to say, 'My girlfriend Ieiri does not like it when I talk to other girls,'" recalls the boy.

"That's a relief. I was actually afraid ... well, never mind," Rachel says, leading them down the road.

"I do not really understand, but I am glad you are relieved," he answers cheerfully.

For a moment, he's right beside her, but soon, he's darting back and forth from one side of the street to the other, picking up item after item and asking, "What is this? What does this do?"

She can imagine the expression on the last merchant's face as he blankly answers, "It's an umbrella. It keeps you dry when it rains."

She tries not to laugh. "I take it that you're new around here? First stop on Tour?"

"Yes, and I cannot wait for it all to begin!"

It's been awhile since she's heard someone sound so excited about being on Tour. "That's actually a pretty good plan: get a little experience in Greenwood then you'll be better prepared for next season."

"No, that is not my plan. I plan on getting licensed this year."

Licensed? Who in the world cares about that? Rachel wonders. It's true that most of the kids on Tour aren't here to get into school, but before meeting him, she could say with absolute certainty that none are here to get licensed. Wysteria's been banned from the World Circuit since before she could remember. The Three Kingdoms hasn't had a team of their own on the International Tournament of Tears for more than a decade.

"That's going to be pretty hard if this is your team's first tournament." *Impossible, really ...*

"Really?"

"Yes, really. It's hard just getting a single win this time of year. And you will be so far behind on points that catching up will be impossible." she says, feeling somewhat sorry for the clueless boy. "Still, I guess you never know. Best of luck to you and your team."

"Thank you, but I only have one of them with me now. I need to find a couple more."

"That's also going to be difficult this time of year. Anyone even halfway decent is already going to be on a team. Your best bet is waiting until points reset in the spring and trying then," Rachel explains.

"I cannot do that. I turn eighteen in a couple days."

"You're not really serious, are you? There are only two stops left on the Tour, including this one. Even if you placed near the top in every event, you'd still be short on points." *And that's a feat even The Royal Team wouldn't try to accomplish.*

"I am always serious," the Fate declares. "If I may ask, why would someone who is already competing need to go to the Office of the Registrar? I thought only first-timers needed to sign in."

"I'm here for my brother. Greenwood will be the first time he's officially competing solo." She gestures to a small building near the entrance to the Tourney Grounds. "Here we are and it doesn't even look too crowded." The walls of the office are thin enough that she can make a good estimate of the auras within.

"You really know a lot about a lot of things," the Fate says. "If I had someone as strong as you, I know I could do it."

"Do what?"

"Win one hundred in a row," he says.

As strong as me? Win one hundred in a row? Why that's just absurd. He must be jesting with me. Rachel can't hold it any longer. She's laughing so hard her belly hurts. "That's a good one, but you know I'm older than you and you shouldn't be teasing your seniors like that."

"I am sorry if I teased you, but I am serious," he says.

"But that's just impossible, you know? This is my second time through and I'm at about a dozen and a half matches. And if you won out the first time through—which in itself is a hopeless goal—there really would be no reason to compete again. Why would you want to try to win one hundred?"

"To be happy, of course," he says. "But you are correct. There is no reason for me to compete in Wysteria once licensed."

At least, he realizes that. "I'm actually between teams right now, but I'm sorry, I need to get on an established team."

"An established team? Please consider establishing a team with me, instead."

"No, thank you," she answers quickly.

"Perhaps, the timing is not right. I will ask you again another time then," he says, holding the door open.

They enter the small wooden building and are met with half a dozen clerks sitting behind their windows, ready to assist. Only one has a queue in front of it and she leads them to that one.

"Do you have a Healer? And just so you know, my brother and I come as a pair. I'm a Specialist and he's a Finisher," Rachel tells him, wondering why she even bothers.

"I have Riser with me, but she has yet to pass the pre-exam."

Riser? Fate? What kinds of names are these? Rachel wonders. "What class are you?" she asks.

"I am a Fate."

"Oh, I didn't realize that was a class. What is that, a Finisher type?"

"I suppose. I am the Captain. I usually fight the other Captain," he tries to explain.

"Is it Home-brew?"

"Home-brew?" he asks.

"You really must be new. Home-brew is when a Crier combines all their favorite skills into a new class. Like, they just threw them all in a big old pot and brewed them together to their own tastes. Home-brew classes aren't proven and always a work in progress compared to an established, well-tested class, so they have a bad rep. But I run one and my brother does, too."

"Daebak!" he says, full of excitement.

"Daebak?" she asks.

"That is what you say in Han if you hit it big, or if something is really amazing," the boy explains. "What kind of Home-brew class are you, then?"

"The truth is I haven't actually got around to naming mine. It's sort of complicated. My brother, Wake, calls himself the Water Knight. No one really uses Water, so a name like that was still available."

"I do not know much about that, but I like the name. It makes sense," the Fate says. "Would that not make you a Sun Knight?"

Rachel can almost see the boy's eyes twinkle at the thought. She holds up her right wrist from which dangles a fine golden chain attached to a bright Yellow Tear. "Like I said, it's complicated. Look closely at the center of my Tear."

"It is Pale Yellow, and oh ..." he says, pressing his face right up against it. "There is a speck of Blue in there."

"Yes, there is; just enough so I can use some of my brother's Water Techs."

"Should you not use Sun Aspect Techs, since your Tear is almost all Light Yellow?"

"Yes, well ... Do you know how much a Sun Shield costs? More than this whole town, that's how much. It's not worth it for someone like me. Besides, I just use that stuff for when I have to draw a match. Really, I'm just here to race the Light Course. Otherwise, I'm best off on the Observation Deck playing strategist. Even though I can't use the Tear Screen to see through the eyes of those on the field, at least, I'm out of the way."

"Out of the way? I do not understand," the boy says. "But to answer your original question, Fates are actually a really old class, but it is still similar to being Home-brew. Each Fate is different, and I often have to make things up as I go along."

"Interesting. I really do wish you and friend well, but my brother and I are right on the border of actually qualifying. You understand, right?"

"No, not really, but I suppose it does not matter. I could not accept your brother, anyway. No matter how strong you are, it is not enough to carry someone else on my team."

Rachel tries not to giggle. "I think you got it backwards. My brother is a much better Crier than I."

"Is that possible? You are perhaps one of the strongest people I have ever met."

"I don't know what you're talking about, but I assure you he is stronger than I am."

"If he is—that would be double daebak! Then both of you could join. What are you signing him up for?"

"Um, just for the One-on-One Finisher's Series." Rachel counts only a few auras left ahead of them. He seems nice. *Once he learns a few things, he may even make a passable Captain.* She's been around worse.

Then she notices that something is crawling right up the boy's back. "Oh, my! There's something on your back! It's gigantic!" The sounds of pens writing and paper shuffling come to a halt, and all eyes turn to the pair. Those closest to them take a step back.

"Something gigantic? On my back?" The Fate tries to reach behind him, his hand searching and his body slowly circling like a dog chasing his tail until he realizes. "Ah, I think you must mean Spikey. He lives inside my hood, but there is nothing gigantic about him. He is just a chipmunk."

"Oh, I am so sorry. I thought because of his dark aura he was a spider, I dislike spiders." Spiders have a black aura, and so did this chipmunk. But when she looks more closely, she sees that it glows golden around its edges. "What a remarkable aura. I've never seen anything like it before: black, but glowing golden. It's absolutely flawless."

The chipmunk jumps over onto her shoulder. A surprised smile greets him, as does a gentle hand. "May I?" she asks, about to pet the little animal.

"Spikey, please do not bite her."

"Squeak, squeak."

"He is his own master. He does as he wishes," the Fate explains. "Which mostly involves sleeping and biting."

Spikey reaches his head up and nuzzles her fingertips. "You are just so precious, aren't you?" she says to the chipmunk and then to the boy, "He's amazing, so soft and so well behaved. I've never seen a Tear Companion like him before. Where did you find him?"

"He came up and touched my Tear a couple days ago. Now, we are stuck together."

"No way!" she says, playfully pushing him away in disbelief. His aura twitches and then shrinks at her touch. *Something's wrong.* Whatever it is, it makes her suddenly afraid—not of the boy, but for him.

Spikey squeals in approval. "I'm sorry. I don't know what I was thinking. It's just that I do that to my brother all the time." *But I don't think I've ever done that to anyone else. What am I doing touching a total stranger like that?*

"Please, do not do that again. I do not like being touched." His voice trembles. Just as Rachel is about to apologize again, he continues on as if nothing happened. "I thought he was just a little chipmunk, but he is a true Tear Fighter. Unfortunately, I did not recognize his true strength and he took a Death Vow to never fight by my side."

"Really? That's such a shame." Rachel wonders just how much of that story could possibly be true as she pets the chipmunk. All of a sudden, the little chipmunk dodges her fingers and pounces playfully back.

"I've been looking for a Tear Companion forever. I've checked every Trainer on Tour, but I just can't find one that I can bind. I want one, so I can use the Scout Vision Tech. That way I can see through their eyes. Wouldn't that be so wonderful? The only hope I have left is to get into Criers College. They say they have a device there that will match anyone with a Tear Companion."

"If you wish, I can take you to my rock after my hundredth. That is where I met Spikey. It is much better than any device you will find at Criers College. You can see the sunset from it."

"Thank you, but I'm pretty set on getting into school," she says.

"I understand," he says before all of a sudden noticing, "Why are we in this line? All the other windows do not have a wait."

"First things first: only crybabies call them lines. We call them queues on Tour, okay? Lines are what we use for Techs," she says. "We're in Young Sensei's queue, so we don't have to keep coming back. He makes sure all the proper forms are acceptably filled out the first time around. Sometimes, he can even circumvent the system. Where another clerk would tell you it's impossible, he'll get it done. It means waiting now, but we'll save a lot of time getting it done right the first time. Trust me."

"I will," he says. "He does the impossible, you say? Is Sensei not an Azurian word? He does not look like he hails from Neverfall."

"He's not. I guess they call him that because he's the one to ask if you have any questions while on Tour, particularly concerning all the rules and regulations. He's young, still too young to even compete, so I guess it would be awkward if everyone called him something like, 'Tour Master.' I think an Azurian started calling him Young Sensei, and it just sort of stuck."

It's not unusual to find foreign-born citizens of Gorgury. Being the third and newest of the Three Kingdoms of Wysteria, Gorgury was conceived by immigrants, unlike Silla and Bae, whose roots trace back to the native Han.

"He must be very strong."

"He's smart and knows how to get things done, but he has some sort of heart condition. Even when he turns seventeen next year, he won't really be able to compete," she whispers. "We're next, so have your Tear ready. And don't ask him about his condition. I'm sure he's sensitive about it."

"Next," the floppy haired young boy announces. His freckles line up in concentration as he gives a final look over of the previous application.

"Welcome to the Office of the Registrar. How may I be of assistance ... Oh, hello, Rachel."

"Hello, Sensei ..." Rachel begins, but before she can say anymore, the Fate is already introducing himself.

"Well met, Sensei, I am Fate. How fare you this fine day?"

"Pretty good, thank you for asking," Sensei says. "It's nice to meet you, too. And just how may I help you today?"

"You could help me by joining my Team," the Fate says.

This guy is just asking anybody, isn't he? Rachel takes it.

As usual, the Fate is met with a chuckle. "Are you serious?" the young clerk asks.

"I am always serious."

"Three years, I've been working here and you're the first to ask." Young Sensei looks the Fate up and down. "Just who are you? Are you here together?" he asks each of them.

"No ..." she begins.

"I am Fate, Captain of the Team that will do the impossible— the hard way. Are you interested in winning one hundred in a row?"

"That does sound interesting." Sensei smiles. "Are you Bae? Which Clan are you from?"

"Yes, I am from the Slate. Now, will you join my team?"

"I appreciate your offer, but I'm not sure how much use someone like me would be on your team. I have this thing with my heart ..."

"That matters not. You must love Tear Fighting as much as I do. I see you do all you can to be a part of it," the Fate tells him. "Be my strategist."

Oh my, that's actually quite clever, Rachel thinks. *A strategist doesn't actually step onto the battlefield. Instead, they oversee things from the Observation Deck. From there, they can coordinate the five actually on the field.*

He'll be a much better strategist than I ever was. At the very least, he'll be able to make proper use of the Tear Screen to see what everybody is doing.

"That's generous of you, but can you really afford to fill a spot with someone who doesn't fight at all? I can't think of a single team on Tour that has a spot dedicated to just a strategist. Well, unless the strategist bought that spot. If, I was to be your strategist, that would mean the other five will have to compete in every event."

Sensei's right, Rachel realizes. *That means, someone like him and I could never be on the same team.* She has no intention of joining the boy, but soon it may not even be an option.

"That is fine. I want the best and you will be the best strategist."

Sensei goes quiet, before finally asking, "You do know that teams that can spare an extra slot usually sell it, right? You can make a decent amount of money if your team is any good. There are plenty of rich families out there willing to pay for even a slight chance at getting their kids out of Service."

"None of that matters to me. Join my team and I promise you will not regret it," the Fate says.

"There's one other thing, too. I don't turn seventeen until just after the season," the young clerk says. "But there is a rule that allows for early participation. And it just happens to apply strictly for strategists.

"But with my birthday still a couple months away, I won't be eligible for early participation until just before the Grand Finale

Tourney. If you'll have me then, I'll give you my all and I'll totally understand if you change your mind between now and then."

"Daebak! Welcome to my team, Sensei."

Did that really just happen? Rachel wonders. *Sensei's far too smart to make such a rash decision. It's just one tournament, but his reputation may be ruined for it. Then he'll have no chance of getting onto a team next year.*

"Thank you. Even though, I won't officially be a part of your team until after Greenwood, just let me know how I can help," Sensei says. "And Rachel, I heard about what happened to you and Wake. I'm sorry. Kearney is a real jerk to do what he did," Sensei says, smiling apologetically. "Never mind that, though. What can I help you with today? Need to sign up for some solo events?"

"Thanks, Sensei. And you're spot on, as usual. But it's not for me. I'm here to sign Wake up for the One-on-One Finisher's Series."

The young clerk already has the proper form out before she even finishes. He doesn't need to ask a single question as he fills out the paperwork. He knows most everyone's information by heart.

"I need to sign up for that as well. And of course, we need to register our new team," the Fate says happily.

More often that not, Arthur Bannister Jr. can be found taking lunch at his desk. What you will never find is anyone actually referring to him by that name. Everyone calls him Sensei, which he's not particularly fond of. But, he's not complaining. It's far better than being called Arty.

Arty is what they used to call his farther back at the Great Library. And Arty used to take lunches at his desk, too. Even janitors are given a desk at Wysteria's largest and most prestigious library.

Sensei's not like his father, though; he's already a level three clerk. He knows every in and out, every loop and hole of how the Tour works.

It's a rather complicated system, set up to deal with the thousands of seventeen-year-olds competing each year. And Sensei is the one to turn to if you have any questions. But registration for the solo games ended at noon and applications for team events won't start until tomorrow, so for the moment, he has some time to himself.

Sensei pulls out the gift that his new Captain had left him. It's a wicked-looking, little drum. The drumhead is made of thick, black goatskin that is stretched and tuned by blood-red ropes that crisscross down the drum's sides.

It has the distinct look of a war drum.

He takes a seat and positions the drum between his knees just as the Fate showed him. He gives the drum a gentle thump. It's louder than expected and he finds himself double-checking to make sure no one else is about.

He can't help but wonder why his new Captain would choose a Zul hand-drum rather than the more common type that you hit with a pair of sticks. Which reminds him, *that's where I heard his name before.*

It's been bothering him since meeting the odd boy. Even though he called himself Fate, it was the name on the application that he could have sworn he heard before. And it just hit him: Kase Shake was asking about a Terrantius Slate, all the way at the beginning of the year.

Kase may be the Top Finisher on *The Royal Team*, and his father, Senzen, a legend in the Three Kingdoms. But before all that, Senzen was a Chieftain of the Zul. They say he fought his way halfway around the world to join his tribe with Wysteria's newest kingdom, Gorgury.

But why had Kase Shake, the Best of the Best , been asking around about this guy? the little clerk wonders. *The Slate Clan's always been small, usually too small to field a full team of their own. But last year's Top Team did have two Healers from the Slate. And there's that girl, the first in the Three Kingdoms to receive an international ranking in a long, long time. Her second name's Skyshadow, but isn't she also linked to the Slate?*

Sensei's far from tough or strong, but what he's always been good at is seeing the whole, even the missing pieces. *This could be it—the start of something really special.*

CHAPTER 5
IEIRI
[THE VILLAGE OF THE SLATE CLAN]

Interrupting the stillness of midday, the slightest of figures bursts through the treetops. To the unfamiliar observer it would appear as if Ieiri Skyshadow is violently climbing an invisible ladder just above the tree line.

In truth, each unseen handhold, each temporary step, is her creation. They exist for barely a moment, just long enough for her to advance to the next. It's an act of incredible physical exertion, usually done as an exercise of the body, but today she climbs for another reason.

He met someone. She felt it.

Trying to clear her head of such thoughts, Ieiri focuses the totality of herself straight ahead. She stares defiantly at the sun, willing it to become ever so slightly larger. It's the only way to measure her ascent. To look down, to lose focus in the slightest, would mean an end to it all.

This is it. Out of breath, her legs unresponsive, Ieiri reaches out with the last of herself. The silhouette of her hand is all she can see; that and the sun. It's so large now, almost in her grasp— almost, but unattainable. *Like that clueless boy.*

All momentum is gone—in its stead, weightlessness. And then she falls. Her hood flails furiously, finally forcing flat against her back. Her eyes, shut tight, leave a glimmering trail in their wake.

Hundreds of feet above the tallest tree, where no soul can see the highest ranked youth Wysteria has ever produced, Ieiri Skyshadow cries.

There was never any doubting her choice—never, not once, not since that day a year ago, the day she tied her fate to that boy. Even though, it's considered the most forbidden act by her people; to Choose someone in secret. Worst of all, she Choose one who couldn't Choose her back and complete the cycle. If discovered, Ieiri would lose everything. She'd surely be recalled to Neverfall. *Father would be furious.*

She can't go back to the Azure, at least, not yet. Ieiri left as a disappointment and long ago decided never to return as one.

The memory is all too clear: the look in the eyes of her parents as her teacher informed them that their daughter was abnormal, that she couldn't hear the Wind as the other children. "Luckily," he told them, "Even though she can never achieve great status herself, she's a pretty enough girl to marry into it."

Ieiri's parents accepted this. She almost did, too.

Her father returned to his duties the very next day. His only words for his devastated daughter were the traditional Azurian greeting and farewell, "Never fall, Ieiri."

That's when she decided if she couldn't be a Stormwalker of Neverfall, she'd find another way.

Barely thirteen, she crossed the narrow sea to reach the Three Kingdoms of Wysteria. Even in a land known for opportunity, there were not many interested in a girl with an affinity to Air, but no talent for it whatsoever .

She was eventually able to find her place in a relatively unknown clan, the Slate, a small but respected village rooted deep in the Earth Arts. Despite her affinity to Air, they were the only ones to accept her, reluctantly at that. If it wasn't for him speaking up for her back then, they would've passed on her, too—just as all the others.

Being accepted was almost enough to make her smile. But it

wasn't until she went to ask him why he had spoken for her that she remembered how. In fact, his answer was ridiculous enough to make her even laugh.

It was amazing the things he didn't know, almost as amazing as the things that he did. A couple of happy years later and she's not just the Pride of the Slate, but of all the Three Kingdoms. She's eternally grateful, but it's not enough.

To him, she's just a pupil, a promising young girl—a teammate, at most. It doesn't matter, though. Ieiri Skyshadow performed the Choosing, the most sacred ritual of the Azure, anyway. It linked the two together, forever—unbeknownst to him.

On that first day, when she felt his ambition run through her, Ieiri trained for three days and three nights straight. She was so drunk on his desire, his goals—she may never have stopped. In the end, they were forced to physically restrain her, binding her tight so she couldn't escape.

She only stopped fighting back when he began gently feeding her as if she were a baby. It would've been too embarrassing to endure if it had been anyone else. But when she looked into his eyes, she knew he understood.

Ever since then, Ieiri Skyshadow's greatest challenge isn't seeking motivation, but rather keeping it at bay. The day she received worldwide recognition came as no surprise to anyone who knew her.

Back then, this day seemed so far away. She was so sure he'd be hers by now. Even with the extra time he lingered waiting for the Old Man, things still didn't go as planned. *Fool boy!*

As Ieiri Skyshadow falls, she takes in a breath so deep that her lungs feel as if they'll burst.

The air flows through her, enriching her blood, delivering the much-needed oxygen to her depleted muscles. This is the secret of the Air Climb. She needs to get to such a height that during the descent, she'll have sufficient time to recover enough for one more Technique or …

Feeling the swift approach of the trees behind, she quickly flips over and faces the forest canopy. She stretches her arms and feet towards the ground like a cat preparing to land on all fours.

The lithe girl arches her back and lets out a simultaneous burst from her clawed gauntlets and Sandals of the Wind. It's just enough to slow her descent.

She eyes the oncoming branches, looking for a familiar pattern in the shadows. Breathing deeply once more, she waits for it ... *Now!*

Ieiri leaps forward, reaching for something solid. She swings, releases, and lands deftly on a large branch, one conveniently flattened with use.

She slips quietly to the ground below. Exhausted, she curls into a ball and falls asleep.

When Ieiri awakes, the moon stares back at her. *Enough of this foolishness*, she decides. She always knew that this would happen. When that boy, the Fate, left the village, her connection to him would weaken. The distance may draw their link thin, but she could still feel it. Something unchanging, deep down inside; it is there. It will always be there.

I'll never regret it, she thinks in defiance, though, she's not exactly sure who she defies.

She playfully fingers the slim braid brushing her cheek. It's her new one, longer than the rest of her thick black hair.

She smiles. Ieiri knows what has to be done. She will become so powerful, so dominant—even he'd have to rely on her. Ieiri Skyshadow will be all the Fate ever needs.

She stands and stretches. *A night climb will do me good.* This time for the body, her soul's at ease once again. After all, her time will come with the spring and she will be with him soon enough. Until then, his promises will keep him safe.

Ieiri slips quietly into the Women's House, a brightly painted building on a particularly lovely stretch of the granite cliffs. Overlooking the beach, it serves as home to the unmarried women of age.

Once, it was her only sanctuary. That was a whole different girl, however. One who had journeyed so far to find a place that would accept her and when she finally had, she ended up hiding in her room all day. Nowadays, she barely visits it.

"Is that you, girl?" an ageless, heavyset woman calls out from outside her room. "Where have you been? Are you trying to worry an old lady to death?"

"Forgive me, House Mother. I was training," Ieiri answers as she crawls into bed. "Please do not worry so much over me."

"You're such a good girl, but you smell like the stables after a midsummer rain. You need a bath—badly," Marli, the Mother of the Women's House tells her, holding her nose good-naturedly.

"Fate never minds what I smell like," Ieiri replies indignantly. *I guess, I have been living in the woods for the last couple days. I really should wash up,* she thinks before saying, "I'll scrub extra hard tomorrow, I promise."

The older woman sighs and sets her lantern down onto a small desk along with a small, covered plate. "At least, you didn't tell me to go away and mind my own business like girls your age are supposed to."

"I would never ... I am a guest," Ieiri begins.

"Don't say that, child. This is as much your home as Neverfall. To say otherwise would hurt this old lady's feelings. Besides, you're not the only one. Fate wasn't born in the village and neither was the Old Man, you know?" Marli sits down next to her. "And I saw what you did to that boy's hair. Though to be honest, I think your plan backfired."

"I know," Ieiri admits in absolute sadness. "He looks like a Northerner now. I thought it would make him look … funny, but it did not. He will be sure to attract some Gorgurien hussy now."

"Don't worry, he has his stick to keep them away," Marli teases before her tone turns serious with care. "But what is my poor Ieiri going to do now, hmm? The Old Man still hasn't returned. Sya and Haenul left last year, and now even he's gone. It just doesn't seem fair to split up such a good team just because of age."

"I'll be fine. We'll be fine."

Marli leans over and puts an arm around her. "Are you nervous about going to Silla? The Daughters of Enyo aren't known to be the friendliest of sorts."

"No, I have been there once before, back when they told me I was not worth their time," Ieiri answers, unsmiling. "Things will be different this time, however. Esperanza told me I will have a very special teacher, someone even she has not trained with."

"I just hope they keep you well fed," Marli says, gesturing to the plate. "But you really should have said goodbye. Who knows when you'll see him again? You may regret it."

Ieiri replies with a glum look that morphs into a yawn.

"Sleep well, child."

"Sleep well, House Mother."

Of course I wanted to see him off, but how could I? I watched him say his farewells all week. Never once did he feel anything but his usual determination. I would die if he said goodbye to me like that, not feeling a thing.

CHAPTER 6

WAKE
[TOURNEY GROUNDS OF GREENWOOD]

Wake Avenoy sits on the sidelines rubbing warm wax over his inner boots. It's a task that usually calms him before a match, but more importantly, it helps keep his feet dry. He can walk on water with his armored Battle Boots, but they're not so great for keeping his socks from getting wet.

It's for that very same reason that his sleeves and pants end three-quarter lengths of where they should. Inevitably, his wrists and ankles will get soaked. Which isn't so bad in the summer, but with winter fast approaching—it's far too cold for all that.

He smears a particularly large glob of wax deep into the last unsealed seam. *It's almost time,* he realizes, braving a look up.

It's hard for him to believe that just a few days ago this place was nothing more than a field full of weeds. But a few days were all the tournament officials needed to transform it into a proper battleground. Now, hastily erected stands line each side, seating hundreds who cheer on friends and family as they clash on well-manicured battlefields.

Clangs of metal on metal, participants shouting out their Techs, and the occasional roar fill the air. Above it all, a loud explosion shakes the very ground itself.

The dust finally settles to reveal a girl floating flat on her back, surrounded by a protective sphere. Her opponent throws his hands up in the air and the crowd lets out a thunderous cheer.

Adding to the chaos are the Tear Speakers set intermittently throughout the grounds. The horn-shaped devices blare out continuously, announcing the result of previous matches and introducing those about to begin.

Having already won his first pairing, Wake Avenoy feels slightly more at ease than usual. Even so, he wipes his palms onto the towel next to him. *I should've made time for breakfast,* he thinks, wondering if the sloshing feeling in his stomach is more from hunger or nerves.

It's taken him almost a year, but he's finally grown accustomed to fighting in front of a crowd. At least, to the point where it doesn't paralyze him with fear. *But that was as part of a team. Now, you'll be out there alone without anyone to hide behind.*

Just as he's about to wipe his palms again …

"Wake, I found some extra towels," his sister says, hurrying over.

"Thanks, Ray." He always feel better when she's around. The fact that he got matched up with a total crybaby isn't bad, either. "I wonder what the chances are that I'd end up fighting your newfound friend? It must be Fate."

"Ha, ha." Rachel laughs unenthusiastically. "It's not all that surprising. This is a seeded tournament, after all. They are bound to match the highest ranked Criers against the lowest. He has no points, while you've got almost enough to qualify."

"But it's still weird. And is this guy really a crybaby? You never see one of those this time of year. I wonder what types of Techs he uses?"

"He mentioned something about Fates being an old class. I would guess that to mean he uses mostly physical attacks. I really didn't want to find out more. He seemed nice enough, but kind of … simple."

Wake chuckles at that. His sister doesn't have a mean bone in her whole body, even when describing an obvious fool. "It's not like I'm complaining; easy points are hard to get this time of the year. Speaking of which, have you heard anything back from the *Knights of Old Town*? Weren't they looking for more?"

"They don't need two."

"That's too bad," he says. "But that may not even matter if I can just earn enough points today. Then, all we need to do is get you on a decent Relay team."

"I don't know if I like the idea of joining a team without you," she says.

"It would only be for one race. Besides, worst comes to worst, you have an open invite from that guy." He points across the field towards his hunched over opponent.

The Fate leans over and throws up violently. After a final heave, he wipes his mouth and looks up with a sickly smile. Noticing them, he waves back cheerfully. *Maybe, it's a good thing that I didn't eat breakfast.*

"From the sound of it, I'd rather wait and try again next year."

Contestant #18 Wake Avenoy, the Water Knight and Contestant #371 Terrantius Slate, the Fate. Please report to Battlefield Three, announces the closest Tear Speaker.

"It looks like I'm up. Wish me luck." *I'll get this over with quick and then we can go get something to eat. I think they're serving dumplings today.*

"Luck, Wake. I know you can do it!"

"Are you ready?" the official asks Wake.

"Yes, sir."

"Are you ready?" the man asks the other boy. The Fate's ridiculous smile disappears for a moment as he looks up at Wake. "Thank you," he says before nodding to the official.

Before he can wonder what exactly he's being thanked for, the official begins backing off the field and counting down. "3, 2, 1 ... Go!"

Wake Avenoy takes no joy in beating up rookies. But this is an official tournament match and he wants to get it over with as soon as possible. He pulls up his sleeve and presses the Water Aspect Tear strapped to his upper arm. Instantly, he is surrounded in dark blue armor.

"Water Grab, Falchion," he recites as he pulls the moisture from the surrounding area to form a long, curved sword of Pure Water.

He wonders if this Fate fellow has ever seen a true-blue Water-User. Criers that use Water are a rarity at this level. Anyone unlucky enough to be Dark Blue always goes Ice, but that just never seemed right to Wake.

Something smells good. *They are serving dumplings today,* he thinks happily. When he turns his focus back to where his opponent should be, there is no one there. Frantically, he scans the area just before something jabs him in the ear. Immediately, followed by a blow to his belly. And then, his chin explodes in pain. The last hit sends him reeling and his sword of Water disperses, totally soaking his well thought out outfit.

A moment later, his attacker is looking down at him with a disappointed smile. "I thought you were supposed to be good."

"That was a waste of a berry," the Fate mumbles. "Fluttering Blade."

In a daze, all Wake can hear is a silent ringing in his ears and an echo of a memory ...

Wake the Waste,
The big Disgrace.
Always crying
all over the Place
Wake the Fake
The lying Snake ...

Anger snaps him out of it. A razor sharp leaf slices into his chest. His Deep Blue Spectral Armor fades close to nonexistence.

"I am not a Waste!" he screams. Something's different. The words come out slow—everything is slow. Instinctively, he starts to sway to the rhythm of the leaf. He dodges the next slice and then the next. Again and again he manages to just avoid the fluttering petal. Shifting ever so slightly, his form blurs, flowing and reforming. Over in an instant, he remains armored and standing after the savage onslaught.

"Water Grab, Falchion," he cries, his hand already in mid-swing before the liquid sword finishes forming. He strikes his opponent cleanly across the chest.

Seemingly unaffected, the Fate reaches out with his Earth Gauntlet and grabs his arm. "Earth Lock," the boy says. And as much as Wake twists and turns he cannot break free.

With his other hand the Fate brings his switch down across Wake's backside, shattering the remnants of his Spectral Armor.

"Brother, that was ridiculous!"

Wake looks up from the puddle forming below the bench, sees who it is, and quickly lowers his head again. "Good game. If you wouldn't mind, I'd like to be alone right now." He grabs another towel and throws it over his head.

The last thing he wants to do right now is talk to somebody, especially this guy. Wake didn't just lose a match, he just lost it all—everything he went through for the past year was for nothing. It doesn't matter that he and Rachel are near the top five percent. They aren't in the top five percent. And that means not getting into Wysteria's Criers College, no excusal from Service, and no to his sister's only chance at seeing.

Why do things always end up like this? I work hard. I try my best. Why can't I ever get a break? It would take a miracle for them to qualify now and he's never believed in those.

"Your sister was right; you are pretty strong," the grinning boy tells him. "What I do not understand is why you did not even try until the very end."

"What are you talking about? Of course I was trying from the very beginning. You have no clue what you're talking about," Wake says. "Whatever, I'm not in the mood for this just now. Please just go away."

"Now, I understand. You must be mad ... like Wolak. It is as if you think of every little thing but ignore the basics. Besides that, we are a lot alike, you and I."

What the fail is this guy talking about? There's only one Wolak in Wysteria worth mentioning, a Master Scholar at Criers College.

The last couple decades have been difficult ones for the Three Kingdoms, having been suspended from the International Tear League. Wolak is the only thing left Wysteria has to be proud of. His work has changed and continues to change the way people view the Color World. *There's no possible way this guy could know him.*

"Look, I thought you said something you didn't. I was angry for a minute there, but I'm over it, okay?"

"I did not mean to say you were angry, just crazy."

"I really don't know what you are going on about, but we're finished here. Good game and goodbye."

"Please, just a moment." The boy called Fate leans in close. "Will you join my team?"

"What? Why? You just crushed me. I barely got a hit in."

"I want you and your sister on my team. Besides, you are already using that." The Fate gestures towards the lobstered-iron gauntlet on Wake's right hand. Beads of water cling to the overlaying plates that form the gauntlet while iridescent rust eats away at its edges.

"This?" Wake holds up his gauntlet. The motion shakes free a few drops of water. Rather than splashing to the ground, the droplets take orbit around his hand. "It's just something I picked up a while back. Do you know what it is?"

"Yes, of course. It is a Hand of Fate. A rare one at that; I did not realize any Hands of Pure Water still remain in existence. The only Dark Blue Gauntlets I have ever seen have all been Ice."

"Well, the guy I got it from pretty much considered it worthless. It's always been covered in rust," Wake says. When it comes to unique equipment, he can't help it; he'll talk to anybody willing to on the subject, even to a guy that just whipped him good.

"Pure Water Gauntlets were always considered pretty useless. That is why they are nearly impossible to find these days, but somehow you found one and figured out how to use it properly. I have no clue what the attack you hit me with did. It did not do any damage as far as I could tell, but I know it did something. Only a true mad genius could figure out how to use one. That is the truth."

Wake chuckles. "I'm pretty sure, I'm not the crazy one here."

"That is exactly what Wolak always says."

Rachel hurries over with a mug full of something steaming. "I'm sorry, Wake, I had no clue ..."

"Hello, Light Tripper. You were right. He is strong ..."

Rachel hands her brother the cup and turns towards the annoying boy. "You stop teasing us! Just leave us alone, we didn't do anything to you."

"Squeak!" The chipmunk climbs out the Fate's hood and leaps onto Rachel's outstretched finger.

"Spikey! Please be more careful," says the Fate.

Rachel's grimace has already turned into a smile, though. She gently cups the little critter in her hands and brings him to her lap.

"I believe it was meant to be." The Fate smiles at them. "Will the two of you please join my Team?"

Wake is shaking his head, but his sister answers for them both. "Could you give us a moment? I need to talk to my brother alone."

"Of course." The Fate turns to walk away, grinning at no one in particular.

"Absolutely not," Wake whispers to his sister.

"Wake, what do we really have to lose at this point? Signups end tonight. We're not going to get another invite."

"But, Ray, this guy is really weird. And I really don't want to get embarrassed in front of everyone. We finally have a decent rep, you know?" he tries to tell her. "At least, we did before that last match."

"We have to try. At least, it's a chance." Without waiting for an answer, she calls out to the Fate. "How do you plan on having me—*a blind girl* and Sensei, a boy who has trouble walking from one end of the field to the other, on the same team? We'll need to field at least five, so one of us will have to be out there."

"I realize this. My job as Captain is to remember what matters," the Fate says. "That is something you can always count on."

"If that's so, then promise us that we will earn enough points to get into Criers College."

"Yaksok," the Fate says, holding out his pinky.

The siblings stare back at him in confusion.

"It means promise in Han. It is my word, unbreakable," he says, reaching over and wrapping his pinky around Rachel's. He barely shakes as he says, "You are the fifth person I touched this year. The third I have touched more than once. Do you see how serious I am?"

Wake looks at his sister and then at the boy who only sort of makes sense. He has a bad feeling about this. But before he knows it, they're wrapping little fingers, also.

"It is settled then," the Fate says. "Riser should be finished retaking the pre-exam and waiting for us back at the inn."

"Wait a minute; we never really agreed to join you," Wake says.

The Fate is already walking towards the entrance. He continues talking, paying no attention to Wake's words. "Then we have to find a Healer. I have a couple in mind already."

Things are happening all too fast. Wake needs a moment to think. Just then, the wind blows, carrying off one of his towels. It flutters and floats through the air, finally losing momentum above a large, muddy puddle. As it plummets, another gust sends it upwards and he watches it disappear above the crowds. He feels himself being swept away, too.

"You can't just leave. What about your next match? I'm knocked out but you're still in it?"

"I have already informed the officials that I am withdrawing."

"What? You're going to need every point you can get."

"There is no way I can obtain enough points to get licensed," says the Fate. "Come on already; we do not have all day."

"Let's go, Wake. We don't really have any other options." Rachel hurries after the Fate and Wake has no choice but to follow. *I just hope that I don't end up in some dirty puddle.*

"I don't know about this," Wake whispers to his sister. They stand before a small inn he's never heard of. Worst of all, it's on the wrong side of town. At least, the wood is varnished instead of worm-eaten. He'll give it that much.

The inn's also so close to the outskirts of Greenwood he can see the forest behind it. And for a moment, he thinks he might have even heard a bird singing back there, too.

Otherwise, it's actually pretty quiet, all of which he finds very strange. It's nothing like every other inn he's stayed at while on Tour.

"I love it," Rachel says. "But they need a new sign." The beat-up old sign hanging over the doorway reads *Stewards & Raiders.*

Otherwise, everything else about the place seems clean and well cared for. But still, it's on the wrong side of town, which means it's away from the block-long row of inns that everyone else is staying at.

Being so far away from everybody means missing out on half the fun of being on Tour. *Not that I really had fun, anyway,* Wake thinks. But at least, he was able to watch, even if he never quite felt a part of it.

He opens the door the Fate disappeared into and follows his sister in.

Inside it's well lit, with large stone hearths to either side. To his right is an open kitchen with bundles of herbs, pots and pans, and all manner of utensils dangling from the ceiling. Small tables are arranged neatly throughout the rest of the inn, most of them empty at this early hour. In the corner is a set of stairs, and along the far wall lays open a dark walnut door that reveals the woods out back.

It does smell good. Wake spies his new Captain pulling up a seat next to a growling girl. *Wait a minute, that looks like a Daughter of Enyo. But, there's no way ... Why would a Daughter be on his team?*

The bronzed girl tears a piece of bread in two and picks the larger half to clean her bowl. She shoves the dripping handful into her mouth. A couple of half-successful chews later and she tries to swallow. A loud thump to her chest and it is done.

"Congratulations, Riser. I assume that you passed," the Fate says to the warrior girl. Turning to his new teammates, he asks, "Have you had lunch?

"Lene, may we get three bowls over here, please?" the Fate yells out, not waiting for them to reply.

The Daughter takes a large swig from her mug and slams it down with a table-shaking belch. "I really hate you! How could you keep me from eating this?"

"It was for your own good." The Fate motions for them to take a seat. "These are the new ones I was telling you about. He was able to dodge out of Fluttering Blade and land a hit on me." He points to Wake.

"You?" the Daughter asks in wonder, pointing from one to the other. "Hit him?"

'I got one strike in," Wake admits, setting down his satchel and showing his sister to what he deems the cleanest chair.

"I do not know what he was doing for most of the match, but when he actually tried—he was really quite amazing." The Fate leans in close to the Daughter. "He is a little off, though."

"What?" Wake says, wondering how he could say that. "No, I most definitely am not."

The Fate shrugs.

"Wake's a good, thoughtful boy," his sister says in his defense, making him cringe inside.

"I am sure he is, but that does not change the facts," the Fate says just as the Innkeeper plops a bowl overflowing with stew in front of each of them. Riser asks for another helping.

"Thank you, Lene," the Fate tells the tiny innkeeper before turning to Wake. "That last match was really important to you, was it not?"

"Of course it was."

"But you did not even try until the very end. I do not know what was going through your head, but it was not what should have been going through your head. You knew you had to win, you wanted to win, but you were barely paying attention."

"That's not quite ..."

"That is what it looked like to me. And I have a word for that—madness." The irritating boy grins at him. "No worries, though. Once we learn how to deal with your condition, I am sure you will be unstoppable."

Wake decides he doesn't want to talk about it anymore. One thing's for sure: his new Captain is really annoying.

"Riser, let me introduce you to our new teammates ... what were your names again?" *Beyond annoying.*

"Hello, I'm Rachel Avenoy and this is my brother, Wake. It's a pleasure to make your acquaintance."

"Nice to meet you," Wake says politely.

"Well met, I am Esperanza, current First Daughter of Enyo.

You can call me Riser." The Daughter grunts and nods. "At least, you two look more promising than the first one." *This can't be for real*, Wake thinks. *She really is a Daughter.*

"Sensei helped you study last night, *after* working all day. You would be sitting here with an empty stomach if it were not for him."

Riser rolls her long-lashed eyes and leans over to her new teammates. "Can you believe this guy? Captain made a rule that I couldn't eat until I passed the pre-exam. He ate three bowls in front of me yesterday. I was this close to sticking a fork in him, I was so hungry." She has to squint to make sure her finger and thumb are close enough.

"You should have passed the first time," he says as the innkeeper brings another serving of stew and a pile of steaming bread.

"Thank you!" Riser tries to smile graciously, but only succeeds in baring her fangs. Two of the Daughter's side teeth extend slightly further down than the rest, ending in a pair of cute points. It's a common trait among Orcs, a feature many a Daughter has also inherited over generations.

"Please eat," the Fate tells them as he breaks off some of his bread and hands it to the chipmunk on his shoulder.

"So what are you two?" Riser asks between chews.

Wake can't decide if it's ruder for him to answer with his mouth full or to leave the question hanging. The Fate answers for them.

"She is going to Shield with you. And he is a Finisher."

"I am most definitely not a Shield. I race the Light Course and if I have to, I try to draw. Though, I'm not very good at it," Rachel says. "And thank you for lunch."

"You are welcome," the Fate says. "What is it that you try to draw? Portraits or landscapes or is there something else?"

"Nooo, nothing like that," Rachel says, trying not to laugh. "Well, I do paint, but that's another story. What I mean is, I can go defensive and try to go for a draw or a tie in games that require one-on-one matchups like, King's Corridor. Anything else, like Flag or Battle Royale, I'm pretty much worthless."

"You make very little sense sometimes," the Fate says. "It does not matter, however. We will figure it out."

Before she can say another world, he hands her a piece of bread. "The bread here is quite delicious—crisp and chewy."

"It is good, isn't it? Makes me want to hurt him all the more." Riser leans in close to the newcomers. "If you guys want to mutiny, I'm in."

Well, this is certainly different, Wake thinks. His new teammates are loud and rude. They say harsh things about each other, but with no real malice. It's the opposite of his last team, where kind words hid darker intentions. Before he can get lost in the thought, the Fate hands him a piece of the warm bread.

The awkwardness of the silence that would have been is instead replaced by what the locals called the inn's specialty, 'Quiet Stew.'

CHAPTER 7

RACHEL

Rachel tries to keep up the best she can. Even though, she doesn't understand just why they have to be in such a hurry. Her eyelids are already closed, but they feel heavy nevertheless. *Maybe, I should've passed on seconds. But everyone else had seconds. Riser even had thirds. Am I really on the same team as a Daughter now? Wouldn't that be wonderful?*

Rachel hurries to catch up to the fading auras. *It's definitely naptime now. And why is he dragging us to the Office of the Registrar now of all times?*

When they finally arrive, her brother waits for her at the entrance. *At least, we're still together.* She thanks him for waiting and asks for his help in finding a seat.

The next thing she knows, they're teasing her for falling asleep. Meanwhile, A new aura has joined them; Young Sensei's.

Unfortunately for him, it's a slow day at the Office which leaves him available for lunch. Their new Captain declares it's a perfect opportunity to get in their first practice together.

I know we don't have a lot of time, but isn't this a bit much? Rachel can't help but wonder. The Fate is still talking, so she tries to pay attention.

"We do need to find a Healer, but any Healer worth their salt will be training this time of the day. Which is what we should be doing, too."

"In front of all these people?" Wake gestures towards the crowds scattered throughout the Tourney Grounds. It seems as if everyone and their mother is out to enjoy the last of the solo games.

"I have gone over the rules and they state that teams may practice anywhere on the Tourney Grounds. Did I misunderstand the rules?" the Fate says, setting down his buckskin pack.

"No, you're right. But no one practices here in the middle of everybody," Wake tries to explain.

He's not going to listen. Rachel already knows that much about their new Captain.

"It is settled then. Everybody, please loosen up and then we will go for a short run." The Fate plops down onto the ground and begins to stretch. Noticing that only Riser's joined him, he asks, "You do know how to stretch, right?"

"Yes, of course." Rachel lowers herself to the ground, gracefully. Her brother and the clerk follow suit. She knows that Wake hates doing stuff out of the ordinary, especially in front of all these people. She doesn't like it much herself.

"Four laps around the Tourney Grounds should do it. Sensei, you just go at your own pace," the Fate tells them. "Last one to finish does push-downs."

"Push-downs?" Wake asks. "Don't you mean push-ups?"

"Yes, those."

Two laps later and a glistening Rachel slows down to walk alongside the strolling clerk. She earns a look of disapproval as the other three lap them. But she's run enough. There's no need for her to run anymore around the grounds like this. It's unseemly. A weary Wake hands his satchel to her as he passes by.

"So what do you think about our new Captain?" she asks the wheezing clerk after the others are out of sight.

"Actually, I think ..." he replies between breaths, "he's pretty great."

She wasn't expecting that. "Weren't you surprised to see Wake and I joining the Team?"

"Not really ... he asked me to set it up so that he'd have the best chance ... of going up against your brother." The little clerk has to stop to spit out the rest of it. "Over the past couple days ... he's asked me to help him with some odd things. He never really explains why, but it's usually pretty obvious."

"Are you feeling alright? Should we rest a moment?"

"No, I'm fine," he says, wheezing for air. "I guess my lungs aren't used to it, but it's really only my heart that I have to be careful of."

"I hope so," she says, full of worry. After he catches his breath, she asks, "Is it really possible to choose your opponent, or even fair?"

"I guess that wouldn't be fair, but it doesn't exactly work that way. There was a lot of luck involved, too. I just made sure his application was near the top of the pile and Wake's was near the bottom. The way they seat the competitors did the rest. I would never have done something like that unless he had Wake's best interest in mind."

"Oh, I get it, you only use your powers for good," she teases. "He also mentioned that we're signed up for the Greenwood's Closing Games. Wasn't the deadline for that yesterday? If so, how's that possible? We don't even have a full team yet."

"Well, we filled out all the proper applications and used a placeholder name to fill out the team roster. As long as the correct names are on the applications before the match officially starts, we'll be fine."

"So you used a fake name?"

Sensei scratches the back of his head and grins shamelessly. "Something like that ..."

The others catch up once again. This time, the Captain signals for them to come to a stop. Wake collapses to the ground, gasping and drenched. He seems long past caring about what others may think.

"Rachel, you are last. You may do your push-downs and run your last lap after practice." The Fate looks over at Wake. "Please sit up."

"I just need a minute to catch my breath."

"We do not lie around during practice unless we are practicing lying around. And I see no need for that," the Fate says. "If that is how you have been training, I see why your guard was down during our match. You practiced letting your guard down."

Wake picks himself up. He doesn't say anything, but rubs his ear.

"Now, let us go over our Fighting Styles ..." the Fate says.

"Why did we have to go for a run if all we were going to do was sit around and talk?" Rachel asks. *This makes no sense.*

The Fate looks at her curiously. "You can sit here and listen to me describe my Fighting Style without going for a run first? You really are strong."

What? The more she learns of her new Captain, the less sense he makes.

The Fate is already moving on. "I have an affinity to Yellow, particularly Earth. I use three pieces of Sharded equipment: Terra Boots, a Hand of Earth, and my Stick. I have been working on switching over to Light Boots, but I am not good enough with them quite yet."

"I use the standard 'Earth Leap' and 'Hold My Ground' techs with my 128's," he explains. *At least, he's not a total crybaby,* Rachel thinks. He called Teared battle footgear 128's, just like everyone else. Which means he probably knows that they're called that because it takes a shard of 128 internal facets to power.

"I use 'Earth Grab' and 'Earth Repel' with my Earth Gauntlet, usually to power up my handsprings to aide in my movement, but sometimes I use them to lock down or push away an opponent." He nods at Wake.

"And my Stick is actually a Rock Leech Root, a parasitic plant that grows on the shells of Basalt Tortoises. That means it thrives off of blood as well as water. Stick's also coated with the sap of Black Iron Wood. This combination pulls the iron from the blood stored within to use my 'Iron Blood Block' Tech."

"Where did you get something like that?" Wake asks. Rachel knew he would. Wake has always been interested in rare Teared equipment. It even led to her brother earning his Appraiser's License and writing a weekly column for their local paper on the subject.

"My Old Man helped me get her, but I raised Stick all by myself. There is nothing else like Stick in the whole-wide world," the young Captain proclaims proudly. "She is still growing, you see. Just this past summer, I planted a seed on her tip, a flowering type of razor grass. After gathering enough blood, the razor grass blooms, allowing me to use 'Fluttering Blade.'"

"That's pretty impressive. I've never heard of a living weapon," Wake says.

"Yes, I have been raising her for almost eight years. Stick has a shard of each primary color embedded in her. This helps keep her nice and healthy. That, a little blood, and sunlight is all she really needs."

"So you're pretty much all physical, close combat melee—using your gauntlet and boots to outmaneuver your opponent and get in close?" Rachel asks.

"Yes, that is what I am best at."

"Rachel told me you're Home-brew. I have respect for anyone who tries something new, and your combination is elegantly straightforward. There's a lot of synergy in that build, definitely Beautiful Design," Wake says. "Is there a standard Fate skill set, though?"

"Not exactly. And if I had to be exact, I suppose it would be more correct to call myself a 'Switch Fate,'" he says, swiping the air with his stick. "Fates existed even before there were Classes, so we are more a collection of ideals than anything else. In fact, everyone here is going to end up being some version of a Fate."

"How's that?"

"We will all be following the Way of the Fate." He straps on his gauntlet and wiggles his fingers. "And we will all be using at least one of these. It is not absolutely necessary that we do, but there are benefits. Please let me show you."

He reaches into his pack and pulls out a pair of gauntlets created of interwoven vines. Each one a different shade of Green, they seem to writhe in the light as he tosses them to the clerk. "Green Hands are popular and relatively common. Go ahead and get used to using a pair for now."

Sensei thanks him and tries them on.

"For the Big Sister we have something very special. This is another one-of-a-kind Hand, almost as rare as your brothers. My Old Man probably would not like that I took it from the armory, but he did say to take what I needed before he left," the Fate says. *He still can't remember my name.*

"Please take good care of this." He places a sleek golden gauntlet in her hands. It is warm and strangely smooth, with hardly an edge or corner to be found. It has weight, but doesn't really feel heavy. She can feel the gilded glove glint wickedly even in the shade of the old tree. "It is a Hand of the Sun. I am pretty sure it was made for you."

"Are you sure about this? I've actually been using a Water Gauntlet for a while now. It's not ideal, but I'm pretty used to it." She doesn't feel comfortable accepting this at all.

"Please give it a try," her new Captain urges. "That way your brother can try using both of the Water Gauntlets."

"Speaking of the Little Brother, you should start getting used to using the pair. With the way you weaponize Water, you will be much better off with two."

"I've kind of always wanted to, but I always saw the second as Rachel's," Wake says, taking back the rusty glove. "But, yeah, thanks for letting Rachel use that so I can give it try."

"You are welcome," the Fate says before turning back to her. *What if it doesn't work?* Rachel worries. Wake seems pretty happy to reunite his pair.

"Why are you not putting it on? As I said, it was made for you. No one else I know besides my Old Man can even use it, and he still has yet to return from his trip. There is a drawback to this particular Hand ... repeated activation of a Sun Gauntlet leads to permanent blindness." *Does that mean his old man is blind too?*

"Really?" Rachel wonders aloud, knowing the armored glove she holds must be forged of solid gold. It's the only metal able to harness Light Yellow Tearstones. "I promise to take care of it the best I can."

She tries it on. It fits perfectly, almost as if it really was made just for her. The warmth she felt just holding it is multiplied. It reaches deep inside her, making her feel strangely calm and restless all at the same time.

When she flexes her hand, it feels strong. Now that it is on, she never wants to take it off. *Maybe this is what I was really afraid of?*

"See, you're just like me," he explains, snapping her out of her little moment of bliss. "Others may view our conditions as weaknesses, but they are what make us unique. This uniqueness is what gives us our true strength, our incomparable strength. Do you understand?"

Rachel thinks she understands.

"The same goes for all of you."

"Sensei, since you have no experience with one, it will take you some time to learn how to even activate yours. But for you, Big Sis, it should come more easily. You are already experienced in using a Hand of Fate. If you used Shielding Techs with the Dark Blue

Hand, you should be able to use this one in the same way. The main Tech is just summoning the Light around you. Just imagine drawing in Light instead of moisture. It is called 'Grab the Sun.'"

"Should I try to here, now?" But she doesn't wait for him to answer. *What could possibly go wrong?* If she fails, she fails. But something tells her she won't.

Just as she practiced a thousand times before, she tries to draw everything she can from her surroundings. Instead of Water, though, she focuses on extracting every bit of Light that she can. It comes easily. "Grab the Sun."

Screams fill the air as day abruptly turns into night. A cloud of pitch-black surrounds them. Thirty paces from end to end, with panicked bystanders caught in its sightless grip, the darkness grows as the Sun Gauntlet continues to steal the light.

There's only one thing visible in the encompassing darkness. It escapes between Rachel's fingertips and hovers there trapped in her grasp. She holds it, but she can't control it. And as much as she tries, she cannot stop it. What it is can only be described as a miniature sun.

"Rachel, let go of the Light!" the Fate yells at her through the chaos.

"I can't!" she yells back, confused and afraid.

"You can. Clear your head and focus," her new Captain tells her. Rachel takes a deep breath and grabs her right wrist with her other hand. She tries to ignore the clamor and clear her head of all other thoughts, except for one: *Stop!*

"I think I did something, but I'm not sure."

"You did good. It is no longer growing. Now, it is just a matter of time. There is a built-in safety reflex that keeps it from returning all the daylight at once. The Sun Orb will slowly release the daylight back into the world on its own."

"We have to do something, someone might get hurt," Sensei says. Already, people are running around in a panic.

"Sensei, can you lead her away from here? Somewhere safe?" asks the Fate.

"I can." The clerk makes his way over to her.

"Everyone, please follow Sensei."

"Ready?" The clerk grabs Rachel's hand and prepares to lead them away before turning to ask the Captain, "What about you?"

"I will make sure everything is fine here." Whistles sound in the distance. The Sitters are on their way.

"Why did he stay behind ... is he going to be alright? Are we going to be alright?" Rachel asks, finally breaking the silence. The four teammates minus the Captain sit huddled in a small clearing adjacent to what Sensei called the Clerks' Dorm. They've been waiting too long. He should've been here by now.

"I didn't mean to do that. Why didn't he warn me?" One second it was fine and the next everything was chaos: screaming, shoving; she even heard someone crying.

"Because he didn't know. How could he?" Riser says. "I've seen the Old Man use 'Grab the Sun' before. All it did was slightly darken the area within arm's reach. Nothing like what you did.

"You practiced all these years with an Aspect you could barely use. And when you finally got to use the one you were meant to ..." The Daughter stares at her. "Even so, no one could've guessed something like that would've happened. Don't worry. We'll be fine, he'll be fine."

"How will he even find us?" Wake asks.

"I'm guessing with these," Sensei answers. "I didn't notice at first, either; not until it got dark and I still felt like I knew where everyone was. If you shut your eyes and concentrate, can you feel him? He's not too far now."

"You're right. I can feel him." Riser inspects her own gauntlet. "How did I never notice that before? I've spent every day of last year training with this thing."

"We've had ours for much longer and never noticed," Wake adds.

"I'm assuming you can only detect gauntlets that are in use and within a certain distance. If you already know where they are, you probably wouldn't realize anything, either." Sensei looks down at his pair of green gauntlets.

The petrified vines covering his hands shift back and forth as he makes two fists. "Perhaps, because I was wearing two it was easier to notice."

Wake slaps his forehead. "I totally forgot my ..." he begins, just as his satchel is thrown onto his lap.

"Keep your eyes open. Even when it gets dark, Wade," the Fate scolds him. "Is everyone okay? I apologize about that, Team."

"Thanks," he replies. "And it's Wake"

"What took so long?" Riser asks. "Are you okay?"

"I am fine. And it looks like you all are, as well," the Captain says. "Everything was fine after you left and you took the darkness with you."

"The Sitters didn't do anything to you?"

"They asked me some questions and then put me on something called The List."

That's not too bad, Rachel thinks, full of relief. Being on The List is pretty much just a warning. As long as he doesn't get into any more trouble, he should be fine.

"I thought I had taken into account everything that mattered. I am sorry. I failed you as Captain. I will not let something like that happen ever again."

"Enough of that. There's no way you could've known," Riser tells him.

"I should have at least warned you of what to expect.

No other Hand of Fate has a built-in safety like the golden one," he says, shaking his head. "It must have been horrible, not being in control of your own power. But without the built-in safety reflex—well, if you released all that Light back into the world all at once, it would have blinded anyone nearby."

"Wow, that's actually quite terrifying," Wake says.

"Yes, a total Moment of Truth," the Captain agrees. He turns to the clerk. "Sensei, how are you on time?"

"I'm not too late yet," the youngest replies, grinning. "Besides, I can't go without seeing that Tech at least one more time."

"That is for her to decide. I do not believe anything else will go wrong." The Fate faces Rachel and asks, "It is alright if you choose not to, but now that we know what to expect, it should be okay. Would you like to try that again?"

"Now?" There's nothing else she wants more than to try it again. But the thought of doing so is just as frightening. "If everyone else thinks it's okay, I'll try it again."

"Ray, are you kidding? I mean, it was a mess back there, but that's just 'cause there was a bunch of people around and we didn't know what to expect," her brother says. "And Sensei figured out we can locate each other using these, even if it gets dark." He holds up his gauntlets.

"Daebak! You learned the lesson and I did not even have to teach it. The Hands allow you to sense the location and well being of anyone else wearing one, friend or foe. It is just a feeling and not very exact, but it is something. I can only tell so much, but maybe some of you will have better luck," The Captain says. "Go ahead, Shine."

"Grab the Sun," she answers as the world goes black around them. *Is this how others feel when they use their Techs? Water never felt like this.* But it's not the first time she's felt this way. It's how she feels on the Light Course.

"Hold it out directly in front of you and don't move," the Captain tells her. "Brace yourself, Shine."

Is he calling me Shine? Rachel staggers her feet, one slightly in front of the other. She holds her right hand in front of her, supporting it with her left. It was a natural position for her, though, she had never used it before in Tear Battle. "I'm ready."

"Ray, you sort of look like you're about to paint with your large brush."

Before she can reply, the Fate is flying towards her, Stick in hand. One, two, three, he strikes. Each blow bounces harmlessly off the glowing orb. "Fluttering Blade," he commands before he is knocked backwards by the fury of his own attack. Spikey finally wakes up and crawls out of his hood to check on what the commotion is all about.

"The Sun Orb is impenetrable by regular weapon attacks and most Techs. I bet Shine could even use hers to block some Power Moves," says the Fate, picking himself up

"My turn!" Riser exclaims.

"I should go next. She's my sister."

"I would like to try that again."

"No, it's my turn ..."

"Squeak."

CHAPTER 8
WAKE
[THE OUTSKIRTS OF GREENWOOD]

The last building in sight comes and goes. It's enough to make Wake start wondering just where the Fate may be leading them.

He mentioned something about finding a Healer, but no one stays out this far. Another block and it'll be all farms and forest.

He stares at the back of his new Captain's head, wondering if he looked for long enough if he could figure out just what's going on in there.

Sensei had to go back to work, and Riser and his sister are giggling about something or other. *She's probably just happy that there's another girl on the team.* Wake wants to think of something to be worried about, but he can't. *I guess we really have nothing left to lose.*

Despite everything that's gone wrong in the past days, he finds himself in a good mood. The training session was nothing like the ones with his old team, *Kearney and the Courageous.* Even though it was a hundred times more difficult, it was actually somewhat fun.

And that's one thing we never had on Kearney's team—fun, he thinks in disgust. Rachel, as sweet as she is, never saw it, but he hated every second he was part of *The Courageous.*

As backwards as this new group is, it's still one hundred times better, he decides.

This afternoon reminded him of something he forgot, long ago. How it was before his sister left for her first time on Tour, back when they'd spend every free moment they could find playing at Tear Fighting—back when it used to be fun.

With all the worrying about points and qualifying, he'd forgotten the feeling. *The truth is I didn't forget. I gave it up*, he admits to himself. *Why? It wasn't worth it. Even if we had made it all the way with Kearney it still wouldn't have been worth it.*

When Wake looks up, he realizes they are passing a farm. "Are you sure we're going the right way?" His sister warned him of just how well their new Captain knew his way around town. And there's nothing else out here except for ... *No, we couldn't possibly ...*

"Where exactly are we going?" he demands to know.

"We are going to get a Healer," the Fate tells him.

"But nothing's down this way except for the Royal Caravan. We'll get in trouble if we try to go anywhere near there."

"We will be fine. Trust me."

Decked from head to toe in regal lilac and white, two guards stand watch at the Royal Campgrounds. Tall and silent, they stand in defense of the entrance, keeping the riffraff out. *Riffraff like us ... Just what is he getting us into?* Wake worries.

The Fate walks right past them.

He may've gotten away with that, but there's no way they'll let us all pass. Wake just knew something like this would happen. All the good feelings from earlier begin to wash away. Wake grabs his sister's arm.

Riser notices their hesitation. "It's fine. This is probably a big waste of time, but he's not going to get us in any more trouble—at least, not today." She begins to laugh. When she sees his doubt remains, she adds, "You have my word on that."

"I'll trust you then," Rachel says, following Esperanza past the pair of well-armed guardsmen. Wake hurries after, not wanting to be left behind. The guards let them pass without a word.

When they catch up to the Captain, Wake asks, "Wouldn't the Lobby be a much better place to look for a Healer?"

"If we were looking for any old Healer, but I want someone good enough to stick with us for the long run. Besides, this Healer needs us as much as we need her."

They come to a stop before a humongous tent, striped in a hue of purple that can only be associated with royalty. The canopy ends ten feet above the ground, below which a ring of wagons circle, forming a wall.

"Fate, this can't be right. This is *The Royal Team*'s Tent. We can't go in there," Wake says.

"That is exactly where we are going," the Fate says. "Let me guess—you must be worried about meeting the Princess? Just remember to belch in her face and you should be fine. She hates that."

"What the fail are you talking about? This is crazy. We have to go *now!*" Wake pleads.

"Have you not learnt the Princess Rules?"

"Princess Rules?"

"Yes, the rules you have to follow in order to protect yourself from their Dark Arts."

"I have no clue what you're talking about, even more than usual," Wake complains.

"I realize you are mad, but even you should be able understand this," the Fate tells him "What is a princess, really?"

"This one is the former King's granddaughter!" Wake answers matter-of-factly. "The current King's grandniece."

"That is true, but none of that is what matters. What is important is how princesses tend to be treated. As soon as they come into the world, they are pampered with luxury, their every whim met—no want goes unfulfilled. They are always being praised for their beauty, intelligence, and upbringing. Most people can not say a word against them. They are usually taught to believe they are naturally better than commoners or other people," the Fate explains. "And they always want things to go their own way."

"That's very stereotypical of you. But I guess it makes some sense, so shouldn't we just avoid her all together, then?"

"You cannot just avoid things in life. That is why the Princess Rules exist. By following them, you can protect yourself from their witchery." He wiggles his fingers as if casting a spell.

"And we are about to meet the worst type of princess— the exception. She was raised the princess way and somehow she is not all that wicked. But do not be deceived—Princess Achylsa Love is dangerous. Believe me when I tell you this: she definitely has her own selfish agenda and she will not bat an eyelash, even if it means crushing your dreams. She is ruthless ... "

"Fate," scolds Riser. "You shouldn't talk about her that way. She's still the Princess."

"I really don't know about this." Wake says.

"You feel it too? It is another Moment of Truth." The Fate beams with excitement.

The Captain's said that a couple times now and Wake hates hearing those words already. *Moment of Truth.*

This isn't happening. I need to get out of here. Wake's mind shrieks at him to turn back even as they approach the entrance to the tent, the one he'd never thought he'd find himself in, not in a million lifetimes.

He stares at *The Royal Team*'s Tent. Above it flies the three banners of Wysteria: the waves of sea and sun of the Bae, the thin, S-curved line enclosed in a blossom of Silla, and the three-legged, red raven of Gorgury.

Two of the banners might as well have been carved from stone for how still they are, while the last flaps mercilessly. Wake can't help but feel sorry for it. He takes a deep breath and hurries after the others.

The canopy overhead is a flood of white, patterned in thin lines of lavender. The canvas rooftop ends atop a wall of circled coaches so pristine they look to be carved of ivory.

The wagons are all exactly alike, except for the doors set at the center of each. No two of those are even similar. It takes him only moments to pick out which one must belong to the Princess, a strikingly plain door painted two tones of violet.

Feeling distinctly like a fish following his school into shark infested waters, Wake tries to keep his eyes on the floor. But at the clang of metal on metal, he braves a look up.

There dances a strikingly tall youth. With a spear in each hand, he keeps a handful of opponents at bay. Simultaneously brutal and graceful, the fighter dodges a pair of coordinated attacks, returning the favor with a stab to one assailant's face and a sweep to the other's knees. They crumple before him. Upon noticing the interlopers, he backs off and gives the command to end the exercise.

"That is enough for now," the fighter orders. He removes his helmet to reveal a dissatisfied scowl. His short rough hair, black against his dark complexion, and unusual height mark him as Kase Shake, the Best of the Best. Undefeated in official solo and team play, he's the true power behind Wysteria's top team, *The Royal Team*.

Wake's watched every available memory of Kase's matches.

No one compares to the Chosen One. His skill and talent are unparalleled.

"Everybody out. Leave your armor on, we will be continuing shortly," Kase commands. Wake and Rachel turn to leave before Esperanza stops them.

"He doesn't mean us, babos." The room empties and only the interlopers remain behind with the intimidating descendant of the Zul.

"Greetings, Brother!" the Fate says happily. "How fare you this fine day?"

"Are you trying to anger me? I told you never to call me that. There is no blood shared between us," Kase growls. "Why are you even here?"

"What are you saying, Brother? Do you not believe we Zul should look out for one another," says the Fate, though, the paleness of his skin indicates otherwise.

Kase takes two angry steps towards the grinning boy before regaining his composure. "Whatever," he spits out before turning to Esperanza. "Greetings, Esperanza, First Daughter. I hope you have been well. Are you here for a private challenge perhaps?"

Riser laughs in his face. "Not even if you suddenly turned into an Orc would I fight the likes of you."

"Still going on about Orcs, I see," Kase says. "You do realize that they are no longer the most feared of the new teams on the World Circuit, don't you?"

"Who pray tell, is then?" Riser asks.

"The Bunny Death Mages."

Riser begins to laugh.

"No, I am serious. Look them up. They are fearsome and undefeated. No country wants to face them right now." Kase turns back towards the Fate. "Why show up now? What could you possibly hope to accomplish this late in the year?"

"We are looking for a Healer. I am here to ask Princess if she wants to join my Team," the Fate says. It's so much worse than Wake feared. All he can do is stare at his new Captain and hope this is all some sort of bad joke.

He can't be serious. That's the Healer we're here to recruit?

Kase just stares back at the Fate. Finally, he takes off a glove to wipe away at his eye and bursts out in laughter. "Look, *Brother*, I'm not sure if you were born this way or someone dropped you on your head, but there's no way under the sun she'd leave *The 'Royal' Team* and join yours."

"I will not know for sure unless I ask."

"If that's what you're here for, go right on ahead." He bows with a flourish and gestures towards the white coach with the two-toned door. "She's in there. I'll warn you, however, this is her 'Reading Time' and she hates nothing more than to be bothered at this hour.

"And forgive my rudeness and your Captain's for the lack of proper introductions," the young nobleman continues. "I am Kase Shake. It is a pleasure to meet you. I believe it is Rachel and Wake Avenoy?"

Rachel blushes as he takes her hand. "Thank you, it is an honor to make your acquaintance." She curtsies.

"It really is an honor to meet you. I'm a big fan." Wake says. The star of all those Tear Memories he used to watch is right in front of him, and he actually knows their names. It's almost too much for him.

What is going on? How can Fate and Esperanza talk to the Chosen One the way they do. How do they even know him?

"Ha, so at least there are a couple among you with some semblance of manners." Kase shakes Wake's hand firmly before pulling him in close. "I saw your match earlier. That was a nice counter, but you should have smacked him with something harder than just Water."

He chortles as he turns to walk away. "Now, if you'll excuse me, I must get back to my training."

Wake stands there doubly dumbfounded. Not only are his new teammates welcome here, but Kase Shake, the Best of the Best, watched one of his matches and gave him a compliment.

Before he is able to get too proud of himself, Wake sees the dreadful sight—the Fate at the top of the most ornate set of stairs, about to knock on the door done in two tones of violet. *Kase warned us she doesn't like to be disturbed at this hour! What's he doing? She can have us beheaded or worse…*

CHAPTER 9
PRINCESS
[THE ROYAL CARAVAN]

Princess Achylsa Love sits at her vanity reading the day's paper, which just happens to feature her on the front page.

Despite that, she finds herself immersed in the story of what befell the town of Glen Forest. Though, you wouldn't be able to tell by the expression on her face.

There is none.

Even in the privacy of her own chambers, she sits uncomfortably straight. Her amethyst hair falls careless, however, ending in so many swirls against her high-collared dress.

It is one of many handpicked by her grandaunt—a woman who has dressed no less than three Queens and more than a handful of Princesses. And now that her husband's come to sit upon the throne, the royal court has never looked so good, which is something the Princess could not care any less about. She's always been fine with her grandaunt's choices, however. That is, until just recently.

Queen Jandice is a classic woman with classic tastes, which means gowns imported from Jasir for the warmer months and Yornian attire for autumn and winter.

However, his past spring, the Princess made it clear she would only wear garments produced in Wysteria.

The Princess even went out of her way to explain *Why to Buy Wysterian*, using quotes directly from the enlightening article. But the Queen didn't appreciate the lecture one bit. Still, her grandaunt went out of the way to find the most promising tailor in all of the Three Kingdoms.

Even now, the Princess wears his work: a dress featuring a sleek silhouette from collar to waist, below which the outer skirt opens to reveal a split, long and dramatic. The clean lines and blocks of color suit the *Doll Princess* well.

No one who actually knows her would ever call her that: the Doll Princess. But that's what the kids on Tour have taken to calling her. She doesn't particularly like it, but she couldn't care less what they call her.

"We have visitors, Your Highness," says the lady in the silver mask. Up until that moment, the Sibyl of Sleeping Goddess was so quiet, the Princess thought the old priestess might've actually fallen asleep. *Just like her goddess.* But she never forgot that the Sibyl was there.

She's always there.

"Tell whomever it is, to go away," the Princess says before returning to her article.

"Hello, Princess, are you in there?" a voice calls from the other side of the door. The Sibyl stands and slips past the piles of newsprint and stacks of books that clutter the otherwise tidy wagon. *That voice ...*

"You may want to come see this," the Sibyl says from the peephole.

The Princess lets out a little sigh and sets the paper she was so enjoying down next to the lilac on her desk. She holds no particular fondness for flowers, but she tries to keep at least one of the potted, purple plants around. After all, they were her mother's favorites.

When she makes it to the peephole and peers through it, a little "Oh" escapes her lips.

"Princesssss, are you in there?" the Fate calls again from the other side.

"This is quite the opportunity. There is more than a bit of *Virtue* at stake here," the Sibyl notes. "Tread wisely."

The Princess nods and reaches for the door.

"Wait, Princess. You should at least brush your hair."

The Princess takes one look in the mirror and acquiesces. "A moment, please," she calls out before returning to her vanity in search of a brush.

The Sibyl in turn tries to bring some semblance of order to the room. In seconds, her arms are full of all manner of papers, from scrolls to books to old newsprint. With nowhere to put the growing pile, she begins shoving them underneath the bed.

"Gently," the Princess orders, putting her brush away. She takes a seat and nods.

"You may enter," she calls out. The Sibyl opens the door with a humble curtsey. On the other side is the Troublemaker, and tugging at his shirt is another she recognizes.

"Hello, Princess," the Fate says before turning to the stately priestess. "Hello, Auntie, I hope you're well ... Oh, and before I forget." He belches loudly in the princess's general direction.

He turns to his friend and signals for him to do the same. The other boy will have none of it, though. *Thank goodness; at least he has some manners.*

"Welcome ... Fate, Esperanza." She tries to make it sound friendly and welcoming.

"Thank you, Princess. And how do you fare this fine day?" the Troublemaker asks before leaning in and staring at her mouth. "Your smile still needs some work ..."

Before he can finish, the Daughter cuts in diplomatically. "Good evening, Princess. Lady Myun and the Venerable send their best wishes."

"How kind of you to relay the message, Esperanza. Please return the sentiment the next time you see your mother."

Never one for formalities, the Troublemaker gets to the point. "Princess, would you like to join my team?" The question is surprising, but not that surprising.

"You very well know that I can do no such thing."

"There are no rules against it as far as I know," he says.

Ignoring the annoying boy, she stands and faces the tall, fair girl. *This must be the older sister.* "Excuse me for not introducing myself straight away. I am Achylsa Love. It is a pleasure to meet you."

A blushing Rachel replies with a curtsey. "It is an honor, Your Highness. I am Rachel Avenoy of Ice Ridge."

The Princess turns her gaze towards Wake as if noticing him for the first time.

"Um, Hel ... Greetings, Your Majesty, my ... I'm Wake Avenoy. Nice to meet you," he manages to spit out. He looks everywhere but at her.

She doesn't say a word. Instead, she waits for him to face her.

When he finally does, he turns red and blurts out, "You're much prettier in real life."

The Doll Princess reveals she is not made entirely of porcelain. Her eyes grow large before she furrows her brow and sits back down.

Esperanza slaps Wake on the back and laughs silently. The Fate looks at him curiously. The nervous boy then extends a hand towards the Sibyl. "Hello, Ma'am, it is a pleasure to make your acquaintance, also."

The older woman is taken aback. Obviously the Troublemaker's rude greeting was to be expected, but otherwise the masked priestess has grown accustomed to being overlooked.

"Greetings to you, young man. You do not have to worry about introducing yourself to me. I am but a simple priestess, nothing more than an attendant to the 'prettier-in-real-life' princess."

Why did she just say that? the Princess wonders, studying the Sibyl out of the corner of her eye. It's unlike her to speak at all in front of others, and even then the Sibyl always keeps it short and to the point. These may've been the first unnecessary words the Princess has ever heard the masked lady utter. Seeing what could only be described as a twinkle in the priestess's eyes, the Princess suddenly wonders if she is smiling underneath the silvery mask. It's a thought that never, ever crossed her mind before.

"Fate, I will not join your team, but instead I will make an offer to you, to all of you. Whosoever among you that so wishes, may join the Royal Team. If you do so, qualifying for Criers College will most assuredly be guaranteed. I ask this of you, not only for myself, but for all of the Three Kingdoms."

Wake can't believe what he's hearing. Even his sister's eyes snap open in shock.

"It is essential that I am the one who leads this year's top team. There's more at stake here than you could ever know," the Princess explains.

The Fate is the first to reply. "No thank you, I am already the Captain of this Team. And there is more at stake than you could ever know."

"Don't be a fool … Fate. You don't even have any points yet." Sensing she's not getting anywhere, she looks to the others. "The offer is for each of you. If you choose to accept, you will be doing a great service to all the citizens of the Three Kingdoms."

Esperanza bows and says, "Thank You, Princess, but I'll stick with Fate."

"I can't believe I am saying this, but I too must refuse. I was just cast off a team and leaving after committing myself would be too similar an act. Please forgive me, Princess," Rachel tells her.

The Princess looks at the only one left to answer, but he is too busy staring at his boots to notice.

"Ray, are you sure about this?" Wake asks his older sister.

"Yes,' she whispers, "I'm sorry. I just can't. But it's okay if you do."

Scuffing his boots, he says, "Thank you. Really, thank you, but I guess I'm with them."

"Very well, then." The rejected girl turns to face the Fate. "You do not know what you are doing. Your actions are harming everyone," she declares softly. The Princess looks straight into his eyes; trying, hoping to make him understand. *This is no game ...*

"Dark Magic! Flee!" he says, bolting for the door. The remaining teammates apologize and follow behind—a little more civilly.

"Are you sure about this?" Wake asks, following the others out of there. "I get it. You want to be Captain. But that may've been our only chance—your only chance of qualifying."

The Fate shrugs. "No, there is always a chance."

"Are you sure? Maybe, it's not too late. We could go back," Wake says, almost pleading.

"No, we are going forward."

"Come on, man, be serious. All of our futures are at stake here."

"I realize that, but I wonder if you do."

"Can you at least tell us what you're planning?" Rachel asks.

"Nothing has changed. We are going to find a Healer tonight. And I know just the cleric. He's the strongest Healer in all of Wysteria." The Fate holds his hands out wide. "Besides, Sensei says we need to have our roster finalized by tomorrow morning in order to compete in Capture the Flag."

"No way!" Rachel says. "We won't be ready in time."

Her brother agrees. "That's just two days away and even you must know that Flag is everyone's favorite event. Everybody's going to be there. And didn't we just ask Princess to be our Healer because she's the best?"

"That was a matter of need, but this Healer is even stronger than her," the Fate says.

"Then why didn't we go ask 'this Healer' first?" asks a frustrated Wake.

"I have," the Fate says. "He has refused me three times already."

"Then why are we wasting our time?"

"Today is the day he says yes. I know it," the Fate says.

"Did you feel the same way about the Princess?" Rachel asks.

The Fate tilts his head questioningly and blinks twice at her before nodding.

"Just exactly who is this Healer?" Riser asks flatly. She's waited silent up until this point, but this is beginning to feel ominous. If this Healer is any good, she should've already known who they are. But she couldn't think of anyone matching the description. Whoever it is, they better be good. Most teams run with at least two Healers.

Having three no-names on the team is bad enough. If they add a fourth nobody, even she would have to start doubting their chances. *Fate is strong. I'm strong. We should be enough to carry the others as long as they don't get in the way. But we need a decent Healer.*

It's not something the Daughter would ever admit out loud, but all of a sudden she wishes the original team were here. *If only Sya and Haenul weren't older and Ieiri younger.*

She trudges along in silent thought before finally snapping out of it. *Enough of this wishful thinking. I need to figure out exactly where we're going,* she thinks. *If this Healer really is any good, I should be able to guess who it is.* She begins listing off the top Healers in her head, but she can't think of a single one not already on a team.

Finally, she gives up. "You've never mentioned any other Healers than our regular pair ... and the Princess."

"That is correct," the Fate says.

There's probably no use in asking for a name, she figures. Esperanza runs her tongue over her fangs as she contemplates just who 'this Healer' could be. The pair of barely protruding points have always been a source of pride and she habitually brings attention to them.

No other Daughter of her generation has fangs as nice as hers. She often wondered how hers would compare to a full-fledged Orc's. Which reminds her of the closest thing to a real Orc around: Brother Monster.

No, he couldn't possibly mean him; anyone but him. That would be ... unforgivable.

Riser groans. "It's not that coward Brother Monster, is it?" *Please, for the love of Enyo, say no.*

Orcs tend to stick with their own kind. The only times you see one away from their homeland is on the World Circuit of the International Tournament of Tears. But there is one so-called Orc in Wysteria. Well, half of one, though, she wouldn't even him describe him as that. They call him Brother Monster and he's known more for being a wimp that refuses to fight than anything else. The coward's famous for taking some sort of vow against it.

The Captain nods his head, much to her dismay. *Unbelievable!*

"Please, no, anybody but him. All he can do is heal. He won't fight back, even if he's getting beaten up. The last thing we need is a weakling like that."

Wake adds his voice. "There's no way he's going to join us, anyway. I heard he's rejected every offer, ever. No one even bothers asking him anymore. I wonder why he even follows the Tour."

"He is just waiting for that right moment," The Fate tells them. "And that moment is now. We will be the best team this country has ever seen and he is the best Healer out there, so it only makes sense."

"With that kind of logic, how can we go wrong?" Rachel notes as she joins Riser in groaning.

"I'll pass. I'm hungry. I'll meet you back at the inn." Riser says, trying to get out of this worthless mission. Things are not going as expected. She doesn't care how well Brother Monster might heal, not if he refuses to fight.

I should've waited till next year. I would've been better off with Ieiri. This year's class is way too full of strong candidates. They say the strongest in years, she thinks before checking her cowardice. *Who cares about the likes of Kase Shake or Daisho Sixblades?.* She might've lost to them before, but she's beaten them, too. Well, at least in practice—sort of.

Either way, I'll beat Sixblades for real the next time we meet. She better; she'll be seventeen in a couple days. And with the coming of her birthday, her Pilgrimage will officially begin.

"No, we are going to do this together as a team. From now on, we do everything together. We are going to go ask Brother Monster to join us together. We are going to stay hungry together, and later, we will eat together," the Captain says. "I also upgraded our room. We will even be sleeping together."

Wake chokes on something, and the others look at their Captain oddly.

"I thought you all would be more excited. I got us a Full Team Room. It has dividers and everything."

"Oh, that actually sounds quite nice," Rachel says, full of relief. "Anything's better than the ones they assign you to on Tour. Let me tell you, there's nothing worse than having to share a washroom with twenty other girls."

Wake thinks about it for a moment. "Wait a minute. If Monster joins us, that will be four boys and two girls. We're going to be totally crammed on our side."

"That is true. Too bad we failed in getting the Princess."

It's Wake's turn to groan.

Riser's far from happy as they enter the House of Worship. It's the largest building in town, with ceilings so high she wouldn't be able to hit the rafters with a stone. She's always been terrible at throwing things, though.

I'd like to throw something at Fate right about now.

She lets the others pass. Hopefully, she can hang out in the back. The less she has to do with this mission, the better.

The Fate leads them towards a corridor on the far side of the Prayer Hall. Their footsteps echo loudly as they pass pew after empty pew. The hundreds of candles lining the walls remain cold and unlit waiting for this week's service to come back to life again.

They enter the narrow corridor at the far end of the Hall. The torches here are spaced so far apart that there are moments they walk in complete darkness. As they near the end of the passage, the chattering of old men can be heard. The Fate comes to a stop in front of a solid oak door.

The Fate knocks three times and calls out, "Hello, Monster? Is anyone there?"

"I don't think we should call him that," whispers Rachel. The voices on the other side continue unabated.

The Fate shrugs and continues to knock. "Hello, Brother Monster, are you in there?"

"Maybe we should go. This is a House of Worship. We can't just go wandering around like this," Wake says.

The Fate ignores the advice, instead, choosing to shove the door open. On the other side, sit three men of varying degrees of oldness: kind of old, really old, and ancient.

The room is bright and warm, lit by a smoldering fire in an oversized fireplace. An incredibly tall youth works a series of stove ranges on the far side of the room.

" ... A Vision is never wrong. It is impossible for it to be wrong. The very nature of a Vision is that it comes true," argues the ancient one.

The one with the most hair shakes his head and answers, "The world is a mutable place. No fate is set in stone. A Vision is true at the time of receiving it, but its purpose is not to show an absolute truth, but to be a guide on what may or may not be. I can quote at least a dozen examples of this being the case ..."

"I've heard your dozen examples before and each one has a counter ..." begins the ancient priest before finally noticing them in the doorway. "And just what do we have here?"

"Pardon us, sirs. We knocked, but no one answered. We are here to speak with Brother Monster concerning a matter of great importance," the Fate explains. His chagrined teammates look anywhere but at the three old men.

The Daughter settles for staring at the back of the beanstalk of a cook—unforgivably skinny, even compared to a normal man. Only his height and pale skin, tinged ever so slightly blue, betray him for his namesake.

"Go away, Fate," the towering cook says without turning.

"Greetings, Monster, are you ready to join my Team this fine day? This will most likely be your final opportunity."

"Are you daft? I would never join your team, *ever*—just because you call me *that*," the tall boy growls back. He continues to stir a large pot in silence. Finally, he picks it up and turns. His prominent fangs shoot upward as much as the corners of his hairline recede backwards, highlighting a strikingly angular face—one that abruptly fills with shock at the sight of them.

The heavy iron pot clatters to the floor spilling hot broth everywhere.

CHAPTER 11

BROTHER MONSTER

[THE HOUSE OF WORSHIP, GREENWOOD]

The fateful day Brun received his Vision was the happiest of his life. It wasn't just the peace and fulfillment he felt, but the fact that he, a Half-Orc, received it, which mattered most.

To a young orphan, it was undeniable proof that he wasn't some unwanted abomination, but that he too was worthy of the One God's love.

Even the doubt that filled the face of Father Arnold upon hearing the news wasn't enough to discourage him that day.

The Head of the Sanctuary has always been known to approach such things with skepticism—it's just how you'd expect a Master of the Doubting Palm to be. But when he finally comes to believe, his belief is unshakeable, a trait he passed on to his prized pupil.

The blessing of a Vision wasn't uncommon at the Vision of Divine Mercy Sanctuary, although, it had been a dozen years since anyone had been graced with such a gift.

At Father Arnould's suggestion, Brun immediately began to fast and pray.

Slowly, the overwhelming experience began to gain clarity. The vision gained focus and the memory of the voice rang clear.

On the third morning of meditation, he finally accepted the path he must follow.

Before only himself and the Maker, he took the Vow of Pacifism, and in doing so everything felt right for the first time in his twelve years of life.

He wanted to scream his vows out for all to hear. Instead, he took them in private. He did not want to cause any more trouble for the Brothers and Sisters of the Sanctuary. The Half-Orc had already been denied permission to take the official vows of Priesthood. No matter how much Father Arnold pressed the matter, The Order was unwilling to set such a precedent.

In the end, they wouldn't even acknowledge the Vision. The case was classified as needing further investigation, which proved to be a difficult matter. Brun would not betray the Voice he heard so clearly during the Vision: *"Speak not of what you see, but only that you have witnessed it. In this manner, follow the Path of Peace for all the world to behold."*

From that point on, his training took on new meaning. With renewed dedication, he began refining the art of Laying Hands and mastering the lore of Herbology. He also continued training in the ways of the Doubting Palm, but only practiced the forms that caused no harm.

Once his studies reached completion, he knew it was time to leave. He always knew his time at the Sanctuary would come to an end, but leaving the only home he had ever known proved hard.

But he gathered his resolve and left all he knew behind. The Half-Orc took only the clothes on his back, a plain tunic that almost fit him, and a blessed rope to cinch it tight—a final gift from the fatherly Priest.

His only other possession was a voluminous dark robe, a self afforded necessity that helped hide his pale, steely skin.

The young Healer traded in his herb collection for the robe. There was even enough coin left over for a new pair of sandals, though, in the end, he decided to remain barefoot as he'd grown accustomed to.

It would only be a matter of weeks before he would outgrow anything he could fit now, anyway.

The coins ended up in the offering box.

His once dark robe is now threadbare. It fails to cover as much of him as it once did. But you'll never find him without it, even though, it's now too tight to properly fasten down the front and rests instead on his shoulders more like a cloak than a proper robe. *That's about to change*, he realizes. He wasn't wearing it in his Vision and this marks its nearing. *Just when I was sure that I'd have to wait another couple years.*

That was until he turned to face the annoying fool and those who entered with him.

Brun barely felt the broth splash his toughened, exposed feet. The scalding drops to the shins, however, were quite painful. They're sure to leave tiny blisters, but the discomfort wasn't enough to make the self-disciplined boy blink twice.

With a grimace he grabs a cool, moist cloth and begins to wipe up the mess. *Could it really be?* he wonders to himself as he steals a glance towards the new arrivals.

"Brun, don't worry about that now. Are you alright, son?" one of the clerics asks. The one able to get up with the least discomfort attempts to do so before the Half-Orc gestures that he is fine.

"Just look at what your rude intrusion ..." another of the old clerics begins before the oldest cuts him off.

"I understand that the deadline to submit final Team Rosters has already come and gone," the ancient priest says.

"There is no problem there. The proper paperwork has already been submitted ... with his name on it," the cheerful boy replies. "I was going to change it, if I had to. I am glad I do not. Brother Monster can still join us."

The oldest one carefully studies the Fate. After a long moment he asks the Half-Orc, "Brun, what do you think of all this?"

The Half-Orc returns from the windowsill holding a long, thick leaf serrated with small white teeth. He sits down onto a stool far too small for him and begins to apply the gel of the prickly plant to his burns.

"This is your team, Fate?" he asks, not looking up from his work.

"Yes, Monster. There is also Sensei, but he is currently at work."

The Healer remains quiet. He grabs a second plant and crushes the broad leaves into his palm. After applying a generous portion of the salve to his shins, he looks up and says, "Why should I join? I have no points, no real chance of qualifying."

"No worries, Monster. With you on the team, we will make it for sure."

"Will you stop calling me *that*, if I join?"

"What, Monster? Is that not who you are?" the Fate asks.

"I don't like being called that. I don't like what it means."

"People will not stop calling you Monster just because you do not like it," the Fate says with a shrug. "Monster, you make the name, the name does not make you. If you do not like what it means, change the meaning, not the name."

One of the clerics chuckles politely. "The boy is right, Brun. And he calls you that with no malice."

"Fine then, grab a bowl, if you're hungry. Somehow, I made too many noodles. It'll take me a minute to salvage the broth, though." For as long as he's been cooking, the Half-Orc has never once made too much of anything. His measurements have always been exact.

I blamed the mistake on being distracted by the deadline coming and going, but ... He takes another look at the group. He tries not to show it, but, tonight, for the second time in his life he feels like he's experiencing the impossible—a miracle.

CHAPTER 12
POE
[THE LOBBY, GREENWOOD]

A slender shadow slips along the side of the road with a large case strapped to their back. Dressed somewhat like a gentleman, the delicate youth wears a broad-collared tailcoat with matching waistcoat over a half-buttoned shirt that's already become untucked. And of course, a three-cornered hat pushed precipitously forward in the manner all bards are famous for.

Hair like winter's sky covers half the bard's face. But it's not enough to hide the scar that runs down from their right eye, ugly as a trail of tears.

The wound may have even appeared dashing on another, but in this bard's case, it's too obvious a flaw on an otherwise flawless face. Poe looks every bit the part of an aspiring bard, except for one thing: a charming smile.

But Poe has no reason to smile. Everywhere the bard looks there is always some reminder to be sad. Even just being bard. Among the first things Poe learned in life were; *Mother's passed away and Father's away being a bard. That's why I don't have parents around like everybody else.*

For the longest time Poe felt nothing but resentment towards the profession. At least, that's how it was until that one day—the day he came back with that song, a song written just for Poe.

It ended up becoming one of his most famous. But the only one who'd ever fully understand it would be Poe.

That's all it took. Just one song and Poe was hooked, fascinated by how a few notes and a string of words could reveal what has always been there.

Ever since that day, Poe followed in his booming footsteps.

But lately, things haven't been so booming.

Why can't I do this? Poe wonders.

I've tried everything. I came all the way to Wysteria just to wake up every day before the sun even rises and play for these backwater bumpkins. I've listened to old favorites until I can't stand them anymore. I've listened to songs I could never stand until I liked them. I even tried drinking that horrid coffee stuff and I've gotten absolutely nowhere.

Why can't I just finish this song?

It's all Poe ever thinks of these days: the song. *At least, I'm finally comfortable performing in front of strangers, now. But there's really no other reason for me to keep following this stupid Tour. It may have worked for him, but it's definitely not working for me.*

Distracted, Poe steps right into a pile of something soft and squishy. Aggravated, the bard tries to wipe off as much of the stink as possible.

That's it. I'm done with Wysteria. It was a mistake coming here in the first place. I've wasted too many months on this backwater peninsula, and for what? Nothing! I'll play one more morning for these ingrates and then I'm on the next ship out of here. It doesn't even matter where—anywhere has to be better than this.

Lately, the conversations in Poe's head have gotten longer. It couldn't be helped, though: the bard needs to talk to someone.

Ever since, Poe ran away from school and arrived in the Three Kingdoms, the bard hasn't uttered a single word to anybody.

As usual, there are at least a couple of 'competitors' passed out on the benches bordering the Lobby, but they don't matter. They'd be kicked out soon enough when the Sitters do their morning rounds.

Other than the rabble, Poe is always the first to arrive. However, this morning someone's beaten the guitarist to the Lobby.

I've never seen him before. He must be new. But why is he running around like that? Poe wonders, almost tripping over the blonde giant sleeping in the middle of the road. *Whew, that was too close.*

The rest of the rabble are harmless enough, but that was Kearney Dim, the self-anointed 'Big League Rookie,' who in reality is nothing but a Big League Brute.

Just last week, he broke some kid's arm over a card game. The kid was on a hot streak until Kearney accused him of having cards up his sleeve. The big bully yanked the boy's forearm free of his sleeve and shattered it across his table. No one ever found the extra cards.

Poe clutches the strap of Desi's case at the thought. The musician would risk broken bones over the song, but not Desi. Never Desi Derata. The guitar that Poe's father made from the better parts of three other instruments is worth more than anything.

This should be far enough, Poe decides, picking the furthest possible corner. After a quick tuning of Desi's six strings, the bard begins to play softly. As the guitar begins to sing, Poe seeks that moment of clarity, that place where the irreplaceable isn't lost, where every day isn't a torturous test.

As much as Poe silently complains about it, the Three Kingdoms of Wysteria are not the source of the bard's torture. In fact, Wysteria's Tournaments have provided the perfect atmosphere for the young bard to safely blend in and get lost. Poe's just old enough to not stick out amongst the kids on Tour.

And though there's no way anyone would mistake the fair-haired bard to be from either Bae or Silla, Poe could always claim to be from Gorgury, the third and newest kingdom.

It didn't take long for a stranger like Poe to figure out how things work around these parts. Really, Wysteria's Tour is just a lesser version of the real thing, the International Tournament of Tears. The only real difference is that instead of traveling each month from nation to nation as the World Circuit does, Wysteria's Tour travels from town to town—that and the level of competition, of course.

Even, not being able to speak hasn't been that big of a hassle. *At least, I still have my tongue,* Poe thinks, remembering an old friend left behind. And as difficult as it's proven, the torture isn't even from having to complete the song. It's from remembering the one who began it—that he's no longer around.

When Poe's eyes open, the new boy stands there bouncing on his heels, staring back as if in a trance. Suddenly, he starts smiling—almost like he'd forgotten to.

"That was beautiful. Why did you stop?" he says, tilting his head "Please keep playing."

Poe nods briefly and begins to play the song a second time. It's been a while since anyone's asked to hear it again. By now everyone else on Tour is more than sick of it. But it's the only song Poe is willing to play, at least, until it's finally done.

Warmed up, the second performance is near perfect. But still no closer to completion.

The new boy starts to applaud. And even though Poe's stopped playing, the boy continues to nod his head to the beat.

"Being on Tour really is amazing!" the strange boy says. "Why do you only play the beginning, though? You play it too well to still be learning it ... Is it possible you are still composing your song?"

Poe nods reluctantly. He's the first to have bothered at guessing the answer rather than being annoyed.

"Really?" He closes his eyes, still nodding his head. "Can you hear the beat?"

Poe shrugs and begins to play it again. Whenever Poe's father worked on a song, he'd play it for anyone willing to listen. So that's how Poe tries to do it now.

The new boy whips out a stick and begins to tap it against the ground in rhythm with the song. His simple cadence frames the melody perfectly. The beat matches the time kept in Poe's head until the boy pauses and begins again. The stuttering of the beat gives new meaning to the melody. *He broke the beat, if I change scales there …*

The odd boy begins to bob his head again. The movement makes its way down his arms and to his legs as he begins to step to the rhythm. One foot after another and then he's sprinting across the Square. Already a blur, he leaps into a series of endless somersaults and handsprings—all in perfect rhythm to the song. He returns just as quickly, flipping and spiraling the length of the field all in time to Poe's song.

It's the first time the bard's seen anything like it. Feeling it, Poe begins adding to the end of the incomplete song. *This is it. This is why I'm here.*

The determined guitarist has been trying to finish the song for so long now, only to realize effort and desire aren't enough. But right now, at this single moment in time, Poe could finally feel it.

"SHUT THAT CRAP UP!" bellows the waking brute.

Oh no, I forgot about Kearney! Poe looks all around, but there's only one who's ever stood up for the bard before and right now Kase Shake is nowhere to be found. *I can't stop now, though. I'm almost there.*

"Didn't I tell you last time, don't play that junk when I'm around?" Kearney screams, stomping his way closer.

I will finish no matter what, Poe decides. The musician continues to strum, eyes closed to the world.

"Please continue," the new boy whispers.

"What are you looking at?" the brute demands, tongue hanging out of his mouth and breathing hard.

Kearney turns back to the musician and bellows, "Why are you still playing? I told you to shut that crap up!"

Poe feels the song coming to an end as well as the oncoming fist. *Keep playing. Just keep playing ...* Smack! *What was that?*

"You dumb bastard! Get out of my way." Smack! Another thunderous blow echoes from near by.

Poe strums the final chord, letting it reverberate through the still morning air. It sounds so very lovely.

The newly minted songwriter opens tear-filled eyes, ready for Kearney's worst. Instead, the bard is met with an unexpected, smiling face, one with two swollen eyes. "Congratulations," he says.

A whistle blows from nearby. The Sitters are finally here.

"Nobody move! What's going on here?" the tall uniformed man asks. He looks directly at the new boy, whose eyes have already begun to swell shut. "You again? Are you causing trouble already?"

"No, sir, there's no trouble here," he replies cheerfully.

The Sitters look Kearney Dim up and down before turning back to the new boy. "What happened to your face, did he do that?" The Sitter points to Kearney.

"Nothing happened, sir. I am just out here getting in a little early morning training and enjoying some good music."

"Well, stay out of trouble, understand?"

"Yes, sir."

The taller Sitter looks at the shorter one and shrugs. He inspects the Tearstones of each boy. "You two are already on The List. If you get caught so much as looking at someone funny, you'll both be banned from Greenwood."

The two known troublemakers nod. The Sitters look them up and down before finally saying, "No rules were broken—this time. But we most definitely have our eyes on you two."

"Don't think this makes us even. Best watch your back—the both of you," Kearney whispers vehemently. The brute turns and stomps away towards his trio of jeering friends.

"Are you okay? Why did you do that?" The bard's voice trembles and cracks, but even that cannot disguise the voice of a perfect soprano. Wide-eyed, the bard clasps their hands over their mouth. *No, how could I be so stupid?*

"I am fine. I just wanted to hear the end of that song. It was worth it." The new boy smiles back at the bard.

Tears fill Poe's eyes.

"Are you crying because you are happy or sad?"

Poe keeps quiet and carefully studies the older boy. He looks Bae ... or maybe not. The bard can't tell.

He's tall, but not that tall. He looks strong, but not really that strong. He's handsome, but not as classically as someone like Poe. He knows music, but he's obviously a fighter, not a musician.

But most peculiarly of all is that the older boy isn't affected by Poe's voice—a voice that caused any to hear it, to do ... strange things, to say the least. *Could he be like Father? My voice never affected him, either.*

"Are you a bit babo? No worries, I am as well," the boy says. "They call me Fate. What do they call you?"

Fate? "Oh, I'm Poe ... just Poe." The musician studies the boy carefully for the slightest hint of the unusual. But Poe's voice seems to have no effect upon the Fate. He remains the same smiling boy.

"Well met, Poe." He looks all around and then back at the small bard. "Will you be fine getting out of here?"

"Thank you ... for everything, but I'll be okay," the bard whispers back.

The Fate points to the east gate where Kearney Dim waits,

pretending not to look their way. Just outside the west gate are his three friends. "I can tell you are pretty strong, but that guy is pretty big and he has friends. Do you have friends?"

This is bad. Kearney's staying at the same inn as I am, too. What should I do? I don't need to go back for my stuff. As long as I have Desi, I can just leave. There's really no reason for me to stay now that the song is done. But I've just found someone I can talk to.

"Can you watch my guitar for me?" Poe asks the older boy. He'll be the first other than family to touch Desi, but there's no other choice. "I'm just going to get it over with and let him beat me up before things get any worse."

"So, you are alone?"

Poe nods.

"I suppose you will be coming with me, then," the Fate says with a shrug. "Come on, I have to get back to my teammates. They are probably up by now."

Why is he helping me? Can I trust him? The answer doesn't matter. Poe's already decided. *"When you find it, grab it and hold on with everything you got for as long as you possibly can. Don't sleep unless you have to, don't eat until you have to, just create ... but most importantly, enjoy." That's what father said,* Poe remembers. *That's what you do when you find inspiration.*

Poe looks at him closely. *It's all around him, swirling back and forth, so strong I can almost see it. No, not just surrounding him; it's coming from him.*

"Coming?" the Fate asks.

Poe looks at him oddly.

"The ones by the west gate seem preoccupied. Now is the time to go. Are you ready?" the Fate asks again.

Poe nods, cries, and smiles the charming smile you'd expect from a bard.

CHAPTER 13
WAKE
[STEWARDS & RAIDERS INN]

Wake, only half awake, stumbles down to the main room. His sister was so kind as to try to rouse him, but he isn't quite up for completing the task. He didn't sleep that well and his body is already feeling the aches from the day before.

At the bottom of the stairs, the scent of fresh bread baking fills him. He ignores it. Someone has opened all the windows, allowing in the morning sun and fresh air, which annoys him. The sight of the Fate balancing precariously on a chair is downright maddening. *Argh. It's too early for all this.*

"Morning!" the Captain calls out, crunching into an apple and somehow maintaining his balance.

Wake mumbles something in reply. He can barely open his eyes, but somehow an errant hair finds itself into his left one. *F'ing hair! Failing eye ... hurting. Just leave me alone.*

"He's not a morning person," his sister warns the others.

"Catch." The Fate tosses him a fresh apple. "We have waited long enough. It is time to get started."

Wake grumbles something about an apple not being a proper breakfast. Riser slaps him on the back and laughs in condolence.

The Captain points to the empty plates. "Would you like for us to sit around and wait for you to eat?"

He guesses not.

"No worries. If we have a good session, there will be a big lunch." *What if we don't have a good one?*

"Come on, then." The Fate is on his feet and his chair is back on four legs. "The Office is giving Sensei mornings off, but we do not have all day."

"Wait a minute. What happened to your eyes?" Wake asks, just noticing that both of them are dark and bruised.

"A fist." The Fate waves thanks to the innkeeper and leads them out.

Wake is the last one out the door and somehow forgets the single step at the entrance. As he tumbles forward, a dozen thoughts cross his mind: *hands forward, break the fall, turn, tuck, roll, save the apple ...* He can't decide on any of them and lands flat on his face.

He curses up a storm.

"Oh my goodness! Are you okay, Wake?" His sister hurries over.

He looks around and realizes he's causing a scene. "I'm sorry, I just can't think clearly when I first wake up. I'm sore all over, tired, and this hair got stuck in my eye and ... I'm sorry."

"Tomorrow, I will wake you before the others. This will give you some time to shake away your early morning madness," the Fate tells him. Wake agrees with a sigh. When he turns to apologize to the rest of them, he almost runs into Sensei's case.

Why is Sensei carrying a guitar case? He rubs the last of the sleep from his eyes and realizes it is not the clerk at all.

"Hey, you're not Sensei! You're that bard from the Lobby." He recognizes the scar. "Why are you here and where's Sensei?"

"He went on ahead to file the paperwork," his sister explains.

"This is our new friend, umm ... what is your name again?" The Fate asks the bard.

The small boy leans close and whispers something into the Fate's ear.

"Poe," the Fate relays.

"I'm Wake. Nice to meet you," he says quickly before his own name can get butchered.

The Fate scratches the back of his head. "I got us into a little trouble. He will be staying with us for a while. He cannot talk with his mouth, though. If he does, bad things happen. Fortunately, I am immune."

Wake greets the new boy and prepares himself for another day as surreal as the one before.

They find the little clerk banging away on his drum in the very same clearing he showed them the day before. When he sees them, he stops and waves.

The Fate gathers them together and asks them to take a seat. Most of them are happy to, all except for Wake, who settles down in the tall grasses with little joy.

He hugs his knees tight to his chest in an attempt to prevent as much unnecessary contact with the itchy stuff as possible. Despite his best efforts, he can already feel an unbearable tickle growing along the underside of his right t arm. Other than that, it's a relatively glorious morning with the chill of autumn muted by a particularly brilliant sun.

The Fate looks over at Poe, who seems unsure of what to do. "Bard, you are welcome to join us."

Poe nods and unhooks the case on his back from the strap running diagonally across his chest. Wake can't help but notice that the bard wears his Light Blue Tear set into the thick leather strap. Once his guitar is gently unpacked, Poe attaches the very same strap to either end of it. The bard notices him staring and gives him a questioning look.

Wake doesn't know what to say. "Um, I was just noticing that you wear your Tear on your strap. It must mean a lot to you …"

The bard shrugs.

Wake tries to say something nice. "That's a fine guitar you got there. I bet it's as nice as The Maestro's." For an instant, Poe looks back at him wide-eyed before getting up and sitting as far away from him as possible.

"I was just trying to be nice," Wake huffs to himself.

Poe's right hand flashes across the guitar's strings, and the other tunes the pegs with quick precision. He looks towards the Fate to see if it is okay to continue. A moment later he does, playing an all too recognizable song. Though as he continues, Wake realizes there are some parts of it that are not as recognizable as he first thought.

The Fate claps his hands and says, "First of all, Team Rules."

He holds up a finger. "Rule One. No touching the Captain unless you absolutely have to."

"Rule Two. Do right by each other."

"Rule Three. Do things together."

"And last, but not least, Rule Four. We are not allowed to lose."

"What kind of rules are those?" Wake asks. "And just how are we supposed to know how to do right by each other? That's just too vague." *And what does he mean by, we're not allowed to lose? Like ever? That's just absurd.*

The Captain shrugs. "Please try your best. I am sure that will be good enough."

"Unusual, but reasonable enough," Rachel muses aloud.

They all agree to follow the rules.

"There will be more. I just have yet to think of them," the Fate says. "But for now, I have a little story ...

"It takes place long ago, before the Age of Tears and after the Clash of Champions. During the dark time, just before Tournaments and Tearstones—a time in which victory was attained through warfare and grievance settled in bloodshed.

"The world was a scramble after the Clash of Champions. After their disappearance, many lands lost not only their heroes but their Kings and Queens, as well. In their place they found chaos and strife.

"Territories changed hands as quickly as the wind changed direction. The cunning and ruthless reigned triumphant and those vicious enough claimed the glory. Until finally, one nation stood above the brutal throng, threatening to conquer them all.

"From a village at the edge of the world was born a great leader of men. One who could outwit the cunning and match the vicious with his resolve. First, he freed his own land and then those that surrounded it. But it did not take long before he realized that this was not a victory, but rather a challenge issued to their oppressors.

"So he marched. Village after village and then nation after nation he set free, and all the while his army grew. All were free to join: man, woman or child, just as long as they could follow orders.

"But a battlefield is fluid and ever-changing, and on more than one occasion the day was saved by those acting in defiance of their orders. What was he to do with these defiant heroes? Dismissing those too selfish or cowardly to do as commanded was one thing, but these men disobeyed their orders to do what needed to be done. When he called upon these defiant ones and looked into their eyes, he had no doubt of their bravery, or that they would do it again. And the next time, they may choose wrong. Either way, he knew he could not depend on these men.

"All he knew for sure was that they had no place in his army. At least within his main ranks, he finally decided. So he created a special unit just for them, a place for those too valuable to dismiss, but not disciplined enough to be relied upon.

"It did not take long for the defiant ones to become known for their skill, bravery, and ... unreliability in battle. His generals hated even the idea of such a unit. Everyone knew that well disciplined soldiers were the key to victory and that exceptions bred complications.

"In order to set an example of the unruly bunch, his generals assigned them the most undesirable of duties, from digging ditches to the most dangerous of missions. To their surprise, the group of soldiers known for their defiance on the battlefield did not rebuke these commands. They took to these tasks, lowly or dangerous, with equal ardor.

"But where they could not be depended upon was where it mattered most: the battlefield. The defiant ones infuriated the generals, doing questionable things such as ignoring a besieged commander to save a group of lowly commoners or breaking rank to fight wherever they pleased.

"Regardless of the respect they garnered, no one actually wanted to join their ranks. Who in their right mind wanted to be sent on the most dangerous missions only to have to clean the latrines as their reward?

"This worked out well enough for the generals. Though they were mystified by how a group could fight so well with no chain of command, everyone doing as they wished, without even speaking a word to one another. The leader, however, was satisfied. If it worked, it worked. And at this point his army had swelled to such a size that it was being called the mightiest the world had ever seen.

"Finally, they reached their enemy's own city at the center of the world. Their enemy, however, still possessed the other half, and too had marched their troops back to partake in one final, decisive battle.

"When that day came, so too did the great leader's first taste of defeat. He saved nothing for another day, not even himself. The leader led the charge himself. He did not need to see tomorrow, only victory that day. But what he saw instead was a nightmare. Their enemy had developed a fantastic new weapon—a horrible magic of unimaginable power.

"It was not the first time he had seen a volley of arrows turn day into night, but these scratched the sky, making the heavens bleed brighter. The arrows flew neither true nor straight, but slithered bloodshot like crimson serpents through the sky. They hissed promises of death with ginger tongues and glared with eyes as bright as the sun.

As they writhed closer, he realized they were not snakes followed by ruby-scaled tails, but more akin to falling stars chased by flickering trails. The hisses were not from the forked tongues of a myriad of serpents, but the sizzle of scorching fire. He had seen a star fall once, but never tens of thousands as he did that day.

"Their adversaries had acquired some horrible, dark sorcery, one capable of raining down endless bolts of fire, and in doing so creating hell on earth. His army had been prepared for the depths of depravity, the atrocities known as war, but in no way were they prepared to dance the inferno. Their only hope was to retreat or face a death of searing agony. So he gave the order.

"Hundreds of thousands of his mighty army, an army who once united had never known defeat, ran from the blazing ruin. In the madness that ensued, men threw down their weapons, trampled their own brothers: anything to get away from the promise of being burned alive.

"All except for one unruly group, who instead marched silent past the fleeing—towards fiery death itself. This battle had been too important to allow the defiant ones to take a valuable position near the vanguard. They had been positioned as far to the rear as possible, and only then, did they take their place at the fore.

"After he could run no more, the leader looked back to see what remained of the battlefield. *They* were at it again. He should have known the men and women of that unit would not follow his final command, even if it was one meant to save their very lives. And he thanked them for it, because for every moment they held the enemy at bay, it meant hundreds more would escape. Still, all was lost. The only thing left was to save as many as he could.

"Night fell before the leader was satisfied they had fled far enough to lick their wounds. It was then, he received the unbelievable news: the small band of warriors left behind had neither retreated nor fallen, but instead, still fought on within the flaming battlefield. Now that he had led what remained of his army to safety, the leader rode back to see to those he had left behind.

"He did not truly believe to find them still standing, and even when he saw the sight with his own eyes he could scarcely believe. There, where he had left them half a day before, the defiant still stood. From so far, they seemed a tiny ring of pebbles and the enemy a scarlet sea.

"The fighters who had always refused to listen, now refused to fall. Wave after wave of soldier and flame crashed down upon them. But the surge of the scarlet sea could not pull the insignificant pebbles under. The mighty tidal waves accomplished the opposite—they drove the pebbles deeper into the sand. The ring remained unbroken.

"The insolent soldiers had not stayed behind in a final act of sacrifice: they had stayed behind to win the war. They fought shoulder-to-shoulder, outnumbered by more than even the learned leader could calculate. Refusing to burn, defying death because if one were to fall, who would watch his brother's back? They continued to fight, not realizing the ridiculousness of their actions, and in doing so, moments crept into minutes, minutes became hours, and day had become night.

"Even so far from the heart of the battle, the leader could feel the heat coming from the flaming battlefield. How did they still stand?

"Then he noticed what was not. Neither was there smoke, nor ash, nor the foul smell of burning. How could this be? He strode forward into the flames to find out for himself. He felt the heat upon his face. The hairs on his arms singed and his armor threatened to cook him alive. But when he threw off his armor, he found the hairs on his arms untouched and his skin not even flush.

"The leader finally began to understand. This really was a strange, new magic. One based on belief more than anything else.

"He gave no command, but drew his sword and charged into the madness. And soon so did the others that had gathered to see if the absurd rumor was true, that the fight was still on. Word of their actions quickly spread, drawing more and more back to the battlefield.

"Now, it was the enemy who could not believe. Every advantage had been theirs. Victory should have been claimed long ago, but it was not. After everything they had thrown at the impudent army, they had not been able to break them. The oppressors realized they would never break them, and in doing so their ferocity faded and fear crept in to replace it.

"As more of the leader's army returned to the battlefield, it became obvious that the pebbles would outlast the ocean. The tide had turned and now receded back to the mountain. Victory was theirs at long last!

"But even the defiant could only defy that which cannot be defied for so long. When the leader came upon the ones who stayed behind, he found many pale and cold. Before his very eyes, the ones too far gone began to stiffen where they stood. The early stages of death were ignored, but the third could not be denied. 'Til this day they stand there still, a ring of ragged statues with contentment drawn on their faces.

"Afterward, those few of the defiant to have survived were asked the source of their courage. How did they do it? How did they know?

"The answer was simple. They had decided even before stepping onto the battlefield that their fate would be to win that day. For them, there was no other option. Once their minds were set, nothing, not the fires of hell or enemies endlessly streaming, could change their will. Even death was made to wait its turn.

"After hearing this, the other soldiers began referring to their headstrong heroes as their Fates."

"Isn't that the story of how the Conqueror took Ver?" Sensei asks, breaking the silence. The clerk was paying rapt attention, even taking notes in his little notebook.

"I believe people call it that. But I do not know why. They only fought to free themselves once and for all and nothing more. When they learned the truth of the Mines of Ver and of the special stones found within, they had no choice but to stay and defend them.

"After the War to End All Wars, the leader sent most of his army home, all except for the surviving Fates. With them he remained behind.

"The Legacy of Ver was one of bloodshed. The Legacy of the Conqueror, however, would be one of peace. For many years, the leader maintained a harmonious existence between most nations, but he knew it to be temporary. As his own end drew near, he realized that war would someday return.

"He needed to name an heir, but he knew of none strong enough to maintain the peace, nor would he damn anyone to such a position. Even more so, he realized he needed to end the cycle.

"After much consideration, the leader announced that he would adopt all the world and all those who wished so, could claim their birthright: a Tearstone and a chance to sit his throne. Anyone who wished to do so would have to prove their worth through a tournament of skill and courage. Thus the Legacy of the Conqueror was born and the foundation of the Tournament of Tears set."

"Most of that isn't in any history book I've ever read," says Wake. "Where did you hear that story?"

"The 'Final Battle' used to be one of my favorite bedtimes stories. I would ask my Old Man to tell me that story every night."

"Why don't the history books mention Fates?" the doubt-prone Half-Orc asks.

"I guess over the years the names of those involved became unimportant, but that does not mean their ideals just disappeared. They just changed with the times. The Daughters of Enyo, my village, and even your Order train in the Old Style, which is based on The Way of the Fates," the Captain explains.

"I always wondered what they called the Old Style when it was new," Wake says. *It's been over three hundred years and even the Conqueror's name has been forgotten. No wonder we don't remember the names of those who helped him. But that story ...*

"How could a story like that be forgotten?" Wake says softly.

"That is a good question." The Fate looks down at his gauntlet. "But by the time we are done, we will make sure everyone remembers. Even more, we will give them an even better story—one, no one will ever forget."

CHAPTER 14
BROTHER MONSTER
[PRACTICE FIELD BEHIND THE CLERK'S DORMITORY, GREENWOOD]

Brother Monster finds them to be a peculiar lot. The tall girl has the look of some young Queen, one who has been tricked otherwise. Her brother looks everywhere all at once, except at you.

When Sensei told him he was raised at the Great Library at the Crossroads, it seemed more than fitting. Their leader is a naïve fool—of that, there is no doubt. And the last ... well, she is a Daughter, true and true, stepped straight out a dream. *A crude and obnoxious dream.*

Despite how different each is, they get along so well it surprises him to learn they only met just days before. They try to make him feel welcome, but the feeling doesn't come easily.

"Monster, these are for you." The Fate hands him a pair of blackened gauntlets. He accepts them with reluctance. They're heavy as iron, but rough and porous, like some sort of black rock or ... Coal, he thinks, wrinkling his nose at the stench. They stink like a newly put out fire. A scent he's always found particularly offensive.

"No, thank you." The Half-Orc tries to hand them back. "I can't use these. My vow keeps me from using any item crafted for warfare; armor or weapon."

"No worries, I will never ask you to break your vow," the Fate says, refusing to accept their return. "You use a knife when you cook, do you not?"

"That's different."

"They are both just things, objects that may be used to create or destroy. It is the owner who decides which. Think of these gauntlets as some sort of tool, one that you will use to help us with. When you wear them you will be able to feel where we are and to a certain extent how we all fare."

Monster stares at the pair of armored gloves not liking them one bit. He tries them on with a sigh. To his surprise, they fit his large hands quite well.

"I added some links to them last night." The Fate inspects the fit. "It seems I guessed correctly on your size. Thank goodness, because I was just about out of burnt iron."

"They stink."

"I guess they do, but you are just going to have to get used to it. Shine and Sensei are new to theirs, also."

"Are you going to insist on calling me that?" Rachel asks, flexing her own gauntlet. She is all Sun and her glove golden. He wishes he had been born attuned to Sun or Earth, Water or Wind: anything but Fire.

Even Blood would've been better.

"Sorry, that is just what comes out of my mouth when I think of you," the Fate says, smirking unabashedly.

"I don't know, Shine. I think the name fits you well," her brother chimes in, visibly annoying his sister.

"I guess so, Wade," Rachel shoots back. It's hard to learn anyone's name, as it seems as though they each have at least two. Everyone only calls Monster by one.

"Apologies, Riser, I know this is all old news for you," the Fate tells the Daughter.

"Not at all, Oppa. I've always liked that story."

"Still, you have heard all this several times before," Fate tells her. "How about you go over the next part, The Fate's Oath?" *He's not so foolish as he may appear,* the Half-Orc realizes. *At least, he recognized just how restless she was becoming.*

"Yeah, sure, I should've been Captain, anyway," she says, leaping to her feet. Monster doubts that. Better to follow a fool than a brute.

She leans over and asks the bard, "Play something new ... something a little more epic." To the other's surprise, the guitarist proves to know more than one song.

Esperanza Enyo clears her throat and recites:

> *"To look back with no regret, I choose what is right.*
> *This is my Will.*
> *To impose my Will upon all that oppose it,*
> *That is my Way.*
> *To Shape the World, with my Will and my Way,*
> *This is my Fate."*

"That's the Fate's Oath. It sounds good and all, but what exactly does it mean?" Riser asks, but doesn't bother waiting for an answer. "The first line, 'To look back with no regret, I choose what is right' is the hardest to answer."

"Shine says to not call them lines but queues, or you sound like a crybaby," the Fate says.

"No, only lines that you wait in are called queues!" Shine tells him. "Not lines in an oath, or Prismatic Lines for the matter. You call those lines, okay?"

"Oh, okay."

"As I was saying, the first line is the most difficult to understand. It has a different meaning to all who take the Oath. It's not just about what would make you happy or content right now or even a year from now, but when all is said and done. What is it that you dream of above all other dreams?"

The Daughter turns to the Half-Orc, "You, Monster, what is it that you ultimately fight for?"

Why is she picking on me? Monster snorts. "I don't *fight* for anything. I have always followed one path, with one goal. I choose to walk the Path of Peace. I do this to show the world what any Man or Orc is truly capable of."

Riser stares at him in disgust. "So be it, Faintheart."

"I wouldn't expect someone like you to understand," he says. The Daughter leans over and pinches his arm hard. "What was that for?"

"It's just what cowards like you deserve."

Monster doesn't know what to make of it. *It kind of hurt, but …* He rubs the spot where she pinched him.

It feels warm.

CHAPTER 15
RACHEL
[PRACTICE FIELD BEHIND THE CLERK'S DORMITORY, GREENWOOD]

"What about you, Unnie?" the Daughter asks Rachel. "Unnie?"

"It's what Daughters call older sisters."

Rachel beams, then frowns as she tries to find an answer to the question. Up until now, her only wish had been to get into school. But she knows that isn't the answer. What really came to mind was something that is always on her mind: a Tear's Memory.

It's a rare gift among Criers, the ability to store what they see within a Shard. Reminiscers, they're called, the lucky few who can record and share their experiences with others. Every tourney would have at least a couple, and through them sights could be seen again. Even by a blind girl.

The only true sights Rachel has ever seen were the memories of others. And those sights were more fantastic than anything she could have ever imagined. She even started her own Tear Memory Fan Club while away on Service.

She wonders how the younger members are doing just now. Next year, a couple of them would be embarking on their own first Tour.

"I can see it on your face, don't deny it!" Riser says. "If you could have one wish, no matter how crazy it may sound, no matter how impossible—what would it be?"

Rachel just shakes her head. *I can't ...*

"Be brave, Unnie. Are we not worthy to share your dreams?"

"I want ... I want to be a hero in a Tear Memory." Shine can't believe the words coming out of her mouth. "Like Lady Seo, Rizky V, Kai Abdul ... I can still remember the first time I saw their matches, how they made me feel—even the looks on their faces. Those were my first true glimpses of the world." *And what I saw was wondrous.*

"I didn't just watch the Memories. I was there with them. I lived them."

Once she admits it to herself, it becomes painfully obvious. How could she not see it before? *Because it is too much for someone like me to ask for.*

She doesn't want to go to school to get a Tear Pet just so she can see, but so she can see to fight. Shame fills her, and she feels the utter fool at admitting it to herself, let alone out loud. But no one laughed.

Spikey climbs up her long, pale cloak and nuzzles her flush cheek. It makes her feel almost brave. There's no stopping the words now.

"My whole world is based on the Memories of others. When I close my eyes and imagine you, Riser. I see a combination of Lena and Priss; dazzling and daring in their leather armor—that fierce look of challenge in their eyes," Rachel tells the Daughter. "I want to be in a Memory like theirs. One that inspires everyone who watches, like all the great ones that have inspired me."

A hand is on her shoulder. *Wake, he heard it all. He must think I'm a fool, too.* She grabs his hand thankfully, realizing he never would.

"They do say I resemble the Pristine One. And that is truly a worthy goal, Unnie." The Daughter thumps her chest. "I will watch your Will come to fruition. I pledge this before Enyo, and in doing so we are Sisters Sworn."

"Esperanza, thank you." *I've just met her and she's so good to me. All of them are.* "I guess I am one too ..."

"What do you mean, Sis?"

"A babo." She sniffles and smiles.

"What about you, Sensei. What is your greatest desire?"

"To be honest, I'm not exactly sure," he says. "All I really know is, I'm tired of being last. Being first sounds nice ... or even better yet, being the first to do something new. Now, that sounds really nice."

"That's not bad. Being first is always good," Riser says, pacing back and forth. "But you need to be more specific."

"I do not think he has to. He wants to be first, not in one thing, but in those things that really matter." The Fate finally speaks up. "Is that not true, Sensei?"

"I guess that wouldn't be bad ..." the strategist admits.

"I like it. That's pretty a good one too, Sensei!" exclaims Riser.

Enthused by her teammates' declarations, Esperanza addresses the last one. "So what about you, Mad One? What do the demented dream?"

Wake, of course, has no answer at all.

"You cannot just ask someone like *him* a question like that," the Fate tells the Daughter. "Besides, I fought him already. I already know his Will ..."

"He wants to not be a waste," the Fate tells them.

"What? How'd ..." Wake asks incredulously. "I never said anything like ..." And then he goes quiet.

"It is fine. We accept you and your odd ways, Wave. Besides it is actually a lofty goal to not want to be a waste on a Team such as this," the Fate assures him. "It just means you want to be useful."

Wake shrugs. "Whatever, and it's Wade, I mean Wake ... W A K E, Wake."

"What kind of goal is that? Not wanting to be a waste," Riser mutters.

"I thought so too, at first, but he is different. And he looks at things differently. He is like half-babo, half-mad, half-genius," says the Fate.

"That's three things. You can't have three halves," Wake says, feeling two-thirds offended, one-third complimented.

"Whatever." Riser reaches over and pats Shine on the shoulder. "It must have been difficult looking after him all these years."

Wake has always been different. Rachel has always known this, but not that different. *He's about the sweetest brother any girl could ask for. He just worries ...*

"I can hear you guys," Wake says.

The Fate moves on. "Riser, now, is a good time for you to share your Will with us."

"My Will ... well, mine is a bit more complicated. To understand it, you must know a little of Enyo." Riser faces them and looks at each in turn. This is a rarity. Daughters do not talk of such things openly.

"In life she bore no children of her own, but still, she is our mother. All I am and everything I ever will be is thanks to her. She was our founder, our sister, our mother and our Champion, true and sure. And as quickly as she brought us together, she was gone. As all the other great ones of her age, she answered the Call of Champions and was never heard from again after the Clash.

"On that day, a statue in her likeness appeared in her gardens. It is a marvelous work, exactly what you picture when you hear of tales of her beauty and might. She stands there still—strong and proud, with a joyous expression upon her face, and eyes full of resolve and kindness both.

"But also, full of tears, for her statue weeps. Day and night her statue cries, though, no Daughter knows why.

"It's the duty of my family to take care of her gardens. I've tended her flowers for as long as I can remember. And every time I see her statue, I get a really sad feeling here." She pounds her heart. "I want to learn why her statue cries and how to stop her tears. My Will is to stop Enyo's Weeping."

"How can you do that? How can we help?" Rachel asks.

"I don't know for sure, but I believe it has to do something with the Pilgrimage. And the first step to that is making it past Wysteria." Only the Fate stares back at her without question. The others know only what they have been told. Stories of how if you beat a Daughter in battle, she is yours.

"Enyo was born to the Han before there was even a kingdom, let alone three. The Age of Beasts was at an end, but a handful still remained behind. The Han befriended such Beasts and soon each village had one for a Guardian. The Beasts protected the Han, nurtured and taught them all they knew—even the arts of war. Women, however, were not allowed training in the martial arts. For them the marital ones were deemed enough.

"Not so for Enyo. No man would teach her the ways of battle, but there was a Beast that would. A winged serpent spurned by all others. He trained her and when he was done, she challenged the world.

"She traveled village to village and attacked them. This is how she became known as the Champion of the Fight. After beating the best they had to offer, she would take the village's sign. She also took their daughters, at least those that would follow. This is how she became known as the Delighter of Discord."

Monster growls. Low and from his gut, he says, "That's horrible. All of it, how could she do such things? She was a ..."

"You don't know anything! Those were different times." Riser's eyes are the storm, her voice thunder. "Every man, every woman is born to do something. Enyo was born to fight, but was forbidden her destiny. It was the world that was wrong, not her! A coward like you would never understand such things."

"Still, she *attacked* people for no other reason than to prove that she could? She *took* their daughters?"

"She attacked because they would not fight her otherwise. The women she took were young and old, slaves or near-slaves, those beaten and used. Three hundred in total and 'til this day each is remembered and honored in Silla. She did not fight out of anger or hatred, but to show the world that anyone, anywhere is capable of any path."

The Pacifist grows silent and mumbles what may be taken as an apology.

"As I was saying, she would take a village's sign ... to help them remember. It is said that once she defeated all in this corner of the world, she created a ship out of those signs. Dubbed *Glorious Defeat*, she then set sail to challenge the rest of the world.

"Enyo brought her lesson to each and every known land, until there was only one left to teach. Sadly, she did not reach it before the Call of Champions. It is thought that if a Daughter completes this journey, her soul may rest in peace."

"What land did she not reach?"

"Ascecia, the Twin Isles, Homeland of the Orcs."

The Fate leaps to his feet. "Impressive."

He starts off by pointing at the gaunt Half-Orc. "Monster wants to show the world how strong his way is—the hard way. Shine desires to become the most awe-inspiring figure in history. Sensei wants to blaze a trail ahead for all of mankind. Riser seeks to fulfill the true wishes of a Champion. And Wake wants to not be a waste on a team with Wills such as these ... the key to it all."

That's not exactly what they said, but there is no use in correcting him.

"Things could not be more perfect. I was not sure our Wills would be compatible," the Fate says. "As for me, I have a pretty simple wish. I want the team I captain to win its next match."

"That sounds easy enough," Rachel says.

"Yes, I think so too," the Fate says. "The thing is that my Will is a hundredfold strong. I want to do it 100 times in a row."

For a moment there is silence, and then the reality of it sets in.

"But that's crazy! There's even that old saying, 100 Victories in 100 Battles is simply ridiculous," Wake says. *He's right. And the more Rachel thinks about it, the more impossible it seems. More than impossible; that would mean ...*

"You would have to continue onto the World Circuit, the true Tournament of Tears," she says quietly. No matter how much you wish it, you can't just do something like that. We're a banned nation and have been for over a decade.

"Yes, to do the ridiculous. Why not? Besides, I cannot lose. The day I do, I have to give up Tear Fighting forever."

CHAPTER 16
RISER
[STEWARDS & RAIDERS INN, GREENWOOD]

Lunch is pink-scaled fish, burnt black at the edges, a salad of flowers that the innkeeper makes them pick themselves out back, two types of cheeses, and black bread. There is no crumb remaining by the time they are done. Riser would've preferred the addition of some sausages like the ones they had for breakfast, *but ... at least, it's not nuts and berries.*

After lunch, the team makes their way back to the little field behind the Clerk's Dorm that has become their temporary training grounds. As they pass the Office, Sensei bids them farewell to return to work.

Riser notices Rachel lagging behind and joins her. The older girl is a mystery, obviously dominant on the Light Course but humble in all other things. *She's faster than anyone I have ever met and stronger than she looks. She reminds me of someone.* But the Daughter can't quite place a finger on it. Either way, Riser likes her.

Who she doesn't, is the coward. Just the sight of him trudging along, slumped and meek, makes her want to smash something.

"We will not begin training in earnest until after tomorrow's match," announces the Fate as they arrive at the clearing. "I do not want you all tired out before our first match. Besides, we still have to get to know each other's fighting styles." *Great, more talking ...* Riser can't help but sigh.

"Monster, can you explain to us how your healing works?" the Fate asks the Half-Orc. "Next, will be Wade. I have been waiting to learn how your Pure Water Techs work."

"Wake."

The Half-Orc gives Wake a sympathetic look as he stands. "I am a touch Healer, meaning I have to be close enough to place a hand on you in order to heal. My main heal is in fact called Lay Hands."

"Please show us," the Captain asks as he activates his Tear. "Riser, if you would ..."

The Daughter activates her Air Tearstone and is instantly surrounded by light blue. The Fate strikes her three times in quick succession, causing her Spectral Armor to dim to half-glow.

The Healer takes his position behind her. He raises his hand and presses it between the blades of her shoulder. "Lay Hands." Instantly, the glow of her armor is restored to full. *Not bad for a wimp. But, still, unimpressive.*

"My Lay Hands should be sufficient to always heal you to full. But I cannot cast it often. I need sufficient time to recover between uses," Brother Monster explains. "I also have a small regenerative heal and one that absorbs minor damage."

"Amazing. Only the best Healers on the World Circuit are capable of healing that much in one shot," Rachel says, her voice full of admiration.

"It has to do with the essence of healing. To truly heal another you must first understand their pain. Others heal from afar. Which is more convenient in many ways, but the connection between souls is weak. There is only so much you can feel at a distance."

"Fate, please attack Riser." The Half-Orc is ready behind her.

The Fate swipes the air with his Stick and nods.

"Don't move," Brother Monster tells the Daughter. She fidgets. *Like I would ever listen to you.*

The Fate attacks without mercy, landing three strikes in a matter of moments. "Fluttering Blade."

Just as her armor looks to fade out of existence, the Healer says, "Lay Hands," restoring the Life of her Armor to full. Riser claps her hands with glee. The Fate tries again, but with the Half-Orc's combination of heals, the outcome is the same. *The coward knows how to heal. I'll give him that much.*

"Ha, I don't have to even lift a finger and you still can't take me down," she lets the Captain know, who slumps low in failure.

"May I?" Wake asks. "It's a good time for me to show you how my Pure Water Weaponization works."

The dismayed Captain nods in approval.

"Water Grab: Falchion," Wake commands. He strikes Riser several times with no effect. *His sister has promise, but this one ... I don't know,* she thinks, barely feeling a tickle from each blow.

"You haven't damaged my Spec Armor a shred. I'm still at full."

"That's true, you are," he says with a knowing smile. He swings once more. The attack seems no different than the last, but this time the Daughter's Armor shatters.

"What the hail was that?" Riser yells from inside the Loser's Ball. She really doesn't like being in there.

"Please don't use that type of language" the Half-Orc beseeches the Daughter, who pinches him in return. *I know he felt that one.* If he did, he doesn't show it. Instead, he turns to Wake. "I don't understand. Her Armor was at full. How did your last attack do so much damage?"

"That last attack was no different from any of my previous ones. My Pure Water attacks don't actually do any damage." Wake gestures to the Captain, who still has his Spectral Armor activated. "May I?"

The Fate nods eagerly.

"Water is the Physical, Dark Aspect of Blue. Anyone unlucky enough to be born Dark Blue usually becomes a Healer or freezes Water. As Ice it is at least useful to attack with, acting like any other physical weapon," Wake says.

"Freeze," he commands, and his sword of liquid hardens into clear ice. He strikes the Captain, whose armor dims slightly at the blow. "But that never seemed right for me. It's just turning Water into a plain old weapon, a fragile one at that. It took me a little while, but I was able to figure out a different way to utilize Water.

"And patience is exactly what I needed, because Water is not like the other Physical Aspects. It is slow and methodical like a canyon formed by a trickling river, a hillside covered in small rifts and gullies from the rain. Even the rust on my Gauntlet itself is a sign of how Pure Water works.

"Erosion, corrosion and even rot are how Pure Water does its damage. You really have to concentrate on it to achieve any noticeable effects, but watch.

"Thaw," Wake commands, and his sword returns to its liquid form. He strikes the Captain once again. Somehow, instead of dimming, the Fate's Tear Armor glows more brightly.

"How is my Armor at full? Did you just heal me?" the Fate wonders aloud.

"No," Wake replies.

"I think, I understand," Monster says. "Your Pure Water attacks do no actual damage; instead, they reduce the maximum hits your target's Spectral Armor can take."

"Exactly! Spectral Armor represents one's Life. The amount of damage that any one person may take differs, but let us say someone's Spec Armor is able to take 100 points of damage, or in other words has 100 points of Life. An average Crier will fall to approximately five clean blows. From this we can assume an average hit does about 20 damage. So after one blow, their Armor will be at around 80.

"My Pure Water attacks affect the total Life of your Armor, but they are weaker in comparison. After one of my hits, you will still be at full. Your full will just be less, something along the lines of 90 out of 90. And then 80 out of 80 until finally you have a maximum of zero, at which point your Spectral Armor will disappear altogether."

"That would make heals useless against you," The Half-Orc realizes.

"Yes, exactly. It may take me almost twice as long to bring down an opponent. But it doesn't matter if they are by themselves or with a hundred Healers. As long as I am able to attack, my target will always go down. And my Water is hard to block. You have a chance of dodging, but if I concentrate hard enough, even indirect splashes add up over time," Wake explains.

Impressive; I've never heard of anything like that before. Oppa was right, Riser thinks. *I should've known his judgment wasn't all that bad. He did pick me. He must have seen something in each of them, also.*

"Daebak! You really figured out how to do that all by yourself?" the Fate asks.

"Yes, it's my ... our little secret. I've never told anyone but my sister how it works. Even our old team doesn't know," Wake tells them. "To be honest, they were never really interested."

"I knew you were like him; you think different," the Fate says. "No one else has ever figured out how to get Pure Water attacks to work, not even the original creators of the Water Gauntlet."

"That's just because they went straight to Ice attacks. They had no need to delve deeper. Not many are interested in studying iron rusting away or observing rotting wood decay back into Earth and Water," Wake says.

"Still, that is hundreds of years that no one has figured it out until you found the way." The Fate grows wide-eyed. "Wood decomposes back into Earth and Water ...

"Earth and Water, two of the Physical Aspects from wood," the Fate mumbles to himself. He looks down at his Earth Gauntlet and draws his Stick. "I wonder ..."

"Unleash: Switch Fate, Water Style!"

Slowly, his Stick breaks apart. It crumbles into smaller and smaller fragments that fly towards his gauntlet. What is left behind is a thin rod of liquid predominantly composed of Pure Water with a thick red channel running through it: a blood groove. The Earth extracted from the wood forms three orbs, which revolve around his gauntlet.

Riser doesn't like what she is seeing one bit. *No, this is not happening. He did not just learn an Unleash before me.*

"This is Monstrous!" the Fate declares, swinging around his liquid stick. "I wonder just what it does ..."

It's not every day you see someone learn an Unleash Technique. Unleashes are Power Moves on a tier all by themselves, second only to Techs that could Defy reality itself. There are Criers who train a lifetime without achieving an Unleash. People do not just suddenly perform one.

And now, he's learned one before me, Riser thinks angrily.

"Fail, Fail, Fail! How did you just do that?" Riser bares her fangs. She's been watching him try to learn one for as long as she's known him. If there was one thing she was sure of, it was that she would learn hers first.

It's his fault. It was something he said. The Daughter stares holes into Wake Avenoy. *Still, it's not very impressive for a Power Move. Mine will be far better.*

"Congratulations, Oppa."

He thanks her. "I gave up on learning one anytime soon. My Old Man tried to teach me so many times, but I could never get any of them down."

The Fate turns to Wake. "You really are a First Master."

"What?" Wake says.

"You have heard of Unleash Masters, right? My Old Man is one. He has taught dozens their Unleashes over the years, but he could not teach me. We tried everything: burying me under a dune for three days with only a long straw for air, sleeping on rocks for a year, breaking rocks, carrying rocks, lifting boulders. Why, I once had to shovel enough gravel to pave half the South Road with my bare hands. The worst was staring at pebbles, though. That was no fun at all and that was only the Earth stuff. I tried other Colors, as well.

"Eventually, he said that teaching me an Unleash was beyond him. And, since I am hopeless by myself, that if it was beyond him, then only a true First Master could help me," the Fate says. "You see, given enough time, most people can learn the basics from another who has already mastered a skill, art or craft; enough, to even eventually become a Master themselves. But who taught the first person to master a field? No one did. They figured it out all by themselves. They looked for a new way, a different way—just as you have with your Pure Water Techs.

"And just now, as I listened to you talk ... I just knew. No special training was even needed. All I had to do was listen. That is how good you are. I have never been able to learn a Tech that way." The Fate turns to the rest of them. "Listen, everyone. I want you all to pay very special attention to anything and everything he says from now on. No matter how insignificant it may seem, I want you to remember his every word and think about it carefully."

"Are you serious?" Riser asks.

"Yes, consider it a new rule." The Fate swipes at the air with his watery weapon. "Riser, armor up, please. Time to test this thing out ..."

"But ..." Wake begins before lowering his voice to a whisper. "But Unleashes just don't work like that. Something's not right."

CHAPTER 17
WAKE

[PRACTICE FIELD ADJACENT THE OFFICE OF THE REGISTRAR, GREENWOOD]

Tired, covered in grime and sweat, they still manage a cheer upon Sensei's return. "Let me guess. Captain said practice is over when I got back?" Everybody cheers again.

"I suppose we are done for the day," the Captain says with some reluctance. "I did promise Lene, I would help chop some wood, today."

"Well, Lene promised me that she would be making roasted hare with her special sauce for supper!" Riser says. "Who wants to race me back to the inn?"

"Me!" the Fate says, already quickening his steps. "Way, Monster, you guys go over your fighting styles with Sensei ..." The Captain and Riser are already out of sight before anyone can reply.

Wake walks with the others, at a much more reasonable pace.

"They're pretty strong, huh?" Rachel says when they're out of sight.

Monster mumbles something. The clerk answers, "Yeah, did you know they're old team beat *The Royal Team* during Pre-Tour rounds last year?"

No way! I figured they weren't the crybabies we had first thought. But to be able to beat the Princess and Kase Shake, even if it was just a scrimmage ... Wake sees that his sister's jaw has dropped just as low as his. Monster seems unimpressed.

A low fire burns in the hearth and the stained pine table is piled high with their empty plates. The Fate talks excitedly about their first match on the morrow.

Wake studies him long and hard, wondering if it could possibly be true. It would explain how they already knew Kase and the Princess. *But if that really did happen, why would they want someone like us on their team?*

The others don't seem to care, however. Bellies are full and spirits are high. The same can't be said of his sister, whose food has gone cold before her. Buttered peas pushed to one side, the sliced beets to the other, she forms rings around the roast hare with her spoon. "Is something wrong, Ray?"

She shakes her head and takes a spoonful of peas before lowering the still-full spoon back to her plate. "How can he expect me to go out there tomorrow? I've never even thought of competing in Flag before. I'm not sure that I won't just get in the way."

That's right. The Fate told her she needed to be out there tomorrow, Wake thinks. He was so caught up in other thoughts that he didn't take time to think of how his sister would feel about something like that.

Riser slides closer to Rachel and places a hand on her shoulder. "You have nothing to worry about. Just let me and Fate handle things tomorrow. You two protect our cowardly Monster and it'll turn out all good and fine." The Daughter flicks her hand dismissively at the Half-Orc. "Anyone up for thirds?"

"You should wait a moment before you order any more," Monster tells her. "Most likely, you're already full and your mind has yet to catch up."

"Are you even craven when it comes to food? Besides, how else am I supposed to eat enough to support these?" Riser flexes her biceps and growls.

The Captain returns from showing Poe the room they're all sharing. The little bard walks up to Wake and sticks out his hand. "He is sorry for acting rudely earlier," the Fate says. "He says, he hopes we can all be friends."

Wake shakes his hand, apologizing for anything he may've said.

The Fate looks at the single plate in front of Brother Monster and asks, "No seconds for you? Why do you eat so little?"

"Gluttony is a sin," Monster says. "I'm used to smaller servings from my days at the Sanctuary. No one ever had seconds there."

"But are you still hungry?" the Captain asks again.

"Yes, but a little hunger is good for the soul."

"That makes no sense, at all. Especially, while training." The Captain shakes his head. "No wonder you are all skin and bones. From now on you have to eat at least as much as she does." He points towards the Daughter.

Riser grins and shouts out an order for three more servings, one for her and two for Brother Monster.

Poe scribbles something into his little notebook. With one hand still penning, the bard pulls out a wallet emblazoned with a thousand snowflakes.

"Put that away," the Fate tells the bard, shooing him with his hand. "I was the one who got you into trouble. This is my treat, just like it is your treat when you play for us. Or is that my treat too? It feels like a treat.

"That reminds me ... Sensei, can you take charge of our accounts and inventory?" the Fate asks the clerk. "I have a lot of treats stored in the room and even more at the bank. I brought everything I could think of, but no one seems to appreciate the way I organize it all.

"There is no rush, but if you could help me with this, I would appreciate it." He hands a pouch bursting with coin to Sensei. "This is most of our money, as well. It should be more than enough for whatever we may need, but if you could keep an account of things that would probably be for the best, also."

The little clerk almost falls forward when the Fate releases his grip on the money pouch. When he cinches it tight to his belt, his pants begin to sag and the weight of it makes him lean to the side. "Consider it done. Do you have an inventory list or an account book, perhaps?"

The Fate stares back at him blankly.

"Like a record of what you have and where? Or maybe an account of how much the team has spent so far or other expected costs?"

The Captain's eyebrows scrunch up in concentration.

"Never mind, I'll figure it out. I guess I'll start with the stuff in the room first."

"Thank you, Sensei. Also, please do not worry about the box with the word 'E.L.' carved on it. That just holds some of my personal items," the Fate says before turning towards the rest of them. "Well, it is officially free-time. Spend it however you wish; just make sure to get to bed early. We have a match tomorrow. As for me, I am going to go chop some wood."

Wake stands. "I'll join you. I saw a second axe by the woodpile." He used to hate the chore, since it meant trekking from the depths of Ice Ridge to the nearest woods. But after a year of not having to swing an axe, it actually sounds like it could be fun.

CHAPTER 18
SENSEI
[ROAD TO THE BANK, GREENWOOD]

The little clerk makes his way past the booths of the eastern market. Merchants hawk their wares from all sides, selling all manner of goods: from buttery griddle cakes to less than savory looking weapons. He almost stops at a cart overflowing with apples—green and red, both. That is until, he sees a girl eyeing his purse. Sure enough, a little ways away he spots her partner, a thin blade barely showing under his sleeve.

There's probably a half a dozen more in the crowds, he realizes after spotting the first pair of pickpockets. He clutches the money purse tightly and continues on.

Beyond the market, the road begins to wind through a particularly quiet portion of Greenwood. He doesn't spot a soul until passing an alley, one known as a gathering place for kids with nowhere better to be. He doesn't look their way as he crosses, but he can feel them watching him. Suddenly, one of the girls cries out for help. He knows better than to, but he looks over just in case.

Surrounded, she looks like she may really be in trouble. He turns away from the scene and continues on. It's just Sue Pricen and her cousins. He wouldn't fall for something like that.

He pats the heavy money pouch with one hand and grips a brand new ledger in the other. He's had the leather-bound book for quite some time, saving it for something particularly special.

It's a true Team Ledger, with pages lined and divided for charts, lists and notes. It even has a separate section for a journal and calendar.

Distracted with thoughts on how he'll fill it, he barely notices the pair of disheveled boys who pass by. That is until he hears their footsteps turn and approach from behind.

"Hey, kid, could you help us out? We're a little lost," the beady-eyed one asks ever so nicely.

"Sure, where are you trying to get to?" the small clerk says, not bothering to stop.

"Hey, buddy, can you slow down a minute?" the larger, greasy fellow asks him. "We're just looking for ... my aunt's house. She's supposed to live next to a ... big red house on this road."

"Sorry, I haven't seen anything like that."

"Well, how about buying us a drink, then? That's a pretty big money sack you got there," the larger one blurts out before his beady-eyed friend sticks an elbow in his side.

"What he means is perhaps you were looking to have some fun this evening?" the beady-eyed boy adds quickly. "We have a little problem. There's these three girls waiting for us, but our friend got sick and we're short a fellow. We don't want to disappoint the girls, you know. Maybe you could help us out?"

Sensei slows down, not wanting to show the older boys just how short of breath he is. He pats the pouch at his waist and feigns a look about. There's not a single other soul on the street. "How much are we talking about here, fellas? I have a couple copper, but ..." Sensei motions them closer.

"But the rest of it is pebbles. It's just a game I like to play." With his breath caught, he continues walking. *Just one more block and I'll be within sight of the Bank.*

"Hey, hey, that's alright, we'll take what we can get," the large fellow blurts out before getting jabbed again.

"Hold up, hold up," The other boy steps in front of him. "What's the hurry?"

"I'm sorry, but I really have to get going. I need to get back in time for supper or Pa will get sore at me. He's a Sitter and he gets mean when I'm late." *This is not good, but I'm so close. Just a half a block more ...*

"Now, now, we don't want that to happen ... but I don't think there are any houses in this direction," the beady-eyed boy says. His friend is now next to him, arms crossed, with a mean grin on his face. "The only thing past us is some warehouses and the *Bank*."

"He's stationed at the Bank, today." With one hand on the pouch and the other his ledger, the little clerk darts right between them. He doesn't stop running until he sees the Sitter stationed in front of the Bank. When he looks back, the street is empty. He leans over, hands on knees, his heart knocking against his chest and his lungs desperate for air.

It was a short distance, but he hasn't run that fast in very long time—not since the Healer diagnosed the problem with his heart.

He isn't sure if it's the sprint or the fear that's making his heart beat like it is. Rapidly and hard, faster than he could drum, it feels like his heart may just beat its way out of his chest. But it passes.

Sensei staggers by the curious Sitter standing guard. Inside, he finds a chair and takes another moment to rest.

It's not long before he figures out which queue is moving the fastest and takes his place in it.

His thoughts turn back to the girl he met at the office earlier that day. She claimed to have spied the scrimmage herself in which the Slate soundly defeated *The Royal Team*. When Sensei asked the Fate if it was true, he shrugged and told him, "Everyone won; it was training." *Anyone else would've bragged about it till no end. But not Captain*, he thinks proudly.

"Next," a tired looking teller calls out.

Sensei limps up to the window. The weight of the pouch makes him compensate with each step and his right knee begins to ache.

It's the first time in a while being on this side of one of these. *I'll deposit most of this copper. A small handful should be more than enough to last the rest of the week. But first I should check the box.*

"I need to check a deposit box." He passes a small numbered key beneath the window.

"This is actually a key for a Personal Vault. If you would still like to see it, it is right this way." The teller stands and motions towards a well-lit hallway.

The teller leads him to a door marked 301. He unlocks it and asks, "Will you be long, sir?"

"Yes, I think so," Sensei says, seeing just what he's in store for. Just as the equipment back at the inn, everything is stacked in neat piles that make absolutely no sense. Only here, he can't even see the floor. *I'll have to start at the door and make a path as I go.*

By the time he's finished, he can make out most of the pattern on the rug. Burgundy birds flit across wheat-colored patterns and a dark blue star holds the center. It's plush and was rather comfortable to sit on, which the clerk is grateful for.

He can't help but be pleased at the sight of his work: armor, weapon, Tearstone, part or tool, each is now on a shelf of its own. Once started, it went quickly enough—everything's now accounted for except for a small cylindrical baton.

Sensei inspects the reddish-bronze rod. It is as thick as his finger and runs the length of his hand. It has a shard embedded on one end and what appeared to be a faded insignia on the other. What remains of the mark looks familiar, but it could be the insignia of half a dozen things.

He wonders if it might've been brought by mistake. *Well, I guess I might as well take it back to the Captain and ask him what it is.* He knocks on the door. Within moments he hears someone fiddling with the lock on the other side.

The same teller opens the door. The banker's worn face takes on a look of surprise at how much the small room has changed. "How may I assist, young sir?"

"I'm done here for today, but I'd also like to make a coin deposit."

"Very well, right this way, sir."

Sensei takes a last look behind him. *There's some pretty neat stuff in here. I'll bring Wake next time. He's into gear and his appraisal skills should help in cataloging it all.*

The banker locks the door and motions for him to check for himself. Once satisfied, he follows the teller back to his window.

There, he pulls free the money purse from his belt and begins dumping its contents into the small divot below the thick glass window.

They both gasp in surprise. Instead of copper, it's gold that falls out onto the counter. *I bet the richest man in the world, The Maestro, wouldn't even carry this much in a single purse ... at least, if he was still alive,* Sensei thinks, seeing all that gold.

His head becomes dizzy just thinking of what almost happened on the way to the bank. *He should've told me it was gold. How could he trust me with all this?*

CHAPTER 19
RACHEL
[STEWARDS & RAIDERS INN, GREENWOOD]

All worries are forgotten as Rachel watches her brother's aura disappear behind the Fate's. It's been a long while since she's been around him like this. *He's happy.*

Spikey squeaks something from her shoulder and she strokes his little head. If only she had met the chipmunk first, she might've been able to see through his eyes even now.

Riser finishes her bowl with a loud slurp. "Still worried about tomorrow?"

"I am ... but I'm feeling better now," Rachel says. "I want to thank you, Riser, for treating me and my brother so well."

"Are you trying to get me to let you take a bath first? Because nothing's going to keep this Daughter from a long, hot soak."

"No, please go ahead. In fact, I feel like working on my brushwork," Rachel says. *It's been too long. I'm going to lose my touch.*

"I'll make sure to leave some hot water for you," Riser says, taking her leave.

"Since Fate and Wake are helping chop wood, I think I'll make myself useful, too." Rachel turns to the Healer, who is just finishing his last bowl. "Brun, could you give me a hand when you're done eating, of course?"

"Sure, I'm done," the Half-Orc mumbles. "You should call me Monster. Fate made it a rule."

"I will, at least when he's around." Rachel giggles . *I would never have gone against Kearney's orders and he's not half the man ... or at least the Captain the Fate is.* "I'll be right back."

Rachel returns shortly with a long mahogany case in tow. After ensuring the table is clear, she sets it down with great care.

"Can you wave over Lene?" she asks the Half-Orc. Rachel can't help admiring his ever-changing aura of crimson and blue. It rages and churns, a storm of indigo and scarlet that knows no calm. She's never seen anything like it.

As much as she appreciates a unique aura, the traces that Tears themselves leave behind can be just as beautiful. All major roads and official buildings are marked with the glowing colors created by a Sharded Brush.

Most private establishments try to maintain a Shard Painted Sign, as well, but that's easier said than done. Practitioners of the Long Brush are in great demand, and smaller towns like Greenwood go many a year without seeing a true Master.

"Another plate?" the innkeeper asks.

"No, it was most delicious, but I couldn't eat another bite," Brother Monster says. "May I ask if that is fennel or anise that you spiced the broth with?"

"Close, young man, but it's neither. It's ground Lovage seed, a special variety Greenwood has always been known for. We call it Sweet Lovage around here. It isn't popular outside of our little town. It has a tendency to lose its aroma when not freshly used," she says with a chuckle. "Ahh, you must be the cleric that's been staying with the priests? You know they used to be my some of my best customers?"

"Forgive me. They have been so kind as to host me while the Tour is in town and in turn I have been helping out in the kitchen. They haven't forgotten you, though. They frequently talk about their meals at the Stew. Would you mind showing me around your kitchen, when time allows? I would be happy to wash some dishes in return."

"Sounds like a deal," the innkeeper replies. "I have a garden out back that you may be interested in, too. I'll give you a full tour once the dinner hour is over."

"Before you go, I wanted to show my appreciation, also," Rachel adds. "I was wondering if you might want the sign out front touched up. I offer you my services as a second-degree Master of the Long Brush. I studied under Master Glasgow of Middleton."

"Really? Could you really do something about that sign?" Lene asks. "It's older than I am."

"It would be my pleasure. No charge, of course." Rachel turns to Brother Monster. "Would you be so kind as to help me take down the sign?"

Monster grunts his affirmation and stands, leaving only the little bard at their once filled table.

Rachel asks Poe if he would like to join them. She can hear him still scribbling madly away. But the innkeeper has another suggestion. "Everyone else is helping an old lady out. Why don't you play something for my customers?" she asks, gesturing towards a small stage.

"Especially, anything by The Maestro. Did you know Lord Hardrime once stopped in here? That was half a lifetime ago, long before he became famous, but even then, you could tell he was something special.

"The stage hasn't been used in years, but it'd be nice to hear some music in here again."

Poe bows politely and heads for the stage with guitar in tow.

To Rachel's surprise, the Half-Orc is able to unhook the large sign without the aid of a ladder. She's never been very good at judging one's height by their aura, but the Half-Orc must be quite tall.

Monster heaves the huge sign over one shoulder and leads Rachel around back. She wonders just how many signs it would take to make a ship like Enyo had.

As they approach the rear of the inn, the sounds of furious chopping can be heard. *I always thought Wake hated chopping wood*, Rachel thinks, rounding the corner.

"If you could just set it somewhere clean and out of the way."

The Healer leans the sign against the back of the inn, safely away from the flurry of wood chips. "Is this fine?" he asks.

"Yes, that should do nicely," Rachel says as she feels out the area. "If I could ask for one more little favor? Could you find something for me to set my case upon?"

He brings over a pair of stools.

"Thank you so much. You're a real sweetheart."

He mumbles something and heads back in.

"Boys, be careful, okay? Don't send anything flying this far," she calls out to the two who have stopped to count how much wood each has split.

"Yes, ma'am," Wake says before turning to his opponent. "You have a quarter of a cord more than I do, but you started well before I did."

"No excuses. I won fair and square," the Fate says. "It is unfortunate that we ran out of wood. I was just getting warmed up."

Wake hefts his axe over his shoulder and starts towards the woods further behind the inn. "I saw a dead hickory back this way. Those burn nice and long," Wake says, trying to get a head start. "And do you really think that a true Northerner would ever let some beach lover beat him in a chopping contest."

"What does a Water boy know of fire or wood?" the Fate taunts back, hurrying to catch up.

"At least, I won't have to worry about them getting in the way," Rachel says to herself. She runs her hands over the sign to get a feel for her canvas. On one side is a faded drawing of what she guesses is some sort of knight on a horse. *Easy enough*, she thinks.

The letters on the other side are going to be more difficult, however. The original artist had a unique style, one that would be difficult to mimic. It took the first two years of her training just to learn how to make her lettering uniform in all ways, especially in brightness.

Rachel opens the large case with great care. Inside are five brushes, each as long as her arm. And though each brush is remarkably similar in size and shape, their bristles are of strikingly different colors. The chipmunk jumps down from her shoulder and scurries between her brushes.

"Please be careful, Spikey. These are very valuable to me." He squeaks twice, short and quick.

She chooses the black-headed brush and holds it in one hand while the other grips her wrist. Her first strokes are broad and sweeping. It's not long before she is lost in her work—all lingering worries longforgotten.

A final daub of red and she's done. The round of applause that erupts surprises her. *When did the boys get back? And Riser too ... I must have been really distracted to not have noticed.*

"Amazing, Shine," the Captain says. Rachel can hear the whooshing sounds he makes trying to mimic her. "After the hundredth, will you teach me how to do that too?"

"I can get you started, but it takes quite a bit of practice to master."

"The way you move with your brush ... it's so graceful," Riser says. "Can I ask you to draw something for me—when you have some time?"

"Of course, anytime," Shine says. "I'm only proficient at the Large Brush, but I also have a smaller set that I've been playing with. By the way, who chopped the most wood?"

"I did," they both answer.

"Well, it was close," Wake admits.

"We ran out of dead trees," The Fate says sadly.

"Good, then you two can take some firewood over to the baths. They're running low," Riser tells them. "Don't forget to wash up while you're there, too."

"Last one clean empties the tubs," the Fate proposes mid-dash.

"Are you really challenging a Water-User to a bathing contest?" The door closes behind them.

"I haven't seen Wake like this in awhile. It's really nice, especially after how serious he's been lately."

"It's good for Fate, too. He's always been the only boy."

"Oh, really?"

"Yeah, him and four of us girls," Riser says. "Which was nice and less stinky." The two share a giggle.

"There were no boys his age in the Slate," Riser tells her. "From what I heard, the older girls used to tease him pretty bad when he first got there."

"Oh, that explains a little. He is ... different," Rachel says. "And what was it that you wanted me to draw?"

"It's just something I saw once, but I'm always afraid of forgetting.'

CHAPTER 20

WAKE
[STEWARDS & RAIDERS INN, GREENWOOD]

The night air tastes crisp and feels sharply cool against Wake's flush skin. *I'll go ahead and empty the tubs, after I get dressed. It should only take one trip with my gauntlet.* There are no signs of the Fate as he enters the team room.

"Oh, hey, Poe, I didn't know you were in here," Wake says, finding the bard alone in the room. The fidgeting musician glances over at the towel-clad boy and quickly resumes arranging blankets in the far corner. "There's still a fresh tub in the washroom. Do you want me to ask Lene for some more hot water?"

The bard shakes his head and continues on with his work.

"Ah, I was thinking of doing something similar, myself," Wake admits. "I can't say I'm not glad there isn't another joining us on the bed."

Earlier, the Fate found out the windowsill was large enough for his bedroll, leaving the bed to just Monster, Sensei and Wake. It's probably the most comfortable bed Wake's slept in since joining the Tour.

Unfortunately, Wake can't decide who has sharper elbows: Monster or Sensei. Apparently, the Half-Orc didn't adhere to his vow while he slept and Sensei has the penchant for jabbing him in all the most painful spots.

"It doesn't seem very fair that the girls get a whole half of the room to themselves. Fortune must be more chivalrous than I ever realized," Wake mutters, noticing the two additional dividers that have been added for extra privacy.

Poe reaches high and attaches a line to one wall and runs it to the other, cornering himself in. The little musician throws a sheet over it, creating a very private corner. A hand sticks up over the self-made curtain and waves as if to say good night.

"So you're a private one too, huh?" Wake says softly, before calling back, "Good night, Poe. And thanks for playing for us. It really made training go by faster."

The door bursts open and Sensei comes barging in with a wild look in his eyes. "Wake, have you seen Fate?"

"He's still washing up, I think. Is everything okay?"

"No, not really," the clerk says. "Let's just say I never knew going to the bank could be an adventure."

"I'm sure he knew you could handle it."

"It was too close for my comfort," Sensei whispers to himself. He reaches deep into his pocket. "I wanted to ask him about something, but maybe you could help me. You're a pretty high level appraiser, aren't you?"

"That's right. I used to even write a weekly column on equipment and appraising back home," Wake answers proudly. "I'm only licensed to appraise armor, though."

"Oh, well, maybe you still might know what this is? I don't know what to make of it. But it seems like it could be important." Sensei pulls out a small, bronze rod.

"Wow, these are pretty rare," Wake says, taking the object and inspecting it closely. "They used to be common not too long ago, but now they make much cheaper and efficient locks. See, it's a key. There's an engraving on it, too. It's pretty scratched up, but I think there's enough left to make out what it was."

Wake holds the key up to the light. "No, this can't be ..."

"What is it, Wake?"

"This is bad, really bad. I'm pretty sure that these three lines are the legs of a bird," Wake says quietly. "This is the Royal Seal, which means it is property of the Royal Family. If we get caught with something like this, we could get into some real trouble. We'd be branded as thieves." *Why does the Fate have this? This key is dangerous just to be around.*

"I have never seen it before," the Fate tells them. "It must belong to my Old Man."

"I'm pretty sure that's the mark of the Three-Legged Raven," Wake whispers as quietly as he can.

"Hmm ... Now, just where have I seen that before?" Fate muses out loud.

"Two days ago, on a flag outside the royal tent. It's the mark of the Royal Family," Sensei explains in disbelief. "Anyone in unlawful possession of a marked item can get into really big trouble."

The Fate dismisses their worries with a wave of his hand. "It is that bird, the one with the extra leg. Either way, there is no need to worry. If my Old Man had it ... it would not have been unlawfully."

"I don't know. Even if he held it by right, it doesn't mean we can. I really don't want to be branded a thief," Wake says nervously.

"That is not going to happen," the Fate says.

"Maybe we should turn the key over to the proper authorities."

A sleepy looking Poe comes out from behind the hung up sheet and whispers something to the Fate.

He hands over the small bronze rod to the bard. "Daebak, Poe says Bards often receive gifts like this. He can safely hold it for us."

"Thank you," the Fate tells Poe. The bard's lithe hand waves back as he disappears behind the curtain.

Sensei looks almost angry as he walks up to the Fate and asks, "Captain, why didn't you tell me how much money was in that pouch? You shouldn't have trusted anyone, let alone me with all that gold."

"I thought I did. I hope I did not cause you too much trouble."

"Just a bit," Sensei says.

"I knew you could handle it," the Fate says, leaning forward and looks the little clerk in the eye. "Who should I have trusted with the task besides you?" Sensei looks stumped at the question.

Wake doesn't really know what they're going on about. He's too distracted by thoughts of the key. *It's true that no one should question why a bard would have something like that. The wealthiest man in the world is none other than the King of Bards, The Maestro, himself. Well, at least he used to be. But still, this wasn't just the mark of any noble house. This was the mark of the Royal Family.*

CHAPTER 21

RACHEL

I t's too hot to fall back asleep. Rachel throws off her blanket, but then it's too cold. At least, Riser's stopped grinding her teeth, but the strange rustling won't go away. She can't quite tell what's making the bothersome noise, but it's definitely coming from somewhere outside.

I need my sleep. We have a match today. But after tossing and turning a bit longer, she relents.

The last thing she wants is for the others to share in her misery. So she dons her thick sweater and long woolen skirt as quietly as possible and slips out the door.

She expected that at least the innkeeper would be up, but there's no sign of anyone downstairs. *It must be earlier than I thought. There's no one else awake except for whoever is out back.* She's pretty sure it's the Captain. His aura was missing from the room earlier.

"Hello," Rachel calls out opening the door to out back. "Fate?"

"Good Morning, Shine," the Fate calls back. "You are up early."

"I woke up and couldn't fall back asleep." She wraps her cape tightly around her. "Do you know what time it is?"

"An hour or two before sunrise."

"Oh, then, I really should go back to bed."

"I also have trouble sleeping in there," he admits. "After Lene does her second bed-check, I sneak out here and sleep on the bench."

"Out here ... in the cold?"

"It is not so cold if you bundle up," he explains. "My blanket is on the bench. You may use it if you wish. I am about to start a fire, so please do not worry about the cold.

"Spikey, would you be so kind as to guide her to the bench?"

She follows the chipmunk's squeaking until she finds the bench. There, she discovers a thick, wooly blanket, which she quickly gets underneath. The little chipmunk finds a comfortable spot on her lap and curls up.

Soon, her shivers are gone. "You're right. It's not so bad under here. You don't need to start a fire on my behalf."

"I have to make a fire, anyway. I need the coals and embers."

"What do you need those for?"

"For the hole I am about to dig," he says, lighting the fire.

"Why exactly do you need a hole and coals? And why so early in the morning?"

"It is a secret."

The flames crackle, filling the air with warmth and the smell of burning wood. Rachel nestles herself deeper into his blanket. It smells like outside. Crackle, hiss and then the sound of shovel scooping dirt.

Today's just another day. He's not worried about it all. We'll be just fine. He gave his Yaksok, she tells herself, feeling the gentle flames caress her face. Having been raised in a city built within a cliff, the clean chill in the morning air is nice. She can almost feel the dew coalescing on one side, and the dry heat of the fire on the other.

Rachel feels cozy, even outside ... with him. Crackle, hiss, shovel, sleep.

"Rachel." Someone is calling her name.

She's back at home, and the smell of dank clay and mud and stone surround her. Water drips in the distance, echoing through the tunnels, and a fire crackles nearby.

"Rachel!" She takes a deep breath and it is all grass and trees; only the smell of smoke remains, and the voice calling her name. Wake? Rachel sits up and yawns.

"She is over here, in my bed," another voice says.

"What?" her brother says, his voice filling with anger and confusion. Something stirs in her lap. *Where am I? I must have fallen asleep. What time is it?*

"She is fine. I kept her warm," says the Fate.

"What?" Wake repeats, louder and full of fury. Rachel stretches her arms high above her head. Her blanket falls to her waist and she scurries to get back underneath. Without it, she can feel the warmth of the fire but also the cold morning air.

Why is the fire over there? Wasn't it on the other side before? She tries to remember, unable to shake away her sleep. *What's going on ... why does Wake sound so angry?*

"No worries, I consider your sister a good girlfriend. I made sure to take good care of her."

Rachel almost chokes. "Excuse me?" she tries to say. The next things she hears are two quick steps and a loud smack. Poe, who must have joined them, lets out a little yelp before clasping his hands over his mouth.

"You stay away from my sister, you crazy freak!" Wake yells down at the Fate.

"Ouch," Fate says, rubbing his chin. "You really are fast when you want to be, Way."

"Be quiet! Enough of that," Wake begins before his sister finds him with her gentle hand. Poe runs inside, returning a moment later with Esperanza.

"It's okay, Wake, I don't know what he's talking about. But I just woke up a little too early and couldn't fall back asleep. He made a fire and I ended up falling back asleep out here."

"What's going on?" Riser asks, entering the yard with the bard in tow.

"I would also like to know," the Fate admits, rubbing his jaw.

"He said some awful things about Rachel. I had to defend my sister's honor."

"Oh, and what exactly did he say?"

"He said that Rachel's his girlfriend and that she's sleeping in his bed ... and he was keeping her warm!" Wake explains, twitching in anger.

Esperanza bursts out in laughter. Spikey climbs onto Rachel's shoulder and begins squeaking in delight, too. Monster and Sensei come out to join them.

"What's going on out here?"

"Wake just laid the Captain out. It was in defense of his sister's honor, of course." Even as she speaks, the Daughter can't stop laughing. "I guess it's up to me to explain."

She turns to the Fate and asks, "Oppa, what's a girlfriend?"

"What? A girlfriend? That is a girl that is your friend, of course," the Captain replies.

"So even though I'm your cousin, I'm your girlfriend, right?"

"Yes, of course, Riser, you are one of my finest girlfriends."

Riser starts laughing all over again. She pats Wake on the back and heads back in. "Blame Ieiri Skyshadow. She taught him that word. She also got him to promise to tell any pretty girl he meets that he already has a girlfriend and that it's her, of course.

"Fate may be a lot of things, but you never have to worry about that. And a word of advice—I would never, ever mess with that girl and her promises." Riser actually shivers at the thought before turning to head back inside.

Monster checks out the damage to the Captain's face. The Healer peers deeply into his eyes before grunting that he's okay.

"Um, I'm really sorry ... uh, Captain," Wake says. "I just thought something else ..."

"That was just silly, wasn't it?" Rachel laughs nervously. "Just a big old misunderstanding."

"Why do people keep punching me in the face?" their Captain asks, getting to his feet.

"Fate, I'm really sorry. I feel horrible. I thought you were speaking basely of my sister. I had a hard time with our last Captain. I was always worried about his intentions towards Rachel. I thought I was defending her honor, but I was the one that was wrong. You weren't dishonoring Rachel in any way. I'm sorry. Really, I am."

"I see it is of the utmost importance to defend Rachel's honor. And you thought I was attacking her honor, so you hit me ..."

"Yes, but I was wrong. Please forgive me. I've never actually hit anyone before in my life. Well outside of Tear Fighting," Wake says," Do you want to punch me in return?"

"I believe, I understand—her honor means a lot to you. If that is the case, it means a lot to me as well. I promise to defend Shine's honor from hereon out. You will no longer have to carry this burden alone. And no, I do not want to punch you. I want to wash up and eat breakfast," the Fate says. "I forgive you and thank you for explaining yourself to me. Just please do not touch me again, it is against the rules. And we must always follow the rules."

CHAPTER 22

WAKE

[TOURNEY GROUNDS, GREENWOOD]

Wake stares at his hand, the one he just hit his new Captain with. *Why did I do that? I never would've done something like that before. He didn't even deserve it.*

It's his old Captain that did, but he never would've tried to hit Kearney. And it's not like Kearney Dim ever beat him as badly as the Fate did, at least in a Tear Fight. *What's wrong with me? I did the exact opposite of what I was supposed to.*

Wake looks up and realizes he's on the sidelines. The stands are already full, but more and more are still arriving. Soon, he'll be taking the field in front of all these people ... with a team he barely knows.

But really, I know them. They are exactly what they seem. They might not be what I'm used to or even ever expected, but I'm lucky to have them. A team where I can be myself, even if it means I do something stupid, like hit one of them.

Riser just laughed, Monster fixed things and Fate—he tried to understand. He even thanked me.

I broke almost every Team Rule, even before our first match. I touched the Captain, I didn't do the right thing, and even though, I spent night and day with them, in a way I stayed apart. Now, all that's left for me is lose us this match ...

The boy he hit earlier comes and takes a seat next to him. "This is great, is it not, Way?"

"Yes." Wake doesn't bother to correct him. The Fate's called him that a couple times now: Way. *It's close enough, and at least, it's not a different name every time he tries to talk to me.* "Look, Fate, I just want to say one more time that I'm really sorry."

"For what?"

"Hitting you, of course."

"What is past is past. I forgave you already," the Fate says, looking all around at everything, all at once, until finally setting his sights upon the fountain in the middle of the field. The officials have moved everything over to Greenwood's marquee landmark, Titan Blue, a gigantic fountain. Its shape resembles that of an arm that reaches from the ground, and it is taller than the tallest of the three hundred-year-old forest surrounding its walls.

Water sprouts from its palm like a river falling from the sky. The roar of the crowd is deafening, but the rushing of the water is loud enough for even the deaf to hear. Low and deep, you can feel it as much as hear it, a trembling beneath you that never ends.

Two teams battle it out below the fountain, but the match is practically already over. One side is already down a Crier. It is only a matter of time now.

"You guys are good. I guess, I'm just not used to that."

"I thought your old team was highly ranked." *That's not what I meant.*

"Way, I will help you with your little condition, but you do not need help being good. You have always been good."

The answer just makes him feel even worse. The outnumbered team puts up a brave fight, but it's not long before they lose another and then another.

Finally, Wake looks up and asks, "How do you do it?"

"Do what?"

"Aren't you nervous?"

"Nervous?"

"If we lose today, aren't you going to have to report for Service and give up Tear Fighting forever?"

"I really have not given it much thought. Why would I?"

"Because chances are it's going to happen!"

"Anything might happen." The Fate looks up at the sky. "Frogs might rain down from above, for all I know. But why worry about that?"

"It's what a normal person would do. Everybody can't be as strong as you. And even then, someday you'll be out there against someone stronger."

"It is not about being stronger or weaker. Anyone can Win the Moment. The only thing is ... you have to try, Way."

"You make it sound so easy, but how? Isn't there anything else? Some Technique or something you could teach me? I've actually learned a lot these last couple days. I'm willing to try anything."

"Daebak, but I do not know anything like that." The Fate scratches his chin. "Actually, I do know one Water Tech. It is a secret one, long handed down by the Bae, but I can teach it to you, if you wish."

Wake's hopes rise at the thought. *He's going to teach me some secret, powerful Technique, one that will change everything.* "Yes, please. Can you really teach me something like that before the match starts?"

"Sure, why not? Go find Riser and a bucket of water."

"Way, please get down onto your hands and knees." The Fate points towards the water filled pail. "Yes, right there, in front of the bucket.

"Riser, we will be teaching him Mul HoHeup. You know what to do, right?" he asks her. She nods and begins to mount the kneeling boy from behind.

"Wait a minute, what are you doing?" Suddenly, she's behind him, straddling him, pinning his arms to his sides with her long legs. He almost falls forward, but she holds him up by his chin.

"I thought you wanted to learn a new Technique?" the Fate asks.

"No, I mean yes, I do. It's just ..." Wake tries not to think about the legs wrapped around him. *Smooth, lean, soft and hard ...* He faces the bucket. "I'm ready."

"This might be a little unpleasant," the Fate warns him. "Riser, go ahead and begin."

The Daughter grabs the back of his head and shoves his face into the water. Her legs tighten around his body, squeezing the air out of him. He's helpless, drowning in a bucket. *I can't breathe. I'm going to die!*

When the bubbles stop, Riser says, "He's ready. There's no air left in him."

"A little bit more," the Fate says.

"I can't hold him much longer. He's stronger than he looks," she says, struggling to keep his head down. *I need to breathe! Please, I'm sorry, just let me up.*

"Way, I need you to listen to me. Try to calm yourself, clear your head. Focus."

"He's not listening," Riser says.

The Captain lowers himself to Wake's ear. "There is only one way we are going to let you up, so listen closely. What is it that you want right now?

"You want to breathe so badly it hurts, correct? When your mind is emptied of all other thoughts, we can begin. Forget everything else except for what it is that you really want. That is the only way you are going to get it. When all you can think of is that next breath, still your mind and body and I will help you get that breath."

Wake gives a final buck, but it's no use. His body quivers and shakes, but he focuses on what has to be done to get out of this alive. *Air, please air!*

"Good, now listen carefully and do exactly as I say and you will get that breath and learn the secret Water Tech of the Bae," the Fate says. "All you want right now is that breath of fresh air. Focus on that, use that desire—and reverse the bubbles.

"Begin slowly, put your lips together and pull it from the fringes of the water. Just focus on that ... like whistling backwards. You can do it! I know you can!"

Wake purses his lips and sucks in. His mouth fills with water and he chokes.

"Focus! Water is your element. You control it. Keep it out and only let what you wish for through."

For a moment, everything is still. *Only air! I only want the air.*

The water begins to bubble.

It tastes so sweet. *Air!* Soon, Riser is rocking gently to the rhythm of his deep breathing.

"I think he's got it." Riser releases him and jumps out of the way. Wake throws his head back and water cascades all around them. Eyes red with rage, he screams, but only water comes out. "You ... glub ... crazy bastard, glub ... trying to kill me!"

Wake takes a step towards the Fate before falling over and coughing.

"I knew you could do it, Way. It took me a good month to learn that Tech, but I knew a Water genius like you could do it in one shot."

Wake looks up. "You could've killed me."

"There was no chance of you actually dying. Did you not want to learn the secret Water Tech of the Bae?"

"How's that going to help me in a match?" Wake asks in disbelief, "And if I wanted to breathe underwater I'd just use a Sharded rebreather!"

"That is true. I guess that is why it is a secret ... forgotten Tech."

"What! Come here. I'm going to break Rule One, one more time!" Wake screams, getting to his feet.

The Fate flees.

"We'll just call it even for me punching you earlier," Wake says, finally giving up the chase. He leans over, hands on his knees, trying to catch his breath once again. *It tastes so sweet, the air. I still can't get enough.*

"If you say so," the Fate says, looking almost out of breath for once. "Did you learn what you asked for?"

"What are you talking about? I thought you just taught me that worthless Mul Haobb Tech."

"It is Mul HoHeup. And I did not really teach you anything. I just made it so you wanted to breathe and you learned it yourself. All a Master can do is hope for his student to thirst. After that, the Master provides the water, but it is up to the student to drink," the Captain explains. "What matters is what you felt. Did anything else in the whole world matter except getting that next breath?"

"No, of course not."

"Remember how you asked me 'how can I not think of losing?' I guess that is why. All I can think of is how much I want that next win. Sometimes, I want it so bad, I feel like I will even forget to breathe," the Fate says quietly.

"Listen, Way," his Captain tells him. "You are strong, but your mind is unfocused, or rather focused on the wrong things. When you go out there today, there are three things I want you to remember. First, find your calm."

"That's easier said than done. How am I supposed to just find my calm?" Wake says. "How do you?"

"This is the way I see it. No matter how crazy it gets out there, deep down I really know that everything is going as it should, and everything will go as it should. That is just how life works. When facing the unknown, you can choose fear or faith. I choose faith." Even, now, repeating it to himself helps. *Everything is going as it should and everything will go as it should.*

Wake nods and wonders, "What's the second thing?"

"Once, I find my calm, I make sure to clear my head of all other things and concentrate on what must be done at that moment. Just as you did when learning Mul HaHeoup. You have to focus."

"I can try to do that," Wake says, the memory still fresh in mind.

"The last thing you have to do out there is to not forget ... Never forget, *you cannot lose!*" the Fate says, leaning forward so his hair covers his eyes. All you can see is that smile. "Those are the things that I believe and will never forget. Most importantly, I believe in you, Way. So believe in me, and the things I believe in, too. It is as easy as that."

CHAPTER 23

RACHEL

[TOURNEY GROUNDS, GREENWOOD]

"Where did everybody go?" Rachel asks the Daughter. Riser sits alone, grumbling over getting stuck watching their gear.

"I don't know. Your brother and Fate ran off playing one of their babo boy games. I guess the other two didn't want to miss out and went after them, leaving me alone to watch our gear."

"That's great." Rachel smiles for the first time since getting to the Tourney Grounds. "I don't mean you getting stuck here is great, but I'm glad they're over what happened this morning."

Riser chuckles. "I guess you could say that."

Rachel takes a seat next to her new good friend. "Riser, are we really ready for this? If we lose here today, will he really never fight again?"

"We won't lose. But yeah, it's true, I've heard him make that promise to the Old Man many times."

"The way we've been training. He's been doing that all his life?"

"Much harder, actually." The Daughter's answer scares her. It's just too much.

"Unnie, he's a babo, but he's not stupid. Though, sometimes, he even makes me wonder on that. To be honest, I was worried when I first met you all, too. I never heard of any of you guys before ... but now, I think he picked the right team. Well, I'm not so sure about Monster—just joking ... maybe."

"I just don't want to fail ... you, him, my brother, anyone."

"Everyone fails, even me. It's part of life."

Rachel is grateful. She wasn't sure how the Daughter would react to her confession. *Coward, I'm a coward* ...

"I bet you think Fate calls me Riser because of how I use the Winds?"

"Yes, of course."

"Truth is, he started calling me that before I mastered my 128's," Riser says, tapping her Gust Boots. "When I first met him, I had just lost an important match. I do not lose matches often. It was the only one I lost that whole year, practice included. Everybody else knew well enough to leave me alone. But I guess he was visiting with his Old Man and somehow, he found me alone after the match. He kept pestering me. I couldn't understand why he wouldn't just leave me alone. He's so failing annoying that way, you know what I mean?"

"I think so."

"Don't tell anyone, but my mother is the High Priestess of Enyo. So I might have been treated a little differently growing up. I wasn't used to people annoying me the way he did. That smile of his, it's unforgivable."

Rachel can't hide the surprise on her face.

"Who my mother is has no bearing on who I am. Anyway, everything came pretty easily to me. I was given every opportunity and no other Daughter could stand against me.

"Oh, I hated him so much back then. I just wanted to wipe that smug look off of his face. But when I tried, he just beat me up. Of course, I got angry. I kept getting up, over and over again ... and he kept knocking me down. I couldn't accept it, though. He just kept smiling and I kept trying. Until, finally, he said he was done and told me that I had won, even though, I didn't manage to hit him once. And then he asked me if I wanted to join his team.

"I thought he was taunting me. I wanted to hit him so badly, but I was so tired I could barely situp. All I could do was ask why and this is what he said. 'You're Riser. Every time I knock you down, you rise up again. When you get up, you're stronger than before. I'm too tired to knock you down any more today, but let's keep going tomorrow and the day after that. You and I are the same that way and with someone like you, I think we can really do it—the impossible.'"

"That's so sweet ... I think."

"Yeah, well, that's why I take pride in being called that. Not because of any Technique, but because when I do fail, I rise up again. I'm not as ridiculous as he is. I know sometimes I'll lose, but I'm no loser if I get up again."

"You could never be a loser, Riser. And I'll try my best, too. When I get knocked down, I'll rise up again, too, just like you."

"Good. We all know this is your first Flag Match so it's okay for you to lean on us," the Daughter says. "Besides, there's only one team on Tour that Fate and I can't take out by ourselves. But don't get me wrong. By the time the Grand Finale rolls around, I expect to lean on you, understand?"

"Finally finished with your little game?" Riser says, standing up from the bench. "It's your turn to watch our stuff. I'm going to go see if matchups are posted."

"Apologies, Riser," the Fate says. "I would also like to see who we will be matched up against. May I accompany you?"

"Yeah, whatever," she mutters. "Whoever wants to, follow me."

"I'll stay and watch our equipment," offers Rachel.

"I'll stay, too," says her brother. The others promise to return soon with word of whom they'll be facing.

Watching them go, Wake asks, "Ray, are you feeling okay?"

Even surrounded, they are alone. The packed stadium shakes and roars to the ebb and flow of the current game. Unlike the last time they were on the sidelines, the whole field is dedicated to each match. All eyes will be on them when they take the battlefield.

"I'm a little anxious. But in a way, I feel kind of lucky, too. Everyone's been so good to us and they are ... I don't know ... just good. Do you know what I mean?"

"I know exactly what you mean."

"And all we have to do is win one match today. That doesn't sound too bad," Rachel says.

"No, it doesn't, not bad at all," a new but familiar voice taunts. I know that voice; it's ...

"Kearney Dim." Rachel looks up to see his despicable aura. Next to the rude boy are the rest of *The Courageous*: Willie Walls, their Shield, and the Mace Brothers, a pair of heavily armored Healers. The other she doesn't recognize.

He must be one of our replacements, she realizes. *They were awful to us at the end, but we were on the same team all year. We're all from Ice Ridge, right?*

Her thoughts go to Wake. After all, he went to school with them. Rachel didn't; she attended a private girls' school in upper Ice Ridge. Her scholarship was a blessing, but it kept her apart from her brother. She would tell him all about her friends and teachers, but he never said a word of his, not until she met them for herself.

It was just over a year ago that she met their old Captain. In many ways, it wasn't too different from how she met their new one. Though, she was the one that was lost, not him.

It seemed like a dream come true. Kearney was almost gallant, the way he went out of his way to try to help her. She didn't realize how much the tunnels of Ice Ridge had changed during her four years away and had somehow managed to get lost.

Even though he ended up leading her in the wrong direction, he at least got her to a place she recognized. Along the way, he mentioned how well his team fared in Juniors. And more importantly, that they were in need of two more. It seemed so perfect, him being in Wake's year and all.

She was feeling guilty that day. Just earlier, she learned that her brother never joined a team while she was away. He refused to be part of any team that didn't promise her a spot, too. And no one was willing to save one for someone they've never met. It was all her fault.

When they were younger, they played at it, dreamed of it: someday entering the Tournament together. Wake would make up the most wonderful games and together they would play in the name of training.

Her favorite was Water Ball. For hours on end, they would go at it, back to back, dodging and blocking as many orbs of water as he could get to bounce around in the small cavern they played in. They'd pretend that each ball was an enemy attack. Her brother would guide her from the dangerous blows with his words. She even gave their little tactic a name—Dual Stance: Flowing Ocean.

But that was all forgotten when they joined a real team. A team led by ...

"What do you want, Kearney?" Wake says. "Don't you have better things to do than bother with us?"

"I always have time for old friends," Kearney says, his voice all but a sneer. "And aren't you doing it backwards, Waste? Aren't you the one that's supposed to be crying and Big Sis babying you?"

"Leave him alone," Rachel says.

"I can't do that. You see, I wanted to come have a look for myself just who we get to crush this round. And it looks like we're up against a bunch of crybabies called Team Fate."

Oh, no. Out of all the teams on Tour, why them? Rachel wrings the bottom of her sweater, stretching it tight. Wake gets up and stands between them. "Something must have you worried. I don't remember you ever bothering to scout anyone else before."

"Shut up, Waste!" the big brute hollers back. "You picked a bad time to grow a pair. Just for that, I'll make sure to take real nice care of you and your sister, too. I'm gonna kick your ass up and down that field and when I'm done with you, I'll pay special attention to your sister's ..."

"That's not going to happen," Wake tries telling him, but the brute ignores him.

"Hey, Ray, did your brother ever tell you about the time he caught me and Willie spying on you in the girls' tubs? It was the first week on Tour. After that, he had to play spoilsport and sit outside the girls' changing room every time you went in."

How could they? They were watching while I ... Rachel thinks in shock.

"Halfway through the year, I started telling everyone he hangs outside the girls' room cause he's an f'ing pervert." Kearney roars in laughter.

"That's not funny," Rachel says, her voice wavering. *How could we ever have been on a team with someone like him?*

"It is though, don't you see? Everyone thinks Waste's a pervert. It's failing hilarious." The big brute licks his lips.

"I never should've gotten rid of you two. You're too much fun to have around." Kearney turns to Wake and says, "And now, I don't have anyone to fetch my stuff and clean my gear. But what I really miss is seeing your sweet sister around."

"Be quiet, Kearney," Wake growls.

"I always knew she had a nice little apple bottom. But damn! When I saw her without that sweater ..."

A familiar eyesore of an aura flashes between them. A clap like thunder reverberates from all around.

"He told you to be quiet. Rachel's honor is not to be messed with," the Fate explains. Unfortunately, the big brute can't hear him from flat on his back with his eyes rolled back.

A loud whistle blows. "Stop right there. You, boy, don't move!"

CHAPTER 24
BROTHER MONSTER
[TOURNEY GROUNDS, GREENWOOD]

T*his is what violence amounts to*, thinks the Half-Orc. *I knew that Fate's a fool, but I never thought he would ever do something like this.*

Monster caught the tail end of what the other boy was spouting and there isn't any denying he should have been stopped. But violence is never the answer. At least, the nasty fellow wasn't seriously injured.

"So who were they?" Riser asks.

"Kearney Dim and *The Courageous*," answers Sensei. "They're who we're up against this round. They're also ..."

"Our old team," Rachel finishes.

"He probably came over here hoping something just like this would happen," Riser says.

Poe points to the Fate, who is still being questioned, and then back to his own eyes. They can't figure what the bard is getting at until he imitates punching himself in the face

"Oh, Kearney Dim is the one that gave Captain his black eyes. He's the one who's after you?" guesses Sensei.

Poe nods.

"It's much more than that. He's a bad person, a really bad person. He likes hurting people," whispers Wake. "Last month, there was this boy, Robbie Thornson. He was making fun of Kearney. Nothing major, just calling him Dimwit for laughs. The thing is, Kearney happened to walk by and hear him. Robbie's as big as they come, but he never stood a chance. The crack his nose made was the most awful sound I ever heard, until Kearney got him down and started stomping on his ribs." Wake cringes.

"I can still hear it. I tried to stop him, but I was too slow. By the time I pulled him off, you could already hear the whistles. Everyone just ran. I ran," Wake admits. "I didn't know what else to do. I guess that means I'm just as bad."

"I know the feeling," the Fate adds, seemingly appearing out of nowhere. "But the mistakes that we make ourselves are the most important ones to forgive."

"But it wasn't your fault, it was mine. I showed you the wrong way. Even in defending someone's honor, you shouldn't hit someone," Wake says. "It's all my fault. I ruined everything."

"No, Everything is fine. And I did not hit him because of anything you said. I did it because it felt right," the Fate explains. "But I was wrong. Afterward, I just felt bad.

"Monster, I think I understand now. Violence is a shortcut. You may get some small thing that you want right then and there, but in the long run you lose even more. I do not like shortcuts like that. He punched me yesterday and then I punched him harder today. I do not like the tomorrow that will lead to."

"He started it," Wake says.

"But I continued it. I wanted him to stop talking. Even more than that, I wanted to show him how strong I really was. But I have been thinking about it. Strength is what you need to do something hard and punching him in the face was so easy. I want to be strong like Monster, instead ... strong enough that I do not care that people think I am weak—strong enough to do the right thing," the Fate tells them. "I do not know much, but my job as Captain is to know what really matters. And for a moment there I forgot what really matters—that it is wrong to hurt other people."

The Half-Orc studies the Captain carefully. *He may be a naive fool most of the time but sometimes ...*

The Fate never stops smiling, even as he tells them, "I am sorry, everyone. They banned me from competing in Greenwood. You all are going to have to win this one without me."

The Half-Orc wonders if he heard the Captain correctly. *Win this without him? Even someone with absolutely no interest in Tear Fighting like me knows no one enters the field one member short.* When he looks at the somber expressions of his teammates, he knows he did hear it correctly.

"Come on, man, be serious," begs Wake. "I know I messed things up, but you don't really expect us to go out there without you, do you? You know how Flag Matches are. It's pretty much over after the first Crier is taken out. And you want us to start that way? Against them?"

The Captain stares back at him and shrugs. "I do not see the problem."

"You don't even know what you're asking," Wake says so quietly they can barely hear him. He takes a deep breath and collapses onto the bench.

"This is a battle that I cannot fight, so you have to fight for me. When you are unable to, I will fight for you. Is that not what it means to be teammates?"

"That's easy for you to say. And ... why are we even doing this?" Wake asks angrily. "The year's almost over. There's no way you're getting enough points to get out of Service. Not that you even deserve to. You should have taken it seriously and shown up at the beginning of the year like everybody else."

Wake picks up the towel next to him and screams into it. "You can't ask us to go out there and embarrass ourselves like this. He's going to try and hurt us. Do you know how he finishes people?

"Kearney uses these iron knuckles and on the last hit he always throws a heavy punch and pretends to drop them. And whoever the poor sap is has to submit or get punched in the face."

"Why would he drop his weapon? If he did that then his fist would go straight through someone's Spectral Armor. It would hit them," the Fate asks.

"Exactly! If the person doesn't want their teeth knocked in, they have to submit. And as soon as they do, he calls them his Flinch Wimp and everyone laughs. I don't want to get hurt. I don't to be his Flinch Wimp. I don't want everyone laughing at me. Why are we doing this? This is stupid ... just stupid."

Brother Monster can't help but agree.

"We need to win this match. It is important," the Captain says.

"You said that already, but why does it even matter?" Monster asks. The Fate promised that they'd get into school, but he clearly doesn't understand what is going on. The Half-Orc has no issues with serving his two years and the situation is becoming obviously painful. *What's he thinking?* Monster wonders. *Can't he see what's happening here? Rachel is on the verge of tears. Wake's a mess.*

"Actually, there is a way for all of us to qualify. I don't know if you'll like it, though," says Sensei. "It involves a Boss Feat."

Even Monster knows that Feats are predetermined milestones. If you attain one you get a corresponding amount of points. And if you accomplish a Feat worthy of being classified a Boss Feat, you automatically qualify for the year. But it's unheard of to actually qualify that way.

"It's called 'Triple Threat,'" Sense tells them.

"That sounds ... pleasant," Rachel says.

"It is more incidental than anything else. All you have to do is place first in the three main events of the Grand Finale," the Fate says all too easily. "And we need to have at least one victory as a Team in order to compete in the Grand Finale."

"So let me get this straight: you expect us to place first in all three events of the final tournament of the year? The tournament that will be held in the capital in one month's time—the tournament that all Three Kingdoms will show up for? That's the plan?" asks Monster in disbelief.

"There's a reason no one's heard of that Feat before. It's absurdly impossible. It's a waste of time to even try," says Wake.

"Says who? Some voice inside of your head?" asks the Captain.

"Yes, of course, it's what everybody's thinking," Wake tells him.

"I for one think that's a fine plan," says Riser. "And the first step towards that is winning our first match here, today." It's just what the Half-Orc would expect someone like her to say.

"I think you guys can do it, too," adds Sensei. "Everything says it won't work, but I think something awesome is going to happen if you guys step out onto the field together."

"Everything does not say it will not work," says the Fate. "Everything says it has to. That is what the Voice inside your head should be telling you, Way."

"No, it says we're about to make fools of ourselves, that ..."

"That it's all a waste?" the Fate finishes.

Wake nods and slumps deeper.

"That is partially correct. You are not just a waste, though, you lay waste. In fact, you are the Waster ... The Waster of Worlds. That is what the Voice should be telling you. If not, ignore the mad one and listen to mine. You are Way, the Waster of Worlds, Destroyer of Dreams. No one can stand against you!"

"What do you know? Really, why should I listen to you?"

Riser scowls. "You're upset, but you should show some respect for your Captain."

"Please let me explain," says the Fate. "Way, did you know that your one punch hurt more than both of his combined? See, he is all swagger and flash. You, though ... you take your opponents out without them even knowing it."

"Yeah, whatever." Wake finally looks up.

"That guy is nothing but bluster," the Captain says. "Think about it, Way. Even though you were on the same team, they have no clue how your Pure Water Techs work. Besides that, you have Riser, the strongest Daughter in generations. And no Healer on Tour can even come close to Monster's heals. And your sister, now, she is the real monster."

Wake sits there shaking his head.

"Little by little," the Captain says. "Just Win the Moment, little by little, and those moments will turn into minutes and the next thing you know, everything will turn out as it should. All you have to do is try. Do not look too far ahead. Focus instead on what you can handle right now."

Monster watches in silence. He still can't figure the Captain out. There's more to him than meets the eye. Maybe he's not the naive, arrogant fool Monster first took him for. *No, he's definitely that, but there is also more to him,* he decides.

"Okay, I'll try," Wake says, surprising them all. "It's just so stupid, but if everyone wants to ... I'll go out there and get beaten up and embarrassed."

CHAPTER 25

WAKE
[BATTLEFIELD: TITAN BLUE]

Right foot ...
Left foot ...
One foot in front of the other, just keep sliding. Mark the trail for Ray, he tells himself. Wake glides through the trees towards something he doesn't want to even think about.

In fact, he doesn't want to think of anything at all, but that is all he can do. *How'd he know about the stupid voices inside my head? Now, I really sound crazy.*

Wake tries to ignore them. They're just dumb memories, meaningless to the rest of the world. But ignoring them meant that he never acknowledged them—never faced them. Over the years the taunts have gained too much say over his life. Even now they're telling him he's about to be shown for the fake he is, by those who it know it best, in front of everybody.

It's just not something he can explain. Who'd understand? It's all just stupid, harmless stuff that shouldn't matter—which just makes it all the worse.

Why do things have to always turn out this way? At first things are fine, but they always end up like this, a failing nightmare.

Right foot ...
Left foot ...
One foot in front of the other ... Mark the trail. He repeats inside his head as he coasts through the forested battlefield.

Another minute and they'll make it to the fountain at the center. *Kearney will take his time like he always does. We'll be there long before The Courageous.*

Wake checks on his sister. She's keeping up. She looks worried. *This is all my fault.* He knows she blames herself, but she never really knew their old Captain; he did. And he never told her.

Before he can even see its gigantic walls, he can hear the rumble of the Fountain's waters. It's enough to drown out his thoughts. He leads his sister through the gate. They are the first to arrive.

Forceful and constant, the water cascades down the gargantuan arm called Titan Blue. The outstretched hand hints at the granite giant buried beneath. Even the unscalable walls surrounding the area seem tiny in comparison.

Every Capture the Flag field is somewhat similar. Teams start off on opposite sides and are funneled to a point in the middle. Still, Titan Blue has a flair undeniably all its own.

Though, flair isn't something that is going to help them today. Not starting off one short. It is a sure disaster waiting to happen. *Why did I agree to this? Four against five isn't even fair. This is so stupid.*

On the far side is the entrance leading towards their opponent's side. He slides towards it, his sister just behind. Once through, he looks for a suitable hiding place. What he finds is a small clump of brush to the side.

"Ray," he whispers once they are hidden.

"Yes, Wake."

"I'm sorry I got us into this. I should have told you from the very beginning what a jerk Kearney is. If I had, then maybe things would've been different."

"No, Wake. I'm the one who accepted his invite," his sister says. "Really, I understand why you didn't say anything. He was our best chance. No decent team was going to take a couple of nobodies like us. I'm the one who should've known better. I just thought you didn't like to talk about your friends or school. I should've known ... I'm your sister."

"Please, Ray ..." Wake almost screams. "I knew the whole time. I knew the only reason I was on his team was that he liked my sister. I knew what kind of scum he was and I didn't say anything. I used that. I used you. I'm horrible."

"No, Wake. It wasn't you who suggested we join Kearney. It was me." Rachel goes silent for a moment before whispering, "They're here."

Still as a pair of stones, they wait for their opponents to pass through the gate. Wake finally lets out a breath. *I need to forget all that other stuff. I need to focus. I need to keep my guard up. What did he call it? Win the Moment, little by little. That's what I have to do, forget about qualifying, forget about everything else. I can't handle any of that right now. I just need to get through this very second the best I can. If I do that, everything will go as it should.*

"Wake, how much longer?"

"It's almost time." *Hopefully, this will be over quick.*

"I just need to stand on the node as long as I can, right?" she asks, wringing her sweater.

"Yes, Ray, that's the plan." He promised to try his best, but he's not sure what that's worth. He begins to worry. It's hard to breathe ... again.

My sister should matter, my own future should matter, but he just doesn't see how they have a chance. No matter how hard he wants to, he just can't believe that this will end well. *I have to get us through this somehow. I have to be brave for Ray. She deserves a better brother than I've ever been.*

"It's time, Ray. Let's go," he says. "If you get into trouble, I'll be there, I promise." *Why did you go and say something stupid like that? You know you can't back it up.*

"Wake, no matter what happens, I'm glad about the way things turned out. I love you."

CHAPTER 26

BROTHER MONSTER
[BATTLEFIELD: TITAN BLUE]

Brother Monster isn't the biggest fan of Tear Battles, Tournaments, or any of that stuff. He understands the rules and even some basic strategy, but you'd never call him a student of the game.

Instead, he spends his time on much more important matters, like healing the sick and injured. Luckily, the two went hand in hand.

This will be his first match of any sorts, but even a crybaby like him knows that no one ever actually tries to capture the flag.

The way to win Flag is by eliminating all of your opponents. If you concentrate on anything else while your opponents are focusing on disposing you—you will lose.

And the best place to fight is by the fountain, especially, if you can get on the node, a small circular mound that, if held, gains you control over the fountain.

Holding the fountain means controlling its waters—which powers up your whole team, making them faster, stronger, more dangerous.

It's still just a game, though, Monster thinks. *Why are they making it into such a big deal? If we win, that's great. If we don't, oh well, it just wasn't meant to be. It's not like the end of the world.*

"Monster, keep up," Riser calls back.

"Riser, can I ask you something?" he asks when he finally catches up.

The Daughter looks at him sidewise, but nods nevertheless.

"Why are we doing this?"

"What?" She doesn't try to hide her disgust at the question.

"Don't you see how hard this is on Wake and Rachel? Shouldn't we think of their feelings?"

"Are you trying to make me angry or are you really just that cowardly?" she mutters, turning her attention ahead. "Unforgivable."

Finally, she looks back and asks, "Why be a pacifist? Is it because you're afraid of fighting?"

"No, it's just what I believe is right."

"Is it easy for you?"

"No, it is not."

"If it gets too hard, are you going to quit?"

"No, I would rather die first."

"I guess, I can't totally look down on you. Why are you looking down on them?" She asks him. "Why hold them to a different standard? Are their dreams any less valuable than your own? I didn't see it too at first, but they're not meant to be mere mortals. Together, we will become legend!"

Mere mortals, legends—what a bunch of arrogant nonsense. She is right about one thing, though. I am holding them to a different standard. But it's for their own good.

"What's the hardest thing you've ever done?" She's already so far ahead he can barely hear her.

"I don't know. I guess, gaining my Master rank in Herbology."

"Was that a good thing?"

She's got a point.

The Half-Orc lags further and further behind. He can see Riser's frustration growing every time she has to slow down for him to catch up. But it's not his fault he can't use 128's like everybody else.

He looks down at his Tear. It swirls from blue to red and back again. His color is too unstable to use Water or Air, and though, he has no problem with Fire, he refuses it. Blaze Boots leave behind a flaming trail, a trail that can inadvertently hurt other people. So he runs along barefoot, covered in sweat and breathing hard.

"We're almost there," Riser says. "Wake and Rachel should be on the other side by now. You understand what to do?"

The Half-Orc nods; of course he does. He may not exactly be an expert, but it's not like he's stupid. He understands the plan Sensei laid out earlier. The element of surprise gives them a chance, even if it meant splitting up an already outnumbered team. It's a risky plan, though; if things don't go just right ...

Monster prays for the well being of his teammates.

"We don't even have a strategist to let us know if they made it into position on time," Riser complains. "I hope they are alright."

She's actually worried about them, too. "They're in good health and on the other team's side. You can't feel them?"

"No, you can?"

He nods and looks down at his gauntlets. *These smelly chunks of metal are at least good for something.*

It's not long before they reach the gate. A gigantic wall looms before them, stretching towards either side of the battlefield. There's one way through and right now it's shut tight.

"They must have closed it," she says. "It's almost time. We need to find the lever now."

"I think I found it, but I can't get it to work," Monster calls out.

"It's really not that hard," Riser says before finding out exactly what the Half-Orc meant. "Oh, you aren't just being a crybaby ... What the hail is that?"

The lever has some sort of glowing wall surrounding it. They can't open the gate.

CHAPTER 27
WAKE
[BATTLEFIELD: TITAN BLUE]

Wake hits the lever and the gate flips open. He activates Wave Step and slides through. Flashing between familiar faces, he marks the way for his sister. Rachel follows, a pale shadow of his shadow. She stops in a blink, directly in the middle of the node—directly in the middle of their old team.

"Grab the Sun," she commands. The area darkens and all those surrounding her are thrown backwards by the force of her summons. This time the blackout lasts for only so long and in its place is Rachel holding a shining orb. *She can finish forming it so much faster, now,* Wake thinks, looking at his big sister. *Now, if we can just hold the node until Riser and Monster get here.*

The sound of half-hearted clapping fills the air. Kearney Dim stands there looking down at them with lazy eyes. He looks amused. "Neat trick, guys. Had no clue you two were even back there."

Why's he just standing there? Wake tries to figure out.

"You look confused, Wake. Let me help you out," Kearney says. "Your friends aren't coming. Willie dropped a wall on their lever. That gate's not opening anytime soon."

"You can't do that ... that's cheating," Rachel says.

"I thought so, too, but our new, *smarter* strategist, is full of dirty tricks."

"Kearney, stop fooling around and hurry up and take them out," says an irritated girl's voice over the loudspeaker. Her voice is familiar. *Where have I heard that voice before?*

"Don't get all bossy just 'cause you were right about the lever. I'll do whatever the hail I want, and right now I want to have a little fun with some old friends," Kearney yells at the sky. He faces Wake, eyes cruel and full of mirth. "Too bad you're cheap-shotting Captain ain't here. I'll just have to settle for you."

Instinctively, Wake begins to draw the brute away from his sister. *If I can just get Willie over here, too, she may have a chance against three Healers.* Suddenly, he realizes the ridiculousness of his plan—him taking two and his sister facing three. He can't help but laugh.

"Kearney's Krusher!" he hears before everything turns white, or is it black? He can't tell. Wake finds himself on his hands and knees. *Keep your eyes open*, he hears in his head, before another voice calls him, *Waste*.

"What the hail are you laughing about?" Kearney growls. His voice sounds far away. "It must of been a *fake* laugh."

Failing Kearney Dim. Why's it always got to be him?

Ice Ridge | Ten Years Ago

"Hey, you, wanna play? We need one more," the fair-haired kid asks young Wake Avenoy. It's the first day of school and everything's a bit overwhelming. But even Wake can't turn down an invitation to play, at least not outright.

"What are you playing?" he asks the larger boy. No one else needed to ask. On top of that, everyone seems to already know everyone else—and what to expect and how to act. Wake doesn't.

"Tear-Tag. You in?"

"Okay," Wake decides, not wanting to seem afraid.

He starts off being 'it' for his side, but is able to quickly tag the proper person. Soon, he's running and screaming like everybody else. *This isn't so bad. School's not so scary, after all.* What's his mother always worrying about?

As the teacher calls the kids in for class, his new friend says, "Hey, Wake, we're going to play again after school. You can be on my team."

Wake and his new friend are the only ones left. He knows he should go home too, that his mother's probably starting to really worry. But he doesn't want to leave his first friend alone.

"I live over there at the top of Duffy Street," the fair-haired boy says, pointing behind him. "Where's your house?"

"Down there." Wake points in the opposite direction.

"You don't live in one of those dirty shacks in The Belly, do you?" the boy asks. Wake was born in Ice Ridge. The town built directly into cliffs of Northern Gorgury is all he's ever known. At the bottom, one can access Wysteria; the top led to the Roh Martyr Highway, and the lands to the north. The Belly is a small neighborhood near the deepest tunnels of Ice Ridge. That's where he lived.

But he's never considered his home to be that dirty, or a shack. "No," he says.

"That's good, 'cause all the people that are a waste live down there. That's what my dad always says. He's deputy mayor. He knows everything."

"Hey, Wake, I thought you said you weren't from The Belly," his friend from yesterday says. "How come Willie says he saw you coming from down there?"

"But, Kearney, I didn't say I wasn't from there ..." he begins.

"You're a big fake, pretending to be one of us, but you're really just a waste," says Kearney Dim

"I wasn't trying to ..." Wake tries to say.

"Wake the fake, the big fat snake, no one is going to fall for your tricks. Go back to the Belly, Waste."

Present

Tears blur Wake's vision. Some things never change. He attempts to wipe them away before realizing his hand is covered in something thick, something wet. He tries not to think of the fact that he's tasting his breakfast for a second time. It's not working. He's going to throw up again.

Kearney Dim laughs hysterically. Everybody's laughing. Nearby, his sister screams out in pain.

Ray! he thinks, trying to stand. He looks over to see her hunched over on the node, surrounded by bad guys. *No!*

"Are you done, Waste? I don't want to get any of that puke on me." Kearney's words come out slow and distant. All Wake can see is his sister. Her cry still hangs in the air. Everything is heavy, he's moving so slowly, but he's on his feet.

The air is thick like water. It doesn't want him to move, fighting him, pulling him into stasis. He has to swim through it to build any momentum at all. *I have to be there*, he thinks, turning his final stroke into a desperate grab.

"Crashing Wave," he shouts, landing in a raging torrent next to his sister. The ring of water crashes down, clearing the node of their foes once again

What was that? Crashing Wave is nothing new, but ... how did I make it all the way over here? Why didn't anyone try to stop me?

Never mind that; I have to help Ray. I'll do it, he decides. *I'll be Wake the Fake, if that's what it takes to get through this. I know we*

have no chance. And if I can't force myself to believe ... I'll even listen to Kearney Dim. I'll Fake it. I'll pretend like I'm one of them. But I'll fake like I'm Fate or Riser, like I know we're going to win. Maybe, if I pretend long enough, Riser and Monster will come save us.

"Back to back, Sis," he says, picking his sister up. "Remember that game we used to play, the one with the Water Balls in the cavern behind the canal?"

"Yes," she says, a smile breaking through.

"We'll do that."

"Blue Summon: Floating Globe," Wake says, calling forth a large glob of Water and suspending it in the air before him. "Water Grab: Dual Falchions."

Armed with two swords of Pure Water, he assumes his stance: one held high, the other low, blades parallel and facing outwards. His sister holds her Sun Orb before her in one hand, the other supporting her wrist, and says, "Dual Stance: Shimmering Ocean."

It used to be Dual Stance: Flowing Ocean, until the day before, he thinks. *But that doesn't really matter. The name may have changed, but not much else ... Except maybe him.*

"What you thinking, Waste? That you'll hold out till your friends come? You think you'll have a chance even then, four against five?" Kearney laughs, walking ever so slowly over.

"I don't need anyone else to beat you!" Wake shouts, trying to hide his desperation. *He's the strongest. I need him to concentrate on attacking me or we have no chance.*

Kearney takes his spot among The Courageous, who have already surrounded the brother and sister. "Cute, Waste, you and your moves that do no damage. How's that going to help you when all I have to do is hit you once and you're on your knees, throwing up. Let's find out what a second hit makes you do."

Wake's ready for him this time. He easily avoids the right. By the second punch, he recognizes the combo. It's one of Kearney's favorites. Next comes the low attack and he always finishes with a left hook. *Keep your eyes open. Win the moment.*

He takes the course of least resistance, dodging the predictable blows. He sees it all, Kearney before him, cursing at missing his strikes, and through the reflection of his Globe of Water, the enemies striking from behind. He shouts out, "12S, 3Y, 9I ... Now!"

Shine thrusts her arm directly ahead to her twelve o'clock and paints the letter 'S' in the air. One of the Mace Brother's attacks is fiercely deflected. She pivots to her three o'clock and marks a 'Y' upon her charging opponent, disarming him and sending him backwards. In a single motion, she stretches one foot back and swivels fully, bringing her orb straight down just in time to block the third and final attacker.

It worked! But he's paying too much attention to what's behind him.

"Kearney's Krusher!" The brute throws all of his mountainous self into the blow. His polarized knuckles multiply his momentum, pulling him forward, faster and faster.

Wake braces himself for impact. "Freeze: Falchions." His wrists ache from absorbing the blow. His swords lay shattered on the ground. But he still stands and so does his sister.

"I'll admit this is fun, Waste," Kearney says, eyes bulging and red. "Why don't you make some more stuff for me to break?"

"What are you guys doing? Get them off the node!" the voice says over the speaker. "Wake is dangerous. He's telling his sister what to do. Take him out."

"Shut up, Juli. Just cause your father paid all that dough don't mean you get to actually ..."

"Water Grab: Falchion," Wake declares mid-swing, soaking Kearney before he can finish. *I have to be careful. I've used up too much Water already. Wait; did he just call her Juli? Was that her voice?*

Is she one of our replacements?

"You should listen to your strategist. At least, if you don't want to get embarrassed out here." Wake's ready for the counterattack, but it never comes. Instead, Kearney's eyes grow large with delight. He stares at Wake and licks the spittle forming at the edges of his mouth.

"Waste, you're a failing moron," he says, grinding his knuckles together. "Why would you defend her? Juli doesn't give a rat's ass about you. She's the reason I kicked you and Rachel off the team."

"Well ... I should thank her then," says Wake. *Stay Focused. Don't let him distract you.*

"She can't even say your name, man. She just calls you the Jerk."

"Kearney!" Rachel yells. "You're the only jerk here. And ... and a pervert, too. I hope your new strategist knows that you spy on your teammates when they're trying to bathe. And she doesn't have Wake around to stand guard outside too!"

"Whatever," the brute grunts. "Everyone knows your brother's the pervert."

"You just spread those lies because you got mad at being caught. But my brother still didn't stop. If it wasn't for him, no girl would've been safe! Perv!"

The crowd grows loud with chatter, and a chant begins to grow. "Kearney the Perv! Kearney the Perv!"

"Shut up! Shut your failing mouths! Or I'll smash them shut!" he screams out with enough rage to quiet the whole arena. The vein next to his bloodshot eyes begins to throb. His sneer begins to twitch. He looks straight at the siblings and whispers, "I'm going to hurt you, now."

Wake stands with his sister, surrounded in a nightmare, dodging and striking in unison, losing precious inches with every attack. He can feel his sister breathing hard, the glow of her armor dwindling low.

Suddenly, something pushes him forward, forcing him away from his sister. Behind him, a massive wall erupts from the earth. Willie is trying to separate them. *It's all over now.*

By the time he sees it, there is nothing he can do; Kearney's knuckles are inches from his face.

He's picking himself up again. He's already taken three clean shots. He can't possibly take much more. *Get up! This is no time to rest.*

"I'll give it to you, Waste, you're tougher than I thought. No one's ever stood up after three Krushers before without healing," Kearney says between his teeth. "But you know what's coming next, right?"

Wake's right eye feels like it doesn't want to stay open, and the sweat dripping into his other stings. *No, not sweat; blood.* Everything's red. He knows what's coming. *Don't look away. I can't leave Rachel alone out here.*

"Circle Step," Kearney says softly. It's his very own personal Dash Step. With his polarized boots, Kearney gets to such a speed that he can't fully control himself. Instead, he relies on his magnetized knuckles to pull him back to his target. It's almost impossible to see. *He's all swagger and flash. He's nothing.*

Wake focuses on seeing the brute—a flicker here, a flicker there. But even if Kearney curves now, there's just no way he'd make it back towards Wake. *No! He's swerving around the wall and towards Rachel. I need to get there first. It's too late to Wave Step, I have to …*

Wake slams his wrists together and points his hands towards the ground. "Gusher," he screams, blasting a stream of Water from his palms, propelling himself directly into the air.

As the top of the wall flies past him, he sticks out his arm and grabs what he can. His shoulder burns, and he feels something in his elbow pop, but it keeps him from flying away. Tethered like a kite gone wild, his body dives back down, slamming into the other side of the wall—onto the side his sister's on. *Fail me! I messed up my arm. Even worse, that was the last of my Water.*

Get up! his new voice says. Wake stands. He knocks his sister out of the way and takes her place.

Kearney's already there, crouched so low it almost looks as if he's tying his shoes. But unfortunately, he's not. The big brute throws himself into a flying uppercut that explodes against Wake's chin. "Earth Style: Straight Up!" he shouts, launching them both high up into the air

Wake finds himself lifted off his feet, flying higher and higher upwards. The force of the blow throws his head backwards. The more it hurts, the more he's thankful that it's him that feels the pain.

He lays there in midair, still ascending. All he can see is the blue of the sky and one little cloud. It looks so lonely, so sad. Something about it all makes him want to laugh ... or cry.

He's caught now; there's no escaping it. The Straight Up Tech paralyzes the victim so Kearney can use his final move, a move no one's ever gotten up from before.

At the height of their flight, Kearney appears on top of him. Wake looks straight at him, really looking at his face for the first time. *He's just another boy. We're not that different in what we want, just the way we go about it. The power he has over me is the power I've given him ... and his face is really round*, he thinks. *It looks like the moon.*

Wake decides to laugh. *I've lost it. I really must be crazy, laughing at a time like this.* The announcer screams something excitedly over the Tear Speaker. He can hear the crowd take a collective breath. *I'm done, tired and sore, without a drop of Water left. Nothing to do but wait. I've tried my best. I have nothing to regret*, he thinks for the first time in his life. *Is that the way everything should go, Way?*

He takes a deep breath. The air tastes so sweet that it changes his mind. *No! I want to keep going. Rachel needs to get into school. I want to keep having fun with these guys. I want to win for her, for them ... I want to win for me!*

It hurts, but it's just pain. All he has to do is take it. His Spectral Armor keeps him from any real harm. There's nothing to fear.

He locks eyes with his lifelong bully and smiles the smile of a madman. When was the last time he spoke honestly, instead of always worrying what other people thought? He's just met some people that live their lives that way—unguarded, unafraid.

"Hey, Kearney. Thanks for asking me to play that first day."

The big fellow squints at him in confusion and then roars. He reaches back as far as he can, only to bring both knuckles down like twin hammers. One moment, Wake is floating weightless, the next he's plummeting back to earth. He's falling so fast he feels the air behind him begin to burn. He wonders if his back is glowing like the face of a falling star.

All he can see is his old tormentor and his own paralyzed arms flapping uselessly in the wind. *It looks like I'm reaching up at him. No, it looks more like I'm waving,* he decides.

"Earth Finisher: On the Rocks!" screams the guy that used to tease him. Wake can hear the giant slabs of rock burst forth from the ground below. Kearney's pressing down on him with all his weight, driving them towards the jagged peaks.

Wake's back explodes, his spine speared by the sharp, hard earth. He feels himself breaking, snapped in two, his insides torn apart. *It's just pain. It's not real.*

His Spectral Armor fades to almost nothing, but he still glows. *How am I still armored?* Wake wonders, but he already knows. The only reason no one's ever survived Kearney's attacks before was because of him ... *Because of my useless Pure Water attacks. I take people out and they don't even know it.*

"Get away from him!" he hears his sister scream from next to him. He's fallen back onto the node. He tries to push himself up. He can barely see out of his one good eye, and what he sees is ... *they're coming for me. I have to get away.*

"What the hail is wrong with you, Waste? Why are you still up?"

"I really did have fun playing that day," Wake spits out, barely able to hold his head up. "Sorry, I lied. I guess I tried to trick myself, but I really knew what you were asking the whole time."

It's my life. I'm going to be brave enough to be myself ... to believe in myself. I won't be ashamed to try my best and fail. He pushes himself onto all fours. Limbs shaking violently, he pitches himself away from his sister's grasping arms—away from the node. Falling forward, he scrambles with everything he's got. *They're following me ... good.*

"I always knew you were weird, but damn, you're failing crazy."

"Guys you have to get that girl off the node. It's about to flip," the voice over the speaker pleads.

"For the last time, shut up! If I hear your voice again, I swear I will sew your failing lips together the next time I see you," the bully bellows.

"Hey, Kearney, I always thought you weren't very nice to me, but I guess I haven't been very nice to you, either. I must have been pretty annoying to be around. If I think about it now, I don't like the old me very much, too. I'm pretty ashamed of all that shame," Wake says, laughing, coughing, sputtering, but moving.

"Julia Redsilk, I'm sorry to you, too. We probably could have been friends. I just didn't think someone like you would want to be friends with someone like me. So I was rude to you before you could be rude to me. Pretty stupid, huh?"

Wake crawls smack dab into another wall. *Fail Willie and his walls.* He stops and props himself against it.

"Kearney, Willie, all I ever thought of were the ways I'd get back at you if I was strong. Now, that was a real waste," Wake admits softly, trying to stand.

"Shut up, Wake." Kearney places a boot onto Wake's chest and begins to press down. "Why are you still even alive?"

Wake laughs long and hard. "Because I cannot lose!"

"Whatever," The big brute leans over his crumpled body and seizes him by the collar. "Water Grab this maggot," he says and spits into Wake's smiling face.

Wake just laughs some more. "I'm sorry for ever listening to you. And you should feel sorry for listening to yourself. But really, most of all, you should've listened to Juli."

A bell rings three times and the fountain named Titan Blue glows. *We did it.* Wake feels the fountain's energizing powers. It's enough for him to knock away his ex-Captain's hold on him. Rachel can barely stand up. *They'll have her off in an instant. But that's all I need.*

"What are you smiling at? Some little fountain buff ain't enough to save you, Waste."

"Kearney, you only got it half-right. It's not Waste." Wake repeats the voice in his head. "I'm the Waster of Worlds, Destroyer of Dreams. And I'm about to bring all yours crashing down." *Oh, god, I actually said that in public ...*

"Wave Step," he says, sliding to the top of the wall. He looks down at his old teammates and reaches behind him, grabbing as much as he possibly can. "Two-fold Water Grab: Tsunami!"

It was never part of the plan, but deep down he knew he could do it, if he dared. And now he dares. *Now, that we have control of the Titan Blue, we have control of its Waters ...* He grips the Air in front of him. Water fills the spaces in between, flooding the sky. It's more than he's ever attempted to control before—more than he ever thought possible. He grabs it all. He can't tell if it's him refusing to stop or the flow of the gigantic fountain. It just keeps coming. The weight is enough to drive his feet deep into the wall beneath him, causing it to crumble and fall apart. Within the palms of his hands he controls an unstoppable force, and with a flick of his wrist he slams it down upon those opposing his Will.

Of all the things that happen at that moment, it's a frog caught in the falling torrent that he notices. He laughs again as he watches it swim away. When he looks up no one is left standing. *Darn, my socks got wet.*

Kearney Dim throws back his head and cackles.

"Is that all you got, Waster?" the brute howls. Wet, but looking no worse for the wear, he gets to his feet and shakes himself dry.

"Freeze!" Wake yells back. The knee-deep water begins to do just that, trapping his enemies in ice. Wake slides out of it.

After all that, there's only one Sphere on the field: his sister's. But still ... "It's over, Kearney."

"Water Grab: Dual Falchions," he commands. "Freeze: Ice Blade Right." One turns into jagged ice.

Behind him, Willie brings his hands together and begins to chant. *What's he doing?* Wake's never seen this Tech before. *Willie must have kept it a secret up until now. This can't be good.*

"Wave Step," he shouts, trying to close the distance.

"North Wall: Ice," Willie says, thrusting his hand to the ground. A line shoots towards Wake, and a giant wall of ice blocks his way. Willie's Walls are almost unbreakable, but they aren't very big and easy enough to go around. He turns to the right.

"East Wall: Fire,. Wake stops before almost running into the deadly flames. *He's trying to box me in.* He turns around and slides the other way, but it's already too late.

"West Wall: Earth," the Waller chants. "South Wall, Blood"

There's only one way. Wake tries to slide up. "Wave Step."

"Sky Ceiling: Air!" Willie finally finishes. "Unleash: House of Tears!" The walls lock together, reinforcing each other to create a prison with no escape.

Kearney bellows in laughter. "Nice one, Willie." He begins to pound the ice encasing his legs. With each strike, larger and larger chunks fly through the air. He'll be free any moment.

It can't end like this. I need help. "Riser, Monster, where are you?"

"Up here," Riser calls down from high above. "Are you done yet?"

"Done?" he asks, confused. *Why are they up there on the fountain's walls? How did they even get up there?*

"Well, earlier you said you didn't need any help to beat them. That was pretty selfish of you, wanting to hog all the glory for yourself. But we didn't want to intrude on any unfinished business."

"Oh, I did say that, didn't I?" Relief washes over him at the sight of the Daughter and Half-Orc sitting atop the huge wall that separates the fountain from the outside. "I change my mind, I need your help ... please."

"Make up your mind, otherwise people just might think you're crazy," she says, leaping down and stretching lazily. "I was about to get really upset if you didn't leave any for me. This is my debut match after all, *and* my birthday."

"Shut up. Nobody cares," says Kearney.

"Presents shouldn't talk," she says to the big boy. "And Wake tied you up with a big fat bow. Besides, you should concentrate more on remembering this moment. Someday, you'll be telling your grandchildren all about how you got your ass kicked here today."

"How'd you get up there? Those walls are supposed to be unscalable?" Wake has to ask.

"Air Blocks. Enough of them properly spaced and you have a set of stairs." She gives him a wink and turns back to their opponents. "Hey, dummies, I'm going to attack this Wall guy over here. You better keep him healed."

The three Healers look this way and that, wondering if she's telling the truth. One begins to chant and soon the other two follow suit.

"Sing, Ehecthal!" she screams, writhing in the wind. Her sword pierces the Waller's armor, shattering it into a million pieces of light.

Riser laughs. "Did you see that? Three Healers couldn't keep him up against one of my attacks. I must be soooo strong."

"Now, I'm coming for you," she says to the Healers. "But just how should I take you out?" She walks towards them slow and deliberate. The trio begins to tremble, their metal armor clanking like pots and pans. She swings her blade almost nonchalantly. They pop into bubbles, like corn in a kettle.

"I must be real Big League Rookie!" Riser exclaims. The crowd cheers loudly at her every word. "Three Healers with one regular attack. That's a record, even for me.

"And now, for you." she says to a shivering Kearney Dim.

"I heard you're the one that punched my Oppa, that you've been messing with my teammates and friends."

He snorts out, "Whatever. You guys just got lucky."

"So you've given up already, huh?" she asks. "You know you had Wake beat way worse than this, and he didn't give up. In fact, he laughed in your face. See, that's the difference between you and him. That's why he's worthy of being on my Team.

"Let's make it official, though. I'll even finish you off with a real Tech." Riser crouches down before exploding through the air, a torrent of wind driving her forward. "Oops, I dropped my sword," she says, sheathing Ehecthal in mid-flight, her knuckles aching for contact.

"I submit."

Riser bounces harmlessly off the protective sphere. Turning her back to the coward, she utters in disgust, "Flinch Wimp." The horn sounds and it's over.

She did it. We won, we really just won, Wake realizes. He's crying; no he's bawling, and in front of everybody, but who cares? He decided a little while ago that there's no shame in being himself. Somewhere along the line, he even stopped faking it.

Rachel's there, and so is Riser and Monster. They're jumping up and down, hugging each other. Well, not really Monster, but still, even he's cracked a smile. Everyone is wishing Riser a Happy Birthday.

Fate, Sensei and Poe come rushing over. He didn't realize it before, but the whole stadium is screaming. They're mostly cheering for the Daughter, but he even hears a few chants for "Waster."

CHAPTER 28

RACHEL

[BEHIND THE STEWARDS & RAIDERS INN, GREENWOOD]

Rachel finds herself sitting on the same bench from this morning, in front of the same fire, listening to it crackle and hiss once more. *Everything's the same, but really, it's not.*

Now, she's surrounded by the sounds of revelry. And even though she sits alone, she's far from alone. There's a smile on her face that just won't go away and she wonders, *how can it feel so good?* It's not like she hasn't been on the winning side before, but this ... *this is different.*

The mystery of the coal-filled pit was answered a short while ago when the Fate unearthed it to reveal a whole boar that was roasting in it all day.

The smell of sizzling pork and charcoal when they unearthed it is something she'll never forget. The least of things of a day she will never forget.

All around her are her friends. Fate, Monster and Lene have each prepared their own special sauces for the occasion. They're going around seeing which one everyone likes best.

It's close, but in the end she chooses Fate's. It tastes fresh, making her think of an island, of sun and ocean breezes. Not that she's ever been, but it isn't hard to imagine.

This is how things should be. Everyone's here. Rachel can't even recognize all the auras. There's the whole team of course, including Poe, the inn's regulars, the trio of priests, half the clerks on Tour, and a slew of others drawn to the sounds of a party. All of them together, celebrate their first victory, Riser's seventeenth birthday and to everyone's shock, Fate's eighteenth, too.

Poe plays a festive ditty, Sensei accompanies, and Riser and Fate try to teach Monster and Wake a traditional Bae dance. *We did it! Wake really did it. I'm so proud of him. I can't wait to see the Memory.*

"Shine, come on, you have to learn this one. We have decided to make it our Team Dance," Fate calls out.

"Alright, but I think I'll need Riser's help to make sure I'm doing it right." She's ready to make a fool of herself. She's never ever tried to dance before, but she's also never ever been in a Flag match, and that turned out just fine.

CHAPTER 29
MY
[ABOVE THE STEWARDS & RAIDERS INN, GREENWOOD]

The feasting continues late into the night, though, those who should be celebrating most have long gone to bed. It's been a long couple days, and their Captain warned them of the long days of training ahead. Which no one has any complaints about, whatsoever.

If anyone could see the top of the roof, they'd find a boy has made his bed up there. Underneath the night sky, he lies there, a knee propped up, hands behind his head, staring up at the stars. He whispers words to someone he thinks will never hear them. The Fate wonders if this is the happiness she spoke of. *It wasn't, but now it really is ... I'm so happy for you.*

PART II

CHAPTER 30
OLD MAN
[PASSAGE TO IMBER, VALLEY OF CLOUDS]

The Old Man walks through the downpour—the rain falling everywhere but on him.

Even on the clearest of days, this stretch of mountain road is considered quite treacherous. But to one whose feet never actually touch the mud, there is no fear of slipping on it. A lifetime ago, he gave up all luxury, but some habits are hard to break.

It's been almost as long since he's last seen Imber, Valley of Clouds. And even though the rain-cursed valley is his destination, he probably won't see it again. That would mean opening his eyes, and the Old Man just doesn't do that anymore.

The outpost is about where he remembered it to be. A little more than halfway up the mountain, the small fort stands guard to the tunnel leading to the valley on the other side.

The two centurions stationed inside are more than surprised by his arrival. New prisoners are rare, and visitors unheard of.

The Old Man knows exactly the type to end up at such a post. Not exactly what you'd call elite, but deserving of respect, nevertheless. Even the sorriest centurion could hold his own against a professional Crier. Upon closer observation, he wonders if even that much has changed.

The senior guard salutes him with a thump to his chest. He does it with the side of his fist, *which means he probably originates from Northern Tyrae. Now, just when did I learn that? Yet, another clue* ... That in itself makes the journey worthwhile. He feels the centurions shrink at his expression and bellows in laughter.

"Young man, I find myself in good spirits on this fine day. Would you be so kind as to put a kettle on the fire for this old man?" he says, removing his cloak. Underneath is a hard, gray man dressed in spotless white. Besides the peculiar choice of color for a muddy day, his clothing is quite plain, except for the fact that his sleeves have been torn off.

"This should explain the reason for my visit." He pulls out a roll of parchment and hands it over.

"Sir, the documents are in order, but ..." the senior centurion begins.

"I realize this must be an unusual request, but I assure you that I have no intention of running off with the prisoner," the Old Man says. "And please, call me Claw. That is what I go by these days."

"Yes, sir, Claw. It isn't that. It's just that ... it's a dangerous thing that you are asking for. The pulley is old, the guideline even older. Really, the whole setup should have been replaced ages ago. We haven't sent anything heavier than a small basket over in a very long time," the guard tries to explain. "And is it really worth it? There's no telling what you'll find on the other side."

"That is fine, I will leap over there if I must," Claw says. "About him, though, tell me what you know. How has he fared?"

"The prisoner is alive is all we really know. The clouds keep us from learning much else." The guard's face fills with worry and fear. "But no one's ever lasted this long. There's no way the prisoner could possibly be sane. He's been alone on that tiny ledge for near thirteen years."

The pulley creaks and groans above him. There is no wind whatsoever, but the light rain comes at him from all directions; from above—from his right and his left, and even rising from below.

More than a couple of times, the Old Man considers taking flight, but the thick clouds and changing rains prove to be quite bothersome to navigate. So he sits cross-legged in the large basket and concentrates on making himself as light as possible.

He doesn't sense his destination until coming right upon it. With an inelegant thud, his ride comes to a halt. The Old Man whistles softly and listens. He can make out a tiny ledge just below from the echo, but the troublesome mist swallows up the rest of the sound. Somebody is down there, though, and their aura is creeping closer. *Did those fools send me to the wrong ledge?* the Old Man wonders, observing the strange aura. *Impossible … Could it be he has changed this much?*

"Is it that time of the month already?" the voice says. A hand wrapped in bloody bandages reaches into the basket and gropes the Old Man's leg.

"Oh, they've sent some meat. And for once it's even still warm," the voice says. "Hateu, we're in for a treat."

The Old Man brushes the hand away and leaps down onto the ledge. "Boy, you are still a hundred years too weak to have a taste of this."

The two stare at each other in silence. The Old Man in all his years has never seen an aura such as this before. Instead of being some amorphous blob of Color, it has a true form. Every detail of the raggedy man comes through, down to his single most hair.

How can this be? the Old Man wonders, staring at the prisoner's whiskers. He plucks one with a single, quick tug and stares in wonder as the whisker fade away between his fingertips. *Truly remarkable.*

"Ow!" the man says, rubbing his chin. "I guess, I don't have to pinch myself now, do I? This isn't a dream, you really are here … aren't you, Old Man?"

The man grabs the Old Man's face and feels it desperately. He begins to sob. "How is Everything?"

"Everything is fine," the Old Man tells him. "The boy is as hopeless as his mother ... and as his father ever were. But he is healthy, happy and just fine."

"Thank you, thank you," the man says, wiping away his tears. "But ... please, could we not speak of her, please? Not just yet ..."

"I see that you are still as weak as ever, Beck Songjinn," the Old Man says. "Very well, then. I will not ... for now." He pats the ragged man on the head and whistles. The ledge is wide enough for two large men to lay head-to-toe against the mountain's side. A low stonewall has been erected along its edges and most curiously of all, there is an opening into the side of the mountain. None of which should've been there at all.

Beck sees his surprise and explains, "I've done some redecorating. It took awhile, but I managed to find the time." He laughs as he walks towards the small opening. "Come in, come in. I'll introduce you to Hateu and show you what I've done with the place. And please tell me more of my son."

Hateu? Who or what could that be? the Old Man wonders. None of this makes any sense. Beck Songjinn was sentenced to spend the rest of his life alone on a small ledge. There are not supposed to be any others to keep him company or even this small cave; just endless days of pelting rain on a small ledge without ever the hope of seeing the sun again. *There is time for all of that later. I shall answer his questions first. The fool deserves at least that much,* the Old Man decides.

"Your boy talks now. I seem to recall that you were always worried about that," the Old Man tells him. "But otherwise, he is much the same. I gave him a fine, new name, but he prefers to go by 'Fate' these days."

"Fate ... please tell me all about him."

CHAPTER 31
BROTHER MONSTER
[BEHIND THE STEWARDS & RAIDERS INN, GREENWOOD]

Monster turns Wake's arm over and presses gently against the elbow.

"How does this feel?" he asks.

"It's a little sore there, but it doesn't really hurt," Wake says.

The Half-Orc grunts and finishes tying the bandage. *He probably doesn't really need it anymore, but another day of wearing it can't hurt.* "One more day in the sling, just to be safe."

We should get going. The others are waiting. Monster takes a final gulp of his tea and helps his teammate to his feet.

Mornings usually start with some light play before they really get into it. Today, Monster and Wake find the others gathered around Poe and Sensei as they act out some sort of battle.

Poe lumbers towards Sensei while growling like some wild beast. Sensei gives a slight nod and says, "Thank you." He pretends to pull something from his belt and declares, "Vine Clone Art: Stick."

A vine spouts forth from his right palm. It twists and it turns, growing wildly, until he whips it into a familiar form—the form of Fate's own Stick.

He swings it wildly at Poe, who continues to stomp towards him as if the blows do not matter. When Poe finally attacks, Sensei leaps backwards onto his left hand and says, "Green Imitation: Earth Repel."

A second vine writhes forth from his left gauntlet and coils into a spring. With its aid, Sensei handsprings back onto his feet, just out of the way of Poe's menacing mock blow. The others clap and laugh.

"He's getting good at that," Wake says.

Monster looks on and although the little clerk is far from matching the speed of their Captain and already out of breath, he does manage to capture the Fate's spirit. Sensei continues to strike with his imitation Stick, but finally, Poe overcomes him with a vicious swipe. The clerk falls to the ground, feigning defeat, only to get up a moment later as a different character.

"How dare you to do that to my Oppa," Sensei says in a voice both higher and deeper than his own. "Unforgivable!" He crouches down low and unfurls himself with his next leaping attack. "Green Imitation: Sing Ehecthal!"

Sensei flies forward ... at a comically slow speed, a half dozen small vines pushing him from behind. Poe cries out and suddenly he appears armless, one of his sleeves flapping in the wind. Sensei places his hands on his hips and cackles.

Even Monster can't help but chuckle at that one. But Poe suddenly comes back to life, roaring and charging forward. When he reaches Sensei, the bard sticks his hand back out of his sleeve and delivers another fatal blow.

This time Sensei gets up and giggles madly. "Fiend! How dare you attack my friends."

Poe roars and pounds his chest.

"Green Imitation: Water Falchions," Sensei says, forming his vines into two large curved swords. "I have figured out you must have regenerating powers, but that will do little good against how my Pure Water attacks work."

Monster watches closely, surprised by just how well Sensei imitates the way Wake moves. They continue to trade blows until Poe stops and grunts something, which Sensei replies to with, "What? You're Tear Armor, it's ... it's over 9,000!" Sensei stops and pretends to do the math in his head. "That would mean I would have to strike you at least ..."

Poe delivers the final blow to fake-Wake as he tries to finish the calculation. Sensei gets up slowly, pretending to hold a fallen friend. "Wake, just hang in there. I can heal you," the clerk mumbles. But before he can, Poe attacks again.

"Green Imitation: Disciple of the Doubting Palm," Sense says, turning away each blow with open hand blocks. Monster's never really seen himself in action before, but the clerk's movements remind him of Father Arnould's own.

After the last block, Poe cries out in agony. "Oh, no," Sensei says, coming over to aid the hurt enemy. "I'm sorry, did I hurt you? It was unintentional ..."

But just as the clerk comes within reach, Poe gives him a pretend head-butt, knocking him to the ground. By now the others are rolling in laughter. *Well, not really Fate. I don't think I've ever really seen him laugh*, the Half-Orc thinks, watching their Captain look on as if mesmerized by it all ... with his usual smile.

Sensei stands and says in a lovely voice, "What have you done to my friends?" Poe grunts and reaches for imitation Shine. "Green Imitation: Sun Orb," Sensei says, forming his vines into a compact ball in his right hand. He grabs his wrist with his left hand and holds it before him defensively.

Poe's hands are thrown back, but he keeps reaching. Finally, he lets out a long series of grunts.

"What?" pretend-Shine says. "You didn't really hurt my friends? They're just sleeping? You don't want to fight me?"

Poe grunts again.

"You wish to court me?" pretend-Shine asks. Poe nods his head.

"I will never go on a date with someone like you!" pretend-Shine says. "Not because you're some kind of fiend. I don't care about that. And not because you hurt my friends ... I'm sure they'll be fine. But because I'm 23 and you're far too young for me!"

With that, Poe and Sense collapse into laughter with the rest of them. *Mornings are pretty fun around here*, the Half-Orc admits to himself, clapping his hands in applause. *But really ... the rest of the day is usually just as good.*

Just as in the days before, the Fate leads them through a now familiar routine: stretching, pushing, jumping, and whatever other exercises he deems fit for that day. Only the Fate does more than the Half-Orc. Monster would smile at the look on Riser's face every time he outdoes the Daughter, but it is not in him to do so. Even the little clerk manages to do more than the day before.

After their first match, Monster gave each a full examination. All of them passed, even Sensei. It's true that the boy's heart beat in an uncertain manner, but so long as he did not push himself too hard, there's little danger to his health. Unlike the beating of his heart, Sensei knows how to pace himself. *As long as he keeps it slow, he'll be fine.*

Once they are properly warmed up, the Fate leads them for a run through the forest. They come across a small stream and follow it deeper into the woods. The cold mud feels almost a caress to the Half-Orc's hardened feet. It feels so good he doesn't stop running when their fool Captain does. They have to call him back, laughing and asking if he would have run forever if they hadn't. He grunts something in denial, but they just laugh all the more.

He's never been fond of laughter, especially directed at him. But he manages not to frown.

"I should've guessed you'd be good at running," the Daughter says between breaths. He's grown used to her barbs. They are nothing like the whispers and stares he is accustomed to. In some strange way it's almost refreshing. *Her every other breath is a challenge. It's just the way she is.*

"From this point onward, we must proceed quietly," the Fate tells them.

Soon, the stream turns into a pool and in the distance, a small outcropping appears where water cascades down from above, casting colors into the air.

"I found this place the other day when I was tracking the boar," the Fate whispers. He points at the reeds growing in the shallows, where three herons stand tall and unmoving. Every so often, one of them dips its long beak into the waters and comes up with a silvery fish. "See the big one? That one is old and powerful."

The one in the middle is large and greying. It stares back at them, unflinching. High above, an eagle screeches. And suddenly, the herons seem even stiller than before. "Watch the strong one."

The eagle circles and circles and just as the sun is cloudless behind it, it dives. The two smaller herons scatter. Only the old one remains. Ever so slowly, it lowers its lance-like beak, keeping one eye on death from above and the other on them. Rachel lets out a little whelp. It's just a bird, and this is the natural order, but Monster has no interest in watching this. He turns away.

The Daughter spies him and sneers in contempt. The Fate orders him to watch, so he does.

Just as the eagle dives, claws hungry and cruel, the heron lifts its head and faces it. Sure and steady, the heron stands its ground.

There is a flurry of feathers and the Half-Orc can't believe what he sees next. There right before him, the eagle is suspended in midair, the heron's long beak piercing its bloody breast.

The eagle's claws grasp air, shudder, and are still. The old bird shakes its beak free and the eagle floats away, it's white feathers reddened with its own blood. *Why is he showing us this?*

Riser cheers and says, "Well played, old bird."

Monster recites the hunter's prayer for the dead eagle. Rachel joins him. Wake and Sensei share the same expression of shock and awe. Poe scribbles something into his notebook. Even the chipmunk is squeaking its admiration.

"She practices The Old Style," the Captain explains, nodding at the old heron. "The Way of Fates."

"They're just birds," Monster says.

"Did your master not teach you The Three Steps of the Right Way?" the Fate asks him.

The Half-Orc nods. Father Arnould had. It was one of the very first lessons the Half-Orc had learned. "Will you recite them for us?"

"Define, Decide, Do," Monster says begrudgingly. They are looking at him now, so he continues. "In any situation, the first step is to *Define* it; to attempt to truly understand what really matters at that moment; to look past illusion and perceive the truth of things. The second is to *Decide* what must be done for the greatest good—now and forever. The final step is to *Do* it: to act without hesitation, doubt or fear.

"Follow this path with pure mind, just heart, and eyes towards enlightenment. In this way, may you live well." When he finishes, Monster sits back down.

"Just like that old bird," the Fate tells them. "She understood just what was happening. If she had fled with her young ones, one of them most likely would have been caught. So she stayed behind as an easy target, ensuring that they got away. But she also decided that it was not yet her time." The two young herons return to their mother and continue to fish as she watches over them.

The Fate stands up and looks each of them in the eye. "There are many ways to view the world, but when we define it with each other in mind, the world becomes something all together different.

"The natural order of things changes; the hunted become

hunters, the weak become strong, and you find yourself not only doing the impossible, but doing things you could not even possibly imagine before, because to not to is unimaginable.

"That is what it means to be a true team," the Fate says.

"I think, I get it," Wake says, "The whole is greater than the sum of its parts, right?"

The Fate looks at him curiously. "No, the whole is always *equal* to the sum of its parts, Way. That is what makes numbers so splendid; they always make sense."

"It was a metaphor," Wake grumbles.

"Oh, oh, I know," Rachel says, raising her hand. "He's calling us his baby birds."

"You are too old to be baby bird, Shine."

"Oh..." she pouts. "But I so wanted be a baby bird."

"Anyone else in the mood for some chicken, right about now?" Riser asks, adding to everybody's laughter ... even Monster's.

CHAPTER 32
POE
[BEHIND THE STEWARDS & RAIDERS INN, GREENWOOD]

No matter how early Poe gets up, he's always there first. Poe can never beat the Fate to the washroom in the morning. It's beyond bothersome.

Luckily, it's usually dark enough that they can't see each other's faces clearly enough for it to matter. What makes it really irritating is how he teases Poe on how long the little bard takes in there.

Poe hoped to avoid getting a silly nickname, but the musician got the very worst one of all.

"Pooh, you are a fortunate fellow. I have never met anyone as regular as you," he says every morning.

In a way, it's better than being called by the bard's real name. *Well, at least it is safer.* Besides, he's the only one to call Poe that. The others know better.

They're always the first two in the yard, as well. The Fate spends that time honing this Tech or that, and Poe watches for the sun to rise.

Afterward, Wake would usually be back from whatever training the Fate had sent him out for earlier and then they would go and gather the others for breakfast.

But those precious moments before they all sat down for breakfast are Poe's favorites. With no one else about, the bard could speak. *Speak!*

The conversations are usually so one-sided that the little bard wonders if the Fate is actually listening, but he always responds just as Poe thinks he's not. He's unforgivable in that way, as Riser would say.

The other parts of the day aren't too bad, either. Poe passes the time writing new lyrics, playing Desi, and sometimes even joining the others in their practice, especially since the Fate gifted the young bard with Baton, an ice reed, Poe's very own mini-stick. The Fate explained how they only grow on the very tips of the most ancient glaciers and that it'd be perfect for an Ice-User like Poe.

He even gave the bard an Ice Gauntlet to match, the common version of the Dark Blue Hand of Fate, the gauntlets that made the Pure Water Gauntlets obsolete. That's how Poe officially became his second student.

On this particular morning, it's the Fate asking all the questions. He doesn't stop all his jumping around and running back and forth to do so either; something, Poe's gotten used to.

"Pooh, how did you learn to speak or even sing so well if you could never talk to anyone before?"

"I used to have this necklace. When I wore it, I could speak as much as I wanted to, but it's lost now. And even before then, I could always talk to my father."

"That is good to know. I wonder why your words don't affect me, either?"

"I'm pretty sure it's not the same reason as my father's. After performing for so long, his hearing was all but gone. He used to say he could still feel the sounds. Whatever that means. He mostly relied on reading lips, though."

"Amazing! He could read lips, like a book?" the older boy asks, standing upside down.

Poe laughs. "No, it means he could tell what people were saying by how their mouths moved. It's not that hard. I can do it, too."

"Daebak," the older boy says, hopping onto one hand. "He must have been really grateful then."

"He used to say that, but I always thought that was a funny way of looking at it."

"He sounds a lot like my parents. He must be a great man," the Fate says, flipping back onto his feet. He was ...

"Yes, well ..." Poe doesn't want to think of all that right now. "What about your parents? Are they coming to watch you in the Grand Finale?"

"No, they are gone, now. I lost them when I was young," he says with that stupid smile. "I have my Old Man, though. Hopefully, he will show up soon."

"So when you talk about your Old Man, you're not talking about your father?" Poe asks. The Fate shakes his head. *I'm so dumb, I don't want anyone reminding me about that ... and I just did it to him.* "I'm sorry. I didn't know."

"Sorry for what? Did you do something wrong?"

"I just reminded you of your ... your loss."

"You reminded me of them. Actually, I am always thinking about them. They were the best," he says. "Thanks."

I bring up his dead parents, and he's thankful for it? Not that anything about the older boy surprises Poe anymore. "But back to your original question. My father tried everything to help me with my problem."

"Condition. It is a condition, not a problem," the Fate says. "Problems are something entirely else."

"Alright, my condition then. Well, he finally found this necklace. It used to belong to a Champion or something. Anyway, when I wear it, my voice is fine," Poe explains. "But after he passed. There were those who tried to use it against me. They tried to control me with it. I had to leave the necklace behind when I ran away, even though, it's mine by right. They can track its whereabouts, and ... and I'm never going back there, ever again."

"You ran away?" The Fate stops and looks at the bard. "You did not call it leaving or escaping, but running away. That is not good."

"Problems, conditions, run away, leave; they're just words. When did you become such a stickler for words?" Poe complains. "I don't really feel like talking about it, anymore.

"Besides, it's my turn to ask the questions, now," Poe says. "You called me your second student, so then who's your first?"

"Ieiri."

"That girl you're always talking about, the one that tricked you into telling any girl you meet that you have a girlfriend? She's your first student?" Poe asks, not liking the answer one bit.

"Yes, but Ieiri did not trick me. She helps me," the Fate says. Now, he's walking on his hands.

"How did you meet her?"

"She showed up at the village one day and asked to join the Clan."

"Oh," Poe says. "Is she any good?"

"Yes, she is very good."

"Is she smart?"

"She is smarter than I am," the Fate says, pushing himself onto his fingertips.

"Well, what does she look like? Is she pretty?"

"Hmm, now that you mention it ..." The Fate flips onto his feet and makes his way towards the bard. Squinting in concentration, he brings his face right up to Poe's and stares.

"Stop that!" Poe says uncomfortably. When one of the bard's frantically waving hands threatens to touch the Fate's face, the older boy jumps back.

"Has anyone ever told you that you look like a cat?" the Fate says, still staring at Poe.

"A cat?" the bard says in surprise before remembering, "My father used to say something like that, but that was when I was little. No one calls me that anymore ..."

"You remind me of Ieiri, sometimes. Almost, as if you're Ieiri in one of her disguises?" The Fate says.

The bard starts laughing nervously. "Disguise? Why would you even say that?"

"You two are just a lot alike," the Fate says. "I suppose she looks like you, or you look like her, one or the other. And I think she must be pretty. Sya and Haenul are always saying that she is."

"Sya and Haenul? Who are they?"

"You do not know Haenul?" the Fate asks, looking almost confused. "Even Sya? I thought everyone knew them."

"I don't think I do. Should I?" Poe says, trying to remember. The names sound vaguely familiar.

"I suppose, I am just used to everyone always knowing who they are. Sya and Haenul are from the Slate, too. Even though you have yet to meet them, consider them teammates. They just happen to be a year older and have already gone on ahead."

"My teammates? But I'm not even really on the Team," Poe says, trying to figure it all out. *So he must have had a team before forming this one. But they got split up because of their age difference. Sya and Haenul must have competed on the Tour last year, while he and Esperanza are doing so this year, and then Ieiri next.*

"Silly Pooh, Wysteria is just where it all begins. Once we get to the World Circuit, we will all be together again—new teammates and old. So just because they list only some of us here, it does not mean you are not one of us. Just like Ieiri, Sya and Haenul are, too. Even, if there are no papers to prove it."

"What about Wysteria being banned and all?"

"Bans do not last forever, Pooh."

"Oh, okay," Poe says quietly. It's probably not as simple as that, but if he's not worrying about it, neither will Poe. "And, Fate ... Thanks."

Just then, the wind blows, swirling the fallen leaves all about. The Fate holds his hands out wide and begins turning with the breeze. Poe joins him.

As the wind dies down, Poe grabs a perfect little leaf that floats by. Looking up at the bare branches, sadness fills the young bard.

"I hate the Fall," Poe says, walking towards the closest tree.

"Why is that?"

"It's just sad. All the flowers and leaves are gone. The trees look naked and ... and dead."

"But they are alive, just waiting," the Fate says.

"It's still sad." Poe reaches up to the closest branch and places the little leaf onto it. For a moment, it stays. "There, that's better."

But with the next breeze it flitters and falls. "Stupid wind," Poe mutters.

"I do not understand. The leaf is just a part of the tree," the Fate says, catching it before it reaches the ground. He hands it back to Poe. "The leaf may fall, but the tree lives on. And all the fallen leaves protect the tree's roots from the cold. They return to the earth and someday return to the tree. And when the time is right, the tree blooms again. Is that not wonderful?"

"I guess, if you put it that way, it doesn't sound so bad," Poe mutters. "But still, I don't like it. They should just all live happily ... together, forever."

"But then there is no promise, nothing to look forward to," the Fate says.

The bard stares at the little leaf. It's a perfect shade of crimson. *He's right, but still* ... Poe pulls out a small notebook and places the leaf inside. "Well, this one isn't going to protect any stinky roots from the cold. This one is going to be a bookmark."

CHAPTER 33

WAKE

[BEHIND THE STEWARDS & RAIDERS INN, GREENWOOD]

"What do you mean, my fighting style isn't Home-brew or Beautiful Design?" Riser growls.

Wake Avenoy shrinks at the Daughter's words. If only he could become small enough to not be there at all. He tries to choose his next words carefully, very carefully. "Riser, you're super strong. Much stronger than I ever will be, but come on ...You're fighting style is unoriginal." As soon as the words leave his mouth, he knows he didn't choose carefully enough.

Riser glares at him. His explanation better start getting better. "You summon chunks of Air, and you hit things with your sword. There's no real synergy besides what's apparent. You're super powerful, but you're not leading up to anything, creating anything."

"What's more beautiful than strength? What more is there?"

"Um," Wake looks around for help, but his teammates have all retreated.

"Beautiful Design is creative, when every move complements every other ... in an almost artistic way. It doesn't really mean it's stronger. But when you see it, you know you're watching something personal, something special. Not to say that when you see brute force, that's not just as special. It's just different, when you see the thought and effort someone has put into creating their own Home-brew Class, you can see a piece of them in it, too.

"I guess that's the real difference. Beautiful Design is not really stronger than a generic type of fighting style. But it says something about the Crier. You know that they put their soul, their heart into it."

Riser thinks on it a moment before starting towards the now trembling boy. "Did you just call me generic?" Wake turns and runs for it.

He finds himself up a tree, too afraid to even peek down. *I think I lost her.* Suddenly, the branch beneath him bends lower, startling him from his perch. He's able to twist himself around as he falls to avoid any real damage, but lands roughly, nonetheless.

He scurries backwards, ready to flee again. "Greetings, Way," the Fate says from above. The older boy leaps down and looks him over. "You seem fine. There is no need to worry. Riser became hungry and Monster convinced her to go back to the inn for lunch."

Whew. Wake slumps down against the tree. He has to really learn to watch his mouth better. "Thanks."

"You are welcome," the Fate says. "I know the feeling—hiding in the woods from girls. But Riser is not so bad. She was just going to hit you a couple of times. It is not as if she was going to tie you up and torture you."

He sure has a way with words. Wake's stomach grumbles.

"Here, I brought you something to eat." The Fate hands him a small package wrapped in linen. "I think she will forget her anger by tomorrow, but you should probably avoid her until then."

"I guess my mouth got me in pretty deep back there," Wake says, taking the carefully wrapped plate of food. "Things like that should be said and known, though. I wasn't trying to offend her."

The Fate nods absently.

"I guess I can't take off my 128's for awhile," Wake says, "As long as I have them on, I should be safe."

"Her Wind Dash is faster than your Wave Step, however," the Fate says.

That's right. I'll never be able to truly outrace her, Wake thinks. Sharded footgear or 128's each have a specific Dash step: Earth has Earth Leap, Sun has Trip the Light, Air has Wind Dash, Water has Wave Step, Fire has Skipping Flames, and Blood has Blood Boost.

The Light, Incorporeal Colors are known to be the faster, though. Dark Blue Water's Dash Step will always be slower than Light Blue Air's version.

"I can teach you how to Wave Step as fast as she Wind Dashes."

"Really? Is something like that even possible?" Wake says before remembering the last private lesson his friend gave him. "Wait a minute. This isn't going to be like that water breath thing, is it?"

"No, this will be much more difficult. It will take some practice. But I am willing to teach you, if you promise to work at it."

This actually sounds kind of interesting. "No water? No buckets?"

"I do not believe so."

Wake manages to avoid the angry Daughter for the rest of the day.

The next morning he finds her sharpening her sword. The sight of her is almost enough to make him turn and go back the way he came. But, he realizes, *I can't avoid her forever.*

"Riser, I'm sorry. I just want to say there's nothing generic about your fighting style. It's just ..."

"It's not Beautiful Design," the Daughter says, not looking up. "I thought about what you said. It's not."

Wake is more than surprised by her answer. In the end, he decides to ask the first thing that comes to mind. "Ehecthal is status locked right? Why are you sharpening her?"

He knows the ins and outs as far as it comes to armor—that's what he's licensed to appraise—but weapons are a whole different matter. What he does know is that when any object is Teared, it does not change, does not chip, nor dull, and should need no sharpening.

"Him. Ehecthal is a him," Riser says. "And don't you know anything? Ehecthal is a +6 Weapon, a true Ethereal Blade."

If memory serves him right, a +6 weapon is powerful enough to slice the intangible; Light, Fire, Shadow, Lightning and Air itself.

"That's really amazing. I never realized," he says. *There can't be more than a handful of weapons rated that high in all of the Three Kingdoms.* "You must think I'm pretty ... babo. I'm supposed to be a high level Appraiser and I didn't even notice."

"Sometimes you're pretty and sometimes you're babo. But in this you are neither. Only a true weapon master could've known by sight alone."

He tries not to turn too red. She continues, "I sharpen Ehecthal, because weapons rated +6 or higher cannot maintain their true sharpness even when Teared. Besides, I want to be able to evolve him to +7 someday."

"That would be really amazing."

The Daughter grunts.

He has an idea. "Riser, the other day while we were training, I happened to barely miss one of your Air Blocks. Anyway, since I just barely grazed it, it ended up sharpening my frozen falchion. Maybe if you did something like that, you could maintain Ehecthal at full sharpness even during battle?"

The Daughter stays quiet for so long that Wake begins to

apologize again, but she waves him away. "Excuse me. I'm going to go try that out, now. Thanks … and Way, speak to me freely on such matters. I might get a little angry, but I promise not to hurt you."

"How much farther do we have to go?" Wake asks the Fate. The sun has yet to rise and the forest is still shrouded in darkness. *No one was awake when we left, not even Poe,* Wake thinks, not liking this one bit.

"We are almost there," the Fate calls back over his shoulder. "Try to remember the way. You will have to come back here by yourself, tomorrow."

"It's far too dark for that," Wake complains, but he starts paying closer attention to where they are going. It's not long before the small game trail their on opens up to the base of a mountain.

"We are here," the Fate announces. Wake takes a look around, wondering just why they had to come someplace like this. There's a small field and the slope of the mountain itself, but not much else.

"I assume you have already gone through the standard training needed to master your Wave Step, correct?" the Fate asks him.

Wake nods. *Of course I have.* Dark Blue is one of the Physical Colors, and to master it requires Physical training. He's practiced his jumps for years.

"Please show me," the Fate says. "From each foot and then both."

It's nothing too complicated. Wake leaps as far as he can from first his right foot, then his left, and then finally from both together. These are the very same jumps that he imagines taking every time he activates his 128's.

"Nice form. Now, please follow me," the Fate tells him as he heads for the steep slope of the mountain. Halfway up, where it becomes more of a climb than a walk, they come to a stop. "Have you guessed the next step in your training?"

Wake looks down the steep slope and sighs. "You're going to make me jump my way down the mountain, aren't you?"

"Exactly," the grinning Fate says. "Just be careful not to twist an ankle."

The Fate is waiting for him at the bottom. "Not bad, but still far from good enough."

Wake's first trip leaping down the mountain was terrifying. He took the tiniest of jumps from each foot and then both, while the Fate hurtled down the mountain with no fear. The second time down was a bit better. On his third, he manages to somehow even keep sight of the Fate, at least for most of it. But now, he's exhausted.

"One more trip and then we can join the others for breakfast," the Fate says.

The next morning Wake finds himself again at the bottom of the steep slope. That's three trips down. *Just two more to go,* he thinks, remembering the orders his Captain gave him back at the inn.

Although, no one's counting except for me. I could just go back now, Wake thinks, lying there on his back.

He turns his head to find a late blooming wildflower staring back at him. Its blossoms are too large for its thin stem, causing it to bend so low that it almost kisses the ground. The straining stem reminds him of how his legs feel right about now.

At least, I didn't get hurt.

Okay, just two more, he decides, straightening the flower and getting up.

Wake makes the final few leaps without fear. The Fate lands next to him a moment later. Wake throws up his hands and cheers. "I win."

He hated this special training at first, but now it's become sort of fun. It's only been a few weeks, but his legs feel stronger and his timing has become fine-tuned.

"Congratulations," the Fate says. "Next time, I will only count to five before starting."

"No, no, let's keep it at ten." Wake laughs. "I like winning once in awhile too, you know?"

"I believe we all do," the Fate says, already heading back up. "One more time, but this time we will not be racing. You are ready for the next step."

"What's that?"

"This time down, you do it with your eyes closed."

It wasn't as hard as Wake first thought. The Fate only asked him to close his eyes just before he jumped. He's allowed to open them before he lands to gauge the terrain and make sure he doesn't break an ankle. Now, he's flying down the mountain with his eyes mostly closed.

"I believe you are ready, Way," the Fate tells him. Wake turns to walk up the steep slope before the Captain stops him.

"Please close your eyes and grab the other end of Stick," the Fate says. Wake grabs ahold and shuts his eyes as the Fate leads him somewhere.

"As you know, each Color has a different Dash Step. And each Dash Step is unique in its own way. Dark Yellow or Earth 128's work by using the natural attraction of objects. We can also reverse this force to make it repulse. Those are the basic principles behind Earth Leap, repelling and attracting against something solid. Even your friend Kerry's Circle Step is a variation of this basic principle."

"It's Kearney, and he's not my friend," Wake says.

"Either way, each Color's Dash Step is different and can be personalized even more so. For the Dark Colors, the only way to do this is through Physical training. But there are limits to Physical training and one of them is ... mental.

"Keep your eyes closed. No peeking," the Fate says from somewhere beside him. "What I want you to do is imagine that you are about to jump. But do not forget that we are on the mountain, so leap accordingly. Can you picture the slope and the angle you have to take?"

"Yes," Wake says, envisioning the flight of his leap. Jumping down a slope requires a much more forward, almost downward trajectory.

"With your eyes still closed, I want you to activate Wave Step down the slope," the Fate explains. Wake is ready for that. He guessed as much that this would be the next step.

"Wave Step." Wake dashes forward.

"Daebak, Way," the Fate yells from behind him. "You can open your eyes and turn around now."

When he opens his eyes, he sees; *We weren't on the mountain? We never left the field.*

And behind him, the Fate is impossibly far away. *What's going on?* Wake wonders, *Did he move back or ... Did I just really Wave Step that far?*

"You didn't move, did you, Captain?" Wake asks. The Fate shakes his head. *I really just covered that distance in a single Wave Step?*

He still can't believe he made it so far in one Dash. *Mental ... He said it was mental limitation,* Wake realizes. *I tricked myself into taking a leap straight ahead as if I was jumping down the mountain, but I was really on flat ground. By doing that I changed the angle so that I was going purely forward. There was no wasted upward movement.*

If I had realized I was on flat ground, I would never jump at that angle. I would crash straight into the ground. My mind wouldn't even allow me to attempt such a jump knowing that I would hurt myself. Wake looks back at his Captain. *That's how he moves the way he does. A normal-thinking person could never move that way.*

"We are done here," the Fate says. "Just keep practicing until you can ..."

"Do it with my eyes open," Wake finishes for him.

The Fate smiles and nods. "Tomorrow, we will invite Poe and Sense along. After all, Poe is Dark Blue like you and Sense Dark Green."

"So you're calling him Sense now?" Wake asks. *Sensei won't mind; he was just complaining the other day of not being Fate-named.*

"Yes, why do you ask? Did I call him something else before?"

CHAPTER 34
IEIRI
[OLD TRAINING GROUNDS, SILLA]

Ieiri comes down from the clouds and gasps, "Water." Only her pride keeps her from collapsing to the ground. Enada, Master of the Dark Wind, tosses her a canteen.

"We're done for today," the imposing warrior tells her.

Ieiri marvels once again at the strength of her new teacher. At first, she had her doubts. The Master of the Dark Wind barely looks older than Ieiri herself. But the outcast Daughter laughed at that, replying that she's old enough to be her grandmother. It's a mystery with no answer, but Ieiri's sure that's one of the reasons Enada lives apart from the rest of the village.

"Thank you for today's training, Master Enada." Ieiri bows deeply.

"You're welcome, and I told you not to bow to me. Daughters bow before no one," Enada says. "I expect a better effort tomorrow." With that, she picks up her long pack and departs.

The fledgling Daughters hiding at the edge of the field come rushing in.

"Ieiri, that was so great!" They clamor around her.

"Hey, Ieiri, do you want some more water?"

"I need a moment," she says, falling onto her back. "And you're not supposed to watch us practice. It's forbidden."

"No, we're not supposed to watch *her*. There's no rule against watching you," the one with the black eye says with a giggle.

"I'll take that water, now." Ieiri shakes the last drop free from her canteen. "Let me just lay here for a little while longer. Then, I'll be ready to take you all on." She wonders why she's allowed to train with Enada, yet the others are forbidden to even speak her name.

"You're ready," Enada says.

"If you say so, it must be true," Ieiri says.

The Master of the Dark Wind stares holes into her soul. "It's been weeks and I haven't taught you a single Technique. Do you have no ambition, girl?"

Ieiri looks up at the Master of the Dark Winds. "Even though you say you haven't taught me any new Techniques, I have learned much just from fighting you, and for that I am grateful." Ieiri bows her head. The leather-clad lady snorts in annoyance.

"When I was your age, I begged my teachers every day to teach me something new. If they refused, I would seek out a new one. Didn't you come to me to learn Air Techs?"

"It may be true that you have not taught me any Techs, but you take time out of your day to spar with me. I have never fought with anyone like you before. It is humbling," Ieiri says. "But yes, when you think I am ready, please teach me some Air Techniques!"

The outcast Daughter laughs. "What about Old Claw? I'm sure he knows plenty about Air. Surely, he humbled you."

Ieiri looks the Master of the Dark Wind's in the eye. "Before you, only Fate was my master. You are the only other person I have called that."

"Old Claw refused to teach you then?"

"Yes, at first, but eventually he offered," Ieiri confesses. "But I refused!"

"Likely story ..."

"It's true. I would never lie. The truth is, I would never have accepted you either, except Fate's not here. I would never choose another, but I need to get stronger."

"So is this Fate stronger than Old Claw? Is his mastery of Air greater?"

"No," Ieiri admits.

"Then he is a poor master, indeed."

"No! You don't understand," Ieiri shouts back. "He begged the Old Man every day to take me on as his student. I knew the day would come when he would finally accept. When that day arrived, I was prepared."

"Please, do tell."

"I said I would accept the Old Man as my teacher, if he could beat me in battle ... And then I defeated him."

Enada looks at Ieiri and laughs.

"Don't laugh, I'm telling the truth," Ieiri says darkly.

"No, child, I believe you," Enada says. "You set him up didn't you? Don't worry, I won't ask how."

Ieiri nods. "So you believe me?"

"I fought him once, a long time ago. I don't care how much older he's gotten. There's no way he'd lose to anyone in a fair fight," the outcast Daughter tells her. "I am not blind. We have fought every day for weeks. You're a lifetime of training away from matching my strength, but even then ... sometimes, I feel as if you are the one leading the dance."

"Master Enada?"

"Yes, girl."

"Please do not talk badly of Fate, ever again."

The Master of the Dark Wind stares at her for a long time. "Now, I know why," she muses to herself.

"I don't understand, why what?"

"Why none of my teachers would teach me their strongest Techniques."

"Oh," Ieiri says sadly.

Enada slings her pack over her shoulder and prepares to leave. As she enters the shadows of the forest, she looks back and says, "Tomorrow ... tomorrow, I will teach you the secret of the Dark Wind."

CHAPTER 35
RACHEL
[PRACTICE FIELD BEHIND THE CLERK'S DORMITORY, GREENWOOD]

"Again," the Fate tells her. Rachel picks herself up from the ground for what must be the hundredth time. The others are off practicing amongst themselves, leaving her alone to be tortured.

This is impossible, she thinks with a sigh. "Don't you think I've tried this before? No matter how hard I try to make sense of your Spectral Armor, it just looks like a mess ... like you took it all off and threw it on the floor. Sometimes, I can make out Stick or a boot or a gauntlet, but most of the time all I see are a jumble of glowing lines."

Why won't he just accept it? Without being able to physically see my opponent, I cannot see the true form of their Tear Armor. I'm hopeless. Her legs are sore from just having to stand up so many times. And her rear aches even more from getting knocked down over and over again. "I can't do it! I can't see where you're attacking from, how you're attacking—anything. I can't see!"

"You can tell when I am coming straight at you," he says.

"Only if you're far enough away," she replies. "And I could already do that before without all this needless knocking around. But that's it. That's all I can make out."

"You will get it," the Fate says.

He just has no clue, sometimes. She reaches down and presses the bottom of her Tear. *I should have done this from the very beginning.*

"What are you doing?" he asks.

"I'm adjusting my Pain Threshold." She wants to adjust the amount of hurt that her Spec Armor lets through. The more pain she feels, the less damage her armor would take, but right now that's not important.

"You should not do that. You should have it set to the same amount in practice as you would in a match."

"Yes, I know that, but this is different. I'm just turning it up one level."

"Keep it at five," he insists.

"I will not," Shine says defiantly. "I know what I can handle and what I can't." She suddenly feels the Fate's aura come uncomfortably close. She can feel his warmth. She can smell his unique scent—earthy, dark, yet, still somehow fresh.

"You set it to one!" the Fate exclaims in shock.

"You saw?" Shine asks. It's her little secret; not even her brother knows. "Please don't tell anybody, especially Wake. My shielding has always been weak. The only way I could even be an average Draw was by setting it as low as possible."

"But after all that getting knocked down, why are you setting it lower?" the Fate asks. She can almost picture his eyes growing wide as he realizes. "Is it possible that you normally fight at zero?"

"So what if I do? Like I said, I know what I can and can't handle." They say to set it so low is dangerous, but she's gotten used to it.

"What if you get hurt?"

"Don't worry, I won't." She never wanted anyone to find out. It makes her look desperate. "Look, I set it to zero by mistake one day. I wasn't trying to hurt myself or anything. By the time I realized that I did, it'd been weeks. Wake's attack don't hurt that much, so it was never really dangerous. By the time I figured it out, I was already used to it. And it helps me last a little longer. I need every advantage that I can get."

"Is that why you always cry out when you get hit?" the Fate asks in awe.

"No, I always did that," Rachel mutters under her breath. "I don't want you to take it easy on me now that you know. And don't tell anybody else, either."

"I will not," he says. She can feel him staring at her.

"I always thought so, but now, I really know ..."

"What are you talking about now?"

"Who among us is strongest," he says.

Shine wonders how much more of this special training she can take. Even the steaming waters of the bath aren't helping as much as before.

She lies there with her head back, arms resting on the sides of the oaken washtub. *Thank goodness the inn has these nice, big tubs,* she thinks, grateful to be able to stretch out her long, sore legs. She dips a small towel into the warm water, squeezes out the excess, and places it back over her face.

It feels so good. All the sweat and dry autumn air is beginning to make her skin feel so dry it hurts as much as the falling. Being knocked onto the dusty ground isn't helping much either, though, it's really her bottom that aches the most.

She hears the door open and someone enter. Rachel twitches in surprise, wincing as her posterior bumps the bottom of the tub. "Hey, Unnie, it's just me," Riser says. Rachel can hear the Daughter hang her towel and begin to tugging at her armor.

"Nothing like a long soak after a hard day, huh?" Riser asks.

Rachel purrs in agreement. Riser splashes gently into the other tub. "How's your training with the Captain going?"

"Painfully."

"It's just been a couple days. You'll pick it up soon enough." the Daughter tells her with all the confidence in the world.

"Esperanza, thank you so much for believing in me, but I'm afraid it may just be a waste of time. I've never been lucky at learning things like this ... *some things are just impossible.*"

"Lucky? I guess that explains why you haven't made any progress," the Daughter mumbles to herself. "I was worried it was something else."

"What?" Rachel asks, unable to quite make out what her teammate said. *Riser is sensible, she'll understand.* "Can I ask you to explain it to the Captain? I don't mind trying, but I don't want to waste any more of his time. Maybe, I could work on something else, instead?"

"I don't think so," Riser says.

"But he'll listen to you. He doesn't listen to me at all when I try to explain."

Riser laughs and says, "Unnie, I'm going to tell you a little secret of the Daughters of Enyo."

"Is this like the secret you guys taught Wake?" Rachel says, getting ready to get out the tub.

Riser laughs again. "No, this is just a story. But it is a real secret. I can tell you, because we're Sisters Sworn, but you can never tell another soul. Promise me."

"I swear," Rachel says, trying to relax once again in the warm waters. "But will you talk to the Captain for me? I don't know how much more I can take of this. I can't even sit, it hurts so much."

"If that's what you want, I'll try. Though, I doubt it'll do any good," the Daughter says. Then she asks, "Did you know that Silla was once conquered?"

"The Daughters were conquered?" Rachel asks in surprise.

"It's sad, but true. It didn't happen too long ago either; during the time of my mother's grandmother. We were conquered not by an army but by one man," Riser admits. "They say it was late autumn, on a day much like today. A mighty warrior approached Silla. First, the Alcendor tried to stop him, but he never stood a chance, they say ..."

"He? I thought only Daughters lived in Silla," Rachel says.

"Yeah, only women are allowed to pass our borders. But Gregory's House sits just at the edge of Silla. It's been around ever since a man, Gregory, followed a Daughter back to Silla. It happens every once in a while. They usually go away in time. But this fella stuck around and built a house. Anyway, around the time Gregory arrived, something unthinkable started to occur. Daughters started bearing sons.

"You have to understand, for many centuries only Daughters were born in Silla. The Daughters of that time didn't know what to do. Because of the confusion and shame, many mistakes were made. As it happens, the Daughter that Gregory followed back to Silla bore a son. She was a good woman and he a good man. She could not raise such a child, so she gave Gregory the boy. He took his son and promised to raise him and any other unwanted children of Silla. No one knows why it started happening, and it's still a rarity today, but when a son is born of a Daughter, we leave the boy at Gregory's House."

Rachel nods, trying to understand. It's difficult to accept, but she realizes it's their way.

"Anyway, the Alcendor at the time—that's what we call Gregory House's best fighter—was said to be strong in his own right. But he didn't last long. The Daughters watched and laughed as he fell. That is, until the wanderer crossed over into Silla. Then of course, they attacked. One-by-one and then group-by-group, the Daughters rallied to stop him, but he just kept on coming.

"The mightiest warriors in the land couldn't even so much as change his course. Finally, he stopped right in the heart of our village and fell asleep. Only then were they able to properly subdue him. Afterward, they left him on a road leading away from our land. The man just got up and walked away. He never even looked back."

"I don't understand. Why did he do that?"

"No one really knows, but you should ask Fate. He might know."

"Why would he know?"

"It was his Old Man. He didn't even bother opening his eyes. He conquered Silla with his eyes closed," Riser explains. "It's how we're cousins. But more importantly, since that day, the blind are held in high regard in Silla.

"We don't expect you to be strong right away. You have a lot of learning left to do, but for someone like you there are no excuses, only expectations."

"So I guess, you're not going to talk to the Captain for me."

"It's kind of late for that. He already beat you to it. That babo came to me after practice, begging, 'blah, blah, blah, she will listen to you. She does not listen to me when I try to explain it ...'"

"I suppose there is no hope, then." Rachel lowers herself deep into the now lukewarm water. Face half-submerged, she exhales a string of bubbles in defeat. *I guess I have to just keep trying. There really is no excuse.*

Someone knocks at the door. "Hello, Shine, are you in there?"

Rachel almost leaps out of the tub at the sound of a male voice, bumping her sore bottom once again. She grimaces and replies, "Yes, but I'm in the bath! You can't come in here."

"I realize that. I just thought maybe the water might be getting cold," he says through the door. "I heated up some more and brought some extra wood in case you were running low."

"Thanks, now go away!" Riser yells back.

Rachel is a little more at a loss for words at their Captain's consideration. She watches his aura fade away through the wooden wall.

Rachel stands. The water itself has cooled, but the steam remains in the air keeping her warm. She grabs a towel and creeps close to the door. After a final double-check, she cracks it open and feels around until she finds what she is looking for. She comes back with a bucket of near-boiling water for her teammate and a second for herself. On her next trip, she finds some fragrant logs and tosses them onto the fire.

"Those smell good," Riser hums more than says.

Rachel opens the door just wide enough for a final search of anything she may have missed. To her surprise, she finds something smooth, soft, and fluffy. She pulls it through the crack and shuts the door tight before any more steam can escape. It's a cushion.

No longer interested in continuing her bath, Rachel offers her teammate the second bucket of hot water and walks back over to the fire. She lays the cushion gently down on the floor and takes a seat.

Finally, it doesn't hurt at all. Even laying, floating in the water barely helped. Rachel stretches her legs straight, reaches her arms up high and sighs. She can't help but think that it's nice that her brother doesn't have to stand guard anymore as she nods off.

Someone is shaking her awake. *Where am I?* she wonders before realizing she's in a towel, in the bathhouse.

"Here, put on your clothes." Riser places them on her lap. "I want to show you something."

"How long have I been asleep?"

"Not long," the Daughter says. "Come on, I don't want you to miss this."

Once dressed, Rachel grabs her new cushion and follows Riser out the door.

The Daughter leads them out back and into the woods. "Shhh ... try to be quiet. He probably won't notice us; he's concentrating so hard. But still, you never know with him."

As they sneak closer, Rachel hears the sound of someone grunting and falling. And then she sees his aura. *What's going on here?*

"Try and guess what he's doing?" Riser asks.

She watches his aura pulse randomly. It sounds as if he is falling down, over and over again. She feels like she should know what is going on. It seems strangely familiar.

"Let me know when you've guessed it," Riser whispers, but the sheer joy in her voice speaks volumes. "Take your time. I could watch this all day."

After several long minutes of hearing him fall, she finally figures it out. "He's trying to Trip the Light?"

"Yeah, he is. And he's failing miserably each time," Riser says. "Remember how you said you had no luck with training? Well, right there, is what luck really looks like. Watch closely."

After a while, the Daughter grabs her gently by the arm and leads them back to the inn. As they enter the empty dining room, she announces, "Let's have a little snack before bed. I should get that wimp, Monster, but I'll let him pass this time."

They take a seat and Riser pulls out a Memory Shard and hands it to Rachel. "Go ahead and link with that. I paid a Reminiscer good coin for that Memory."

Rachel forms the link and concentrates. Flashes of this and that fly through her mind until they slow to form a picture that begins to move. She sees the Fate doing just what they left him doing—tripping over himself and falling onto his rear, again and again. Each time, he gets up, rubs his backside, and tries again.

Riser returns with some leftover pie and two plates. "That's his cushion, you know?"

"Oh," is all Rachel can say.

"That Memory's older than a year. He's been falling like that every night for ... who knows how long," Riser tells her. "I watch it when I need a pick me up. I like watching him fall like that ... but it also makes me want to try harder every time I see him get up."

Rachel is silent. Her teammate continues, "I used to think the same thing when I met someone strong, too; that they were lucky. But he taught me that when I did that, I was dismissing all of their hard work. What makes *him* strong isn't what takes place in a match. It's what he's doing alone in the woods right now, and there's no luck involved in that."

She listens to one teammate and watches the other in her head fall. It's enough to make her want to cry. "I'll try harder," Rachel sobs.

Riser wraps an arm around her. "You're doing just fine."

"I'm the older one. How come you're always teaching me things?"

Riser laughs that laugh of hers and says, "Actually, I was just *lucky* enough to have really good people to learn from along the way." Rachel can't help but laugh also, wiping her face with a sleeve.

"I'm just repeating things smarter people have taught me. And I've learned way more from you and your brother than you may realize. I know you won't believe me when I tell you this, but you guys are really something. Don't tell him I said that. It's just that no one taught you the basics. And even a babo like me can pass that much along."

"Don't say that. You're the best! Him too," Rachel says, wiggling around to make herself comfortable on her new cushion. "Should I give this back? It's like magically soft or something."

"Nah, you don't have to worry about that. That boy's fallen so much, it doesn't even hurt anymore."

CHAPTER 36

HAENUL
[CITY OF ARIZ, CURRENT STOP OF THE INTERNATIONAL TOURNAMENT OF
TEARS, THE WORLD CIRCUIT]

"Sya, this is serious. What are we going to do about him?" Haenul asks her life-long friend. Who seems far more interested in fixing her ponytail right now than paying attention to the conversation.

They're both Bae, but Sya's hair is as fair as Haenul's is black. Her partner's face is a mirror of her own, however; small and heart-shaped, with eyes like half-moons.

Though, that's where the similarities end, especially in their choice of clothing. The feathered robes covering Haenul and the velvety leathers of her companion make them look more like they were born a world apart rather than in the same village.

"It's too loud in here. Let's go back to the room," Sya says, twirling one of her fair locks. The tavern is just like the last one, loud and stinky. But it is the best that they can afford.

The smell of stale smoke hangs in the air. *Which is probably a good thing*, Haenul thinks, lifting her shoe to find wet hay stuck to the bottom. But she knows that going up to the room won't be any better. Sya can fall asleep anywhere, anytime, but Haenul will inevitably end up staring at the bunk above her for hours.

"Let's go for a walk," Haenul decides. *At least, we can afford to do that.*

"Daebak, that's a great idea," her friend says all too cheerfully.

They step out of the tavern and onto the road muddied from heavy travel. The moon is out, but that doesn't scare the two girls. At least, not anymore than they already are: nighttime is no more frightening than day in these faceless cities. It's the first thing they learned on the Circuit, to always be at least a little bit wary. The only time they could really relax is when Houk is around. He may be a pretty useless fellow, but at least, they could trust him.

"I hate the city." Haenul stabs her staff into the ground. The tips of her black hair begin to brighten red and the twin pins in her hair start to smoke. A sure sign she is getting angry. But it passes just as quickly as it began. "I miss home. I'm tired of the smell, of everything being dirty and grey. But most of all, I'm tired of all the rudeness."

"Complaining isn't going to help anyone. For someone who flies so high, you're such a downer." Sya makes for the boardwalk on the other side of the road. Haenul has no choice but to follow. Halfway there, a carriage pulled by a giant walking bird passes by. She whistles three short notes and the muddied bird turns its head and snaps a treat out of the air.

"You're going to get in trouble if you keep doing that," Sya tells her. "And can't we talk about something pleasant for once?"

Haenul knows that complaining is just making things worse, but she can't help it. She understands that worrying is a waste of time, but her friend is too much the opposite. "I can't just ignore things like you do. We have a lot to worry about, right now."

"If you insist." Sya finally gives in. "It's not like I haven't thought about it, too. There's just nothing we can really do, is there? What is there to do but wait for Fate to show up?"

"What about Houk?"

"There's not much we can do about that. Once Captain shows up, he'll decide what to do with Houk."

"But you know Houk's too weak."

"That may or may not be true." Sya shrugs. Her golden ponytail bounces without care. "It is not for us to decide."

"How can you just say it like that? Houk may not be strong, but he's been there for us." Haenul isn't sure why it bothers her so much, but it does. "I'm sorry, I know getting upset about it won't help."

"You're just being you," Sya says with eyes that understand. "Hey, remember that time you found that squirrel and took care of it until it got all better?"

"The one I found by the waterfall?"

"I was thinking of the one that fell out of the big oak," Sya says. "Either way, it's like that. Except that Houk's not some hurt fuzzy little creature, he's a big boy. He can take care of himself. And the last thing he wants is you pitying him. Guys hate that, don't you know?"

Haenul starts pouting. Houk's been with them since Wysteria. He's one of those rare individuals that chose to leave their homeland to join the Three Kingdoms. It used to be quite commonplace just a couple decades ago, but not anymore. There's not much reason to defect to a banned nation.

"I hate him." Haenul almost begins to fume again. "He won't even try to get stronger." *Him and his stupid Firepoint.* He uses that tiny lancet of fire like someone would use a weapon, but it does less damage than a plain old dagger. It makes her mad just thinking about it.

"It is what it is. Houk's just like that. You aren't going to do anything but annoy him by trying to get him to ..." Sya stops short as a hand reaches for her out of nowhere. She steps to the side and reaches her hands deep into her pockets. Haenul grabs the stone staff from her back and slams it on the ground before their attacker.

A dainty boy floats backwards, palms forward as a sign of peace. "I'm sorry, no harm intended. I just thought I heard you say the name Houk?"

"Yeah, so what of it?" Haenul says, slamming her staff onto the boardwalk a second time for emphasis. Several more lithe figures pour out of a carriage nearby. The final one to step out is a fiery-haired beauty. Haenul recognizes the statuesque young woman immediately. She is Lady Teori of the Roc Riders of Ramaya.

"You, girl." Lady Teori points to Sya. "What do you know of Houk Bosh?"

"Hmph," Sya answers, turning her nose upwards. The easy-going girl changes when she feels directly challenged. She turns away as if to continue walking. Haenul grabs her by the arm. It's her turn to be reasonable.

"Forgive the rudeness of my friend. She's not feeling well," Haenul says. "But yes. we do know Houk Bosh. We're friends of his."

"Likely story." The tall red head scowls, looking them up and down. "If it is somehow true, where is he?"

"I'm sorry, but we don't know where he is at the moment," Haenul says.

"Look, little girl, if you are lying ..." Lady Teori begins, before being stopped by the dainty boy who originally approached.

"Enough, Teori, let me handles this," the boy says to the scowling leader of the Roc Riders. She looks ready to explode, but the boy gives her a gentle look and says, "That's an order. You can go back to the carriage and wait there, or be quiet and listen."

He turns to the two girls and bows deeply. "I'm sorry. Please allow me to introduce myself. I am Ighy of Ramaya." He points to those behind. "All of us here are friends of Houk. Perhaps, he's mentioned that he hails from Ramaya?"

The two girls shake their heads.

"Oh, I'm sorry to hear that," the little boy says sadly. "It's not surprising I suppose. He left home two years ago and we haven't heard a word from him since. But please believe me when I say that we are his friends and that we hope only for his best. All of us here wish for him to come home."

Haenul looks at Sya. Without words, they decide to not say too much.

The little boy, who just before ordered the leader of the Roc Riders to silence, notices and continues. "The reason that we are here is because one of our party, Aule, claims to have met Houk earlier today," he says. "But it is hard for us to believe his story."

The two girls stand there in silence. The young boy throws his hands up and says, "We don't know what to make of Aule's story. What he described was a Houk that we do not know. But at the same time they were classmates for many years, so how could he have mistaken him for anyone else?"

Haenul shrugs one way and Sya the other.

"See, someone claiming to be Houk approached Aule and asked for money. This is something the Houk we knew would never have done," the boy says, pacing back and forth. "For all my life, Houk was my hero. The Houk Bosh we know wouldn't beg anyone for anything—ever."

Houk a hero? It's almost enough to make her laugh. Instead, she says, "If it was earlier today, we were with the real Houk Bosh. Your countryman must have encountered an imposter. I can assure you that the real Houk Bosh would never do something like that."

"But ..." the one named Aule begins.

"Houk has plenty of money, and he has us. He doesn't need to go around asking for anything. We take care of Houk."

"They're lying," Lady Teori blurts out. "You know they are, Ighy. They didn't even know he was from Ramaya."

"He is our friend!" exclaims Haenul. "Houk Bosh is a man who refuses to use any Tech but one, Firepoint. And as weak as that Tech is, he'll ... well, he has us. And you'll never find him without Streak, a yellow dog who follows him anywhere and everywhere. Sometimes he does stupid things because all that matters to him is being The Comet!" Suddenly, Haenul wants to cry. Half her locks blaze red. "The stupid Comet ..."

The tall redhead looks at them for a good long while before turning to walk away. The rest of the party follows behind, all except for the young boy. He pulls out a money pouch and holds it before them. "If you see Houk, could you give him this?"

"No, never!" screams Haenul. *He doesn't want you to feel sorry for him. Guys don't like that.*

The boy looks deep into her eyes and says, "I know you lied, but you also told the truth about the things that mattered most. I'm a truth-reader, you see. Not only can I detect the truth, I can only speak the truth."

She's heard of those with such a gift.

"If you won't accept this, please return this to him. It is not a gift. It is something he left behind," the boy says, holding out a slightly misshapen bronze-colored orb. "He had an accident, and that's why he left us. When we cleared the site, we found this. It's all that was left of Nix. It's not enough to bring Nix back, I know. But maybe ... Please, just take it. Maybe, it will remind him ..."

Haenul accepts the imperfect sphere. "Are you sure you can't give this to him, also?" The boy pushes forth the money pouch again. Both girls look at it and shake their heads.

"Excuse me for asking, but are you crying?"

Back at the tavern, the two girls sit quietly in the corner. Even the ever-bright Sya looks sad for once. "We should have taken the money."

"I know," Haenul says. *But we couldn't.* Just then, the door slams open and a gallantly shady boy bursts in. The young man is typically tall, dark and handsome, with scruff surrounding a daring smile. A yellow dog follows close behind, tail wagging. He smiles and slams two lobsters down onto the table.

"I found a couple of big ones. They're from the sea, not some little freshwater ones that taste like mud," he says happily. Haenul picks one up and throws it at his face. She jams a finger into his chest and almost says something, but instead marches upstairs, her hair flaming red.

"I don't understand. She's been going on forever about wanting something good to eat, lobster in particular." He picks the lobster off the ground and tries to dust it off. "These aren't easy to get this far inland. You don't know what I had to go through ..."

"Yes, we do," Sya says with a cute smile. "These are going to taste great. I'll make sure she eats hers, too." She picks them up and takes them back to the kitchen.

The ever-dashing but hopeless weakling Houk Bosh slumps down into a chair. He nuzzles his bright-eyed dog and sighs. "Girls ..."

CHAPTER 37
RACHEL
[BEHIND THE STEWARDS & RAIDERS INN, GREENWOOD]

She can't get the image out her mind. Falling, getting up. Falling, getting up, again and again, never a moment without a smile. She has to help him. She is the only one who can. After all, it is her that he is copying. Every little detail, right down to the smallest movement, is a mirror of her own. *He does everything else so well, except this. It's like we're complete opposites.*

"Fate?"

"Shine, is that you?"

"Yes, Captain, is it alright if I join you?"

"Sure, but I cannot practice with you right now," he says, falling hard to the ground. She winces at the sound, her own aches and pains all but forgotten.

"Why didn't you ask me for help?"

"You have already helped me without me having to ask. I would not have gotten this far if it was not for you." He's on the ground again. "I watched you do this a thousand times."

"But I can help you better than a Memory," she says, trying not to sound like she's pleading. *He's right, though. There's nothing more I can do. From what I saw watching Riser's Memory of him practicing, he's already doing everything right. If he hasn't gotten it by now ... I have to get him to stop.*

Rachel studied the Memory all night. She knows better than anyone. *The Fate will never be able to do it, Trip the Light.*

And with no ranged attacks, Earth Boots won't be enough for him to compete on the World Circuit; not against flyers, not against those who can attack from afar, not where the footing is not solid, not against so much more. *And he knows, that's why he's doing this.*

"When I found the Memory you made explaining how to Trip the Light, I knew I could do it, too. You really explained it in a way that even I could understand." Thump. He gets up and recites, "The secret to Tripping the Light is just as the name suggests. The Tripper must actually trip himself, causing himself to fall. At the very beginning of the fall, there is a moment where the Tripper is actually falling upwards. During that instant of instants, before the apex of the fall, is when the Tripper must catch the line. Once your Light Boots contact the line, the Tripper may then use the line to regain their balance."

Shine listens. It doesn't surprise her that he even copies the way she spoke on the recording. "How long have you been practicing Tripping?"

"For the last year and a half, one hundred fifty times each night," he answers. "74,324 times to be exact."

"No way!" she says, but even as she does, she knows he is telling the truth. "How many times have you been able to catch the Light?" That's the part he seems to not be able to get right. He's trying to hook the Line as he falls upward correctly; it's just that his feet don't seem to ever catch the Light.

"Zero."

That's impossible. Even if by accident, even if he had almost no yellow in his aura, he should have caught a Line by now. *This has to stop.*

The Fate looks up and asks, "Why are we crying?"

Rachel realizes that she's not the only one. "Why are you crying?"

"I am crying because you are crying."

She can't help but laugh at that. "You have to stop this. And I don't mean crying."

"Just eighty-four more and I will," he says before falling back down. "Please do not worry. I will get it for sure on this next one."

"How can you even believe that?"

"It is the only way," he says. "I may not know much, but I do know that believing that you can, matters. If you do not believe, it will never happen. I learned that from my Old Man."

"So he told you to do this?" Suddenly, she doesn't like his Old Man very much.

"No, he does not teach by telling," the boy says, getting back to his feet. "It took 5,178 battles and an earthquake for me to learn that lesson."

"First of all, how do you keep track of all those things? Are those numbers for real?"

"How do you not? Yes," he answers.

Rachel knew he'd say something like that. Maybe he'd explain the earthquake comment a little better. "How did all those battles and an earthquake teach you?"

"I suppose the lesson began even before that. Ever since we arrived at the Slate, my Old Man would play with me every day. And every day I would ask him to train me to Tear Battle. One day he said yes and our games turned into real battles. He always won. I got better and better, but he is very strong.

"At some point, I came to the realization that I was not yet good enough to beat him. But it was still so much fun, and I felt like I was getting stronger. I thought that was enough. Then one day while we were really going at it, the earth shook and he lost his balance and fell. But I was not looking to win. I was not looking to finish him off and I missed that instant—my only chance up to then to have beat him. I let it slip away, all because I did not think I could win. I will never believe that I cannot do something again, because that will just make it true."

She now understands that he isn't going to stop. There's nothing else but to ... "On this next one, I'm sure you'll catch it, for sure." She puts on her Slippers of the Sun. Out of habit, she taps each toe to the ground and says, "Follow me, exactly."

As graceful as a feather floating up, she kicks one foot out from underneath her and falls. Before she feels the pull of the earth, she catches the line. In a blind girl's blink, she's on the other side of the clearing. She gasps out loud as she realizes the Fate is next to her. She decides she's not that surprised, after all. "I knew you could do it."

No matter how many times the Fate tries it by himself, though, he can never get it just right. But every time he follows Shine, he's beside her like light's shadow. He still can't do it on his own, but at least, he doesn't have to fall by himself anymore.

CHAPTER 38

BROTHER MONSTER
[BEHIND THE STEWARDS & RAIDERS INN, GREENWOOD]

"I believe it is about time that you learned to put those to proper use," The Fate points at the Half-Orc's gauntleted hands.

"No, thank you. I'm perfectly fine just using them to help me sense everyone."

"But there is much more your Hands of Flame are capable of," the Fate says. "Just as there is much more to Fire than just burning."

"That may be true, but its mere existence could harm—even unintentionally. Don't you understand? No matter what you say, I will never wield the flame. I will never take that gamble," the Half-Orc says. *Why doesn't he just leave me alone? I've already agreed to wear the awful-smelling things.*

"And I will not ask you to." The Fate pulls out a candle and a small rock from his belt. He strikes the rock against his gauntlet, creating a spark. "There is something I wish to share with you. Whether you want to learn it is up to you."

He sets the burning candle down. "Is it not beautiful, the way it dances to the breeze?"

Monster frowns, but nods.

"Fire does not know right from wrong. It is hungry, however; so hungry, it will consume this whole forest if we let it get out of control," the Fate says. "But if we can control it—contain it—it will warm us when we are cold, cook our food, or even forge something of use."

"Yes, I understand this," Monster says. "But you can never truly control it. At some point the flame will betray you."

"You are correct. One may never truly control anything, but maybe just for a short time we can try?" the Captain says. "You were born of the flame. Even though, you are as much Blue as you are Red, you have no talent for Water or Air. You are meant for Fire.

"And even if you did not start the fire, perhaps, you should at least know how to put it out?"

Monster reluctantly agrees. Fire eats, fire consumes. He can feel its hunger. It eats everything it touches, even the very air surrounding it. Worst of all, it is the Aspect most favored by Orcs, who use it to destroy. But perhaps, he should learn of a way to at least extinguish it.

In a way, that is what he has been doing all his life. "Alright then, show me."

The Fate looks at him and then at the candle. "It is not something I can really do myself, but I learned the basic principles behind how while at school."

"What school teaches Fire Techniques?"

"Criers College."

"You're telling me you've already been to Criers College?"

"I have been there before." The Fate shrugs. "Now, back to the flame."

Monster stares at the candle. The flame moves faster than he expected. Red, yellow, orange, and where it meets the air, it dances invisible, cloaked in haze. It's so quick there's no way his eyes can keep up when the wind blows. So nimble, it's without pattern, but there's always a tip. Whether low or high, it reaches.

Half the wax is melted before he looks up and asks, "What exactly am I supposed to be looking for?"

"I am not sure," the Fate says, grinning. "But if you can, close your eyes and see the fire within your mind."

After staring at it so long, it is not difficult for him to visualize the flame. "Now what?"

"You can see it?" the Fate asks in surprise. "Can you make it stop moving? Can you stop the flame's dance and make it totally still?"

Brun tries to stop the flame in his mind from moving. When he opens his eyes, the candle has gone out.

"Daebak! But snuffing out the flame is no good," the Fate explains. "I want you to picture the fire being still, not going out. Please keep trying."

Monster continues the exercise for the rest of the day and again the next. Every day, he tries to stop the fire from moving without extinguishing it.

The day comes when he finally does it. The candle is still burning, but the flame is still. Unmoving, it looks like a small blade painted red, orange, yellow, and even white.

He reaches his hand out and can still feel its warmth. The act breaks his concentration and it flickers to life once again. He does it once more to be sure, before going in search of the Fate.

When he finds him, Monster shows him what he has achieved.

"Impressive," the Fate tells him. "There is just one more step, but you have already mastered the hard part."

The Fate picks up the candle and puts it away. He sits down and takes the candle's spot.

He stares into Monster's eyes and asks, "Are you sure you understand the difference between extinguishing the flame and making it still?"

Monster nods. *Of course I do, it's what I've been practicing all this time.*

The Fate points towards his heart. "You will need to activate your Spectral Armor for this. Look, right here. Every person has a fire within them, some stronger than others, but it is always there." To Monster's surprise, he sees the Fate's flame quite easily. It's so bright that he wonders how he's never noticed it before.

"Close your eyes. Can you still see it?"

Monster grunts in affirmation.

"Okay, the Tech is called 'Still the Flame.' Say the words and try to calm my flame. Please be careful not to extinguish it."

Monster closes his eyes and concentrates. The Fate's flame is so clear. He stretches his hand towards it and calms it. "Still the Flame!"

When he opens his eyes, the Fate is frozen in mid-air. The sight breaks Monster's concentration and the Fate lands roughly, his elbow cracking against a small rock.

"Monstrous! I knew you could do it. With Still the Flame, you can immobilize nearly anyone for a limited time. The more you practice, the longer you will be able to hold them."

He doubted it all the way up 'til this point. *But this was actually worth learning.* "You didn't have to jump, just to show me. Here, let me look at your elbow. It's bleeding."

The Fate waves him off and picks up a handful of dirt. He rubs it onto his elbow and says, "This is nothing. All I need is to rub a little dirt on it."

This would infuriate anyone with any knowledge of healing, whatsoever, but the Half-Orc knows better than to argue. Instead, he looks down at his blackened gauntlets, grateful to have them for the first time.

"Also, I owe you an apology, Monster," the Fate tells him. "For I have taught you a Forbidden Tech. Still the Flame has two versions, but now that you have used and named it, you should not have to worry about activating the forbidden version by mistake."

"Another version?"

"It is a true Death Tech. For some reason, the two Techs share the same name; Still the Flame. But now, that you have used the Tech against another Crier, you have locked in the proper one to your Tear."

"You mean, if I did that wrong just now ... If I extinguished the flame instead of causing it to be still ..." Monster mumbles before yelling, "I could've killed you!"

There is nothing more he wants than to smack some sense into the fool boy. *How could he risk it?*

"You said you could do it," the Fate says.

Monster's anger doesn't subside. He grabs the Fate by the collar and screams, "How could you be so stupid? Why would you risk it?"

His Captain looks at him and says, "Because that is how much I believe in you."

CHAPTER 39
RISER
[PRACTICE FIELD BEHIND THE CLERK'S DORMITORY, GREENWOOD]

Riser screams in frustration. She pounds on the bubble that marks her defeat, before turning to Sensei and Wake, who cringe under her glare. "Again! This time, try harder!"

"Wait, Riser," Sensei says ever so meekly. "I think we need a better plan."

Riser doesn't say anything, but stomps over to the edge of the field and sits down.

Wake shouts over to the three standing on the other side of the field. "We need to go over some things. We'll be ready in a little while."

Fate, Shine and Monster wave back and begin to discuss things on their side.

"We're not going to win at this rate," Sensei says as he and Wake catch up to the angry Daughter. "Let me explain. The longer the fight goes on, the more we are at a disadvantage. They have healing and we don't. Even without it, their endurance is better than ours. I mean better than mine and Wake's."

Riser growls. "We just have to hit them harder and faster, before their healing gives them an advantage, then. We really shouldn't be having this much difficulty with this game. We have one objective: eliminate Monster. We just aren't trying hard enough."

But whenever they finally get the other three on the defensive, Monster would Still Rachel's Flame and wield her like a shield. None of their attacks have been able to get past the combo. And because Shine doesn't try to breakout of the Monster's hold, they could keep it up for quite a while. Once the two synched, Shine's Orb would fully neutralize any of their attacks. Together they suffered no recoil, allowing them to block multiple times in quick succession.

What angers Riser the most is that Wake and even Sensei are doing their part. Surprisingly, the young clerk figured out a way to neutralize the Fate for a full five-count. And they all know, Wake is capable of making short work of any Healer. It should be enough.

In this scenario, it should be Riser's responsibility to take out the other side's Shield. It's as simple as that. If she could just do her part, they wouldn't be in this predicament. Wake could take out Monster if he just got the chance. Sense could neutralize Fate during crucial moments. If only she could do her part. "Argghh!"

"Hello, over there," the Fate calls out to them. "Shall we break for lunch?"

"No, thanks," the three reply in unison.

"One mind, one voice. Good for you," the Fate says, leading the other two away, along with their music. Shine yells something about bringing them back some food when they return.

"It's not your fault, Riser," Wake says.

"Who says it's my fault?" she screams.

The two boys start cringing all over again. "Sorry, I just meant ..."

"What he is trying to say is ..." Sensei tries to explain more tactfully. "It must be frustrating teaming up with us. No one person can break through their combo. We have to find some way to combo, too.

"And I have just the idea," Sensei says. "It's a little tricky, but I think you two can pull it off."

"Don't think just because you brought us back some food that we're going to take it easy on you," Riser shouts to the other group. Monster mumbles something, Shine apologizes, and the Fate smiles back. All of which makes Riser just more angry.

"3, 2, 1 ... Go!"

Riser draws Ehecthal and charges in. Shine Grabs the Sun as Monster places his hand upon her back, and chants "Still the Flame," paralyzing her in place. He picks her up and positions her between him and the charging Daughter.

Wake slides to flank them. The Fate intercepts, as expected. Sensei steps forward and holds out both hands. "Green Art: Vine Lash," he says. A writhing tendril sprouts forth from each palm. They seem to grow forever, a surging green, thicker than the clerk's own arms.

Even in mid-air, the Fate manages to change direction. But the vines do so, as well, grasping first a stray arm, the second wrapping tightly around his waist.

Riser bounces off Shine's Orb. With no recoil to deal with, Monster is able to swing her around and deflect Wake's attack, a moment later.

Four more seconds until Fate is free. It's now or never, Riser thinks, landing beside Wake as planned. She hears him intone, "Water Grab: Riser's Channel."

A tunnel of Water forms in front of her, just large enough for her to slither through, but she doesn't have to do that. She kneels low and launches herself, shrieking, "Sing, Ehecthal!" She shoots through the narrow opening. With her Winds funneled and focused, she flies faster than she ever has before. Her sword stretched before her, she screams, "Dual Combo: Jetstream!"

As her blade meets the Sun Orb, she feels it sink deep, deeper than ever. But just as every time before, it does not pass. The Daughter ricochets backwards, landing roughly on her backside. The Fate charges her before she even stops bouncing. And once again she finds herself cursing the Loser's Ball surrounding her.

"It didn't work," Riser says flatly, trying to control her frustration. She knows her group is doing all they can. *We're closer than ever, but ...*

"Guys, I got it!" Sensei says, looking up from his calculations. "All you have to do is spin."

"Spin?" the Daughter asks in disbelief. "This isn't for show. This is serious. If we lose one more time ... I'm going to lose it. If that happens, you two better start running ..." *This is unacceptable.*

"Don't worry, we will get it this time," Wake says. "I think I understand, Sensei. She was close. If the next time she adds a rotation while maintaining the same speed, the force of the attack may be just enough to break through Shine's Sun Orb."

"Exactly! With this slight adjustment, Jetstream should have enough force to break through."

"What the hail are you guys talking about?" Riser asks. "Sensei, have you gone mad too?"

"It's simple. Force equals Mass times Acceleration," Sensei explains. "If you can maintain the same speed, but add a spin, you'll increase the distance that your sword travels, thereby ..."

Riser turns her back to the clerk and faces Wake. "Please explain in Common."

"If you spin, but don't slow down, your attack will hit harder."

"Really?"

"It will. Imagine, just the very tip of Ehecthal as you sail through the air. That's where you're putting all your weight behind during that attack, right?" Wake asks the nodding Daughter.

"Pretend there's an imaginary line that follows the tip of your sword. For your regular attack, it's a straight line, but if you spin, the line is a spiral." Riser nods in understanding.

"If you straighten that line out, it's longer. If it takes you the same amount of time to travel those two lines, it's going faster, see?"

"And I'll hit harder! That makes total sense." She looks over at Sensei and whaps him upside the head, "You need to learn how to communicate more clearly. Good idea, though." The young clerk smiles and rubs the back of his head.

They execute the plan exactly as before. The other group responds in kind. This time around, just as the Daughter enters the tunnel of Water, she begins to spin. As the tip of her blade meets the Sun Orb, she shatters the Light. Before her opponents can respond, she's onto Verse Two. Wake and Sensei clean up.

Riser sheathes Ehecthal and places her hands on her hips. She throws her head back and cackles. *This may be the final touch that I have been searching for. I think I can finish 'that' now.*

CHAPTER 40
SIR GROCK
[MAIN STREET, GREENWOOD]

The rain falls in waves. Ever so often, an errant sunbeam peeks through the morning gloom to remind everyone that the sun is indeed still there. It's enough to keep the streets of Greenwood clear of all but the bravest of fools.

Not that Grock Hardrime would ever be considered either: brave or a fool. A true gentleman has time for neither.

Short and proper, he walks purposefully through the downpour under the protection of a baby blue parasol. His associate lumbers behind, face fully pelted.

"You should have taken the pink one," he calls back to his traveling companion. His eyes twinkle at the thought, the dreaded Scourge Kutz under such a thing. Unfortunately, for anyone old enough to regret their youth, the stores in town are stocked against them.

The large barn of a man snorts in reply.

Grock stops to laugh in the rain. He likes to give The Scourge a hard time but realizes if the rain truly bothered him, Grock wouldn't be the one with the umbrella. Kutz grins to himself as if thinking the very same thing. But the large man's grin turns into a squint as he peers down the road ahead.

The skies choose that moment to clear, revealing an upside down boy hurrying towards them. Upon reaching them, he promptly flips upright and begs their pardon before jumping back onto his hands and taking off once again.

"Just a moment, young man!" *This may be just the type of lad we're looking for.*

The upside down boy pauses, then scampers back towards them, legs flailing like bent straws in the wind. He flips upright just before losing his balance. He grins wildly and bows deeply.

"Young man, may I ask why you are walking on your hands in the middle of the rain?"

"Yes, you may," the boy says. "I do so because it is faster than actually walking and I promised my mother to never run in the rain."

Grock chortles at the young man's exquisite sense of humor. "Are you a performer, perhaps?"

"That is possible, perhaps, even plausible ... after all, I performed a Calling rather perfectly. Although, I must admit—it was not done purposely," the boy replies.

This "Calling' must be the name of a Wysterian Play. He also highlighted his alliterative boast with mock humbleness, Grock thinks, clapping his hands together. *A well developed wit and the dexterity of an acrobat. What's a talent like this doing in a backwater town like this?*

"Bravo. You must be a clown of rather high-rank?" the elderly gentleman asks.

"I am called that often, yes," the boy replies. "Though, my friends call me Fate."

"Well, Fate, My name is Grock. And I am here on other business, but normally, I manage talent of your caliber. May I ask who you studied under?"

"The Old Man is my master. People such as yourself usually call him Claw."

Hmm ... a clown named Claw? Doesn't ring a bell. "I'm afraid to say I haven't heard of your master, though, I must admit it's been quite some time since I've delved into the world of clownery."

"You were once a clown?" the Fate asks him.

"A lifetime ago I studied to be one, yes. Grand times, those were," Grock tells the boy. "But that was a very long time ago."

Kutz clears his throat. The rain has stopped, but it's no time for chitchat.

"But back to the matter at hand," Grock says, "By chance have you seen any pretty girls around town carrying a large wooden case?"

"I know a very nice girl who often carries a large wooden case which holds her brushes, and I have another friend who never goes anywhere without his guitar, which he also carries in a case."

"This girl ... are you sure all she carries in this case are brushes?"

"Yes, sir, I am. Shine's a master of the Long Brush. If you would like to see her work, you can find a fine example of it hanging outside the Stewards and Raiders Inn located not too far south of the Lobby."

That can't be her. "Thank you. And this guitarist fellow you mentioned; could you also tell me a little about him?"

"Well, Pooh's a little fellow. He is mostly quiet, but get him alone and he will talk forever," the Fate says. "He is also is very regular, if you know what I mean? That is how he got his name."

"Interesting," Grock says. "Guitars are rather uncommon around these parts. Do you happen to know where your friend came by his?"

"It was his father's."

"Ah, very well," the gentleman says in disappointment. "Thank you so very much for your time, young man. I won't hold you back from your training any longer. If you ever find yourself looking for representation, please look me up." Grock hands him his calling card.

In a sense, he is relieved to find out that the guitar the boy spoke of couldn't possibly be Desi Derata.

CHAPTER 41

SENSE

[BEHIND THE STEWARDS & RAIDERS INN, GREENWOOD]

"What's that, Sense?" the Fate asks. The Captain started calling him that at some point and now they all are. He doesn't mind at all, though, he rather likes being Fate-named.

Sense looks down at the small metal box on his lap. It has a couple of adjustable knobs, several buttons, a slider, and even a small set of keys akin to that of a piano.

"It's my Echo Box," Sense tells him. "In case I get tired of talking with just the drum, I can use this."

By now, everyone has picked out a favorite beat. They range from a simple broken one for the Captain to a complicated, evolving one for Wake.

When he plays any of his teammates' favorite beats, they know he is speaking to or about them. But it is getting to the point where just the drum is not enough. So he's been working on this.

He presses a key and the box emits a wavering note. "I'll also be able to give more detailed information with the different sounds that the Echo Box can create. It can also play back anything I record—like an echo."

With the assistance of Poe and Desi earlier, and a couple of finishing touches just now, he's ready to unveil to everyone.

"So I guess you can boss us around even more with that," Riser says with a grin. She leans over and musses up his hair. "It's sure to help us reign victorious."

Sense finishes off his apple, core and all. He inspects the stem between his fingers before deciding there's nothing left to eat.

Poe makes a sound of disgust. Sense looks at the bard and says, "I can't help it. I love apples. Sweet ones, sour ones, red ones, green ones. I prefer crispy, but I'll eat a mushy one, too."

Poe shakes his head and shrugs with his palms held forward.

Sense has no problem reading the bard at this point. "Why? Well, because they taste good of course. Besides, they don't allow apples anywhere near the Library."

The bard nods slightly, a sign for him to continue his explanation.

"I guess it's really the Crossroads, the area where the Library is built, that doesn't allow them. Apparently many of the native town folk are allergic to apples or something.

"So how did I start liking apples in the first place? Well, that's a good question. I always remember the taste of my first apple, but who gave it to me ..." Sense's memory is usually perfect. It's odd that he hasn't thought of this in so long, but all of a sudden, the memory comes flooding back.

"I must have been very young. I think it was before they diagnosed my condition, so I was still running around playing with the other kids. Anyway, Fall was just beginning, and we were all out by the main road. I remember Bennet was there; he was always there."

Poe shrugs and rapidly waves his hand to get on with the story.

"It started to rain. I remember everyone running back inside, but I happened to see this little old lady making her way down the road. She just looked so small and so frail and the autumn rain was very cold that day. She didn't have an umbrella or even something to keep her head dry. I remember feeling really bad for her, so I ran up to her and threw my scarf around her head."

Poe looks at him, probably wondering what this has to do with why he likes apples.

"Well, about a month later there's a knock at my door. My mother answers and it's the little old lady. She came back to return my scarf and to thank me. She was actually very scary looking; now, that I think about it. But she must have been pretty nice. I remember she pulled out this apple, the first I had ever seen. She cut it in half, straight through the core and shared it with me. It was so delicious. I never tasted anything so sweet and tart and juicy and crisp. It was really good.

"I've never had another apple as good as that one. Honestly, every apple I eat is like a ghost of that apple. They never taste as good as that first one, but they remind me of it, I guess."

Poe doesn't look very impressed by the story.

"You asked," the young clerk answers. "The funny thing was that it was so good I ate the stem and all. I remember the scary looking lady suddenly looking scarier. Or maybe she was just scared. She must have been worried that I'd choke. She even stuck her bony little fingers down my throat, but I had already swallowed it all.

"She just stared at me for a while after that. Then she started laughing. She didn't stop. The little old lady laughed all the way out the door and down the road.

"I wonder why I never thought of that story until just now, though?" Sense asks himself quietly.

Poe stopped listening a little while ago and is already fiddling with the Echo Box.

One of these days, though, I'm going to find an apple as good as that one. Shiny and gold just like that first one. In his mind he can still picture how it reflected every flame that swayed in the hearth that night. It's enough to make his heart start to ache.

CHAPTER 42
BROTHER MONSTER
[ROAD TO THE CITY OF SARANGHAE, CAPITAL OF THREE KINGDOMS OF WYSTERIA]

As he watches the small town of Greenwood disappear behind him, he can't help but think of the day he left the Sanctuary. This is different, though. He never looked back as he walked away from his first home. *But really, what's different is that I'm no longer alone.*

To his right, Esperanza and Rachel play a guessing game involving flowers. The Daughter picks whatever she finds growing along the roadside, and Rachel tries to guess its name by scent alone. Spikey sniffs them from Rachel's shoulder, as well. Every once in a while, the chipmunk takes one and shoves it into his mouth.

On the cart behind him, Poe strums away. Whenever they hit a bump in the road, the bard flicks the Half-Orc with his little, switch-like Reed and laughs. Monster growls back at him, which just makes the bard laugh all the more. Still, Poe goes out of his way to play the old hymns, the Half-Orc's favorites. And when he works up a sweat, Poe comes and wipes his brow since he needs both hands to pull the cart.

To his left, Wake riddles the Fate with impossible questions. "If a tree falls in the forest and there is no one about to hear it, does it make a sound?"

"What is your definition of sound?" the Fate asks back. Wake thinks on it a moment and moves to the next.

"What came first, the chicken or the egg?"

"If I showed you a chicken and told you it did not come from an egg would it still be a chicken?" the Fate asks back. "If not, then the egg came first."

"If you could change one thing about the world, what would you change?"

"The past, because anything else I can change already."

"What is the meaning of life?"

"Wonderful."

Wake doesn't ask him the everyday ones, those he has no answer for.

Every so often, someone offers to take their turn at pulling the handcart, but Monster assures them that he's fine. It weighs nothing at all. In some way it reminds him …

He left the Sanctuary with nothing, and now, he has everything. The journey to the capital for the Grand Finale is underway, and he travels the road surrounded by friends.

They pass peddlers with packs as tall as they are, merchant trains—dozens of wagons deep, and families on foot with little ones riding on shoulders or gently wrapped and strapped onto their mothers' backs. And though they haven't come across any herds so far, the road is littered with hoof prints and other less pleasant signs of their recent passing.

Overall, the people are friendly, but more often than not, the other travelers give the party a wide-berth once they spot the Half-Orc. They whisper too, but he is used to that.

As the day goes on, the road grows only more and more crowded, a sure sign they are nearing their destination. And then they finally see it, shining in the distance even as evening creeps up upon them is Saranghae, the largest and most beautiful city in the Three Kingdoms.

Saranghae is all a capital should be, a gleaming city of pale stone and intricate bronze workmanship. Towers, gilded with birds and flowers, and rooftop gardens dart the skyline to no end. Below, an army of custodians keep the roads of white sand paved with translucent stones sparkling in the morning light.

"I used to do that," the Fate tells his teammates, never leaving Monster's shadow. Even on the most crowded of streets, the people move over to the other side of the road for the Half-Orc.

"What do you mean?"

"I was Head of the South Main Sweepers. I served every summer since I was old enough to. The southern roads were never so spotless."

If Monster didn't know the Captain any better, he'd have to wonder if the fool boy was making up these stories as he went along. But the nonsense that comes out of his mouth is just too farfetched to imagine. *South Main Sweepers, indeed.*

"Welcome to Saranghae, where Love is King! Welcome one and all ..." someone shouts in the distance, reminding Monster that ever since the Bae, Silla and Gorgury were brought together under the flag of Wysteria, a Love has always sat upon the throne.

Only Fate and Esperanza have visited the capital before. For the rest of them, it's a wondrous sight, familiar and exotic at the same time. They walk wide-eyed through its pristine streets, gawking at this and that.

The Half-Orc takes a moment to admire a particularly tall spire capped in crystal that reflects all the colors of the rainbow on to a building nearby. The Fate follows closely behind, stopping when he does and hurrying after when he moves onto the next sight.

The crowds begin to recede as they venture further in. Once the roads are clear enough to walk about without fear of being jostled, the Fate frees himself of the Half-Orc's shadow and begins to stroll happily along.

"Right or left?" the Fate asks, strutting ahead, elbows held high.

Wake looks at the map, trying to figure out how to get to the building marked by Sense. Their strategist had departed a couple days earlier to fulfill his obligations as a clerk.

"Right, keep an eye out for a statue that looks like a lion with long legs. It should be fairly large."

At the end of the block, the Fate shouts back that he's found it. It's not far from there that they find their home for the next couple weeks: the Seven Corner's Inn.

"Daebak, Sense!" Riser exclaims, checking the building out from top to bottom. Large glass windows cover every side and flowers every shade of sunrise line the entranceway.

A short, wide man greets them with a deep bow. "Welcome to the Seven Corners. I am Arniolio, but you may call me Arni. I am the proprietor of this humble establishment. Team Fate, I presume?"

They nod cheerfully.

"I hope your journey has been pleasant. The young master has reserved our very best rooms, and it would be an honor to personally show you our many amenities. But, first, I have very exciting news—a courier is here.

"It is an honor to have such important guests," he says, clapping his hands in delight. "A *Royal Courier* awaits you, right here in my very own lobby."

CHAPTER 43
WAKE
[SEVEN CORNERS INN, SARANGHAE]

"Woodman?" the Fate asks the courier who awaits them in the foyer. The young man, decked head to toe in royal violet, bows with a flourish.

"Fate, Esperanza, it is good to see you again."

"Greetings, Gerald," Riser says almost nicely.

"Why do you wear purple?" the Fate asks, looking him up and down.

"As dense as ever, I see," the courier says with a laugh. "I've been accepted into Our Majesty's Royal Service. I have the honor of being a Royal Courier now and ..."

"What about the Wood?" the Fate asks him as if the answer means everything.

"*And*, I am apprenticing under Estavon, Master Dendron of the Royal House."

The Fate stares at the courier questioningly.

"Dendron can be translated as master of the wood," the courier explains.

"Good for you," the Fate says.

"Thank you," the courier answers, rolling his eyes. "As much as I'd like to catch up, I'm actually here on a rather urgent matter.

"Greetings to all of you Team Fate, especially you, Wake Avenoy. I have a top priority summons requesting your immediate presence at the Palace."

Wake isn't sure he heard the courier correctly. But his sister assures him, "They must need your appraisal skills, or maybe they want you to write an article. Either way, do your best, Wake!"

That makes a little sense, but not much. There are plenty of other higher-level appraisers in the capital. Wake looks to his friends for any additional guidance, but belching is the only advice he gets.

As he follows the messenger out of the inn, his mind races with possibilities—all of them quite frightening.

Wake has seen pictures of it all of his life, but nothing that's prepared him for the sight of it; the Royal Palace. In a city of wonder, it is the most wonderful.

Before him stretches palatial walls, bricked in ivory, with vines of the very same color, carefully grown to paint scenes that make him feel insignificant and proud all at once. *That one must be Lady Seo and the marks of her invisible dragon.*

The courier leads them through an inconspicuous side entrance. *Who from the Palace could possible want to see me? And why? He said it was urgent. And how do Fate and Esperanza know this courier? There is something familiar about him ...*

Wake follows the mysterious courier past the wall and into the gardens; a menagerie of sculpted hedges that frolic amongst amethyst blossoms. The scent of lilacs, violets, and lavender dizzies his head and for a moment all worries are forgotten. At least until they come upon a long building grown from the very same vines used to paint scenes on the castle walls.

"It's a great honor, you know?" the courier says as he pulls out an ornate key.

"More than I deserve. Do you perhaps know who called me here, or why?"

"That is not for me to say," the courier tells him, unlocking the door. "And that's also not what I meant. The honor is in entering this building. There are only a handful of people outside of the Royal Family who have ever entered the House of White Vine."

"Oh."

"Even though it is located within the gardens, the House of White Vine is under the authority of the Master Dendron—a fact that the Master of the Gardens has always been sore about. But it was Filus the third Dendron, who first introduced the White Vine to the Palace Grounds. You need a key for the Gardens from one Master and a second from the other to even step foot into this building."

Wake tries to pay attention, but it's not as interesting as the courier makes it sound. *How can someone talk so excitedly about vines and gardens? Fate called him Woodman. Esperanza called him Gerald ...*

And then it hits him. "You're Gerald Evergreen, Captain of the top team from two years ago."

"The one and only," Gerald says with a bow.

"It's really an honor to meet you. That match in the semifinals, the one in Culmore was one of the greatest of all time!"

"I'm glad to see I am not all but forgotten." The courier opens the door wide and leads him into a long hall carpeted in lush green. "I have to ask you to remove your shoes before we proceed any farther. I also recommend removing your socks."

Gerald takes off his own boots and places them in one of the small cubbies lining the hall. Wake follows suit. When his bare feet touch the ground, his toes sink deep into the thick plush green. The sensation is quite pleasant. Upon closer inspection, he realizes that it is not carpet at all, but moss.

"So how do you know Fate and Esperanza?"

"I know them from school. I used to beat Fate up every day. That boy is as hopeless a Crier as I have ever seen."

"School? Do you mean Criers College?" *What were they doing there?*

Gerald nods and goes on. "Yes, is there any other school worth mentioning? I haven't seen either in quite a while, but some things never change. That boy is as backwards as ever."

"He's a good Captain," Wake says.

"If you say so." The courier stops to inspect a stray vine climbing the wall. "Look, it doesn't take a genius to figure out what you guys are trying to do. You're going for the Triple Threat Feat. Am I correct?"

Wake gives a shrugging nod. *How does he know that?*

"If someone with no stake in the outcome such as myself was able to figure it out ... Well, you'd be a fool to think she hasn't.

"Let me give you a piece of advice. Things aren't that easy. The Fate you see, he's a dreamer. He has nothing to lose, but you ... you seem a more practical sort. You may even be able to get an appointment here at the Palace. Take what she has to offer, get into school, make a decent life for yourself." They come to a stop before a set of colossal doors.

"Did you know that every year there is only one top team? But gaining a position in the Royal Palace is even more rare than that. Many a year goes by where they do not appoint anyone new. It was easier for me to captain the top team of my year than to get here. Do you understand?"

"But my friends ..."

"Friends are one thing. The rest of your life is another." Gerald Evergreen inclines his head to the large double doors. "She's waiting for you in there."

"Thank you ... I think."

"Just my opinion; take it as you will. He's a dreamer, but people like you and I ... well, we know that's just not how the world works. In the end, he'll be left with nothing but those dreams, broken and alone. Like I said, he used to challenge me every day. And every day I had to put him in his place."

What exactly is going on here? I was actually beginning to believe we could do this, but ... No, what he's saying just isn't right. I believe in the Captain. "One question. The last time you fought Fate, who won?"

Gerald throws back his head and laughs. "You got me there ... he did."

The only light comes from the pale of the moon. In the near darkness, flowers blush like soft stars and though, he's inside, it's as if he's walking across the night sky. The main chamber of the House of the White Vine is as magnificent of a place as Wake's ever seen.

And none of it compares to she who sits in the middle of it, Princess Achylsa Love.

Ever since that fateful day he walked through that two-toned door, he imagined what he would say if given a second chance to talk to the Doll Princess. He bows with less grace than he imagined, but she has the grace enough for the both of them.

"Wake Avenoy of Ice Ridge at your service, Your Highness."

He keeps his head lowered until she responds with the proper words. "Please rise, Wake Avenoy." Her voice is calm, stoic. His head is a storm, his heart the center, calm with one satisfying thought: *she just said my name.*

"Welcome, and thank you for answering my call." She looks at him almost shyly. "I summoned you here for two reasons, first of which is this." She holds forth a pair of iridescent gauntlets seemingly carved out of pearl. They are the finest, most delicate of their type he's ever seen. "It is the only pair of Hand of Mists known to be in existence, very similar to your own, if I understand correctly."

She nods for him to take them. The exquisite gauntlets look more a piece of art than a piece of equipment. Though, their luster pales in comparison to the hand that holds them.

"Apparently, your Hand of Water is the original, but was

considered a failure. This is the second attempt. Unfortunately, these too were considered inadequate, leading to the creation of the final version, the Hand of Ice." She points to one of the Hands of Mist. "The left one has been in my family for generations. It was long ago converted from Blue to Violet to match the predilection for Violet that runs in my family. After many years of searching, we have just recently found its match. But there seems to be something amiss."

"The craftsmanship is extraordinary. I've never seen such fine detail," Wake says, his nervousness replaced by awe.

"May I?" he asks. The Princess nods acquiescence. The gauntlets are much too small, but he manages a partial fit. Right away, he notices one's lack to respond. "Something is definitely not right."

"Yes, I was hoping that you could rectify the matter."

"I'm not sure where to even begin with something like this. A failure to respond in this manner often means one thing, that the equipment is dead. I need more testing to say with absolute certainty." He turns over the dead gauntlet and looks for any signs of what may be causing the problem. But he cannot detect any flaws, whatsoever.

"If you are so inclined, I could loan it to you." She stands from the stone bench and draws closer.

"I am sure you could get the faulty one to function properly. You know, they may just possibly be the most valuable pieces in the Royal Armory. If you'd like, you could even keep one for yourself. We would have a matching pair," she offers, watching him closely. "That is, if you were a member of *The Royal Team*."

So that's what this is really about, he thinks as she continues. "It is not too late. If you join *The Royal Team* now, I can assure your and Rachel's acceptance into Criers College. Perhaps, even the others ..."

Why me? Does she think of me as the weak link that will betray my friends? "If that's what you asked me here for, I'm sorry, Princess ..."

"Wake Avenoy, I do not think that you understand," she says. "This isn't just for me that I ask. It's for the good of the people: not just Wysteria, but the whole world."

He sees it in her eyes that it is true. They are filled with a determination that *is so sad, so lonely.* All he wants to do is help, but ... "I can't betray my friends."

"Maybe there is some other way I can help?" Wake asks. *Her expression is like a painting. It never changes. No, that's not quite it, either. She has no expression.* Even without one, he can tell this is all quite difficult for her.

"I have to be the one that leads the winningest team in this year's Grand Finale," she says softly. Even her voice is a caress to his ears. But it's her awkward manner that makes his heart break beat. *She's as nervous as I am,* he realizes.

She wants to lead the top team and the Fate wants to captain it. There's really no compromise. "Princess, I am sorry. Truly, I am. But I cannot betray my friends. Perhaps, it's better that I leave, now."

She looks at him for the longest time before finally giving the slightest of nods. And just like that, their meeting comes to an end.

He doesn't want it to, though. Enough that he promises the impossible for a moment more. "Don't worry, Princess. I'll find a way to help you." *Why did I say that? Next time, I'm just going to burp loudly instead.*

It's all enough to make him scream. A passing gentleman gives him a questioning look. For once, Wake doesn't care. *Could what she said somehow be true?* He wants to believe her, but he wants to believe him, too. *Fate is so hard to understand, sometimes.*

But, he really has been right when it counts.

He almost walks straight past the Seven Corners Inn. Thankfully, its owner waves him down.

"Young Master!" the innkeeper calls out. "I hope all went well with your visit to the Palace."

"Yes ... yes, sir, it did," Wake assures the innkeeper as well as himself. "Everything went well."

"It pleases me to hear that." The old man smiles at him curiously. "If you would be so kind as to follow me, I will escort you to the courtyard where your friends are currently resting from your long journey."

"Thank you."

"It is my pleasure, especially for such an important guest." The innkeeper gestures for him to follow. "It is not just for the royal summons that I say that. I have served many guests and seen even more. I was born in this inn and spent all my life under this one roof and I know when I see something special. And there is something special about you and your friends."

Wake manages a smile, even though, he imagines that the innkeeper must say that to all of his guests. "I don't know about that, but I can tell you this is the finest inn I have ever stayed at."

The innkeeper smiles proudly at that. "I have a feeling someday I may brag that a member of Team Fate blessed this establishment with such kind words." The round, little man gestures towards the coming bend in the hall. "The courtyard is at your disposal for the remainder of your stay. It is of modest size, but I hope adequate for your training sessions. Young Sense has already paid, in full," he adds happily.

If Sense picked this place out, it must be well within their budget; nothing for him to worry about. With his eyes lowered, he can't help but notice the various colored lines painted along the floor.

The innkeeper also notices. "Those are done by a Sharded

Brush. My late mother, rest her soul, began losing her sight near the end. She could manage without these lines to guide her about, but I added them to make things a little easier. They begin at the main entrance. The green leads to the courtyard, the red to the dining area, and the blue to the hall in which your rooms are located."

Leave it to Sense to find the perfect place for us to stay. The thought of his friend going out of his way to make things easier on his sister makes him feel better.

"Here we are," the innkeeper says at the sight of the courtyard. "And please do not hesitate to call upon me if you need anything at all."

Wake thanks him once again before reuniting with his friends.

"What happened?" They clamor around him.

"Nothing, it was nothing. They wanted me to assess a piece of equipment," Wake explains. "I guess they asked for me because it was another version of a Hand of Water, but I couldn't get it to activate." He's not lying, but he doesn't feel very honest.

"Was the Princess there?" the Fate asks. Wake nods. "Did she touch you? She does that you know, even if you do not want her to."

Wake shakes his head.

"That is good to hear, Way. You have also returned just in time for a late night practice," the Fate says, which doesn't sound too bad right about now to a boy whose mind is filled with thoughts of a girl he would like to forget.

"Wake, you seem out of sorts," Sense says.

"What?" Wake looks up from his plate. He picks at it for a while and then asks, "Sense, can I ask you something?"

"Always."

"Is there a way for the Princess to lead the winningest team and the Fate to get what he wants, too?"

Sense looks at him in an understanding way. "Girl troubles, huh?"

"No, absolutely not," he stammers and stutters.

"I'm just fooling with you, Wake."

Wake looks down at his plate before pushing it aside. He explains it all. Sense listens carefully.

"So that's her goal ... She says it's important, not just to her, but the whole world. And Fate wants to be the Captain of the team that never loses," Sense repeats. "Their wishes sound similar, but there may be a way."

"Really?"

"*The Royal Team* is actually classified as a guild. That's why there's so many of them. Anybody who wants to could set up a multi-team guild, too; it's just that no one else bothers. Why go through all the trouble, when most teams barely get enough points to split six ways?" Sense explains. "And I guess, technically, each group could have its own Captain. I'll have to check out the guild application. I've never actually had to fill one of those out before."

"Is that really possible?" Wake asks. "So the six of us would be considered a sub-team of *The Royal Team* which is led by the Princess and the Fate could still be our Captain?"

"I can't make any promises, but I'll check into it."

The next day, he learns the bad news.

"Wake, I'm really sorry, but I don't think it's possible," Sense tells him sadly. "There's no real way to designate captain status within a guild. Here, take a look at the form. There's no space for it like on a regular team application."

Wake takes the piece of paper and sees exactly what his

friend means. "I appreciate it, Sense. It's not your fault. It was a long shot to begin with. Thank you for checking into it." He wasn't expecting much, but still, he can't get the image of the Princess asking for his help out of his head. He studies the application carefully before tucking it safely away.

Later that afternoon, he fills the application out and asks the Captain to sign it. The Fate does so without a second look. *If I give this to her, I'll have helped her. And if what she said was true, maybe even the whole world. Everything else would be the same. We could still compete ... even win,* Wake tries to tell himself.

But then, Fate wouldn't really be our Captain. She has to be telling the truth. The Princess wouldn't lie, would she?

The final week before it all begins comes and goes. They practice long and hard, honing their teamwork and each of them preparing in their own way for the Relay.

Every morning, Wake swims the cold waters of the nearby canal in preparation for his own leg. More often than not, the Fate joins him, which makes it almost bearable.

Spikey would sit atop the Captain's head as he strokes with all his might. Every time the chipmunk gets wet, the Fate lets out a little yelp—a sure sign Spikey is living up to his namesake.

Having them around helps him forget how much he dislikes the cold, at least, until he climbs out of the canal on the windy days.

Afterward, they check on the others: Rachel at the local Light Course, Riser scaling the side of some building, or Monster on a run through the city. The Fate always wants to join in and somehow, Wake usually ends up getting dragged into joining, as well. Sometimes it's a pain, but it's always fun.

At least, it keeps his mind off things.

The night before the opening games comes quickly. Wake finds himself siting alone in the courtyard wondering exactly what he should do. He thinks about the application stuffed deep within his pack. He hasn't really done anything wrong ... yet.

Lost in worry, he doesn't notice someone has come out to join him.

"Way, may I join you?" the Fate asks, sitting down next to him. "Excited for tomorrow? I am. I can hardly wait."

"I'm just worrying about tomorrow and ... other things."

"Why do you worry?"

"I don't know ... I just worry about stuff. It's just the way I am."

"That is good, I suppose."

"No, it's not. It's horrible. I wish I was more like you."

"I do not think that is a good wish. I think it is better this way. I remember what matters—what has to be done. I can even define things. But you ... you can interpret. There is a difference, you know?" The Fate leaps to his feet. He can never sit still for long. "And we need both."

Wake sits there, staring as the moon goes behind a cloud. "Aren't you ever afraid?"

"Afraid?"

"Yeah, afraid, scared," Wake says to the boy staring blankly back at him. "Fear, that feeling you get in the pit of your stomach when something bad is about to happen."

"Hmm ... I think you are doing it wrong," the Fate says. "Fear is that feeling that comes before something important is about to happen."

The Fate looks up at the night sky. "That is what my father used to tell me. But he had another name for it. He called it the Moment of Truth—that instant you do not know what to do and everything you know to be right suddenly seems like it may not be."

Wake looks at him but the other boy doesn't notice; he's too busy smiling at the stars. The moon comes out from behind the clouds as the Fate tells him, "It is a test. Sometimes, you have to fight, sometimes you have to flee, but never lose faith in the face of the unknown. Never stop believing what you believe."

The Fate smiles down on him. "That feeling ... I look forward to it, actually."

He's so different from anyone I've ever met. Even fear means something else to someone like him, Wake thinks. *I wonder what sort of things my father would've taught me if he'd been around.* "You're lucky."

"Thank you. I think so too," the Fate tells him. "I am glad I got to make a boyfriend like you. You are my first. Well, all of you: Sense and Monster, as well."

Wake laughs. "Guys that are your friends are just called friends. Not boyfriends."

"I see."

"And ... well, you're my first real friend, too. At least my own age," Wake admits. "My best friend, actually." Suddenly, the Princess seems far away. What's important is here.

"Is that what it is called? Yes, Way, you are my best friend, too."

"It is time!"

Wake nods absently, too busy taking it all in to pay attention. *They used to hold real Pro Races in this very stadium. Now, I'll be racing here.* The thought is actually quite frightening.

This is Saranghae Memorial Stadium, a whole other world from the bleachers he's used to. A true coliseum filled with row after row of alabaster stone seats, all of which are filled this day.

They qualified for the Grand Finale with a single win in Greenwood, but without a single Race beneath their belts, they are dead last in the Relay Standings. It comes as no surprise when they find out that they're matched against *The Royal Team*.

In some ways, it doesn't really matter. Unlike any of the other games, each team is only given one shot at the Relay Race. Whatever time they finish in is all that matters. There is no second round, no final round. They have one chance at it, and it's here and now.

This is really happening. We're about to go out there in front of the whole country, matched against The Royal Team. The thought is worrisome, but the way Sense explained it earlier makes it, so even, he can believe that they have a chance.

"Shine gives us nearly a half minute advantage over any other team on Tour. Wake's times rank in the top ten in the Whirlpool; only seconds differentiate between him and first. Fate says he won't lose to Kase on the Obstacle Course. I've never seen anyone climb as fast as Riser, and the times that Monster has been running the Long Leg are more than good enough. As long as everyone does what they're supposed to, this should be the easiest of the three to win."

He watches his sister laughing at something Riser's said. She is so full of confidence when it comes to the Light Course, but he knows deep down that she is just as full of concern as he is. Everyone else is, too. *Everything we've been working so hard for starts here today or ... ends here today.*

Next to him, he finds a small pouch. It's the Fate's, the one he keeps his "special" berries in. According to his friend, the small berries are necessary for him to compete.

Wake picks one up and sniffs it. *They don't really have much of a smell. If they help him, maybe they'll give me a little boost, too.*

Wake pops one into his mouth. As soon as he does, he regrets it.

Immediately, his stomach begins to churn. His very core begins to clench and spasm. *Is this why he was throwing up that first time? He called me a waste of a berry* ... Wake closes his eyes. The lights are suddenly too bright, the colors too vivid.

"Help!" he manages to scream before doubling over in pain.

CHAPTER 44
BROTHER MONSTER
[SARANGHAE MEMORIAL STADIUM]

"Fortunately, he only ate one," Monster tells them. "He's going to feel like his insides are flipping inside out for the next hour or so, but he should be fine by this evening. We can't let him enter the water like this, however. It's just too dangerous.

"Apparently, Fate takes one of these berries before each match. And Wake thought there wouldn't be any harm in also trying one.

"Fool," Monster growls. "These are Nune Berries and they're poisonous. It only takes a handful to kill a full grown man." Monster turns to the Fate and asks, "Why do you even have these?"

"I need them. They are the only medicine that helps with a condition that runs in my family," the Fate says. "I have taken them for years. I am used to them, now." Monster throws the pouch of berries at him.

"Don't leave them out in the open. Never take more than one in a day. And never take them for more than a couple days in a row." It's still risky, but Monster knows of a few other medicines that work in a similar manner.

The Fate may claim to have built some sort of tolerance to the Nune Berries, but as far as he understands it, the main toxin in the berries should be cumulative. *He should feel worse after each, not better. I'll have to read up on this when I have more time.*

"I feel better," Wake tries to say before hunching over again and groaning. *He's full of pain, but he still wants to try.*

"Look, one berry won't kill you." Monster explains to him. "But if you get into the water like that ... that may."

The speakers blare. The announcements begin and the crowd cheers wildly as the favorites, *The Royal Team,* are introduced. The Half-Orc tries to ignore all the noise as he retrieves a bundle of dry leaves from a pouch. He hands them to Wake and orders him to, "Chew these slowly. Try not to swallow the juice. Let it sit in your mouth for as long as possible and then spit it out."

The announcer finishes, "... the newest team on Tour, *Monsters To Believe In.*" *What?* The Half-Orc thinks angrily.

"That is us," the Fate says proudly. "Do you like our new Team name? I thought of it all by myself."

"Do you take enjoyment in torturing me?" Monster doesn't like the name one bit. *Why does he always got to be like this?*

"It is a great name, is it not? Everyone else names themselves after something gallant or noble—after some hero or champion from their favorite tale. But I wanted a name that really described us."

He looks Monster in the eye. "We are what we are, and what we are here to do is defeat them all. And if they are a bunch of heroes ... well, who better to beat them than a bunch of monsters!

"Besides, we are here to change things."

CHAPTER 45
SENSE
[SARANGHAE MEMORIAL STADIUM]

"You're going to have to race two legs," Sense tells the Captain.

The Fate grew up on the shores of western Wysteria. Everyday, he would dive deep into the ocean's waters in search of its bounty. He may not be as fast as Wake in the water, but he's close enough. He'll just have to race two legs of the Course; not too uncommon of a thing.

They'll just have to request a transporter carriage to carry him between the two legs. Even though they didn't reserve one earlier, the officials keep a spare for just such emergencies.

"Way, the battles that you cannot fight—I will fight for you. All you have to do is get better," the Fate tells a miserable Wake.

The Whirlpool is the first leg and the Obstacle Course the last. It should be easy enough to arrange transport between the two. Sense reassures everyone as much.

"I'm sorry," Wake tries to say, not realizing everyone is already gone. Sense hooks one arm underneath him and nods for Poe to do the same.

"We can't leave you alone like this. You're coming with us to the official's table."

"I'm sorry, but ... unfortunately, the other team has already reserved the transport," the official tells them. Sense looks over the other team's roster. *They changed their lineup at the last minute. The Princess won't even be out there.* "But they don't even need it. That's not fair."

"They reserved it. If you want to use it, you'll have to ask for their permission. I'm afraid the spare is out of commission." The rules are clear. Sense knows better than to argue with the official.

"Let's try asking," Wake says before bending over and heaving. His stomach is already long emptied, so there's no real mess. Poe tries his best to help prop him back up.

"Okay, let's try," Sense says without much hope. *Still, there must be another way. I have to think of something.*

They hurry over to the other side of the field. Once there, they find the Princess in the Royal Box surrounded by her many retainers.

"Princess, could you please release your claim on the transporter carriage?" Wake asks as they try to hold him up.

She doesn't even look at them. "You very well know that I can do no such thing."

"But don't you want to win fair and square?" Wake begs, shrugging his friends off and falling to his knees. "I made a mistake—a big mistake. This is all my fault and if we have the transporter, at least, then, it would be somewhat fair."

The Princess turns away from the groveling boy. "My answer is no. Please do not ask me again."

Wake is silent as they escort him back to the official's table. Sense wants to say something to comfort his friend, but nothing he can think of sounds any good. And for once, it's probably a good thing Poe can't.

The bard's face changes from angry to worried and back again with each step. The scoreboard shows they have little time before the horn blows.

"Is there any other way?" Sense pleads with the official.

"I wish I could help, but there's no way around it," the Head Official says. "Without the transport, once he's off the course, he's out."

What to do? What to do? "But if he stays on the course, he's fine?" he asks. *We're almost out of time,* the clerk realizes, his chest pounding harder than is good for him.

"Sure, kid," the official laughs. "As long as he doesn't touch or interfere in any way with the other racers."

"Great, thank you."

"Hey, kid, I guess just finishing means a lot to you guys. Good luck."

"Oh no, we race to win."

"Captain, you have to run the whole course," Sense says.

"I understand." He doesn't even blink an eye.

Nothing surprises him, which doesn't surprise Sense. "You're allowed to stay on the course, but you cannot touch or interfere with anyone in any way."

The Fate shrugs. "I will do as you say, Sense."

"I sent Poe for your Light Boots. He'll bring them to the start of the Light Course. I have to go now and let the others know, too."

Sense makes his way towards the service path that acts as a shortcut between legs for nonparticipants. And for the first time he notices their opponent.

The opaque skin between her fingers and toes mark her as at least partially Gilled, however, her full head of hair and bronzed skin make it obvious she's not pure.

But there are no Gilled, half or pure on Tour this year. The Princess must have brought her in just for Relay. This new information may throw off his latest calculations. He thinks back to the roster he saw earlier and realizes there was another name that he didn't recognize.

He passes right next to the Whirlpool. It reminds him of a gigantic stone well, full to the brim. Slowly, the waters begin to swirl as if stirred by a giant spoon. In moments, it becomes a full-fledged vortex, ready to swallow any swimmer not strong enough to swim against its current.

"Captain, good luck!" he yells. "If anyone can do this, it's you!"

The Fate waves back. "Is that what your calculations say?"

"No, it's what my heart says."

"I always thought your heart may be stronger than they say, but I did not know it talked, too." Sense can't tell if it's a joke. The Fate's a funny fellow, but Sense can't ever remember him telling a joke before, at least, on purpose.

The Fate kicks off his boots and readies himself to dive.

"3, 2, 1 ... Go!" A horn blares and the crowd erupts. The very first game of the Grand Finale is officially underway.

The two swimmers dive into the Whirlpool and are quickly swallowed by its turbulent waters. Stroke after stroke, they swim with all their might towards the center of the maelstrom, their valiant efforts barely adding to the force of the current propelling them towards its eye.

Just before she gets swallowed into its depths, the Half-Gilled girl shoots out of the water, her arms pinned to her side like a hawk diving upwards. At the apex of her leap, she reaches out and grabs one of the rings hanging above the swirl.

The young clerk watches as the Fate mimics her movements exactly.

The most dangerous part is over, but now the hard part begins: swimming out, against the whirlpool's current.

Sense explains the new plan to Monster. He understands at once and promises to relay the message to Riser when he reaches the next leg. Monster doesn't look worried at all. Instead, he goes back to his stretching, reaching down and grabbing his toes. His bare toes ... *Monster's used to running around barefoot, but the Fate will have to go barefoot, too. I should've thought of that. I should've grabbed his regular boots.*

The Half-Gilled girl climbs out of the Whirlpool and passes the ring. She flops onto her back, gasping to catch her breath. The Fate pulls himself out of the water, not too far behind. He hands Monster the ring and they're off. *He's breathing pretty hard already.*

Sense is back on the service path. He won't have time to stop and explain everything to Riser, which should be fine. But he has to make it to Shine in time. Even if Poe gets there with the Captain's boots first, the bard won't be able to explain a thing.

Sense jogs towards the end of the service path. He can see the bottom of the Sheer Cliff and the lift that will lead him to its top. His legs are already weary and with each step, each breath becomes more and more difficult.

But it's his heart that worries him most. It beats so hard it scares him. *He thinks it's stronger than they say. And right now I have to believe that, too. I have to make it to the lift in time or all he's doing is for nothing.*

The service path is straight and level compared to the hills and twists of the Long Race Course. Even then, he barely makes it before the racers. He's gasping as he enters the lift. *I wouldn't have been able to do that even a month ago*, he thinks, proudly. Before he can get too full of himself, he sees their opponent handing off their ring.

The Royal Team's climber tucks the brass ring into his waistband and begins flying up the cliff side. He darts from one handhold to another, flying between impossible distances with ease. Monster barrels in afterward with the Fate matching him stride for stride. The Half-Orc yells out what's going on as he reaches forward to pass the iron ring.

Riser grabs it without a word and attacks the rock face. As Sense watches her flutter from one handhold to the next, he can't help but be reminded of a hummingbird flitting between flowers.

It's then that Sense notices just how jagged the rocks along the cliff really are. He winces as he looks down to see the Fate scurrying after her. By now, the announcer has caught on to what's happening. "Folks, *Monsters To Believe In* are not only keeping up with the rank one *Royal Team*, but one of them is attempting to run the whole race by himself." The already rowdy crowd roars even louder as it dawns upon them just what they are witnessing.

The lift stops and he jumps off. Poe is there holding a pair of boots. *Thank god he made it in time with the Captain's Light Boots.*

He gives Poe a huge hug of joy. *Something was weird about that*, but he has no time to think about it as he watches *The Royal Team*'s climber pulling himself up over the top.

It's just as Sense thought; he's a ringer, too. *I've never seen him before. He may even be a Tripper from the World Circuit—a real pro.*

"Shine, Captain has to run the whole course. It's the only way. You have to let him follow you exactly." Even with the short rest on the lift, he's barely able to spit it all out. "But you still have to go your very fastest, or we don't have a chance."

"We're not too far behind. I'll lose him if I go too fast."

"No, you have to go faster than you've ever gone before. I know the Captain will keep up. Believe in him. It's the only way." Sense nods to the other team's Tripper. "He's a Pro-Racer from the World Circuit."

"But ..." The other Light Tripper takes off. His first step explodes in a boom. The sounds of his footsteps follow after. *This is not good, he realizes. Even Shine doesn't always hit that speed on her first step.*

Riser is there in a heartbeat. She flies towards them and with the last of everything she has, she hands off the ring. Right behind her is their Captain, who jumps onto his backside as Poe shoves the Light Boots onto his feet.

"Go," the Fate shouts, leaping to his feet, covered in sweat. *I've never seen him look like this. He never gets this tired, Sense worries.*

"Faster than you've ever raced before. It's the only way." Sense shouts, but she's already gone with a boom, a second one stuttered just behind. The Fate is so close to her they are nearly touching. *Don't touch her or we'll be disqualified,* he wants to say, but it's too late, they are gone. The sound of Poe crying brings him back to reality.

When he looks down, the bard is sitting there, his hands covered in blood. *Fail me. I really should have brought him his regular boots earlier.*

CHAPTER 46
KASE
[OBSTACLE COURSE, SARANGHAE MEMORIAL STADIUM]

K ase counts his heartbeats. They rate at which they beat is perfect.

He tests the wind. It is at his back—perfect.

He feels loose, warm, ready. Today, he will be perfect.

The Best of the Best looks over at the empty space where his opponent should be. *Does that fool really expect to run the whole course?* he wonders in disgust. *Just what is he thinking?* Kase has the top four times this year, his fastest being the best in a decade.

And, it's not by accident. In Kase Shake's backyard there is an exact replica of the Obstacle Course, one he built with his own two hands. Each morning he ran it; twice on weekends. He knows this course inside and out—every step, trick, shortcut and pitfall. All the best of the rest can do is dream of coming in second. *Even him ...*

Just the existence of the Troublemaker annoys him beyond words, but right now, the Princess comes in a strong second. *When will she realize that victory without honor is no victory at all?* Bringing in these other racers is something he would never have considered or even now condones. *That's why she didn't tell me until just before the race. I'd rather lose ...* But he will do what he is tasked with. There is no honor in refusing.

As the racers come into view, he takes a look at the scoreboard. *At this pace, we're going to shatter the record.*

In that moment, he sees the ridiculous. It's hard to really make them out. They're nothing more than streaks, but the twin streaks on the other side are actually closing the distance. *We had almost a ten-second head start, and they're actually going to catch the best Pro Racer the Princess could find.*

He readies himself, crouching low, his hand stretched out behind him, ready to explode forward as soon as the ring touches his palm. Among his many titles, he's always been particularly proud to be known as the Perfect Anchor.

He hears someone come to a stop beside him. It doesn't surprise him that it's not the Pro. He knew it would come down to this, *me versus him.* He feels a mixture of dread and anticipation. Kase Shake chooses the later and promises himself, *I will not let him beat me. No matter what, this I vow.*

"Shine, down!" the Fate screams, unable to stop. The fool boy manages to somehow leap over the fair girl as she sprawls onto her belly. The sight of him is loathsome, though, Kase can't help but admire how the two work as one. If they had so much as brushed against one another, this would have been over.

Before he even lands, the Fate pulls off both Light Boots in one swift motion. He lands and receives his ring just before Kase feels one pressed into his own palm.

The Perfect Anchor bursts out the gate, quickly, pulling ahead. He runs with a natural smoothness, each step familiar and accounted for. The Fate jerks forward, a reckless fool, scrambling on all fours with the ring between his teeth.

The crowd is so loud even Kase has trouble ignoring the clamor of their cheers. It doesn't matter that the whole world is watching. He'd want to beat the Troublemaker just as much if there wasn't a soul in the stands.

They approach the first obstacle, the Web. Kase leaps on to the closest vertical thread and climbs forward, careful to avoid the sticky horizontal ones. When the thread he is on comes to an end, he jumps to another and continues on to the top.

As he gets to the Pumpkin Roll, he counts his steps and hits the Jump Pad perfect, sending him soaring to the sweet spot atop a round pumpkin, which is twice as tall as he is. Underneath him, it begins to roll ever so slowly. But with each passing step, he forces it faster and faster.

Somehow, the Troublemaker is still beside him, trying to match Kase's grace with his own desperation. He can't keep this up, not against the Chosen One.

As he nears the end of the runway, he leaps off the giant pumpkin just before it splatters itself against a wall of stone. The crowd screams in delight as chunks of pumpkin rain down onto those close by.

Three long strides and he reaches the base of a towering Beanstalk. He grabs a leafy handhold and pulls himself up and in no time he is at its very tip, high above the crowds. He grabs on tight and leans back with all his might. Soon, the whole Beanstalk is swaying back and forth. On the third swing, he throws himself forward and leaps.

He lands safely on the next platform, which immediately begins to fall away beneath him. He leaps to the next and the next, each platform smaller than the one before.

As much as he makes each movement seem effortless, his opponent matches each step with his own negligent style. *Is he too ignorant to know when he's outmatched? He can't luck his way through this next one, though,* he thinks, leaping off the final platform.

Kase aims for the small dot, impossibly far below. He takes an instant to look over at the Troublemaker, who has the audacity to smile back. *Fail him! I hate that guy!*

He focuses on the fast approaching jump pad below. At this speed, if he's off by even a finger's width, he'll be launched into one of the many surrounding nets.

The Chosen one hits it dead center. He glides upward, graceful as smoke in the wind. At the very apex of his jump, he snatches the first of many rings hanging from a thick rope that leads all the way to the final platform.

Next to him, the Fate flies past, just missing his own handhold. Kase Shake catches a glance of his rival falling. He almost feels a tinge of regret knowing that the Fate is out of the race.

Gaining momentum with each swing, he flies forward from one ring to the next. The thick cable holding the row of hanging rings sways back and forth with the force of his passing.

Suddenly, the crowd erupts. Their screams reverberate through the whole stadium. *He must have gotten lucky and hit the Jump Pad a second time, but still ...*

Kase almost hurries, giving up a little of his finesse. *Don't rush,* he reminds himself. *You know what the perfect pace is. Any faster just leads to mistakes.*

The spectators are in such an uproar it begins shaking even the Course itself. It doesn't matter what that fool does. *This race is mine!*

He reaches the last of the ropes before realizing the cause of the clamor. The Fate has somehow managed to get on top of the cable itself, bypassing the hanging rings all together. The fool is sprinting along it like a tightrope.

I should've known better than to count him out. But there's not enough Course left for him to make up the distance. Besides, no matter what he does, he can't beat the Shake Roll. These are Kase's personal finishing steps, the ones everyone tries to imitate. But no one can.

The Chosen One leaps from the final ring, launching himself at the perfect trajectory to land on the marble platform. Next to him, he hears the desperate footsteps on the other cable and a sudden twang as his opponent also leaps.

Neck and neck, they fly through the air. *I couldn't have asked for a better ending,* Kase thinks, preparing himself for his favorite move. It is nothing fancy, just the fastest conceivable way to reach the finish.

In one elegant movement, he tucks himself into a ball and flips once in midair. By doing so he maintains all his momentum, not even having to pause to land. With his legs still tucked close to his body, he feels the slick marble dais below him as he gently rolls forward. At the exact right instant, he straightens his legs with all his might, catapulting himself forward with uncanny speed. It's a beautifully simple maneuver, but there is no feasible way to finish the final few steps faster than the Shake Roll.

As he comes to a stop, he can barely hear the buzzer sound over the cheers of the crowd. He raises his arms high in victory. *Finally, I did it! I beat him!*

To the Chosen One's surprise, he finds the Fate grinning next to him. He looks up at the scoreboard to check his team's time on the Course—a full five seconds faster than the all-time record.

When he looks at their individual times, he sees that he beat the Fate by less than a second. He doesn't begrudge his opponent a close finish.

Then he sees the other team's total time, *The Royal Team's* is a half second slower than their opponents. Even though he just ran the perfect race, it wasn't enough. *How could I forget … they handed off first.*

He lowers his arms. The announcer shouts, "MONSTERS TO BELIEVE IN WIN! *Monsters* win in it with a history making time! Can you believe it?"

This can't be happening. Failing Fate! I hate that guy!

CHAPTER 47

SIR GROCK
[FRONT ROW, SARANGHAE MEMORIAL STADIUM]

Sir Grock Hardrime jumps out of his seat, screaming with the rest of the crowd. Even, a worldly gentleman such as himself can't help but get caught up in all the excitement. The race was simply one of the most thrilling he's ever seen.

The young clown put on a magnificent performance—truly remarkable, borderline unbelievable. The boy somehow ran every leg of the relay himself and put his team in position to win it all. With a time like that, Sir Hardrime doubts any of the following teams will even come close.

Drama; the boy has a knack for it. At the end there, it seemed as if he was surely done for. At least, until he jumped onto the cable and began running across it as only a true acrobat could.

His opponent was clearly a generational talent himself. The anchor of *The Royal Team* executed a perfect dismount and roll, not losing an iota of momentum. Yet, the remarkable clown somehow slipped past him, literally.

Arms thrashing in the air to maintain his balance, the boy wasn't even able to land squarely. *Instead, he slid the final few paces across the marble platform on a blood-covered foot. Amazing, truly amazing!*

What an act of sheer determination. *Such is the margin between victory and defeat*, Sir Hardrime thinks.

Suddenly, he remembers something of much more importance than the race's miraculous ending.

He tugs on the sleeve of the silently cheering giant next to him. "Kutz, you saw her, didn't you?" It isn't surprising that the behemoth is caught up in all the excitement. The Scourge has officiated more than his fair share of matches over the years. The large man nods his head.

"Let's go. We don't want to lose her again," he says to the mute giant. Kutz retrieves his hat, which must have fallen off during the excitement and nods.

"She looked healthy, didn't she? I've known her all her life, and this must be the first time I've seen her show care about anything. I think she's been doing just fine."

CHAPTER 48

BROTHER MONSTER
[SEVEN CORNERS INN, SARANGHAE]

Monster finishes wrapping the Captain's feet. Small cuts cover the left one, which may cause some mild discomfort, but should heal quickly enough. The right one, however, is much worse—with a single large gash, running from heel to mid-foot. *Thank goodness they sterilize the Field; at least there's no chance of infection. Even so, how could he be so reckless? People feel pain for a reason. It's for their own good.*

Wake is still suffering from cramps, but he won't stop apologizing. As much as there is reason for celebration, the mood of the group is somber. Except for, of course, their beaming Captain.

"One down, two more to go," he says, not understanding everyone's worry. "I do not need all of this bandaging. Just rub a little dirt in it and I will be fine."

The worst part about it all is the fool is actually serious. "Enough! When it comes to anybody's well being, I have final say." Monster tells him.

The Fate nods reluctantly.

"I've stitched up the deepest cut and applied ointment to the others. If you are careful and stay off your feet for a day or two, they have a chance of healing enough to continue competing."

The Fate throws his hands up in celebration. Everybody else joins him.

"But," Monster interrupts, "Absolutely no putting pressure on them. That means no walking, no standing, and absolutely no training for the next couple of days."

To everyone's surprise, the Fate actually follows doctor's orders, except for the one to stay in bed. But Monster lets that one slide. Their Captain hasn't been sleeping in one of the many plush feather beds provided by the inn, anyway.

He's been camping out in the courtyard ever since they first arrived. And even though winter is here, Poe and Wake have been joining him out there, as well. Brother Monster can't complain; having to only share the room with Sense is pretty nice.

As fortune would have it, they raced on the first day of competition. It takes another couple for the rest of the field to all get their shot at beating their time. With the additional days of rest, the Fate's feet heal well enough to avoid any worry over reopening any wounds. *He was lucky ... this time. But he can't keep acting so recklessly.*

The days go by quickly. While the Fate rests, the rest of them continue to train. Afterward, Monster spends most of his free time exploring the culinary offerings the big city has to offer. He's still under Captain's orders to match Riser, bite for bite.

He grumbles about it, but it is just an act at this point. The reality is, it's him who's now dragging the Daughter around. From one end of the capital to the other, they search for new tastes. She complains about it loudly, but always listens intently as he describes the history and makeup of each dish. As long as the portions are large and the dish contains some sort of meat, she seems happy enough.

This particular afternoon they are visiting a particularly hard to find noodle cart. He wonders if the trouble they went through searching for it is adding to how delicious it tastes. As the Half-Orc slurps up the last of his broth, he looks over to see the Daughter has barely eaten anything at all.

"Riser, are you feeling well?"

"I'm fine, why are you even asking?" She stirs the noodles in her still full bowl. Despite their difference in sizes, Monster has never once finished his plate first.

Grunting seems like the safest answer.

Finally, she looks up and says, "Can I ask you something?"

"Sure."

She puts down her spoon and takes a deep breath. "You know how I'm always saying I'm the strongest Daughter?"

Monster nods.

"Well, that's true and all, but I can't claim to be the strongest from Silla."

He's more than surprised to hear her admit such a thing. That's quite out of character for his dining partner.

"You know about Gregory's House, right?" Monster nods again. He's learned more of Silla than he would care to admit with each passing meal.

"The current Alcendor In-Training ... well, the truth is ... he's beaten me." she tells him, staring into her bowl. "Well, aren't you going to say anything?"

He shakes his head.

"Do you understand what I'm even telling you?" She raises her voice, but lowers it just as quickly. "Even if I am First Daughter, I'm not the strongest in Silla. It's the first time ever that the First Daughter has lost to someone from Gregory's House!"

Even though the concept is foreign, maybe even trivial to him, he understands just how difficult something like this must be for her to admit.

"He's beaten me more than once," Riser says. "Do you know how unforgivable that is?"

Monster looks down at his empty bowl and shakes his head, wondering just who it is she can't forgive.

"It's never happened before!" she tells him. Monster tries his best to look understanding, but just ends up baring his fangs.

"I won't begrudge him. Daisho Sixblades is skilled, but ..."

"I understand. You're the mightiest Daughter. You should be the strongest in Silla. I don't know much, but I know this much: if it's involves a match between you and anybody ... I'd bet on you, any day," Monster says. "If I wasn't against gambling, of course."

"Yeah?"

"Yeah," he answers. "I thought you were strong when we first met, but you're even stronger now. You may not think that anyone has noticed, but I've noticed how you've been sneaking off to practice alone all this time. I don't know where you've been going or what you've been up to, but I do know that you come back exhausted ... and smiling.

"He might have beaten you once, even many times, but I know this: the next time you face him, he doesn't stand a chance."

Riser cracks a half-hearted smile and nods to herself. "Good, 'cause he just joined *The Royal Team*. We'll probably see him before all's said and done."

"Good." Monster reaches over and takes the bowl of cold noodles from his friend and orders her a new one with double meat.

"You should try a bowl while it's piping hot. Do not let something you cannot change like the past distract you from enjoying the present."

"You sound like ..."

"I know, I know. But please don't say it."

CHAPTER 49

MASTER OF THE DARK WIND

[TRAINING GROUNDS, SILLA]

That girl never ceases to amaze her. It only took the Azurian from the Slate a couple of weeks to grasp the basics. And already, the girl moves like a mirage. *Though, it will be years before she truly masters it*, the Master of the Dark Wind reassures herself. *Still ...*

"Enough! We are done for today." Her student makes her jealous as much as proud. Even more, it stirs something deep within in her. A memory of a feeling, a feeling that the world holds wonders.

Even, the Outcast Daughter has caught word of it by now. It's all anyone talks about these days: how the current First Daughter's Team came out of nowhere to win the first event.

The stories are enough to make her want to see it for herself, this Fate and his teammates—especially the Half-Orc. A smile plays across her lips and she spies her student looking at her strangely.

The Master of The Dark Wind was once on a team that came out of nowhere to win it all. In fact, she made it all the way to the Twin Isles of Ascecia during her pilgrimage. She fought the last Orc Chieftain himself, but the journey ended only in disappointment. She came back to a home grown foreign, with questions that she could not answer.

Still, the infatuation has never gone away. *I must see this Half-Orc for myself.*

"Ieiri, would you like to go see this Fate of yours?"

The girl eyes her warily, but her answer is desperate, almost a plea. "Yes, but ..."

"If we leave tonight, we may have a chance of catching the conclusion of the second set of games. If they make it that far, that is." Enada points to her pack. "I packed last night. Go gather your things and we'll depart upon your return."

A thousand questions flash across the girl's face, but she simply asks, "Why?"

"The same reason anyone does anything ... I just want to."

CHAPTER 50

BROTHER MONSTER
[MIDNIGHT AUDITORIUM, SARANGHAE]

"As Captain, I should go first," the Fate declares before their first King's Corridor Match. It's a very special event, one reserved strictly for the Grand Finale, and Monster's just learned its full history and rules a few of days ago.

The game is named for a famous battle between twin brothers, both vying for a kingdom long ago forgotten. The war was said to have started on a battlefield between armies as evenly matched as their prospective kings.

It ended, however, in a hallway so narrow that only one from each side could face each other at a time. As one would fall, he was replaced by another, and so on and so on, until finally only two brothers stood, and in the end ... neither.

King's Corridor pays homage to the tale. The hallway is long gone, replaced by a large ring, but the concept remains much the same: only one Crier from each team fights until a side has none.

It's not as popular as Flag, which has always been the favorite of the Three Kingdoms, but it is a close second. The fact that it's the only event to take place indoors, surrounded in darkness, only adds to its pageantry.

According to Sense, the order in which each team fights is as important as the skill and talent of its members. It often leads to a game before the actual game, one in which each side tries to guess the other's lineup and how to best match it.

But the Fate doesn't care about any of that.

As soon as Monster cleared him to fight, the Fate began insisting on going first. There isn't much anyone can say.

Monster wonders what the auditorium would look like with the lights on. Would it be just as fancy as all the other buildings in the city? It's far too dark to tell. He can't even see how many there are in the crowd, but he can hear them—ten thousand hushed whispers that echo back and forth through the darkness.

He shifts his weight once again trying to find a comfortable compromise with the far too small chair. *Why couldn't they just have benches like they do for every other event? Just because we fight alone, doesn't mean we have to sit that way also.*

But he realizes that they do. There is a title for each seat and they determine the order that they will fight in. He can't remember any of the silly names, just that the last one is called King. Though, the Captain doesn't care at all about that; all he wants to do—is go first.

Suddenly, a single light shines down illuminating the large ring before them. He can make out the shadowy forms of their opponents on the other side. They look rather comfortable in their chairs.

The announcer says something, but he can barely hear it. The crowd, however, does and they cheer—more loudly for the Fate than even his more well-known opponent. *I did everything that I could. His wounds are more than sufficiently healed. He'll be fine as long as he doesn't do anything very, very stupid.* The thought scares him more than it should.

To Monster's relief, the Fate dispatches the first and even the second of his opponents with relative ease. The third is a Healer and he uses his Unleash. The crowd likes that. The fourth is no easy matter, however. And by the end of it, the Captain is limping, favoring his stitched foot. Already having faced three opponents, the Captain struggles against the worthy opponent.

In the end the Fate prevails, but the cost is high. Crimson footprints cover half the ring.

From the sidelines, they begin to beg and plead for him to submit. He's more than done his fair share. Riser curses him and Rachel sobs for him to stop. As his doctor, Monster tries to order him to leave, but he knows it will do no good. *The fool doesn't know how to quit.*

But the crowd loves it, bloody footprints and all. By the time the other team's King is down, the circle is covered in them.

After inspecting his stitches, Monster has to tell him the truth. It is not good for him to fight on it, but to do so will cause no further injury. The stitches held. Only after the Fate agrees to be King for the next match do they begin talking to him again.

The next round, Riser makes it to the fourth member of the opposing squad, but it takes Wake to finish him.

The semifinals end in a similar fashion. For the rest of the afternoon, the championship match for King's Corridor is all anyone else can talk about. The Fate once again begins to insist on going first. *If he won't listen to common sense, I'll have to make him.*

"Something is very wrong. I cannot move my legs," the Fate says.

"It's the tea I gave you," Monster says. "You gave me no choice. You needed to be stopped for your own good."

"I am still going first," the Fate declares. "I do not wish to miss another match. I only get so many, you know?"

"That's fine. Just realize you're paralyzed from the waist down," Monster says. "And with the amount of Sandman's Root that was also in there, you'll be fast asleep, sooner rather than later."

"Monster," the Fate says in his most threatening voice. "I will no longer drink tea of your making."

"I'm sorry, it's for your own good." He is genuinely sorry, but there are some things more important than a game. "If you hadn't insisted on going first this wouldn't have been necessary."

The Fate tries to stifle a yawn. "This is not enough to stop me."

"I know," Monster says. "Can I at least have the white flag?"

"No, that is for the Captain to hold and I am the Captain," he replies stubbornly.

"I give you my word that I won't throw the flag unless absolutely necessary."

The Fate stares back at him, trying to decide what to do.

"Look, I believe we can win this. I believe we have a chance at the Triple Threat Feat. I promise that I will do everything I can to see that we achieve victory. But you can't go out there and have another setback. There's still a lot of competition left. We need you."

"Yaksok?" the Captain asks, eyelids already drooping.

"I vow it," Monster promises, sticking out his hand. The Fate pulls out the white piece of cloth and hands it over.

CHAPTER 51
PRINCESS

The darkness becomes her. She is surrounded in it, her champion to her right, her keeper to her left, and behind them, the rest of her people. Still, she feels alone. *Maybe, someday ... after this is all over, they'll understand.*

The crowd has gotten so quiet that the pitch-black auditorium seems to go on forever. She knows why they hold their breath and it's not for her Team.

This year's Grand Finale is the most exciting in recent memory. No year before has a team come out of nowhere to cause such a stir. More times than not, the bet-makers are spot on, but this year, they didn't even place odds on the no-name team making it this far.

The Relay Race is one thing—many a year a specialist team takes the Race. But for the very same team to fight so far into King's Corridor is more than unexpected. Everyone wants to see if *Monsters To Believe In* can pull off another miracle. Almost everyone.

The Princess sits front and center in the Royal Box. Beside her, Kase Shake fumes in silence until he can take it no more.

"I should be out there."

"It's a game of styles and matchups. You know this better than anyone," the Princess tells him. "I told you before, if the Fate was to go last, that you would be in. But if Esperanza was to be King that we would go with this lineup. And I just happened to find out that the Troublemaker will be going first."

"Still, it makes no sense for me not to be out there. I *can* beat any of them one-on-one."

"Of that, there is no doubt, however ..." She knows there is no use in explaining it again. He'll never accept it. But she is the leader of *The Royal Team* and it is up to her to do what is best for them all. "The tacticians have run every scenario imaginable. This lineup has the highest chance of success: 99.9%, to be exact. Victory is virtually guaranteed.

"It is unfortunate that you're not as good with a sword as you are with your spears," she adds. "We need someone who can wield *it* as our King."

"Whatever," Kase huffs. "This still feels wrong."

She looks over at her one true friend. "I'm sorry, Kase. This is the way it has to be." *I can't risk losing either: the match or your confidence.*

Finally, a huge spotlight pierces the darkness. All eyes are drawn to the center ring. The announcer's voice echoes through the stadium. "Introducing, the lowest ranked team ever to make it to the Finals once again. The one, the only *Mooooooooonsters To Believe In!* First up, their Captain, the one who ran it all, the Faaaaaaaaaaaate."

Wake and the Half-Orc carry the Fate onto the battlefield upon their shoulders. When the uplifted boy raises his arms high, the crowd cheers wildly. *Since when did he become such a showman ...*

"And representing the best that Wysteria has to offer, the Chosen Few, handpicked by their leader, the Princess herself, *The Rooooooooyal Team!* In their initial slot is one half of this year's Top Duo, the Conflagrator, Cales Cent"

The crowd applauds politely, but the Princess is surprised at the few boos that are mixed in. *That's never happened before*, she thinks. *Not that it matters.*

A wisp of a boy wrapped in robes of red enters the ring. He stretches his arms out wide and sends out a burst of flames. For that, the crowd oohs and aahs.

The Fate draws his Stick and holds it before him. The official begins counting it down. Cales Cent assumes a defensive stance and waits. So does his opponent. Neither makes a move even long after the horn has blown.

After a long moment of staring, the Conflagrator asks, "Aren't you going to do something?"

The Fate just looks at him and yawns. He actually looks sleepy. *Something is wrong here. This is not like him, at all.*

The Fiery Mage was prepped to expect an aggressive offensive. This lack of action confuses him. But Cales Cent is not one to be thrown off by the unpredicted. The Conflagrator and his partner have reigned supreme over two-on-two matches all year. He is more than experienced.

Cales conjures a ball of fire. He tosses it at the smiling boy, who deflects it with a swipe of his Stick.

For his next attack, Cales summons two and throws them in quick succession. The first is blocked, but the second actually grazes the Troublemaker.

"What are you doing?" the Princess shouts at her subordinate. "Just stick to the plan!"

"But I can beat him," Cales says. "Something funny is going on here. He hasn't moved at all."

"Do as you're told," the Princess commands.

The Conflagrator grumbles something underneath his breath, then sets himself on fire. "Sacrificial Flame: Blow to Kingdom Come!" the burning boy screams as the whole ring erupts into flames.

"Double Knockout," the announcer declares. The fires subside, revealing two spheres.

Even though, everything is going exactly as planned, the Princess can't help but feel as if something is not quite right.

"Second up for the The Chosen Few of *The Royal Team*, the other half of Wysteria's Top Duo, The Molten Kid, Crag Melti!" A large round boy bounds into the ring and clasps his hands together for his adoring fans. Even as he does, he closes his eyes and begins to chant a complicated verse.

"Chances are good that he'll finish the rest of them all by himself," the Princess says confidently. "And that shall be the last we hear of these so-called *Monsters*."

Kase snorts.

"Could you beat this combo?" she asks her champion. He doesn't say a word.

"And second up for *Monsters To Believe In*, The Water Knight, Wake Avenoy!" Wake is slow to enter, instead wasting his time checking on his fallen Captain. Even as he ensures the Fate is seated comfortably, Crag Melti finishes his chanting. A large boom erupts, filling the still burning ring with smoke.

The crowd, disappointed by the previous round, comes back to life as the smoke clears to reveal a gargantuan meteor floating in the middle of the flaming ring. The burning rock spins in place and opens its single monstrous eye.

Bolide the Colossus has entered into play. He can only be summoned under precise conditions. The Conflagrator didn't just sacrifice himself to take out the other team's Captain but to prepare the field for its arrival.

The audience gasps at the rare sight—an Unleash-level Summon. The humongous floating rock roars back at them, belching fire and spitting molten gravel.

The Princess, however, pays no attention to the living boulder. Instead, she turns her gaze to their opponent, Wake Avenoy. If he would've only paid more attention on entering the ring, instead, of focusing on the well-being of his Captain, he might've stood a chance.

He's lost before the fight has even started. For some reason, she expected more of him.

And for a moment, she remembers the look on his face before the race. *How could he even ask for something like that? He doesn't understand anything at all.*

Bolide roars again and she can feel the heat of its breath from even there. Summoned creatures of the Unleash-level are truly frightening. Their powers are equal to that of a full-fledged Crier. That's two versus one right there, but there are even more surprises awaiting Wake Avenoy. She almost feels sorry for him. *The choice was his.*

The other team's strategist, the young clerk, whispers something to Wake. Whatever it is, it won't be enough to help the Water Knight. Wake nods his head and summons a Shield of Water in each hand before diving headfirst into the inferno. *At least, he's intelligent enough to do that much.*

CHAPTER 52
WAKE
[BATTLEFIELD: TWIN KING'S CORRIDOR]

I have to get rid of the Molten Kid, but how? Wake wonders. He's actually making it sound easier than it really is and he knows it. Sense explained it all on the sidelines. Their strategist also told him that they have no chance ... unless he wins.

As soon as he enters the fiery ring, he realizes just how wise he was to have brought some Water in with him. Cales Cent's sacrifice did more than take out the Fate—it totally changed the battlefield, transforming it into a burning nightmare. There isn't a drop of useable moisture left in the whole area.

All he has is what he brought in: his two shields. Even under their protection, he's already beginning to burn. *My only chance is to keep running and dodging. The more I use my shields to block, the more Water I will use up.*

He knows what he has to do, but he still needs to find a way to get it done. For now, he has no choice but to dance. Fire and burning rock fly all around him.

The Molten Kid, cloaked in the flames his partner left behind, flings small meteors to no end. Bolide vomits a stream of lava that chases him like the line of a kite.

Even the flames of the field seem to lick at his every footfall. *I can't even hit the Molten Kid through his Cloak of Flames without my Water evaporating.*

At least, I'm not the one throwing up this time. He can't help but start to giggle at the thought.

Crag Melti, the Molten Kid sneers at him. "It's true, you really are daft, aren't you?"

There goes his smug look, at least. And even better, he stopped hurling those hot rocks for a moment. Wake laughs even louder. Facing a field of fire, a giant horror of molten rock, and an opponent who can hurl meteors without end are what he's up against.

He looks into the crowd and for a moment, his eyes fall upon the Royal Box and the girl that sits at its center, a girl who's looking at him just now. Time is still for an instant as their eyes lock. *Clear your head and find an answer! But there is no answer.* There's only what he has learned in the past month. *If I don't think I can then I ... no, we have no chance.*

"Is the heat getting to your head? It can do that, you know ..."

Even Bolide stops to stare at the sounds of him giggling. *Just win the moment, Way.* "When you're expected to lose, do the unexpected," he whispers to himself.

"What the hail are you mumbling, now?"

Without any moisture to draw upon, his 128's are useless. They're just weighing him down, so he takes them off. A flame licks his hand and singes his fingers. He quickly runs his hand though one of his watery shields to lessen the pain. He tucks his dripping fingers deep inside of one of his Battle Boots and flings it directly at the Molten Kid.

Crag Melti sidesteps the attack easily and laughs himself. "Man, I've seen some really desperate moves before, but I've never seen anyone so desperate as to throw a shoe. Just give up before you make any more of a fool of yourself. Your Water can't get past the heat. I'll vaporize your Water and melt your Ice into nothing."

Wake throws his other boot at him.

"Just finish him already!" the Princess yells from the stands.

The Molten Kid glares at her, then back at him. Then he begins to chant.

> "Heavenly fires
> Rain down on my enemies
> Obliterate all.

"Orange Summon: Meteor Swarm," the Molten Kid commands. *That sounds bad*, is all Wake can think.

Slowly, the dark above the ring begins to fill with tiny burning rocks. Wake tries to move out of the way, to be anywhere but there. But there's nowhere to go. Behind him is the edge of the ring, and an angry one-eyed behemoth holds its center.

He dodges the first and then the second wave of meteorites, but soon they rain down in all directions. The meteorites know no end, growing larger and more frequent with each passing moment. With every hit, his armor grows more faint. *I have to sacrifice one of my shields or I won't make it ...*

Wake tucks one shield behind him and blocks with the other. The scorching rocks explode as they smash against the Water.

It reminds him of the time he brought home some particularly interesting rocks he found in the river. His mother wasn't very pleased with the wet stones cluttering their already cramped home. On a lazy whim he disposed of them in the fireplace. How was he supposed to know that heating up the wet rocks too quickly would cause them to explode? *Sorry for the vase, Mom.* He thinks before realizing, *that might just work!*

As the meteorites stop falling, the flames come to life and reach toward him with deadly intent—just as Sense warned him they would. Ready, he jumps out of their way.

"You may as well come out, Cales Cent. I know you're still here." Things would've been much easier if he wasn't keeping his back to the edge of the ring from the very beginning. But he wasn't about to leave his back exposed after what Sense told him. Thanks to his friend's advice, he's still standing. *But I've already used up half my Water.*

From the flames rises the fiery form of a boy.

"How did you know?" says the living flame in the shape of Cales Cent.

"I didn't really, but our strategist guessed as much," Wake says, thumbing behind him at the grinning clerk. "He's watched every match this year and he happened to notice that every time you two ran into any real trouble, you'd resort to that Sacrifice Tech. And even though your body would be asleep on the sidelines, somehow the flames would conveniently strike out at the most opportune of moments—almost as if they were being controlled."

The fiery form scowls. "Congratulations on figuring out our little secret. It doesn't matter, though, since this will be the last match we ever fight."

Crag Melti, the Molten Kid reluctantly agrees. "But still, let's make him pay for figuring it out."

"Yeah, let's make him pay."

Wake just looks at them and smiles.

Two Weeks Before

"It's okay, guys. It's not as scary or crazy as it may seem," Wake tells them. "Just go slow at first and focus on a safe landing. The most important thing is making sure you don't twist an ankle or stumble."

Poe and Sensei look at him the way he must have looked at the Fate his first time down the slope. *If you think this is bad, wait until you have to do it with their eyes closed*, Wake thinks.

"Why are you smirking like that?" Sense asks him.

"Am I?" Wake tries not to laugh. "I'll see you guys at the bottom. Be careful to watch your step and good luck." He takes off down the mountain, trying not to show off too much. Behind him he can hear the Fate reassuring their more junior teammates.

Halfway down the steep slope, just as Wake closes his eyes and envisions his next leap, he hears a loud rumbling behind him. The ground beneath him shakes and a small rock rolls past him. He turns around and sees ...

"Landslide!" he screams. The Fate is barely ahead of the wall of rolling rocks ... with Poe and Sense tucked beneath each arm.

"Go! Wave Step!" the Fate yells at him as he leaps past. *The four of us jumping around here all at once must have disturbed the rocks above*, he thinks before activating his boots and sliding the rest of the way down.

"Is everyone alright?" he asks, catching up with his friends. *Thank goodness we had on our 128's*, he thinks, until he notices ...

"Fate, you don't have on your 128's?" he asks in confusion. That doesn't make any sense, though. He just saw his Captain move like a flicker, blurring in and out with each step.

The Fate releases his grip on Sense and Poe and shivers. He steps away from them and begins rubbing his legs. "I did not wear them today," he says.

"Then, how ..." Wake begins to ask.

"Barefoot Dash Step," the Fate says as if it's nothing. Wake's heard tales of it before, how the great warriors from long ago could do such things without Tears. But he never really thought those stories could be true.

"How's that even possible?" Wake asks.

The Fate looks at him for a long time before finally saying, "I will tell you how, but I want you to promise not to try it unless absolutely necessary."

Wake nods.

"In truth, you already know how," the Fate says, "The concept is the same as the one used to improve your Wave Step, just without boots. And over and over again."

That doesn't make any sense, Wake thinks. *If I tried to jump on flat ground while I thought it was really a slope, I would smash into the ground halfway through what I thought was my jump. It'd be like leaping into a wall ...*

But ... If I keep my feet tucked in tight, I would smash into the ground feet first. it would hurt like hail, but I would already be crouched in a perfect position to jump again. If I pushed off as hard I could just then ...

Wake looks at the Captain as he rubs his knees. *It's not even something any ordinary person would attempt. You really have to trick yourself into thinking the ground isn't there. But if you managed to— you just might be able to move the way he just did, so fast that someone watching couldn't even keep up with their eyes. It would just hurt a lot.*

That's why he doesn't want me to try, he thinks. *But he just did it, over and over again.*

Present

Wake grabs his remaining Shield of Water and tears it in two. "Blue Transform: Water Rapier, Water Buckler," he says, forming a much smaller, round shield and a thin blade of Pure Water.

I promised not to try unless absolutely necessary. And right now, it's necessary ...

"Want to see the impossible?" he says, all laughter gone.

His opponents wonder what he's talking about. Whatever it is, they decide they don't want any of it. Cales Cent disappears into the flames. Crag Melti begins his chant anew.

Wake closes his eyes and squats low. He imagines the slope he's jumped down a hundreds times until he can almost see it before him. And then he leaps. Before he smashes into the ground, he opens his eyes and braces for impact. The bottoms of his feet feel as if they've been struck by a gigantic mallet. His knees crack and his whole body quivers, but already he is thrusting forward with all his might.

First he's a blur and then a flash, then he disappears all together, only to appear once again in front of Bolide the Colossus. Behind him, flame and burning stone strike out at where he once was. *Barefoot Dash Step! I just really did it! But I'm not done yet.*

He thrusts the thin sword of Water deep into the living meteor. His Pure Water attacks would evaporate before striking the flames surrounding the two Criers, but Cales hadn't bothered cloaking Bolide in flames. Why would he? It's already a giant burning rock.

Wake's not exactly sure what's going to happen, but he has an idea. Whether that idea is actually possible is a whole other story.

Inside of Bolide, his Water begins to dissipate into something else—something, he's never even bothered trying to control before. Liquid and flowing is one thing, solid and hard as Ice another, but this ... this is too absurd to even imagine.

He tries to control the Steam.

If you can see it, you can do it. And for that split second he sees it, every single miniscule drop.

He can't quite control it, but he can keep it from escaping, from disappearing into nothing. Bolide the Colossus howls. Its mouth splits in two and the howl turns into a whimper. Inside of the monstrosity, something's wrong; it quivers and shakes—blinking molten tears, cracks form like so many empty veins where there should be none.

"You guys must have been better at listening to your mothers than I was," he says, cackling maniacally before diving out of the way.

Bolide the Colossus explodes into a million pieces. *Like a wet rock in the fire.*

The field is covered in smoke and flying chunks of dead meteor. The inferno still rages, but there's no longer a gigantic behemoth holding its center. Instead, there is his laughter.

"Waster! Waster!" the crowds chant. Wake's on his back, looking up at the half of the buckler that survived. It's all the Water he has left. He wants to lay there forever. But now, he sees a way. He gets up.

He's weary from all of the running and burning, his palms red and blistered from trying to direct the Steam. When he looks at the Two-on-Two Champions he sees it—fear. Why can't he stop laughing?

"One down, two to go," he says, dusting himself off. He doesn't know if he's faking it or if he really believes what is coming out of his mouth. Whichever it is, it really doesn't matter. He's already figured out his next move.

"What did you do to Bollie!" the Molten Kid cries, while his dumbfounded partner asks, "How did you just do that without 128's?"

They both look at him in disbelief. Cales Cent snaps out of it first. "It seems we took it too easy on you, but there's still no way you can touch me. Not as long as I am in this form."

Good, they don't quite realize what just happened.

The old Wake would have been inclined to believe the words of his opponent, but not this one.

The new Wake no longer dwells on a problem. Instead, he defines it, answers it, lays that problem to waste. He looks back at his teammates and gives them a crazy grin. *Everything is going as it should and everything will go as it should.* "I bet you two thought that I couldn't even scratch the big guy," he tells the top duo in the land. "Be prepared to be wrong, again."

"Tsk," utters the boy of Fire. He looks at his partner and says, "Leave this to me."

The Molten Kid retreats. The fiery form of Cales Cent floats slowly towards the center of the ring, all the while drawing in more and more of the flames around him. His blazing body swells larger and larger absorbing the fires burning the battlefield.

Cales Cent hovers menacingly in his new form as he cries out, "Fire Form: Flame Elemental!"

The towering pillar of flame reaches down with one massive arm and takes a swipe at the Water Knight. Wake dodges easily.

"Too bad you didn't get any faster," Wake giggles. "In fact, you just gathered all of yourself into one spot, which is just what I was trying to figure out how to do."

Cales Cent flaps once and then twice and is high above him, a fire floating in the darkness overhead. And then he dives. Wake stands his ground. *He thinks nothing can hurt him. That Water will just vaporize at his touch, that metal will pass right through him, but ...*

"No flame burns forever!" Wake yells. "Prepare to be wasted." *I really have to stop saying that.*

He holds up the tiny buckler and dissipates it with a single command. "Blue Transform: Steam Dagger!"

Using the heat of his adversary, he boils what remains of his Water into vapor. His vision blurs in concentration; he can barely see his target. Fortunately, it's a gigantic glowing flame. No one can control a million tiny droplets of Water all at once, it's insane to even try ... *I guess, I just may be a little mad, after all.*

Wake loses some of it, but not all. The little bit of Steam he manages to hold onto, he shapes into something sharp. Like a heron that spots the diving eagle too late to flee, but too brave to die, he calmly faces his attacker and waits. Instead of a long thin beak, it's a Dagger of Steam. All he has to do is hold it sure and straight.

The Conflagrator wails an awful battle cry as he dives. His mouth gapes so wide, it threatens to swallow his own face. And that's just what Wake takes aim for. *Keep your eyes open and look*, he thinks, even as his dagger pierces the fiery elemental. Cales Cent's final attack is earsplitting, but there is little more to his defeat than the dying sizzle of a flame.

"I guess Steam can be hotter than Fire," Wake says as the last of his Water disappears. Cales Cent's real body comes to life on the sideline with a scream and the battlefield stops burning.

Wake begins making his way towards the round boy, who backs up with each approaching step. When the Molten Kid runs out of room, he stops and says, "What are you doing? You don't even have anything left to fight with."

Wake leaps towards his opponent. He vanishes mid-step, landing next to one of the boots he threw earlier. From it, he pulls out the glob of Water he hid there for safekeeping. With it, he forms a second Dagger of Pure Water. The Molten Kid's eyes grow wide with fear. *He's just now realizing that he no longer has the flames of his partner cloaking him. He should've kept his guard up.*

The Molten Kid doesn't even try defending himself as the Water Knight leaps at him. Wake sticks the small blade in the boy's ear and again into his crumpled form. *That used to be me, but not anymore,* he thinks as he watches one of the top-ranked Criers in all the land fall before him. *Define, Decide, Do. That's all it takes. Well, I guess laughing doesn't hurt.*

So he does.

Is this really happening? Wake wonders, listening to the crowd chant his name. But it's only the voices of his teammates that really matter.

His head pounds as he comes back from that place. He never left the field, but for a moment he existed on a different level, a zone all its own. *That's where the Fate goes. No, it's where he lives,* he realizes, understanding his friend a little more.

"Ladies and gentlemen of Wysteria, the match is not even midway through and we've already witnessed a miracle. Can these no-name *Monsters* steal another one from *The Royal Team?* Not if our next Crier, Ossei of Bloodgrip, has anything to say about it. Please welcome Bone Sunder to the ring!" the loudspeakers announce.

Still basking in his victory, Wake barely acknowledges the small boy. His new opponent has no fancy weapons or anything else intimidating about him, whatsoever—except maybe the look in his eyes. The heat is gone and most of the moisture has returned. "Water Summon: Dual Falchions."

His head still swimming from his last victory, he can't decide what to do as the smaller boy walks towards him with his palms facing forward. Backing up seems ridiculous after everything he's just gone through. He slashes out at his opponent, but Ossei Bloodgrip ignores the attack and grabs ahold of Wake's wrist.

"Blood Clamp: Bone Breaker," the unassuming boy says. Wake instantly feels an ache where the boy grips his arm. He screams as the boy's grip grows tighter and tighter. When he looks down at his hand it is almost as blue as his Water. Just before the bones in his wrist shatter, his opponent stops and walks away.

Wake realizes he is in a Loser's Ball. When he looks around, he sees that someone from his side has thrown the white flag.

He was able to overcome so much, but after all that, he still lost. He lost his focus. He just let everyone down.

CHAPTER 53

BROTHER MONSTER

[BATTLEFIELD: TWIN KING'S CORRIDOR]

For the very first time, Brother Monster is beginning to see just what it's all about. He used to think that Tear Battling was just another frivolous way for the strong to show off. Now that he's come to care about those giving their all, he knows he's assumed too much.

That's not all he's been wrong about. He also once thought that healing was only about medicine and proper treatment. *But the wounds you can see are the easiest to heal*, he's realized. *The other ones, the ones that you can't see, that you don't even know you have— those require something more.*

Wake's wrist is fine. But by the look on his face, Monster can tell he is hurting, just not physically. The Half-Orc picks him up and gives him a monstrous hug. He tells his friend, "You did great out there. Just leave the rest to us."

It just makes Wake cry harder. All he can say through his tears is, "I'm sorry."

"You were wonderful, Wake. You have nothing to be sorry about," his sister tells him.

Riser comes over and adds, "Thanks for leaving some for the rest of us." She pats him on the back. *How did I not see it before? This is really what the Tournament is about*, Monster thinks as he watches everyone try to comfort their victorious yet fallen teammate. *It's not just some display of brute force, luck or foolery, but of determination, hard work and courage. One man's Will versus another. And where one man's Will is greater than just his own ... well, that just means he has good friends.*

I really have been a coward this whole time—afraid that someone like me could never have friends like this.

He looks at each of them, his gaze finally falling upon the Daughter. She's trying to look anywhere but towards the other side of the field where the boy on the throne watches her every move. *That must be him, Daisho Sixblades.*

The blaring of the Tear Speakers interrupts his thoughts. "Back and forth, expect the unexpected. Who knows what will happen this next round? If you have to relieve yourself, I'd suggest you hold it, because the two teams in the King's Corridor are dead even at the midway point. Next up for *Monsters* is the fairer Avenoy, Rachel of Ice Ridge, the holder of the all-time fastest time on the Light Course. Let's see how she fares in the ring!"

Wake looks up from his own disappointment to offer a word of encouragement for his sister. They all do.

As Rachel enters the ring, Monster studies her awaiting opponent. When he looks into the eyes of the small boy, he sees something unexpected: sadness. A sorrow that only comes from having to do what he must. Even though physically they could be no further apart, Monster is reminded of himself, his old self.

"Way ..." the Fate calls out. Wake rushes over to his side. "Way, you were awesome ..." he says before his eyes close again.

Monster leaves Wake in the care of their Captain and returns to the uncomfortable seat he's supposed to sit in. He catches Sense's eye and waves him over. "Tell me about the remaining three," he asks the young strategist, who seems surprised by his interest.

"I've never heard of this guy before. But it appears he has a serious advantage over Shine. Since he uses his bare hands, her Sun Orb will be useless."

"I was afraid of that," Monster says. "What of the other two?"

"The only one I know anything about is Stacy Iss. They call her the Perfect Draw. She's pretty much unbeatable. The best we can hope for is to force her to use her specialty and draw," Sense tells him. "All I've been able to learn of their King is his name, Daisho Sixblades."

So that really is him, Monster thinks, wondering just how Esperanza must feel.

Monster watches closely as the fighting begins. He has a bad feeling about this. Of all the different styles he's seen, this opponent uses the most reprehensible.

If he hadn't thrown the flag the round before, Ossei Bloodgrip would've surely broken Wake's wrist. He holds onto the white flag tightly.

Ossei Bloodgrip rushes Rachel. She holds her Sun Orb before her.

It does nothing. Ossei reaches his hand straight through the Orb and grabs her by the arm. "Blood Clamp: Bone Breaker."

The young strategist explains, "His hand passed right through because he isn't wielding any weapons. His hands are his weapons and they aren't Teared. He must be using a Blood Technique to strengthen the force of his grip."

Monster studies the Blood-User, trying to understand just how someone could sacrifice his own body to master such a Technique. Blood is the Physical Aspect of Dark Red. To make use of Blood in such a manner and at this age means he is sacrificing his future for the present. *How long has he been using Blood? How much of himself has he forfeited to master such a style?*

There's nothing Rachel will be able to do against this type of attack, but he gives her every opportunity to perform a miracle. He knows she's capable of something like that. But today is not that day. He throws the flag before it's too late.

Rachel comes off the field and sits down without a word. It's not hard to know what she's thinking. *She's holding it in. She doesn't even think she deserves to be comforted.*

Monster has been wronged more times than he'd care to admit, but all of those wrongs combined do not make him as angry as watching Shine sit there trying not to cry.

He picks up the white flag before making his way into the ring. *It's my turn now.*

The light washes over him as he steps into the ring. The stadium is louder than sin, so loud it feels like complete and utter silence. The announcer introduces him, but all he can hear is the word *Monster*, though, it doesn't sound as bad as it used to. When your friends call you something, whatever it is, you look forward to being called that.

I won't let that word define me. I'll change what it means instead.

Esperanza tries to comfort Rachel. "Styles make fights. Your honor is intact." Her words ring hollow. Similar words were said to her the last time she lost to that unforgivable boy from Gregory's House. The words didn't make a difference then and they don't make a difference now. Rachel hunches over in silence.

Riser leaves her Unnie with her brother and returns to her seat. She's familiar with Bloodgrip's Technique. *Monster has no chance. At the very best, he may draw,* though, she doubts he'll even accomplish that much. *What I really have to do right now is figure out a way to get past Stacy Iss.*

She finds Sense next to her, so she asks, "How can can the Perfect Draw be defeated?"

He just shakes his head. In some small way, she feels relieved—she won't have to dance with Daisho Sixblades, after all. When she remembers the look that Monster gave her as he entered the ring, she suddenly feels ashamed.

"Kick his ass, Monster!" she shouts.

He actually turns slightly and nods his head. *When did he grow a backbone?* she wonders.

Surrounded in darkness, Brother Monster enters the ring of light. He bows low to his undeserving opponent. Surprisingly, Ossei Bloodgrip returns the gesture.

It's a strange sight. On one end stands the tallest Crier on Tour, slumped forward and humble. On the other, erect and proud, is poised one of the smallest.

Monster strides towards the center of the ring and assumes his stance. *He looks good like that, almost like a real fighter.*

He stands tall, right foot forward, one hand above the other, palms facing his opponent. Looking at him like this, she realizes just how much bulk he's put on in the past weeks. *At least, he can thank me for that.*

The Blood-User eyes him warily, as if he's not ready to believe that his opponent is the Pacifist they say he is. Monster inches forward. Bloodgrip retreats step for step until the Pacifist stands at the dead center of the ring and beckons for his opponent to to attack. The smaller boy shakes his head.

Monster begins to chant something. Riser realizes it's all a farce. He doesn't use any Techs that require such chanting. But his opponent doesn't know this. Bloodgrip charges with a quickness so abrupt that his shadow strains to keep pace.

Monster, Disciple of the Doubting Palm, stands his ground and faces the oncoming boy. Serene and calm, no movement wasted, he knocks the smaller boy's hand away. They stand there, legs unmoving, but arms alive. Low, high, from one side and then the other, Bloodgrip attacks. Monster turns each attack away.

Once, Esperanza saw two vipers fight, heads raised high. They circled and lunged and dodged with frightening quickness. Now, it seems as if she is watching four such vipers in action. Each hand, fanged; one bite could end it all. *Except Monster's fangs hold no poison.*

Can he keep it up long enough to end this in a draw?

The Blood-User manages to land an odd strike or two, but whenever he tries to grab ahold of his opponent, he comes up with nothing but air.

Step for step, they continue, trying to gain position or any small advantage to turn the stalemate of styles. As the little one lunges forward, mixing in feints with real grabs, the Disciple of the Doubting Palm avoids and diverts. The attacks come faster and faster, until even Riser can't follow the blurs that their arms have become. *Unbelievable!*

Just as she thinks her dining partner may just have a real chance of outlasting their opponent, he stops fighting back.

Even Ossei looks confused by how easily he is able to grab ahold of the Half-Orc's arm. "Blood Clamp: Bone Breaker."

What in Silla is he doing? Is he trying to lose on purpose? No, never ... Riser thinks.

The Blood-User cannot hide his surprise.

He looks up at the much larger Half-Orc and says in a quiet voice, "Please submit."

"No. I am sorry, but that is something I cannot do," Brother Monster says, his arm growing pale.

Ossei's own arm pulses and flexes as his grip tightens by the moment. Given enough time, those of the Bloodgrip Clan have been known to bend steel with a single grasp. *He's lost his mind,* Riser worries.

She begins to search the sideline. *Where exactly did the white flag go?* She has to stop this.

In a stadium used to shaking with cheers, the beating of hearts is all that can be heard. Monster pulls out the White Flag of Surrender. Displaying it for all to see he says, "If you're looking for this, don't bother."

He's watching her at a time like this. *The babo.* He who refuses to use the Fire he was born to control, activates his gauntlet. The small piece of cloth disappears in a puff of smoke. It's the first time she can remember seeing him burn something. It all happened so fast that she isn't quite sure she saw it clearly, but for a moment there ... *his flames looked white, so hot that they burned Blue.*

"Submit!" she screams, watching his hand turn unnaturally pale. "You've taken this as far as you can. Submit ... Please!"

"But then you'll keep calling me a coward," he says, not turning around.

"I'll never call you that again. Just please stop! Please ..."

CRACK!

Riser almost throws up. Behind her, she hears someone doing just that.

The Half-Orc's only response is, "Still the Flame." He frees his fractured arm from his enemy's deadly grasp.

"Orc bones are much stronger than those of a regular human. And yours are probably even weaker than that from your training in Blood." He stares deep into the eyes of his enemy. "I doubt you would be able to release your Tech the same instant as I release mine. I wonder what would happen during that split second before you're able to cancel your Blood Clamp."

Monster moves the smaller boys paralyzed hand so that it grips the Blood-User's own arm. "Please, I ask that you submit."

Ossei Bloodgrip stares wide-eyed at his arm clamped in the grasp of his own Blood Clamp. The small boy looks up at the Half-Orc and shakes his head. He too is prepared to make the very same sacrifice.

"I thought as much," Monster says as he pulls the boy's hand away from his own arm. And then he does the most ridiculous thing Riser's ever seen. He places his own neck between his enemy's fingers.

The Blood-User's unmoving eyes widen even larger.

The Half-Orc let himself be caught; he sacrificed his arm, he destroyed the only chance for his teammates to save him, and now this.

"I am Brun of the Sanctuary of the Divine Image. My friends call me Brother Monster. I walk the Path of Peace, a path with no shortcuts. Though we are born with violence in our hearts, I refuse it. Never is there a reason to harm another. For violence leads to violence, an escalation of hurt, pain, sorrow and hate. But I will fight! The only way I know how …

"I am a Pacifist. This is my Will and those who oppose it shall fall to the fury of my love and forgiveness. No matter what you do, I love you and forgive you. I offer you a choice. I offer you my life as redemption. I do this because I believe in the goodness of man. The goodness that is in you."

His words start as a whisper and finish a roar. The Blood-User's Inner Flame begins to flicker back to life.

This is no bluff.

"I submit," Ossei Bloodgrip says so softly that if all of Wysteria weren't holding its breath, no one would've heard.

Riser wipes at her eyes. "Big Babo," she mutters to herself. She can't even hear herself over the crowd. From a stunned silence to a raging roar they chant his name. "Monster!"

He's done it, but is it enough? His friends are quiet; even they are shocked at what just occurred. He looks over at them and says, "It's just a slight fracture. I'll be fine."

"No, you won't. Your bone has a crack in it. We all heard it!" Riser yells at him. *Just how babo can he be?* "Do you want to break it clean in two? That's what will happen if you keep on …"

"Fighting?" The Half-Orc doesn't turn around. Instead, he bends down and picks up some dirt. "I'm fine, I can still do what needs be done." He rubs some dirt on his arm. "There, I'm fine now."

"Argh! I hate you," she screams in frustration. *Unbelievable!*

"… The Perfect Draw, Stacy Iss!" the loudspeaker proclaims.

A cute, short-haired girl skips into the ring.

Brother Monster brings his hands together in prayer and bows. With his uninjured arm, he makes a wide flourish and slowly pushes his palm forward as if pressing against the heaviest of doors. His injured arm remains in the prayer position. "Doubting Palm Style: One-handed Prayer."

Why now? Why of all times pick now to fight? "Stop! Stop this right now!" But her cries are lost among the cheers.

She buries her face in her arms. She feels the lightest of touches on her shoulder and when she looks up with reddened eyes, there is a chipmunk trying to pat her on the head with his little claws. A comforting hand clasps her other shoulder.

"Have faith. He knows what he's doing," Sense says, "But still, let's show him our support. Stacy's small but she can pack a wallop. She'll save her Perfect Draw until he proves without a doubt that she cannot beat him."

The tiny girl is vicious, purposefully focusing her blows directly at Monster's injury. But she can't break through the Disciple of the Doubting Palm, Master of Stilling the Flame's defenses.

With each savage strike, each jarring blow, Monster's teammates wince. But in the end she is forced to use it. "Unleash Stasis: Perfect Draw," she commands in a huff.

By the time the Half-Orc lumbers back to their side, Riser is so angry that she won't even look at him. But in the end she wraps her arms around him and squeezes so hard it would hurt a normal man. He feels solid as a rock.

She buries her face into his chest until his robes are soaked. The Half-Orc raises his injured arm high above his head to save it from further injury, but doesn't protest.

It's her turn now.

If anyone asked the Daughter what she feared most, her answer would of course be nothing. But the true answer unfolds before her.

Now, because of him, because of them, she can leave her fears behind. There's no other imaginable option. She's learned a lot from their time together; something more than just her physical training, something she's been missing all this time. *This time I will beat him. This time there is more than just my legacy at stake!*

"Take care of the Babo. I'll take care of this," Riser says as she strides into the ring.

Inside the circle of light stands a dangerous boy. The past, too painful to think of, is all she can think of.

Five Years Ago | After The Third Loss

"Esper, it's just one loss," the curly haired girl says. 'Everyone loses, even you."

No, I don't! Young Esperanza wants to yell back, but instead, she just says, "Delores ... please just leave me alone."

Delores is her closest friend and always has been. And even though she's just trying to help, there's nothing her friend can say to make Esperanza feel any better.

She's just lost for the third year in a row to the boy from Gregory's House. The First Daughter not winning Silla's Harvest Tourney is unheard of. Coming in second three years in a row is downright unacceptable.

For the first loss, Esperanza had an excuse. Back then, she knew she didn't work as hard as the others—she never had to. Her natural talent had always been enough before.

That is, until that first loss three years ago. The taste of defeat had been so bitter she was forced to learn from it. She finally understood why her mother called her lazy. For the entire year after, she outworked everyone and anyone around her.

But when the second time came around, she lost yet again. As much as she felt shock and regret from the first defeat, she felt anger in the second.

After the outrage subsided ... somewhat, she once again asked her mother for guidance. Her mother told her that she was proud of how hard Esperanza had worked, but that sometimes even hard work isn't enough—she needs to be better prepared.

That year she took the Equipment Exam. That year she acquired Ehecthal, a katana wielded by Enyo herself, a true Weapon of Legend. A sword with the soul of a Beast; she couldn't have hoped for more.

But when this year rolled around, she lost again. She didn't even want to think of facing her mother right now.

"Esper, everyone knows that styles make fights. And no one sword is great enough to match six. Daisho's on another level. Everybody knows it but you."

Esperanza shakes her head in denial. *That's not true*, she thinks. *I'm just doing something wrong. I need to try harder ...*

She looks up at her best friend—always as tough and rugged as she is becoming. Delores is the second most popular Daughter of their generation. Delores has always been there for her. *She's the only one I can really trust and really talk to—the only one who truly understands.*

Young Esperanza gets up and says, "Whatever, I'll beat him next year."

"How, by cheating?"

What? "No, of course not. I'm going to figure out what I'm doing wrong and if I can't, I'll ... I'll just try harder."

"That's not going to be enough."

"It is," Esperanza says. "I'm just missing something. I just don't know what it is. But I'll figure it out."

Her best friend throws her hands up in exasperation. "Just face it, he's stronger. He's just better. No matter how hard your work, he will work just as hard. You'll never catch up."

Esperanza doesn't understand. *What's wrong with Delores? Why is she being like this?*

"What's wrong with you?" Esperanza says. "I'm the one who lost. Why are you acting like this?"

"Come on, Esper, you know it and I know it. You'll never beat Sixblades," Delores says. "It's just the way it is, just like you're on another level from all the other girls. Why can't you just accept it? We all had to."

"No, I *will* beat him. Never has the First Daughter lost to a boy from Gregory's House. And I'm going to make things right."

The friends sit in silence, neither understanding the other. Finally, Delores says, "If you had a secret, one you never told anyone, you'd tell me, right?"

"Yes, of course."

"So you've told me everything, right? It's not like you have some deep dark secret you're keeping from me ..."

Esperanza nods, wondering just what her friend is talking about.

"You can just tell me, you know?" Delores says, confusing Esperanza even more.

"What are you talking about?"

"Don't play dumb, Esper. Everyone knows," she says. "Ehecthal is the singing serpent. All of his previous wielders were Bladesingers, they all sang in battle, but you can't sing."

"So?"

"Just admit the truth; you can tell me. We're best friends, right?" Delores asks. "I would never tell anybody. I just want to know how you did it. I want a Weapon of Legend, too."

"What? I know I can't sing, that I can't use Ehecthal the way his previous owners have. Is that what you want to hear?" Esperanza says, full of confusion and anger. "But I didn't do anything except exactly what the examiner asked."

After a long moment of silence, her oldest friend says, "Fine. Be like that. I really thought we could tell each other anything ..."

That was the last time Esperanza talked to her friend. The next day, Delores finally took her Equipment Exam. She was caught cheating and expelled from Silla forever. As she was escorted to the borders of their homeland, she shouted, "It's not fair. I just wanted a Weapon of Legend, too. Esperanza lied and got herself one. Everyone knows it. Just because her mother is High Priestess, she can get away with it ..."

Four Years Ago | After the Fourth Loss

"Hello, First Daughter," the annoying boy says. Esperanza knows him, but has never really talked to him before. He's like the great-great-grandson of Old Claw or something. The two of them are the only two males allowed within the borders of Silla.

"Go away." She wants to be alone right now.

"That was a great match. Would you like to go a couple rounds against me?"

"Didn't you hear me? I said, go away," she yells, reaching around for something to throw at the smiling boy. She finds a twig and hurls it at his head.

Unfortunately, he ducks out of the way. "You got him to draw four of his swords. That is pretty good."

Esperanza finally looks up at the annoying kid. His smile is too big for his face. "I don't care. Go away."

"Please spar with me?" he asks. "Sitting there is not going to make things any better."

She shakes her head and buries her face back between her knees.

A long while later, the annoying kid asks, "I wonder why we have two eyes right next to each other."

Esperanza tries to ignore him. She doesn't have the energy

to listen to the babo things coming out of his mouth right now.

"Would it not be better if we had one eye on the back of our head and one in front?" he asks. "That would be much more useful."

She wants to ignore him, but can't. "Why are you still talking?"

"Because I wish to fight you," he says.

"Why?"

"Because I think it will do us good."

"If you want to fight someone, go fight Daisho," she says.

"I already did. Now, I want to fight you."

Esperanza goes back to trying to ignore him.

After another long while, the boy says, "I think I have figured it out ... "

"What?" Esperanza can't help but ask.

"We have two eyes up front because all that matters is what is ahead," the kid muses aloud. "Being able to see what is behind us would be nice, but it is not worth splitting our focus."

Esperanza thinks long on his words. When she finally looks up, she's not surprised to see that he's still there. "Yeah, whatever. I'll spar with you. If that's what you really want."

"Thank you!" he says, before knocking her down.

Present

"Esperanza, current First Daughter of Enyo, Wind Dancer of Ehecthal, I request this match be a formal Engagement of Silla." The annoyingly gallant boy bows before her.

By Enyo, I hate him. She bares her fangs. *He knows I can't refuse without looking the coward.* "Very well, I accept."

Unlike every battle she's been in until now, if she loses this time, she'll have no choice but to submit to the victor, to become his student and he her master. *Unthinkable!*

He actually has the audacity to smile. *He really takes this whole Alcendor thing way too seriously.* She studies her hated foe for the first time in four years. She can see why all her sisters are always talking about Daisho Sixblades. But to her, there's absolutely nothing attractive about the boy.

Fanned out across his back are his six swords, all of them on a level with her own blade, but each as soulless as their master. As he bows, she spies a seventh strapped straight down the middle. *That's new and why is it so heavily wrapped?*

He notices her eyeing the new blade and says, "Forgive me should I draw that one." *I really, really dislike him.*

The blacked-out auditorium murmurs with excitement as the Kings take the field. She draws Ehecthal and he draws Floe, a sword as cold as Ice. The horn blares.

They clash in the middle. The crowd screams for more as their swords dim in and out of view. The clangs of their blows are the only way to keep up with the fury of their strikes.

Twice the speed of the previous Criers—up, down, left, right, above and beyond—their selected blows start to whirlwind faster and faster. After a final exchange so fierce they're each thrown back by the clash, they relent for the slightest of moments.

"The level of your improvement stirs my heart," he says, blocking a slice at his head

She replies with a glare so fierce it would keep any ordinary man's heart from beating.

"I only do what I must," Daisho Sixblades says. "Shall we end introductions and proceed to the next act?"

Riser grunts her approval and lowers her sword. They slowly walk back to opposite sides of the ring.

The Alcendor In-Training draws a second blade—in his left, he wields one as cold as Ice, in his right, one blacker than its name, Night. Together they are the twin edges of NightFloe. They assume their stances once again.

His form is perfection, but so is hers.

Esperanza knows those blades all too well. Now, is her best chance for victory—before they're fully released. Daisho's father left him six such weapons, all of them quasi-sixth ranked weapons, meaning they could cut even the incorporeal of a certain type.

One Crier possessing more than one blade of such a rank is unheard of, and of course now he has seven. But Esperanza wields Ehecthal, a true sixth level blade.

She charges and he waits. It's her turn to lead. For every step she takes forward, he takes one back or to the side. When he takes two in an attempt to circle, Esperanza executes a pirouette so perfect it shames the battlefield for not being a proper stage with curtains and an orchestra to match.

This is going nowhere. But she knows she cannot rush; a misstep here would add to his legend and mean an end of her own. There is no choice, however. For every second that passes, the twin edges of NightFloe grow in power.

She pivots on her supporting leg and arches just out of range of his next blow. Floe comes for her and she drives it back with Ehecthal, pinning it to the ground. But Night returns, slicing at her from the shadows. She barely manages to greet the blade with her gauntlet. Before he can pull away, she tightens her grip around it and smiles at him, full-fanged. *I got him now.*

But he returns her look with smiling eyes. When she follows his gaze, she realizes Ehecthal is trapped beneath his boot. No matter how hard she tugs, she cannot free her blade.

"On one, shall we?" he asks.

"Fine," she growls.

"One." She releases his blade and he hers, the both of them leaping back and away. She activates her boots and dashes forward. He meets Ehecthal's kiss with Shadow and Ice.

"It really has been too long, Esperanza," he tells her, his blades locked with hers. Their faces are inches apart. "I've missed you."

She answers him with a headbutt. He falls backwards, but as he does, he slices the blade called Night at her legs. Even as she leaps clear of the blow, she knows it's too late. Esperanza watches Night cut at her shadow and cringes in pain.

The boy from Gregory's House picks up the shadow of her foot and feeds it to his dark blade. In some small way it takes away from her and adds to him. The difference is not noticeable yet, but ...

She charges, almost dragging her sword along the ground. When she gets within striking distance, she pulls the blade upward with all her might. Her cornered opponent has no choice but to block. The force of the blow lifts him up, and he lands with a loud thud. As he stands, he reveals another piece of her shadow in his grasp.

When she looks down, she sees that only half of her shadow remains. *Fail him. He blocked with just Floe and used Night to carve my shadow in two*, she realizes. *That's enough for him to ...*

"Release Night, Black Summon: Shadow Twin," Daisho says, letting go of his dark blade. Before it hits the floor, his Shadow comes to life and grabs it mid-fall.

The boy and his Shadow reach behind him as one, each drawing a new blade. The Shadow of Sixblades wields a flaming sword, one too hot for any mere mortal to wield. Daisho draws a shining sword, Sun's Edge, and his Shadow grows darker, stronger.

He's already at four, and I've barely scratched him.

A hush falls over the crowd as they marvel at the boy's exquisite style. The cheering begins. "Sixblades!" Up until now, all they knew of Daisho Sixblades was that he was the one chosen to replace Kase Shake himself as King. But now, they are beginning to see just why.

It's not over, yet. You can do this, Esperanza tells herself. She knows she can handle four blades for a short while; it's only when all six are out that she has no chance.

It's his turn to lead, now. She has no choice but to defend. "Air Block," she commands before leaping behind it. She can keep dancing away as long as she avoids getting cornered. But she's already breathing hard and worst of all, she can see her own breathe. *Which means Floe is almost ready, too ...*

The two Daishos attack in unison. She leaps high, landing on her Block of Air. He shatters it just as she dashes away. All she can do right now is avoid check and mate, her one king against his two. *I have to find an opening, some weakness.*

The Daughter creates another Air Block and scrambles behind it. As she does, she finds herself staring at her teammates. They're still cheering, they're still smiling ... they think she somehow still has a chance.

What's wrong with me? she wonders. *Of course I have a chance. I will not let the past predict the future. They believe in me and they don't even know what I've been practicing on my own.*

She forgets how tired and cold she has become, gets to her feet and stands tall. *It's now or never, and it may as well be glorious.*

"You might as well draw all six of your swords. You're not going to beat me with just four. As you like to say, time for the Final Act."

He studies her carefully and inclines his head. "Very well."

Daisho holds the Ice Blade high above his head and drops it before him. As it falls, he stares at his reflection in the blade. "Release Icefloe, Blue Summon: Reflection Twin."

The chill in the air subsides and icy crystals coalesce all around him to form his mirror image in frost. His cold reflection grabs Floe before its tip pierces the ground. It leans over and draws a crimson sword from his master's back—a true Blood Blade, one that boosts the user temporarily at the price of future health.

By having his Reflection bear such a weapon, the cost has no consequence for the power gained. Daisho himself draws a sword that crackles and snaps with bolts of blue and silver, Lightning's Edge, a sword that cannot be blocked.

He shines dominant in the darkness of the auditorium, a gleaming blade of sunlight in one hand and one bursting and snapping white-blue in the other. The audience gasps at the three of him and the six blades they wield.

Riser knows what she'll see when she turns around, but she does it just so she can remember the sight.

They don't look worried at all. They're actually enjoying this, she thinks, even the one with the broken arm, the one who knows I've never beaten this guy before.

She grips Ehecthal loosely and for the first time in all their battles bows before Daisho Sixblades. For once, he looks surprised.

"To Glorious Defeat!" he says, all three of him bowing low.

"To Glorious Defeat!" she repeats. *Yours ...*

The outcome is inevitable. Against an opponent as skilled as hers, it's only a matter of time before her only piece on the board is cornered by his three. But she's ready for that. He better be, too. No beast fights so fiercely as one with no chance of escape.

She leaps backward, twisting and turning in midair, landing, defending—barely eluding his blows. *Every style has its weakness. There's a pattern here. If I could just see it.*

She picks her spot, one where everyone will have a good view. This is where she will make her final stand. Already, Daisho, his Shadow, and his Reflection surround her.

"A noble effort," he tells her. "I would expect no less of you, but this ends here." For the first time, she notices that his face is sterner than usual, almost angry. *No, he's just concentrating really hard.*

She thinks back on their past battles and finally understands exactly what is happening. The Reflection and Shadow do not think for themselves. They are simply an extra set of arms and legs for him to control. *That's why they always attack in unison ...*

"You're right, it ends here, but not in the way you think," she says. "You probably thought I was forced to chose an incomplete Class like Wind Dancer just because I couldn't become a Blade Singer, huh?

All three Daisho Sixblades stare back at her with no answer.

"Allow me to show you the truth!" Riser says. "I'll admit, your style is pretty impressive, but now, it's time for you to have a taste of my Home-brew."

The arena grows quiet as she begins to spin in place. It was one of the very first things she learned to do, one leg for support, the other working her round.

If it weren't for her teammates, though, she wouldn't have bothered mastering it. She spins, she focuses—she has no blind spot.

"Air Dance: Spiral Form," she says. *If he can concentrate on all three of him, then so can I.*

They attack. She deflects with her sword, then with her gauntlet and then again with her sword, never stopping her turning. She knocks back the Original and the Reflection, but the Shadow goes for what's left of hers. She shouts, "Blue Summon: Air Petal!"

Wake was right; there is no creativity in a chunk of Air. *Beautiful Design, huh?* She still doesn't quite get it, but there's one thing she knows. She's always thought flowers were beautiful. So that is what she decided to master the creation of.

She did it alone, with no soul around, so the moves would be personal, hers and hers alone. *I put myself into these Techs—my heart, my soul. They are mine and mine alone.*

Layer after layer of petals she summons, until she is surrounded in them. And when she is done the Air rushes around her, forming a perfect flower ready to bloom. "Perfect Defense, Roaring Rose."

All of him attacks, slashing and cutting away at her creation. But it holds.

"This is unlike you, Esperanza," he says, hacking away. "A Technique like this could almost be called stalling."

"Fool!" she says. "Didn't you hear me say I'm about to show you my new style? I don't just fight with brute force anymore. Haven't you heard of Beautiful Design?

"My Techs no longer end where they begin. They build upon one another, to achieve what one cannot alone!

"And besides, I've figured you out," she adds with a smirk.

"Figured me out?"

"Someone once asked me, 'If we have two eyes, why are they both right next to each other?'" she says. "I thought he was telling me to look forwards and not behind."

Riser lifts her sword and watches it glint in the spotlight. "But it's really because we're at our best when we focus on one thing. And you ... all three of you can't keep up with that" she declares. "But I haven't changed that much; I'm still a brute at heart. Let me share with you my savage heart. Behold my Brutal Art!"

She begins to spin once again, and this time, she slices at the Flower of Air surrounding her. Ehecthal was once a Blessed Beast; his form was that of a winged serpent that soared through the clouds. As he flew, he sung from his cold-blooded heart. Now, he lives in a sword, but right at this moment, he flies again.

And as he slices through the Air, the serpent sings once more ... a song of pure joy. It surprises even his wielder. *What's this? Ehecthal has never done this before.*

"I'm sorry that it's come to this." Daisho looks at her sadly. "Soulless Blade Style: Release." His twin and reflection disappear and all six of his blades clatter to the floor. He draws the seventh sword from his back. It is a plain looking weapon of ordinary steel.

"Truly, I'm sorry, Wind Dancer. Whatever it is that you are planning, it's not going to work," he says. "This is the most powerful sword in all of the Three Kingdoms, a truly despicable sword.

"It is why I'm the anchor and not the Chosen One, Kase Shake. There's only a handful in all of Wysteria that can wield a Rank Six Swordbreaker."

Half the crowd whispers their disbelief over such a sword appearing within the Tournament. The other half tries to ignore them, not wanting to miss a single thing.

A Swordbreaker is beyond uncommon. It is a blade that can shatter any other of equal or lesser rank. And one of such a high level is unimaginable. Daisho's seventh blade is one of the rarest in all the world.

The Daughter cannot attack or even block such a weapon— doing so would destroy her best friend.

Riser does not slow. The Flower of Air surrounding her is nearly gone; its petals once taller than she, are now sliced miniature and float all about. *Perfect!*

"My Brutal Art: Roaring Rose Bloom." The tiny, hovering blossoms reunite behind her, cloaking and winging her, driving her forward with unbelievable force. She hears the cries of the crowd and her teammates' worried shouts, but most of all she hears Ehecthal. *He's singing.*

Daisho Sixblades charges her. She shouts out her final Tech. "Air Sharpened Ehecthal! God Sword." With this, she claims, "Sharpest Blade in the World!"

The edge of her sword glows fiery blue and she points it straight at the heart of her opponent.

The Alcendor In-Training realizes just what she has achieved. He lowers his weapon before it is too late.

She cleaves his armor in two.

All that remains is a Sphere with Daisho in the middle and seven blades scattered all around him. And of course the crowd goes wild.

"What the hail just happened?" Wake asks as they throw Riser up on to their shoulders.

"Ehecthal, leveled up to a Rank Seven Weapon," Riser explains. "A true God Sword."

"What, how? Swords can level up mid-fight like that?"

"Kind of ... The difference between Rank Six and Rank Seven is possessing one of God's Six Attributes. I used Air to sharpen him to temporarily gain the title of Sharpest Blade in the World. My Petals are made of pretty tough stuff," she explains. "Even, Ehecthal can only hold such an edge for a couple of moments. See, he's already back to his regular self." She holds up her sword.

"Daebak! A sword breaker facing a higher ranked weapon would've broken itself against it. He had no choice but to lay down his sword," Wake realizes aloud, eyes wide with wonder. "Riser, your Brutal Art ... that was the most Beautiful Design I've ever seen."

She hugs him fiercely. "It's thanks to you. You showed me the way. Thank you."

She turns to the Half-Orc and pinches his cheek and where it turns red, she gives him a little pat. "Thank you, too, for everything." His cheek turns redder from that than the pinch.

The Daughter turns to all her friends. "That goes for all of you. Thank you," she says.

"We didn't do anything. That was all you out there!" they shout, tossing her up into the air.

After they finally let her down, she walks over to the boy from Gregory's House, who is packing away his fallen blades. "Daisho Sixblades!" she yells out. "Good fight."

He sheathes the last of his swords and nods. He almost walks away without saying a word, but without turning, he asks, "How did you become so strong?"

She answers, "Because of you. Thank you! You're going to be the best Alcendor ever. I know it."

He gives the slightest of nods.

"I know you were just trying to do your duty, that you would've deferred your claim," Riser tells him. Ever since there's been one, the Alcendor would challenge all Daughters at the onset of their Pilgrimage. Those he defeated, he deferred his claim, allowing them to continue. If that Daughter later fell to an unacceptable foe, she could claim Alcendor's Right. In doing so, the unacceptable foe would have to travel to Silla and fight the Alcendor for First Claim. In this way he protected the Daughters of Silla. This Daughter, however, needed no such protection.

Daisho turns around with those smiling eyes of his. "Perhaps, I never cared about being the Alcendor. Maybe, I just wanted to beat one Daughter ..."

Riser being shocked into silence is a rare sight, but it's one that happens this day.

"Oh well, I guess I have no choice in the matter, now," he says, turning back to face a very unhappy looking Princess.

CHAPTER 55
PRINCESS
[BACKROOM OF SOME INN, SARANGHAE]

O n days such as today, it really seems as if everything is against her. She would laugh at the thought, but a Love never laughs. It is something few would ever understand. But for her, a lesson learned early. Another is that life is never fair, a lesson that needs no reminder just now.

No matter what it takes, I will win the final game.

The Princess studies the small room, checking once again for any possible lack of privacy. Normally, she wouldn't invite Kase to such meetings. The Chosen One has no taste for such things. *But if he really wishes to win, he better swallow his foolish sense of honor and pay close attention.*

In the back room of some small, nondescript inn, the Princess and her champion sit at a wide, wooden table. The Sibyl stands behind them. Her silvery mask hides her face, but not the frustration in her eyes.

"Look, Princess, I want to beat them as much as you do, but Mindreaders?" Kase Shake says when he finds out why they're here. "Really now, do we need to resort to such things?"

"Kase, I would like for you to be here, but if you wish, you may leave. There is but one match left. I will not walk away from this without at least, a single victory. I will do anything ... anything to ensure that."

"Calm down, Achylsa. I want this as much as you. I'll stay."

"Don't tell me to calm down," she says before calming down. "Thank you for staying, Kase. I'm sure this will be most informative. Please call the first one in." The Sibyl exits through the single entrance on the far side of the room.

"Oh, and wear this. It will keep your thoughts hidden." She passes him a silver band, which Kase promptly slips onto his finger.

"There's more than one?"

"Of course. I hired three."

Kase rolls his eyes in disapproval.

The Sibyl reenters the room escorting a young girl, who promptly curtsies and takes the single empty chair.

"Miranda Ducer, of Chastetown," the Sibyl announces. After an exchange of greetings, they get down to business.

"It was kind of hard. I couldn't follow his thoughts at all until the match actually began. His thoughts are like a bunch of gobbledygook, but once he started fighting his thoughts became crystal-clear. He's very simple, really. All he thinks about is one thing—what he wants. Over and over again, all he could think was *Everything*."

"That's it?"

"Yes, he repeated it over and over, like he was singing a little song," she says. "And now, I can't get the dumb song out of my head; Everything, everything, everything!"

"Was there anything else?"

The little girl shakes her head.

"Thank you very much, Miranda. The Sibyl will show you to your mother."

As the young Mindreader is escorted from the room, Kase whispers, "This is a waste of time."

"She is just the first. Let's hear what the others have to say."

The next entrant is hidden in a long dark cloak, with hood pulled low. The lanky fellow bows in a gentlemanly manner and sits down. He pulls back his cowl with a flourish. Beneath it is a familiar face. Nester Hocke, the Royal Family's personal Reader, smiles back at them. A simple nod for a greeting, he gets straight to his report.

"He is a simple, young man; painfully simple. I couldn't make heads nor tails of what he was thinking before the fight. Looking back on it, I'm surprised he didn't give his injury more thought."

"Anyway, he is certainly a determined lad. All he thought of was pushing himself. Over and over he repeated one word to himself: *Everything.* I'm sure he used the thought to describe what he had to give. He gives all of himself in battle. It was a rather short match, but I am willing to bet if he had manged to get an attack off, it would've been *simply* marvelous."

"Was there anything else, at all?" the Princess asks.

"I'm afraid not," the gentleman says. "I am sure there was more to the boy, but that is what he concentrated on most. To be honest, the whole experience was quite straining and I've had the most awful headache ever since."

"Thank you for the report, Sir Hocke."

The Court Reader bows deeply and makes his departure.

Kase holds up a finger and begins to speak, but the Princess cuts him off. "I am sure the last one will have something useful for us."

Her champion gives her a doubtful look, but doesn't protest.

"She is an outsider that reads professionally on the World Circuit," she says, reassuring herself as much as her companion.

An older lady enters next. She gives them a grandmotherly smile full of understanding and takes a seat. She straightens the folds of her dress and eyes their rings. "He's an unusual one, that one."

"How so?"

"He is not like you and I. His world is full of ghosts and he sees people not as they are, but what they may become. He lives with one eye on the past and one upon the future, leaving him often blind to the present. Only when his match began did he fully join us in the now.

"His level of focus is unparalleled. I have never felt the world to be as frivolous as when I touched my mind to his. There is a beauty to his order of things. One that I cannot even begin to understand. He makes connections of the seemingly unrelated, but lacks to desire ... or should I say ability to comprehend what is obvious to you and I.

"What I can tell you is, that his memories are not like yours or mine. His memories are alive. They breath and they speak. And it is them that call out for Everything."

"I must admit, I found the experience to be quite frightening. He will not be denied. I would not wish to go against one such as he." The old lady shudders.

"How do I beat him?" the Princess asks.

"I am no Crier or strategist. My best advice is ... you don't. At least, not directly," the experienced reader tells her. "If I had to try, I would attack his teammates. Which, from what I have seen, is not going to be much easier of a task.

"And as unusual as that boy is, he is not the one that I found the most interesting. That would be the Water Knight. Now, that was a truly delicious mind, one that I could wander around in for days. The fascinating thing was that for a moment there, he really had no chance, and he knew it. But then, he looked up and saw someone, someone he wanted to prove something to ... perhaps, even to impress?" The old Reader grins from ear to ear. "If I had to guess, it looked as if he was looking your way, Princess."

CHAPTER 56

WAKE

"Wake ... Wake! Over here," a girl's voice calls out as *Monsters To Believe In* leave the Auditorium. The Award Ceremony and fanfare that followed their victory were nice, but they're all more than eager to return to the inn and get some rest.

When he sees who it is, he tells his teammates he'll catch up with them later.

"Um ... Hi, Juli. Julia, I mean ..."

"It's alright, Wake. You can call me Juli, Julia. Whichever is fine," she tells him.

Even though she was with Kearney in Greenwood, she was on the Observation Deck during their match. He hasn't actually laid eyes on her since her stay in Ice Ridge. *That was over three years ago*, he remembers.

Her father was and still is one of the most successful textile merchants in the Three Kingdoms.

Four years ago, he came to Wake's hometown to set up his northern base of operations and brought his daughter with him. *What was it that they called him? ... was it the Emperor of Silk?*

They only stayed for half a year or so, and for some unknown reason, Julia Redsilk ended up attending the same school as Wake rather than the more prestigious all-girl school in upper Ice Ridge.

He met her first, even before anyone else. He even helped her in some small way. But that was before he found out who she really was, and of the family that she came from. After he did learn her name, he knew better than to bother someone like her.

"You were really amazing back there. You guys are so good," she says.

"I guess, we got pretty lucky back there." It's winter and he's outside, but his face feels warm. "At least, I did. Monster and Riser are always that good."

"No, what you did was amazing, Wake. I don't think anyone else in the whole world could've won that matchup besides you," Julia tells him. For some reason, Wake always finds the ground interesting to look at when talking to girls. But he does notice the doll in her hands.

"Oh, you still have Eveline," Wake says, nodding at the doll. She used to carry the silken doll with her everywhere back then. At first, the other girls teased her for having such a childish habit, but within a week, all the girls were carrying their own dolls, too.

"You remember her name?" She clasps her hands together. "I never had the chance to properly thank you for saving her."

"I didn't really do anything, but I'm glad she's okay," he says. All he did was help clean her that one time.

"Maybe to you, but it was about the nicest thing anyone ever did for me," she says. "Thank you, Wake. I always regretted not thanking you back then, but you didn't have to ignore me like you did afterward."

"I didn't ..." he begins.

"No, Wake, you did," she says. "But it's okay."

He never saw it that way. If anything, he was trying to help her fit in with the other kids, but ... "I'm sorry," he says.

"Truly?" she says, eyeing him warily.

He nods.

A huge smile covers her face. "Then I forgive you, Wake

Avenoy," she says. "Just don't let it happen again."

He continues to nod, unsure of what to say next.

"Wake?" she finally says.

"Yes?"

"Before I forget to tell you and regret it for another couple years, I wanted to thank you for sticking up for me in Greenwood," she says. "I left *The Courageous* after that match. And I would have had a much more difficult time finding a new team if you hadn't said what you said."

"I think anybody would've done the same ... but I'm glad it helped," he tells her.

"It really did," she says. "If it wasn't for that, I would never have gotten enough points to qualify."

"That's great," he tells her. "Congratulations. I'm glad things worked out."

"It's not official yet, of course," she says. "But I should be joining you in school next year. I hope you remember your promise not to ignore me this time."

He still doesn't understand why the daughter of one of the wealthiest merchants in Wysteria would care about something like that. "I won't."

Just then another girl's voice calls his name "Wake ... Wake Avenoy!"

"I didn't know you had a girlfriend." Julia stops smiling.

"No, no I don't." His face is now downright on fire. "I don't know who that is." *Though, the voice sounds eerily familiar.* He looks around but can't find its source.

"Whoever it is, she's over there." She points behind him. Her neutral expression becomes a frown. "Oh, I didn't know you were friends with The Doll Princess."

"We're not really friends. But it's probably best that I go see what she wants."

"Wake, before you go ... I also wanted to say, I'm sorry," she says. "About what Kearney said ... I didn't know he was going to kick you and your sister off the team when I joined. I never ..."

"It's okay, Julia," he says. "I know better than to believe anything he says. Besides, things sort of worked out, anyway."

The curtains to the Royal Carriage are closed, but the voice coming from behind them definitely belongs to her. "I was hoping we could talk, Wake Avenoy."

"I don't know, Princess," he says, not sure if wants to.

"Please, just for a moment." The door swings opens. From where he stands, all he can see are the shadows within ... and her pale, delicate hand. *What exactly is going on today? First, Juli and now her ...* He wonders. Julia Redsilk was obviously just being nice, but the Princess ...

I shouldn't be here talking to her, he tells himself even as he enters and takes a seat across from her. Strangely, her ever-present chaperon isn't there. She notices his look of confusion. "The Sibyl is elsewhere at the moment, but she is listening through this." She pulls out a small shard from the folds of her dress.

Why am I here? What does she want? he wonders. Wake doesn't know what to say; what comes out his mouth is, "So you're never really alone, are you?"

She shakes her head. *I shouldn't be here ...*

He's always had a hard time looking at people directly, a problem he's never noticed until Esperanza told him how annoying it is. He's worked on it since, but this is different. He can't look at the Princess for a whole different reason.

For others, it's painfully awkward to look into their eyes. With her, it's painful to look away. *Dark Arts! Selfish Agenda! Ruthless,* he tries to tell himself, but he doesn't really believe that. What he really sees is someone who is never alone, but who is still somehow so alone. *She needs me—Why do I have to think that?*

"Wake, I ..." she begins

I can't deal with this right now, he realizes. "Look, Princess, I'm not going to help you ... not anymore. I really believed you. I thought you needed my help to do what's best for Wysteria, but ...

"But I just can't believe that anymore—not by the way you've acted. If you cared about anything or anyone beside yourself, you wouldn't have ... you couldn't have done the things you've done. You'll do anything to win, including trying to use me. I'm not the weak link you think I am."

If he had looked up just then, he would've seen a genuine expression on her face for the first time since they'd met.

"I do not think that, " she says, her voice barely a whisper. "I'm sorry that you feel that way."

They sit quietly in the dark of the carriage. He keeps his eyes down, afraid of falling back under her spell, but there's still the scent of her. *How can someone so heartless smell so lovely? Like flowers blooming in some dark forest, but not so sweet as much as savory. Snap out of it, Wake! Now's not the time to be thinking of the way she smells.*

"Wake, I bear a burden, one that I don't expect any to understand. But I was hoping ... I was hoping that somehow you might."

"Stop!" he says, wanting nothing more than to feel sorry for her. *How can I fall for this again; am I that stupid?* "I don't want to hear it. You brought in a Pro-Tripper to beat my sister. You wouldn't allow us to use the Transporter! You had that guy break Monster's arm! You tried to break Riser's sword!

"And what did those things mean? Fate paid in blood; imagine how much he was hurting—running and fighting on his cut-up feet," he says, shaking his head. "What if Esperanza lost? She'd have to give up everything ... everything! Everyone would have!"

"I am truly sorry, Wake," she says. "But that is the way things had to be. You're the ones who declared yourselves against me. Fate and Esperanza would have done the same in my shoes. And as awful as those things may seem, I would do all those things again. What I regret is ..."

"No, they wouldn't have," he almost screams. His mind is a muddle. His eyes feel wet. *I have to go now*, he decides. But as he stands he finds himself frozen.

There, on his arm is her hand, so delicate it burns. *Why do I have to be so weak?*

"Wake ..."

"If you had acted even a little bit human," he tells the Doll Princess, finding some last bit of strength within him. "If you had believed me when I said I would've made things right, things may have been different."

He shakes his arm free of her touch. The sound of the door shutting behind him sounds so final that he has to run to get away from the echo it makes in his head—to get away from her.

A light winter rain begins to fall. Half-frozen flakes melt against his skin only to rise again like steamy thoughts from his head. A few drops are all it takes to start scattering what remains of the day's crowds.

The lucky ones find spots beneath one of the many brightly colored canopies lining the small street. As it begins to really pour, the less fortunate jostle for a spot beneath the canopies' edges.

Wake Avenoy trudges through it.

Between raindrops, all that can be heard are whispers of the day's matches. That is, until someone mentions that the Glissade are in town. Word of their arrival jumps from one island stranded in the rain to the next, until each and every canopy is abuzz with the news.

Even a boy deep in thought can't help but hear the rumor between icy raindrops. Not that he gives it much thought. He already has too many other things to worry about right now. He did just do the right thing, didn't he? After all, he fought off temptation and remained loyal to his friends. But then why does he feel so bad?

The last flurry falls just as Wake makes it back to the inn. Inside its white stonewalls, Sense paces back and forth, tapping a finger to his forehead. The tapping stops when he looks up to find Wake standing there, silent and wet.

"Wake! Thank goodness you're back." Sense sighs in relief, but the worry quickly returns to his eyes. "We have a big problem."

"Problem?" Wake asks. "Did someone get hurt? I mean more than ..."

"No, no, nothing like that. Listen, everybody's already out looking for him. We couldn't stop him ..." Wake's never seen him like this before.

"Stop who? What are you talking about?"

"It's the Captain. He's gone missing. He took off looking for the Glissade and no one was able to stop him." Sense takes a deep breath and it all comes spilling out. "As we were coming back from the match, everyone in the city was talking about it. The Glissade are here."

When he first heard the whispers of the Glissade, Wake hadn't given it a second thought. Their arrival portends prosperity and although rare, it is not unheard of to find them at a tournament—no matter how small.

But other than bringing good luck, the Slithering Men aren't known to bring much else. *Except for their Challenges of Honor*, Wake suddenly remembers. *How could I forget about those ridiculous challenges that no one can ever complete? No one ever takes them seriously and no one ever would. Except for ...*

"This could be really bad," Wake says. "You think he went after them seeking a Challenge of Honor?"

"Yes, he even said as much as he took off." Sense stands there shaking his head. "It was the darnedest thing. One minute, he's sound asleep in the back of the cart and at the first mention of Glissade, he's up and running down the street, yelling something about challenges and honor. The others went after him right away. I came back here to wait for you."

"Thanks, Sense," Wake says. "How long ago did this happen?"

"It's been a quarter hour or so since I last saw them. We still have time to find him before it's too late." Sense looks up at Wake. "Wake, I've been thinking ... the others are already on the Captain's trail. Maybe we should go see if we can find the Glissade before he does."

"Excellent idea. Let's go."

The storm clouds are but a memory. And just as the fair weather has returned, so have the people, though, the crowds are of a different sort than before. Dressed in their evening finery, young and old stroll through the streets of Saranghae as performers breathe fire and juggle light for their delight. Teared lights and torchlight, both, combine to make the streets seem almost as bright as day.

As the search grows longer, so does Wake's worry. *This is really bad*, he thinks. *Things are already hard enough as it is; impossible, really. And if the Captain were to make it even more difficult by accepting a Challenge of Honor ...*

It's not hard to find word on the Slithering Men. Depending on whom they ask, the Glissade are everywhere and anywhere but where the pair happen to be.

Sometimes, they're recognized as members of that team, the one that came out of nowhere to cause such a stir. Often they're congratulated, and always they're asked if they can really do it—sweep the Grand Finale. All of which just makes the search that much more difficult.

Finally, they meet a pair of young ladies who swear up and down that they saw the Glissade with their own two eyes. The problem is that one saw the contingent of Slithering Men in Upper Saranghae and the other swears to have seen them in all their splendor along Phenry Street in Middle Saranghae.

There's nothing left but to split up. Sense takes Upper and Wake heads for Phenry Street.

Finding Phenry Street proves more difficult than he first anticipated. The small road connects two other small roads that really don't need connecting. Without stopping multiple times to ask for directions, Wake may never have found it at all.

Off in the distance, he can hear the sounds of the harbor: sailors singing in a thick accent as they unload their wares, a dock master yelling something or other, shouts declaring fresh fish for sale and the occasional wave, knocking hull against pier.

But Phenry Street itself is strangely silent. No living soul is in sight. The buildings loom lifeless, making Wake wonder if he's still really in Saranghae, the city he's come to know for being as bright in night as it is during the day. What there is however, are long, line-like tracks that lead to an almost dark corner

But they suddenly stop here, in the middle of nowhere, Wake thinks, staring at the middle of the small, winding road. He checks the nearest buildings, but all he finds are shops already shuttered or closing for the evening. He makes his way further and further down the winding street, but finds no new sign of the Slithering Men or anyone who may have seen them. *Maybe Sense is having better luck*, he hopes before thinking to put his gauntlet on.

There's another Gauntlet-User nearby. *Could it be Fate? Or maybe Sense found nothing in Upper Saranghae and has come to help.*

Wake tracks the Hand of Fate to the narrowest alley he's ever seen. *Whoever it is, they are definitely in there,* he thinks, looking into the deep, dark opening.

"Sense?" he whispers once, but silence is all that answers back. He steps into the darkness. First one tentative step, then a second. On his third, he begins to make out a towering metal gate not too far away. The other Gauntlet-User is close, now. He's almost on top of them. "Fate? Sense?" he whispers. "It's me, Wake."

Once again there is no answer. Wake gives the gate a gentle tug, but it doesn't budge. There is no sign of a lock, but on its other side he can make out what seems be a counterweight. It connects to a chain that surely must pull the gate open. *If I summon enough Water to weigh it down, then just maybe ...*

"Blue Summon: Water Globe ..." he begins, but before he can finish, he finds himself hunched over in pain. *What's going on?* There's a sharp pain between his shoulder blades that wasn't there before. Nothing comes out when he tries to speak, not even a gasp.

"Not another word," comes an angry whisper. When Wake looks up, he's met with a stare so fierce he forgets he can't breath. All he can do is nod.

"Are you daft?" the shadowy figure asks. Without waiting for an answer, the shadow thumps him hard on the chest and suddenly his lungs begin to fill. A claw-like finger is held up to his lips. This close, he can see it belongs to a girl who can't possibly be older than he is. She's no taller than even young Poe, but her eyes ... her eyes are old. Her eyes are frightening, even more so on such a young and lovely face.

She is dressed head to toe in black, and her gloved fingers end in claws. She looks at him and asks, "Wake Avenoy, do you know who I am?"

He does. Who else could it be but, "Ieiri Skyshadow."

CHAPTER 57

IEIRI

[ALLEY OFF OF PHENRY STREET, MIDDLE SARANGHAE]

"**G**ood," Ieiri tells Wake Avenoy. At least for a dolt, he knows that much. He's supposed to be older, but by the way he acts, you'd assume she's the senior. His obvious discomfort is discomforting. He's just the sort of boy she hates most.

She grabs him by the chin and forces him to face the ground, where many circles are inscribed within one. "Don't you know what that is?" she asks, more than a bit irritated.

His eyes grow wide. "It's a Rune of Detection. It will sound an alarm if anyone uses a Tech anywhere near it." His dumbstruck look disappears when he notices her gauntlets.

He grabs her hands and brings them close to his face. "Are these really Hands of Air? They're nothing like Riser's ... Oh, and I suppose, I should thank you for stopping me."

Ieiri pulls her hands back, barely suppressing a growl. "Don't touch me."

"You're like that too, huh?" he asks.

"No, I'm not like *that*," she hisses. "But I am a *girl*."

"I'm sorry, I just get excited by equipment I've never seen before." He circles her, pointing out this and that. "Even your sandals are clawed. All that's missing are whiskers and a tail."

Her glare is enough to let him know what she thinks about that idea.

This one is definitely odd, but, at least, he has a passion for something, she thinks. *And he wasn't half bad during their match today.* Though by the way he lost his last matchup, she couldn't really call him good.

Even with Master Enada's Guiding Winds, they didn't make it in time to see the Fate take the field. She hasn't even had a chance to change out of her Sandals of Air, which if she were to be caught wearing within the city would mean trouble.

All that running and we still missed Fate's matchup. But she knows that if Fate didn't make it past the first round that something must surely be wrong.

"How badly is he hurt?" she asks.

"Who?" he asks.

She hates stupid questions. It takes another silent glare for him to figure it out. "Oh, you mean Fate. He has a cut on his foot. It's somewhat deep, but nothing serious. He'll be fine."

Thank goodness. She stares at the older boy, wondering just what to do now. It had been easy enough following Fate this far, but sneaking past the gate that he and the procession of Glissade entered, is a whole other matter. She mustn't be discovered.

Enada made it more than clear that she is not supposed to make contact with her first Master until the games are officially done and over with. *I am not a distraction! And never would be!* she thinks, trying not to fume at the memory of the Master of the Dark Wind's words.

The older boy is actually cringing at her. "I'm sorry," she says. "It's not you, even though, you almost just messed everything up ... I guess, you were just trying to help him."

He smiles weakly at that.

"They went in there—Fate and the Glissade," she tells him. "I was planning on waiting to see if they would come back out this way." Ieiri doesn't want to admit it, but bypassing this particular gate without the use of any Techs is proving difficult ,even for her.

Sure, she could do it if she really tried, but what if she missed something, just like the daft boy had almost missed the Tech-detecting Rune.

Along with the Rune, there are inscriptions on each bar of the iron-gate. And for the life of her, she hasn't been able to figure out which are meant to be decorative and which may be for real.

Wake Avenoy is no longer cringing and instead, inspecting the gate for himself. "Hmm, each of these bars is made of a different metal. These two are blue-steel, that one is black-iron ... I see blood-iron and ones made of plain old metals, too. I don't know what the inscriptions mean, though. Do you?"

She shakes her head reluctantly.

When he looks up at her, he looks a different sort of afraid. "I think he needs us, right now. I don't know why for sure, but I feel like he really does."

She feels it, too.

CHAPTER 58
SENSE
[UPPER SARANGHAE]

By the time Sense reaches uptown, the Glissade are long gone. They were last seen making their way towards Middle Saranghae. So, Sense heads that way, too.

Wake's not too far ahead, he thinks, feeling his friend through his gauntlet. But, Wake's not the only one he can feel. There's someone with him—someone he doesn't recognize.

It's not surprising to find another Gauntlet-User within the capital. On more than one occasion, he's felt the presence of other Hand of Fate users—even, from the Palace itself.

If he tries hard enough, Sense can feel all of his teammates. *All of them, except for the Captain*, he thinks, trying not to worry.

And all of a sudden, he can't feel Wake either.

He begins to hurry.

Why did the Glissade have to show up now, of all times? There must be a good reason. Sense has never been a big believer in coincidence.

Despite their bad timing in this matter, he's always felt some strange kinship towards the Glissade. They observe, they even help, but they can't participate themselves.

The Slithering Men cannot be Teared, making them the only true neutral race. And as the only nation with no stake in the World Circuit, they are often brought in to settle disputes.

Over the years, he's read every book, scroll and article he could get his hands on about the Slithering Men. What he's always found most interesting about the unusual race are the Challenges of Honor that they issue.

Once, these Challenges were quite rare, but in recent years, they have become much more frequent. By now, there couldn't possibly be a soul in all the Three Kingdoms who hasn't heard of their ludicrous Challenges.

Everyone knows well enough to avoid them, he thinks. *That is, everyone except for ...*

"Rope! For goodness sake, does anyone have a rope?" yells someone, pounding on a door at the end of the street. *Thank goodness, It's Wake!*

"They came this way," Wake tells him. "And, boy, do I have a surprise for you ... You'll never believe what else I found."

Sense follows him into a moonlit alley and soon they come upon a large gate. It's made up of seven metal bars, each as tall as three full-grown men. A thick beam near its top holds it all together. There's also a Rune of Tech detection set into the ground, along with more markings all around the gate.

"I'm back," Wake whispers. "And I brought some help."

"Is there somebody else here?" Sense asks. "We should be more quiet."

"You're right, strategist," a girl's voice whispers directly into his ear. It takes all his self-control to keep from jumping out of his pants. He turns around to face a grinning Wake and a more shadowy figure.

Short and slight, with hair as dark as night, garbed in well-fitted yet flowing black, she is unmistakably Azurian.

And not just any Azurian, but one of their legendary warriors of stealth, a real-life ... Sense begins to think before she asks him in a voice so soft that it makes the world stop to listen. "Strategist, do you know who I am?"

He does. "Ieiri Skyshadow, highest-ranked youth in the Three Kingdoms, representing the Slate by way of Neverfall, Student of Fate ... and his girlfriend."

"Well met, Arthur Bannister Jr., otherwise known as Sense," she says. Her smile is small but pleasant. "I can see why at least you were chosen."

"Oh, well, I guess that's Sense for you," Wake says, scratching away at the back of his head bashfully.

"Did you find a rope?" she asks.

"No, unfortunately, there isn't a single store open along this whole street, but Sense is much better than any rope."

Sense studies the strange gate carefully. "It's a good thing you two deactivated your gauntlets. There's more than just the Rune of Detection you've obviously noticed. Any Tear activity beyond this point would've alerted whoever is trying to keep us out," he says, pointing to a row of shards embedded into the wall on the far side.

"The rope would've been noticed, too. At least, if you tried to throw it over the gate. That beam's pressurized. If so much as a bird lands on it, those inside would be alerted. Very tricky, indeed," Sense says. "But not totally impassable."

"See, I told you the rope was a dumb idea," Ieiri growls at Wake.

"At least, I had an idea and it led to me bringing back Sense," he retorts.

Sense can't help but chuckle. "What are you laughing at?" they both ask him.

"I'm sorry, guys. Are you sure you two just met?" Sense asks. They look back at him, equally confused and annoyed. *They bicker worse than an old married couple,* he thinks before deciding it's probably better to move on.

"This gate's set up in an unusual way. It's designed to be difficult to pass. But if they truly wanted to keep people out, there are many more effective and simpler ways they could have gone about it.

"As long as we are careful to use only the plain old metal bars, one of us should be able to make it to the other side. It's not going to be easy, but between the two of you, I think we can get past this."

Sense turns to Wake. "I need you to climb as high as you can and then brace yourself. Then, Ieiri will go up after and use you almost like a step to get over the beam without touching it. Do you think you two can do that?"

"I think so," Wake says. "Is she going to step on my head, though? That doesn't sound very comfortable."

Ieiri looks at him in disgust. "Comfort is the dream killer."

"You ... you're the dream killer," Wake mutters defensively.

Sense tries not to laugh too loudly.

Wake climbs the two bars until just short of the top. Ieiri goes up after him. She uses his head as a step and leaps over to the other side.

A moment later, the gate begins to rise. A short celebration ensues when they join her. But that ends as soon as they notice the set of stairs leading down into the darkness.

The tunnel is dark and long, with a gentle downward slope. Ieiri goes on ahead, checking every nook, cranny, and crevice they pass. Wake looks wide-eyed and sweaty. Sense just tries to keep up.

The corridor continues on; torch after passing torch are the only signs of their progress. Eventually, the tunnel opens up and voices can be heard in the distance. Ieiri motions for them to wait before disappearing into the darkness.

She returns, whispering, "Follow me exactly. Move as I move."

Easier said than done, Sense thinks. A shorts ways more and she gets down onto her belly, inching her way towards the voices growing louder in the darkness.

Now, that they are closer, he can tell it's predominantly just one voice and though, he can't make out what it says, its tone is calm and reassuring. Every once in a while the voice stops, and its words are repeated by a chorus of others.

In the far distance, he can make out the tunnel's end and the two Slithering Men who stand guard before a set of doors. *They'd be able to see us too, if we weren't on our bellies.*

The voice stops and a new voice answers. *It's the Captain,* he thinks, happy and worried at the same time. He can't make out what he's saying, but it's definitely the Fate.

Doors line each side of this section of the hall. Ieiri disappears into one of them and they follow just behind, still crawling on their bellies. *Now, we're slithering men, too,* he thinks as he nudges the door closed behind him.

It's so dark that he can't tell if they're entering a ballroom or a closet. But a hand grabs his own and pulls him up to his feet. It guides him along gently until they come to a a small opening in the wall. *This must be some sort of air hole or vent that connects to where the Captain is.*

" ... the sins of the father?" a voice echoes through the opening.

"I will, sir," the Fate says.

"The son of Beck Songjinn seeks his redemption," a chorus repeats.

"And for whom do you quest?" the voice asks.

"I am here in the name of the Three Kingdoms of Wysteria."

"The burden of one is unbearable, but the burden of a nation will crush you. This much is assured. Still, do you wish to continue?"

"Yes, sir, let the burden try to crush me," the Fate says. "For I am here to crush that burden."

"Well said, Hero," the voice says. "But failure of such a Challenge does not come without consequence. Are you willing to accept such a fate?"

"I am, sir."

Then there is silence. "Do you understand what's going on?" Wake whispers in one ear. "What burden do they want him to take on?" Ieiri whispers in the other.

"I'm not sure," is all Sense has for an answer. Already, this is far different from what he expected. *Burdens? Consequences? There was no mention of those things in any Challenge I've ever heard of.*

As far as he knows, there were numerous Challenges of Honor issued in the past decade—all of them outrageous, none of them ever taken seriously. *Everyone's always treated the Challenges as a novelty, but this ... this seems serious.*

A large bell rings in the other room. The voice continues, "Before Honor comes Redemption. The Challenge of Redemption is sought."

"Redemption before Honor," the chorus chants.

"To redeem thy name and that of your father, you must conquer the final game of Wysteria's Tournament without stepping onto the battlefield."

"Conquer without might," the chorus chants.

"To claim your honor, you must tell no soul of our meeting tonight or what it is that you attempt."

"Gain trust without words," the chorus echoes.

"Your punishment for failure is that you will never fight again."

"Fail and give up your greatest joy," the chorus says almost sadly.

"The Challenges have already begun," the voice says. "May good fortune shine down upon you."

There is applause and the sound of shuffling. *I wonder if Fate's father had something to do with the incident twelve years ago, the event that no one speaks of,* Sense thinks to himself.

All Memories of that day have been wiped. Even just mentioning it, is outlawed. All he knows for sure is the Three Kingdoms were banned from the International Tournament of Tears shortly thereafter. *Could these Challenges somehow be related to that?* he wonders.

"Fate, may I have word?" the voice from before asks. Though the tone is much more hushed, it is even clearer. *What luck. They must have moved closer to the vent.*

"Yes, High Lord Jhezza, it would be my honor," Fate says.

"Among my people, there is an oath that we hold sacred above all others. It is a pact of loyalty that will tie our destinies until the end of days. I have watched you since before you could walk and have come to admire the man you have become. I wish to take this oath with you."

"I will be honored to take this oath," Fate says. "Is it right to take it before I have completed my Challenges, however?"

"As in all things there are benefits and drawbacks to when the oath is taken. But this will in no way influence the outcome of your Challenges," the Glissade says. "As for myself, I am willing to accept the risks. Shall we continue?"

"Yes, sir."

The Glissade clears his throat and speaks loudly. "I come before you as Jhezza, son of Adzz. The paths we have traveled are our own, but let our ways become one. From this day forth, I shall witness the world through your eyes and listen to its song through your ears. In turn, I will pledge my entirety in support of your dreams. Do you accept me, Fate of lost name?"

"I do," the Fate says.

"Now, we are united. And I will never betray you as long as you stay true."

Suddenly, the door behind the eavesdropping trio bursts open and light fills the room. A Slithering Man stands in the entranceway, spear in hand. "What are you two doing in here? Guards!"

Two? Sense wonders. His question is quickly answered when he finds only Wake at his side. *Ieiri must have hidden in time,* he thinks, trying not to look around.

The Glissade in the doorway is as tall as Wake and in many ways similar to an ordinary man, all except for the trail of cloth that flows behind him, almost like the train of a long gown. Except that underneath the trailing fabric, Sense can make out his thick tail. But Glissade are supposed to be taller than most ordinary humans. His features are also smoother, less refined. *Could he be younger, like us?* Sense wonders.

"Guards!" the Glissade yells out once more.

"Wait," Sense says, standing up. The Glissade youth stares at him for a moment before yelling a third time.

"We mean no harm. We were just worried about our friend and Captain, the Fate," Sense tries to tell him. That, at least, stops the Glissade's shouing. But now, his spear is pointed directly at Sense. *What to do? What to do?*

The Glissade youth looks at him expectantly and the words that come out of his mouth surprise Sense as much as anyone. "I come before you as Sense, son of Arthur Bannister, Sr. The paths we have traveled are our own, but let our ways become one. From this day forth, I shall witness the world through your eyes and listen to its song through your ears. In turn, I will pledge my entirety in support of your dreams. Do you accept me, Glissade?"

The Glissade youth looks at him for what seems an eternity before finally bursting into laughter. The clanking of armor grows closer, but before the guards arrive, the young Glissade closes the door behind him.

"Zzan? Are you in there? Did you call for us?" the guards ask from the other side of the door.

The young Glissade lowers his spear and places his hand on the wall. Something clicks and a light turns on in the center of the room.

He's no longer laughing, but instead, staring intently at Sense.

Finally, he answers. "My apologies, it seems to have been just a couple of rats. Two of the biggest rats I have ever seen, but just rats, nonetheless."

Grumbling can be heard on the other side and then the sound of clanking armor moving away.

The Glissade that the guards called Zzan speaks. "How can a human see through a Glissade's eyes or listen through his ears?" He laughs again. Behind him a shadow grows and suddenly, Ieiri is behind him, claws outstretched.

"No, stop!" Sense says.

"I can't," Zzan says, hunched over in laughter. "You humans are so preposterous, sometimes." His laughter turns to confusion when he notices the single claw at his throat.

"What is the meaning of this?" Now, it's the young Slithering Man's eyes that are large with fear.

"Not another word ... or else," Ieiri whispers. Sense thought the Glissade was pale before, but now he is truly colorless. *The Colorless Race; that's what they're called in the West,* Sense remembers. *Though, it's probably more for the fact that they can't be Teared than the color of their skin.*

"Ieiri," Wake says, "He already sent the guards away. I don't think ..."

"We can't trust him, " she says. For the first time tonight, she looks unsure.

"I'll take the Oath of Understanding," the young Glissade says desperately. "You'll be able to trust me then."

"Is that the same Oath that the Fate took?" Wake asks, "What does it mean."

"It is our most sacred oath," the Glissade says. "By taking it, a Glissade swears support of a human in exchange for being able to view the world through their eyes. It is a great honor for both. Any of my people would sooner die a thousand deaths than betray one they have sworn to understand."

Sense nods for her to let him go. Everyone knows that the Glissade are neutral, but it is not by remaining uninvolved. They remain neutral by offering an equal amount of assistance to all. Nearly every man or woman to have sat the Conqueror's Throne did so with the assistance of the Glissade. But in the same token, the Slithering Men also played a hand in each of their dethronements as well.

Ieiri doesn't look as convinced. "You better be sure about this, Sense," she says before finally lowering her claws. The Glissade brings his hands to his neck as if to reassure it is still in one piece. "Oh, thank you, thank you," he says. "You will not regret this, I swear."

He smiles nervously. "I was actually wishing for something like this to happen," Zzan says, "Not the almost losing my head part, of course, but to find my first to-understand on this journey."

"Time is short, however. Shall we begin?" Zzan lays down his spear and rubs his hands together excitedly.

He faces Sense and begins to speak. "I come before you as Zzan, son of High Lord Chezza. The paths we have traveled are our own ..."

When he finishes, Sense answers, "I do."

Zzan smiles and clasps Sense's hands within his own. "This has all come about in a very unusual way, but still, I believe this is a good thing—a very good thing, indeed. Now, we are brothers, and your friends are my friends and shall be until the end of days." He eyes Ieiri warily.

"I wish we had more time to share, but that time will come," Zzan tells them. "Already, the others of the main party are headed to the Palace. If I do not join them soon, I will be missed."

Zzan turns to Sense and adds, "But what you need to know right now, is that from this moment onward, I will be able to view the world through your eyes whenever you activate your Tear. If you need to ever speak to me directly just do so and I will hear your every word. For now, I will not be able answer, but hopefully that time will come. I will never be able to assist you with direct action, but what I will do, is provide you with any information that is at my disposal—which I assure you is most vast."

It's more than Sense could've hoped for. Glissade are known as information gatherers, and now Sense knows the how and why. *They must make such relationships with many Criers and use the knowledge gained to gain even more.* Sense smiles and Zzan smiles back warmly.

"Very good, you understand," Zzan tells him. "We shall speak again soon, but for now, I must go before I am missed. Please tell no one of our meeting, especially the Fate. At least, not just yet. It will be a delicate matter informing my father of this. I prefer he learn it from me. I will need some time to find the right moment, however."

Sense assures him it will be so.

"One more question, please?" Wake asks. "That wasn't the usual Challenge of Honor that the Fate accepted, was it?"

Zzan shakes his head. "If you wish, I could tell you more, but that would most assuredly mean his failure. But is it not obvious what is at stake?"

The three decide it best to leave it at that.

"This whole compound will be empty within the hour. All you have to do is wait until then and then you may leave by whichever way you entered." Zzan turns off the light and opens the door. "We should turn this off to avoid any suspicion. Also, I have one more piece of information that you may find valuable. Your friend the musician has gone missing."

"Poe?" Wake asks. "Poe is missing?"

"How do you know this?" Sense asks.

"We keep tabs on the people that we have interest in. Your Captain is one such person and the bard is as well. Poe, as you call the bard, was last seen talking to two males, a large one and smaller one. Since then, we have not been able to locate … him."

"What does that mean?"

"I'm sorry, it was my first time sent to observe. It was much more exhilarating than I ever anticipated, but I digress," Zzan says. "I do not know exactly what was taking place. All I can say for sure is that the bard did not look happy, but left willingly with the pair.

"My people hate conjecture, but I think I can safely say something wasn't right."

While they wait in the darkness, Wake and Sense explain to Ieiri that even though Poe is not officially on the Team, he is just as important as any other teammate.

When they finish answering all her questions, she tells them, "You must know by now that Fate lives only for one goal—to be the Captain of a team to win one hundred in a row?"

"Of course, it's all he ever talks about," Wake says.

"Even I don't know who put the notion in his head, but he's been obsessed with the idea since long before I met him," she tells them. "I know it wasn't from the Old Man, either. He hates the idea. What else I know is that—his every breath, his every thought and action are dedicated toward achieving that goal. Do you understand what that means?"

"Yes," Sense says, just as Wake says, "No."

"It means he wouldn't have accepted the Challenges unless it has something to do with his goal," Sense explains.

"Oh yeah, of course," Wake says quietly. "I knew that."

"Do you think it has something to do with ..." Sense begins to ask.

"It doesn't matter what we think," she says. "What matters is what I know. And what I know is that Fate has always been there for me, so I will always be there for him. I do not have to understand why he does what he does, because I have never known him to be wrong, at least, not when it really matters."

"I agree," Wake says. "But I can't help wondering ..."

"If you want to waste your time wondering, so be it," she says. "But if I ever catch you not believing in him, I'll ..."

"Don't worry about that," Sense says. "Wake and I know better than anyone that if there's one thing we can believe in, it's the Captain. He believed in us when we didn't even know we needed it."

"Good," she says as she stands and dusts herself off. "The hour's up; it's time to make our leave."

Ieiri cracks the door and investigates the corridor.

Just as Zzan said it would be, the tunnel is empty. The torches have been extinguished and silence and darkness surround them. They make their way through the pitch-black hall, wondering if it took this long on the way down. Eventually, they come upon the entrance.

"I should be going, now," Ieiri tells them under the moonlight. "This isn't a social visit. I am still in training, and Master Enada is awaiting my return. Do not tell anyone that you met me here tonight. I'm under strict orders to observe and lend aid to Fate without alerting him of my presence. I think my second master finds it amusing. She has somewhat of a dark side."

"The apple doesn't fall far from the tree," Wake says.

"She's not my mother," Ieiri replies flatly.

Sense assures her that they will tell no one. "We'll do what we can to help Fate on our end. But first, we have to find out more on what happened to Poe."

"You two, just concentrate on the games. I'll find the bard and bring him back before the final match," she says.

"What should we tell the others?"

"Tell them what you have to," she says before disappearing into the night.

"I blame you." Esperanza shoves a finger into Wake's chest. "Disappearing like that to talk to some girl.

"And now you think that you can just come waltzing back and tell us that Fate's not going to fight in Flag? You two have some nerve—expecting us to accept that with no further explanation?" she says, looking for something to take her anger out on. The poor bush next to her takes the brunt of it.

It's the wee hours of the night and finally everyone's returned to the Seven Corner's Inn. The Fate is fast asleep on his bench, while the others are huddled around the small fire pit sipping warm cider.

The sweetly sour aftertaste on his tongue is a small comfort to how tired Sense is feeling just now. He takes another sip and swishes it until it turns cool enough to swallow. Hopefully, the Daughter will do the same.

"I'm sorry, Riser," Wake says. "I should've stayed with everybody."

"It's not your fault, Wake. I'm pretty sure things would've turned out the same either way. At least, we learned something important this way." Sense says.

"Riser, I'm sorry that we can't tell you more, but this is important and you have to trust us. I wish we could tell you everything that we saw and heard, but if we do, we may be causing more harm than good," Sense says. "Things could be much worse. We could've shown up for our first Flag match and found out then that the Captain wouldn't be stepping onto the field."

"This is unthinkable, beyond unthinkable. It's un ... ununderstandable,' Riser says, pulling the poor bush right out of the ground and throwing it against a tree. Brother Monster picks it up and begins replanting it.

"I'm sure there's a good reason for all this," the Half-Orc says. "This can't be easy for him, either. Actually, I can't think of a single thing that he would find more torturous."

He's exactly right about that, Sense thinks. *This Challenge is really tailor-made to be as difficult for the Captain as possible.* The strategist couldn't have come up with a more agonizing scenario for the Fate if he tried.

"Monster's right. This must be harder on the Captain than any of us," Sense says. "He's been taking on our burdens as if they were nothing, but he never talks about his. Now, that we know he's in need our help, we have to do our best to be there for him, too."

"Sure looks like he's suffering," Riser says, gesturing towards their Captain snoring on the other side of the courtyard. She stops pacing and sits back down. "Argh! I know I'm not helping matters. I'm just hungry and tired and aching all over and hungry."

"You said hungry twice."

"Well, it's that important!" She grabs Wake's shoulder and gives it a squeeze. "Sorry for blaming you. It's just a lot to take in all at once. But to be honest, I always knew something like this was bound to happen." Just as her anger towards Wake wanes, it grows again at the thought of their Captain. "It's why I should've been Captain!"

Monster moves to block her path towards the closest remaining bush. He looks over at the others and says, "She'll be fine in the morning. We all will. A good night's rest and all of this will be easier to accept. But what's this about Poe leaving?"

"I'm worried about Poe, too," Shine says, sharing her cup with the chipmunk in her lap. "Could you please read the note that he left, one more time?"

Upon their arrival back at the inn, there was a message waiting for them from their friend. Sense pulls the note from his pocket. "'Friends, I have to go now. Thank you for everything. My two greatest hopes are for you to remain ever victorious and that I will see you all again soon.' Signed, Poe."

"It just doesn't make any sense," Shine says, shaking her head. "Poe wouldn't just leave like that, would he? He would at least tell us face-to-face, right? It just doesn't feel right."

"It is a lot to take in. Especially with everything else going on right now," Sense says. "But I talked to someone who saw Poe leave with two fellows after our match. A rather large fellow and a small one, both of whom Poe seemed to be well acquainted with.'

"Hopefully, he'll take care of whatever business he has elsewhere and comes back to us soon," Wake says.

Ieiri will surely find out exactly what happened to Poe, Sense thinks to himself. "I know it seems callous, but right now, we have to concentrate on Flag. I'm sure that is what Poe would want, too."

"Squeak, Squeak." Spikey climbs onto Shine's head.

"It sounds like he has something to say," Shine says. The chipmunk continues to chirp at them excitedly. Spikey jumps into Shine's cupped hands and she lowers him down to eye-level. "You want to help, too, don't you, Spikey?"

"Squeak, Squeak!"

"Two squeaks usually means yes," she tells everybody. To the chipmunk, she asks, "But you don't like Tear Battling very much, do you?"

"Squeeaak," the chipmunk says.

"One long squeak means no," she says quietly. "Does that mean you want to Tear Battle with us?"

"Squeak, Squeak!"

"That reminds me of something Fate told me when we first met. He said that Spikey's strong, but that he took a vow to never fight with him," Shine says. "Maybe now that Fate won't be out there ..."

"Yeah, he said something along the same lines to me too," Riser says. "And I know for a fact that the little pipsqueak's not as useless as he looks."

Spikey growls. Riser growls back. "Actually, if it wasn't for him, I'd probably be Captain right now."

"Spikey, are you really going to help us in place of the Captain?" Shine asks.

"Squeak, Squeak!"

He's just a chipmunk, but, at least, it's something. I'm going to have to come up with all new formations and strategies, though, Sense realizes.

"We can make this work. We have to." He manages to sound almost confident. "It's been a long couple of days. For now, let's get some sleep." But for him there will be no rest, only preparations to make.

As the sun comes up, Sense puts the finishing touches on their new game plan. He's done his best to include Spikey, but in reality they're losing their strongest and replacing him with a chipmunk.

It's more than fitting that the formations and strategies that they'll implement during their final practice together in Wysteria are based on the words the Fate said during their very first. "*Others may view our conditions as weaknesses, but they are what make us unique. This uniqueness is what gives us our true strength, our incomparable strength ...*"

And what makes their newest addition unique is his size. There's no other pet on Tour that can fit in a pocket. That combined with the way they have seen the chipmunk defend should be enough.

Spikey possesses no real attacks to speak of, but he can block all but the most powerful of attacks. *He can only do it a couple times a match, though. We'll have to make sure to only use his ability when it matters most.*

An apple lands on his lap and all else is forgotten. "Have you been up all night?" the Fate asks him, crunching into his own.

"I couldn't go to sleep," Sense tells him.

"Have you seen Poe?" Fate asks. "I cannot find him anywhere?"

"He had something to take care of, but hopefully, he'll be back soon," Sense says, rifling through his pockets. "He left a note, though. Here, take a look."

The Fate looks it over and nods absently.

"Thanks for the apple." Sense brings the fruit right up to his nose and inhales deeply. It smells delicious and tastes even better. "Captain, I've been doing some thinking and in order to beat *The Royal Team*, I believe we are going to need a totally new game plan."

"Is that so?"

"Well, the way the Princess set up their lineup for King's Corridor shows that defeating you is their primary focus." This much is true even though, it's not really the reason behind the switch. "We will be utilizing a new formation to take advantage of this. One where you will be fighting apart from the rest of the Team."

"I see," the Fate says. "Very well, I approve. What do I need to do?"

"I'll be implementing the new formations during today's practice," Sense tells him. "But you don't really need to be there for that, since none of the new strategies will include you. It may be a better use of your time if you were to practice by yourself, today."

"So you all will be practicing fighting without me for the next couple days?" The Fate looks at him curiously. "I did not tell you anything I was not supposed to, did I?"

"Of course not, Captain. You would never do that."

While the Fate trains alone on the other side of the courtyard, the rest of the Team gathers around Sense.

They look better, but they still look tired, he thinks.

"As you all know, Spikey will be replacing the Captain. We will be losing our strongest attacker, but we will be gaining Spikey's unique strengths. First, of which is his size. He is small; easy to carry, and easy to hide. The enemy will have a hard time figuring out where he is or who's holding him. And that crazy block that Spikey does is almost as strong a defense as Riser's Air Petals and Shine's Orb.

"Spikey's ability to defend is limited, however. He can only use it a couple times per match, but with it, he can nullify all but the strongest attacks. If used wisely, it may mean the difference between victory and defeat.

"There are additional conditions we have to keep in mind also. Our Brother Monster is injured and only has the use of one arm. The cast on his injured arm should prevent any further damage, but we do not want him jumping all around or taking too many hits. Fortunately, his healing should be unaffected. But please remember to stay on his good side to make things easier on him.

"We also have to look out for Rachel. After all her hard work, she is now able to read an attacker's basic location and has about a 50% chance of detecting attacks. One-on-one, she is at a disadvantage against any quick moving opponent. She is best off facing opponents using straightforward attacks.

"Without the Captain, we are going to have to lean on Wake and Riser more than ever for damage. Keeping them up will be a priority."

His teammates listen intently. None of them looking all too worried. *They're already used to this—doing the impossible*, he realizes.

He goes over the new formations and what they need to practice today. When he's done explaining it all, he falls asleep on the spot.

"So what is that you learned today?" Master Enada lounges lazily in her thick-padded chair, but her eyes are that of a hawk.

The room the outcast Daughter chose for them is barely large enough for two, but it does have a fireplace and a window that overlooks one of the main streets.

In one hand, the Master of the Dark Wind swishes a goblet half-full of wine and in the other she twirls one of her long needles.

Nothing, Ieiri wants to say, but that will just earn her another hour of sitting. "I found the bard's hat," she answers. At the very least, that's better than the day before in which she really found nothing at all.

Enada throws her head back so far that she's practically looking at the wall behind her. With that exaggerated sigh of hers, she just as quickly leans forward until she is on the very edge of her chair. "You are as short-sighted as you are short. Do I have to wait for you to grow too, before you can see what is right in front of you?"

"Sit," the Master tells her with a wicked smile.

Now, it's Ieiri's turn to sigh. She sits down in the chair across from her master. Enada finishes her wine and places the empty goblet onto Ieiri's head.

She circles Ieiri once before coming to a stop behind her and pulling the chair out from underneath her. Ieiri remains still, her legs bent at a perfect right angle, her bottom touching nothing but air. For the hundredth time, Ieiri wonders if there has ever been another so evil as her current master.

After 'sitting' for so long, it's all she can do but to sit some more. But at least this time, it's on the floor. If her legs would only respond just a little, she would be washing up from the long and fruitless day.

"Is that your first Master I see down there?" Enada says from the window. Ieiri tries to stand, but all she manages to do is fall back onto the floor. Even crawling is beyond her, but by digging her fingertips into the floor she manages to drag herself to the windowsill.

"I guess not," Enada says, watching the disappointment on her student's face. "Goodness gracious, girl, get a hold of yourself. I've never met anyone with as much, yet, so little pride as you."

The Master of the Dark Winds picks her up by her collar and sets her back onto the bearskin rug in front of the fireplace. "You are far too easy to read. Where is your guile?"

Ieiri could say something right about now, but decides it's wiser not to, or that she's too tired to—She can't think clearly enough to be sure which. When the outcast Daughter moves close, to pat her on the head, she can't help but cringe.

Enada laughs her way all the way out of the room at that, leaving Ieiri alone with her thoughts. *Three days and all I've found is this stupid hat*, she thinks to herself.

For three days and two nights all she has done is chase rumor and shadow. She did manage to reunite a pair of lost boys and even a little girl with their parents, but that didn't bring her any closer to her real goal—finding the bard.

She can't remember the last time she's sat down for a real meal. She's slept more standing than in a real bed. Her hair is a mess, and her cleanest outfit is days beyond needing a good washing. Still, she has nothing to show for it.

She did stop her search to catch a few moments of the Team's first match of Flag earlier that day. *At least, they won with little trouble.* Even with Fate never leaving the Staging Area, the others had somehow managed to win. She could tell how miserable he was, though.

It was almost too painful to watch. The way the crowds jeered and taunted made her want to claw their eyes out. *Fools, what do they know?* It was enough for her to skip the following matches. Concentrating on the search is more important, after all. *Tomorrow, they'll fight once more during the day, and then when night comes, they will face the Royal Team in the Finals. I promised to find the bard and bring him back by then, but all I've managed so far is to find his stupid hat.*

She even tried renting a dog, but the supposedly best tracker in the capital only managed in tracking down the Seven Corners Inn. Ieiri picks the three-cornered hat up and holds it high above her head, ready to toss into the fire. But the door opens behind her and instead she's getting laughed at once more.

Enada drops a small tub onto the ground next to her. Warm water splashes against Ieiri's face. The Master of the Dark Wind begins tugging at Ieiri's jacket. Once, she is in just her underclothes, Enada scoops her up and dumps her unceremoniously into the small washtub. She's too tired to say anything as the outcast Daughter begins singing one of her less bawdy tunes, while scrubbing at her with no mercy. She begins to nod off even as Enada begins attacking her hair with a brush.

When she awakens, she is clean and mostly dressed. A bowl of something that has long ago gone cold is by her bedside. It still smells good, though, and soon, she's slurping up what little remains of the soup.

The ground feels like it is shaking when she stands, but, at least, her legs are now working. Before she can even think of making for the door, Enada pokes her with a single finger, knocking her back into bed.

The Master of the Dark Wind sits down on the edge of Ieiri's bed and squeezes her calf hard enough to make her yelp. Then, she presses even harder against her lower legs and begins knuckling her way to Ieiri's thighs. It is the most painful massage Ieiri's ever had, but once it's all over, she can stand once again without swaying.

"Girl, do not forget that you are here to also learn and grow," Enada says.

Ieiri can feel her Master staring at her even as she stares at the floor. *Learn and grow? How can she talk of lessons when I have a promise to keep?*

Enada sighs once more. "Since, you are refusing to learn the lesson at hand, perhaps, there is something else I can teach you," she says, pulling out one of the long needles holding up her hair.

"Give me the hat," Enada tells her.

Ieiri hands it over. Enada extinguishes the fire in the hearth, leaving only a single lamp to light the room. She holds the three-cornered hat up to the lamplight and points at the shadow created on the wall.

"This wasn't so bad a find, after all," she says. "The bard must have worn this almost every day for a good long time. I'd say for at least, a year."

Ieiri watches as the Daughter ever so gently probes the shadow of the hat with her long needle. "What I'm looking for is the place where the hat's shadow and its owner's most often became one." She finds the spot and slides her needle through. Half the needle disappears into the wall and when she pulls it back out, there is a dark, ghostly thread attached to its end.

"A shadow has no soul, but they do have preferences. They form relationships; not just with their owner but also with each other. This is what we call the Affinity of Shadows." Enada hands her the needle. "When we have more time, I will teach you more on the subject, but for now, you can try following this thread."

"Will this really lead me to the bard?"

"Maybe." Enada falls back into her chair and motions for Ieiri to pour for her. Her student does just that. "This should be easy enough, even for you. As for me, the shadow of my backside will stay with its newfound friend, the chair's—at least, until tonight's final match. I will be sorely disappointed if I do not see you there ... with the bard."

"Thank you, Master Enada," is all Ieiri can say, wondering if ever a woman so wonderful as her current Master has ever existed.

The thread leads Ieiri to a large house near the river. She learns from the old crone selling flowers on the corner that the high-walled manse belongs to the Royal family.

From somewhere inside, a guitar cries the saddest song she's ever heard.

CHAPTER 60
SENSE
[SEVEN CORNERS INN, SARANGHAE]

That was closer than it should have been, Sense thinks.

All around them are the sounds of festivity, but in their little corner off of the main battlefield there is only quiet.

Riser is helping Monster rewrap his arm, while Wake sits with his sister—none of them saying a word.

Spikey is curled up in Shine's lap, tired and breathing hard after a hard-fought match. And Fate has barely spoken a word in days. *How can someone's smile look so sad?* Sense wonders.

During their first match, when Fate stayed behind in the Staging Area, all he could say was 'Sorry.' Yesterday, for their second and third, he couldn't even manage that. When he tried to speak there were no words, only tears.

The crowds didn't understand what was going on. Those nearest questioned, heckled, and jeered. *We might have been the same way if we hadn't spied on his meeting with the Glissade,* Sense thinks.

At least, they've been managing to win. But now, the news is out, the Fate is staying in the Staging Area and a chipmunk replacing him.

But that isn't even what's worrying them most.

Just before entering the battlefield, Wake's friend came to them with a message. Julia Redsilk wanted to warn them that

Kearney Dim and Willie Walls were spotted in town. No one wants to say it, but they're all thinking it—*Where exactly is Poe?*

They all know that their friend was last seen leaving with two fellows. A very large male and smaller one were the exact descriptions, Zzan had given them—the very description of Kearney Dim and his friend.

This changes everything, Sense thinks. *Ieiri has no clue of our history with Kearney ...*

Sense can tell by the look on Wake's face that he's thinking the exact same thing.

But, it's the Fate who finally stands up and says, "We should go look for Poe," He's not even pretending to smile anymore. Of all things, this frightens Sense most.

"Yes," Wake says. "This is all my fault ..."

"Way," Fate tells him, shaking his head, "It is my job to remember what really matters. And for a moment there, I forgot, but I will not let that happen again."

"I'll search between here and the North Gate," Riser says, already on her feet. "Monster will check the South ..." The Half-Orc tests his newly wrapped arm and nods.

"I'll take East, then," Wake volunteers.

Suddenly, they're all up and moving. Fate is already heading towards the West.

"Everybody, please leave your gauntlets on," Sense tells them. "We'll meet back at the inn before ..."

"We will meet back at the inn after we find Poe," Fate says. His voice is calm but clear. The Captain has never given them a command as serious as this. They all know what the order means: stay out there until Poe is found. Do not come back to eat. Do not come back to sleep. Do not come back even for the final round. Do not come back until their friend is found.

"If ... no, when you find Poe, deactivate your gauntlet so that we all know," Sense says. Even though he knows most of them won't be able to feel each other throughout such a large area as the capital, it's still better than nothing.

"Shine, how hard is it to distinguish an aura in a crowd?" Sense asks.

"Not impossible," she answers.

"You and I will scan the crowds exiting the Grounds," he tells her as the others leave. "I doubt we'll find Poe here, but ..."

"I'll also keep an eye out for Kearney's," she says.

"I'd stay far away from that house if I were you," the old crone tells Ieiri. "The men who are staying there are no good. No good, whatsoever. One is as big as a mountain and has less teeth than I do. Once, I saw him open his mouth and he had nothing but a black stub where his tongue should've been. And the little one is far worse—always pretending to be friendly and twiddling his tiny mustache while asking about for young girls. Sickening." The old crone spits.

"What about boys or bards?" Ieiri asks. "Does he ever ask for them?"

"I wouldn't put it past him." The crone shivers. "I had half a mind to inform the Palace just what kind of men are staying on their property, but who's going to listen to an old woman like me?"

"I will," Ieiri says before pointing towards the blue roses in the crone's cart. "Thank you for the warning, and I'll take one of those." Ieiri pays and tucks the flower into her wide waistband.

Her hands feel naked without her claws, but she doesn't want to draw any unnecessary attention. Enada made it more than perfectly clear that she isn't to alert Fate of her presence.

This isn't like her first night in town, where she saw the Fate leave his gauntlet behind to chase after the Glissade. She can't risk activating her Hands, now. And the use of 128's in the capital has always been forbidden. She'll have to do this without the use of her Tear.

Ieiri has her eyes, though. *There are two guards at the gate, two at the front door, and at least, one patrol.*

She continues to watch until completely sure.

There are actually two separate patrols circling the grounds. Inside, there is only one. Ieiri watches the interior guards pass by every window except for one—the very top one.

She pulls out the needle and concentrates on finding its shadowy thread. The thin, dark line points towards the building's top floor.

She stares long and hard at the manse. *Breaking in will be no easy matter, but it should be doable,* she thinks. *Leaving undetected with the bard will be a whole other matter, though. Maybe, I should go to Master Enada for help?*

No, she's probably already left for the final round by now. There's no guarantee that I'll find her in time. I'm going to have to do this myself and do it now.

The afternoon sun blankets the city in shades of crimson and gold. Ieiri pulls out a pouch of nuts and pops one into her mouth.

Just a little more and it will be dark enough for me to begin, she thinks, eyeing the setting sun. It looks so different here compared to their spot on the cliff.

The final match of the year always begins once the full moon is high above. *Things have to go just right. I'll make them.*

While waiting for an opening, she listens in on the conversations of those making their way to the Stadium. All the talk is of how *Monsters* are trying to win it with just four. Some say they're crazy, some say they're daft, but each and everyone of them is fascinated.

The moon is overhead all too soon. *It's now or never*, she decides, getting to her feet.

She pulls her scarf up and reaches back for her hood.

"Ieiri!"

She searches for the source of the voice to find a thin, freckled boy hurrying towards her. *The strategist? What is he doing here?*

"Ieiri, thank goodness it's you," He says as he reaches her.

"Sense, what are you doing here?"

"It's about Poe," he says taking a deep breath. "We have some new information."

"I told you I would take care of finding the bard," she says. "You're supposed to be getting ready for your match."

"I know, but we couldn't," he tells her. "Not after we found out Kearney was in town."

"Kearney?"

"He's an enemy we made in Greenwood," Sense says. "He's kind of a bully and has it out for Poe in particular. If Kearney got his hands on him ..."

Sense shakes his head. "I'm sorry, I know we promised to leave it to you, but we couldn't just sit around doing nothing. Not once, we found out Kearney was in town."

They should've left it to her as planned, but ...

"He's lucky to have such good friends, but unless Kearney is a middle-aged man, he's not the one that Poe left with." Ieiri nods towards the manse across the street. "The bard's in there. I was just about to go in and get him."

"Really? Oh, thank you, thank you. We were so worried," he says. His face suddenly looks even more tired; even his freckles seem to sag. "I have to let the others know."

"It's not over, yet," she says. "The building's heavily guarded and from what I've learned so far, the people staying there aren't very good people."

She eyes Sense's gauntlets. "Actually, it's a good thing that you showed up. I could use a hand."

"Now," Ieiri says, listening, watching.

A vine shoots out from Sense's gauntlet and Ieiri flies up it. Sense waits for the signal and pulls himself up behind her.

Once on the other side, they scramble behind a perfectly manicured shrub and wait for the patrol to pass.

"You were right, Sense. They do seem to have something plugging up their ears." *That should make things a bit easier.*

Sense nods, wide-eyed and shaking. *He's not used to this sort of thing. But, at least, he's trying to be brave.*

The patrol enters the building through the side entrance. Ieiri tosses one of her throwing knives to keep the door from shutting tight. She manages to duck back behind the shrub just as the other patrol passes the window above.

Ieiri catches Sense's eye and shows three fingers, then two, and then one. They make a break for the side entrance. She gathers her knife and closes the door gently behind them. Sense points towards the stairs halfway down the hall and they make a run for it.

The guitar playing starts again. As they go up and up the stairs, the sorrowful tune grows louder. They get to the fourth and final landing and she takes a quick peek down the hall.

She was afraid that this would be the case. At no point does the patrol leave sight of double doors at the end of the hall. *Time's running out, we are going to have to fight our way in,* she thinks, looking over at her partner.

Sense is busy checking out the single, small window set into the stairwell. He motions her over.

"Over here," he says, opening the window and creating another vine. She can hear it wiggle its way out and latch onto something beyond her sight. "This should take us to the right window." Sense disappears out the window and she follows just behind.

The guitar stops all of a sudden and is replaced by the sound of tears. Their so close, now, just inches away.

"There's someone up there," someone yells.

"Stop, intruders!" More and more guards show up below.

"Fail us," Ieiri mutters, practically scooping Sense underneath her arm and leaping through the window. Glass and wood shatter. The world spins and rolls until they come to a tumbling stop.

She's staring at a pair of feet that come up to meet the hem of a fine silken gown. When she looks up, she finds a girl with reddened eyes. *Fail, fail, we got the wrong room*, she thinks in disgust.

"Sense?" the girl says.

Ieiri takes a closer look at the girl. She's just the type you'd expect bad men to kidnap—about as pretty as can be and just as helpless looking.

Someone is pounding on the door from the other side. Ieiri rushes over and throws herself against the double doors. "Sense, help me!"

But it's the helpless girl that gets there first. Side-by-side, with their backs against the door, she says, "Ieiri Skyshadow, I presume?"

"How do you know my name?" Ieiri asks, trying to remember if she's met her somewhere before. Sense just looks at them with his mouth open.

"It's nice to finally meet you," the girl says. "My name is Poe. Fate's told me all about you."

CHAPTER 62
POESY HARDRIME
[INSIDE THE HIGH-WALLED MANSE BY THE RIVER, SARANGHAE]

For as far back as she could remember, Midwinter has always been her favorite time of the year. There's nothing quite like watching her breath disappear into the wind or feeling the bite of the cold against her skin. It always makes her feel so alive.

Snowflakes and icicles, hot chocolate and warm scarves—she loves them all. But the very best part of winter was that—it would mean he was coming for her.

The Maestro himself, the great Lord Hardrime—her father, would be all hers for a couple of uninterrupted weeks.

They would play and sing, eat all day, talk about nothing and everything, and go for walks in the snow until she couldn't feel her little toes and he'd have to carry her back. She would laugh a year's worth of laughter in those few days. And then, just like that, he'd be gone.

After all, the world needs its Maestro. Beloved by all, his music brought happiness to the miserable, taught what could not be taught, started wars and ended them as well. But most of all, he inspired. Little girls need their fathers, though. And he couldn't do it all.

But he could if she helped. That's what he promised her the day she entered finishing school. All she had to do was to graduate. Then they could tour the world together.

But that was all a lie.

No one would ever call Poesy Hardrime a good student. Unmotivated is how most of her teachers would describe her. She wasn't always that way. When she was very little, she did try her best. But it didn't take very long for even a young girl to recognize the look she received for her efforts—disappointment. Her teachers never said it out loud, but she could see it in their eyes, more was expected of the Maestro's only child. It became far easier to not try at all.

But her father never looked at her that way. Whenever he would go over her most recent marks, he would simply pat her on the head and say, "I see the dragon has yet to wake." She didn't know what that meant exactly, but the words always made her feel better and worse at the same time.

His promise changed things, though. She stopped caring what others may think. She took every extra class she was allowed. And even though Poe rarely finished at the top, she did well enough. The shock on her teachers' faces was almost as annoying as the disappointment it replaced. *They didn't believe the dragon would ever wake.*

She kept it a secret. She was going to tell him when he came with the snow—that his daughter would be graduating a whole year early. But that midwinter break, he never came for her. He died somewhere far away.

He never even said goodbye.

Eventually, she forgave him. She was used to forgiving him. But she couldn't go back to school after that.

The one who was supposed to take care of her now, her uncle, couldn't understand why.

How can the lecture hall remind you of him? Or the library? Or the yard? he would ask her. Because every day that I sat in class, or studied in the library, or memorized songs in the yard, I did it thinking I would someday soon be with him, was the answer she could not say out loud. It was easier to run away.

Even in running away, she did so thinking of him. Poe wanted to follow in his footsteps, to finish their song, to be like him.

The stories he would tell of his younger days were the best. Tales of back when not a soul knew his name and he played for a meal or place by the fire were his favorite to recall. He would talk of meeting her mother and how she looked so much like her. He said Wysteria was a magical place where anything could happen. So that is where she headed.

She had to leave her special necklace behind. In doing so, she lost her voice, but not her good sense. Poe disguised herself as a boy. It was safer that way. It was more fun, too. It was almost as if she really was a younger version of him.

Finally, she reached the Three Kingdoms of Wysteria. She was nervous. She was terrified, but she did it. She marched straight towards where all the kids gathered and unpacked Desi. Before she could talk herself out of it, she began to play. She played her heart out.

But she wasn't met with disappointment or shock. She was met with nothing at all. No one paid her any attention. No one even bothered to listen.

Why won't they listen?

Life is not like in the songs. There's no such thing as dragons. What's the use in finding something good when it just gets taken away? she tells herself.

Poe didn't even know she was searching, but she found it. But then her uncle found her and her happy little world came crashing down. And now ...

The world is crashing down all around her.

No, really, it's shattering. Glass and splinter fill the air and where once there was a large window there is nothing but a giant hole.

The wintry wind blows in as ferocious as a wild beast unchained. It swirls all around her, grasping at her thin gown and sending chills straight to her heart. She feels her tears stop flowing as if they've been frozen in place. Her flush cheeks feel the bite of the cold and suddenly, the world is so clear.

At her feet is ... *Sense! Could it really be Sense?* And with him is a blur of a girl that moves like moonlight over dark waters even as she tumbles across the floor.

"Sense?" she says in disbelief. The strategist staggers to his feet. He looks wild-eyed, disoriented, but the strange girl is already up and bracing herself against the door.

"Sense, help me!" she says as the door threatens to be beaten down from the other side. Sense is still staggering, but Poe can help, so she does.

Foolish Poe! Wallowing in your own self-pity. Haven't you learned anything? Poe thinks to herself. Something about the other girl makes her want to try hard. From her dismissive glance to how she orders Sense around like she knows him—everything about this new girl bothers her.

And then she figures out why. All the pieces fit. This girl is ... "Ieiri Skyshadow, I presume?"

"How do you know my name?" Ieiri looks at her with eyes that will not be denied. *Eyes as dark as overlapping shadows and skin like milk. I knew she'd be strong, but why does she have to be so pretty too?*

"It's nice to finally meet you," she says. "My name is Poe. Fate's told me all about you."

The dark-haired girl sizes her up in a single glance and sneers. "I don't like liars or fakes." Ieiri turns away from her and yells, "Sense, hurry up and come help me."

What Poe wouldn't give right now to put that other girl in her place. *What's wrong with her? I was just trying to be nice.* She grinds her teeth so hard, they feel as if they'll shatter.

"Poe?" Sense asks, taking his place between them. The next blow to the door is so hard it sends them reeling. It slams against Ieiri's head, dazing her. But they recover in time to keep it shut tight. Poe tries not to smile too much.

"Sense, I'm so sorry. I wanted to tell you ... to tell all of you," she says. "I just didn't know how."

"Now's not the time for that," Ieiri hisses. "We need to get out of here, now!"

"I have an idea," Sense says, stepping back and holding his gauntlets forward. "Green Art: Vine Lash." Tendrils sprout from his palms and bind the handles of the double door tight.

"There, that should hold up long enough for us to come up with something," he says. Even before he's finished, Poe is giving him a hug.

"I'm so glad to see you," she says. "But what are you doing here? And with *her*?"

"We're here to rescue you," he says. The banging on the door continues, but the vines hold fast.

"Didn't you get my notes?" she asks.

"Notes? We got one," he says. "But it just didn't seem right and when we found out that Kearney was in town, we really began to worry."

Poe begins grinding her teeth all over again. "Uncle!" She screams at the door.

"Poesy Hardrime, you open this door right this instant or ... or ..." a voice calls back from the other side.

"No! I will not," she yells back. "You didn't even deliver my second note like you promised to."

"Poesy Hardrime?" Sense's eyes grow wide.

"Never mind, Scourge is here," the voice from the other side says. "Tell your friends to step back, unless they want to get hurt."

"We better do as he says," Poe says, grabbing Sense and backing away from the door. There is a small commotion outside and then the double doors explode, showering the room in splinters for a second time.

When the cloud of dust clears, a mountain of a man stands there, grinning. Sense goes from shock to total fear and even Ieiri cringes at the sight of the near toothless giant.

But it's only for a moment. Before Poe can even scream for them to stop, Ieiri is already pulling out her blades.

A little man steps gingerly through what remains of the doorway. He tries to wave away the dust with a handkerchief.

And then, the world goes dark. Poe finds herself in a blackness so deep it's as if the world has been stolen away. The room is gone. The wind is gone. Even the floor beneath her feet is no longer there.

What in the world is going on? Poe wonders as she tries to scream, but no sound comes out.

And just as quickly as the darkness came, it is gone and standing there is a woman that for some reason reminds her of Esperanza, but a little older and a lot meaner. Underneath her right arm, she has one man in a headlock and underneath her left she has the other.

"Master Enada," Ieiri cries. "You've come!"

"Of course, I have," Enada says. "Did you really think I wouldn't be watching over my one and only student?"

"Stop!" screams Poe. "Please, just stop."

It takes a little explaining on Poe's end before Master Enada agrees to release the men. But eventually, she does.

"Thank you for letting my uncle and Scourge go," Poe says.

"As I was saying, I wasn't really kidnapped—at least, not legally. Uncle is my appointed guardian and Scourge, my father's best friend.

"It is true that they were holding me against my will, but they didn't really mean me any harm," she explains. "Sometimes, they get a little overprotective due to the fact that I am his only heir."

"You are not just any heir. You are the heir to one of the greatest fortunes the world has ever known," her uncle says, throwing his hands up in exasperation. "Do you not understand what that means, my dear? You are worth more than kings and queens, yet you walk around without a single guard. Haven't you learned by now, just how dangerous that can be?"

"It's not as if I walk around with treasure in my pockets," Poe says. "The only thing of value I carry is Desi."

"You still don't understand. It's not the fortune we are worried about. It's you," her uncle says. "How many times have you been kidnapped, now? Three, four? When will you learn—*who you are* makes you a target."

"Five, if you count this one," Poe mutters under her breath.

'What was that?" Sir Hardrime raises his voice and brings his face right up to hers. "This is not a game, young lady!"

"I can take care of myself," Poe says, not backing down. "My friends came for me, didn't they? They're far better than any guards you ever hired. And if worse came to worse, I could always use my true voice." She grabs the necklace around her neck, threatening to tear it off.

Why does he have to always be like this? Poe wonders, noticing for the first time that everyone is staring at her. *Of course, I realize that this isn't a game.*

"Oh my goodness, game!" Poe says. Even though she wasn't allowed to leave the room, she still managed to keep track of how her friends fared.

She runs to the hole where there once was a window and sees

that the moon has risen. "Sense, shouldn't you be at the Tourney Grounds by now?"

Sense manages to finally close his mouth and stop staring. "Yes," he says, running over to join Poe by the hole in the wall. "How could I forget?" he says, fiddling with his gauntlet "We're supposed to deactivate our gauntlets if when we find you, but I think they're too far off to notice."

"What? The others aren't already there?" Poe asks.

"It's a long story, but everyone's out looking for you," Sense tells her. "We were worried ..."

Poe turns to her uncle, who tries to smile. "Perhaps, I should have sent along that second note. I just thought that no good would come of it. For that I am sorry, Poesy."

"Never mind that now, Uncle," she says. "Right now, we have to make things right."

Her uncle still looks hesitant.

"Fine, I'll take the oath," Poe says. She was avoiding it in hopes of rejoining her friends, but right now, that doesn't matter.

Sir Hardrime pulls out a black, leather tome from inside his coat and hands it to her.

Poe grabs the Promise Tome and places her right hand upon it. "I, Poesy Hardrime, swear to finish school and never run away again." The book glows golden and chimes three times.

"There, it's done; now you have nothing to worry about," she says. "Please let me go help my friends." *But how? They're spread all throughout the city. We'll never be able to find them all in time.*

"We should go to the Tourney Grounds," Sense says.

"Have the others noticed your signal?" Ieiri asks.

"No, unfortunately, not yet," Sense says. "But still, it's our best chance."

Sense has that look, like he knows something that no one else does. Usually, Poe hates that look. But right now, there's no other face she'd rather see.

"Uncle, send for the carriage. Sense has a plan."

"Why am I bringing Desi?" She's never without the guitar, but the fact that Sense went out of his way to tell her to bring it, bothers her.

But he's far too busy fiddling with his gauntlet to answer.

Finally, he looks up and says, "Good, Monster's noticed. It should only be a matter of time now, before the others do, too."

"The moon is almost above the Tourney Grounds," Ieiri says, hanging halfway out the window. "There's no way that everyone will make it in time."

"It's okay as long as we make it in time," Sense says.

"Yes! Then maybe we could explain everything to the officials and ..." Poe begins to say, but her hopes are dashed at the looks on the others' faces. "Fine, so that's not very likely to happen, but then just what are we trying to do?"

"You're right; they won't postpone the match for just any reason. But maybe there's another way we can buy some time," Sense says. "Can't this thing go any faster?"

Ieiri climbs out the window and encourages the driver to make haste.

"Another way?" Poe asks. "What other way?"

But Sense is back to tinkering with his gauntlet and not answering questions.

"Now, I remember just why I hate Wysteria," her Uncle says, wiping at his brow.

Scourge begins to make that clucking sound that means he's finding all of this very amusing. When he stops laughing, he signs something with his hands and Poe translates for him. "Scourgey wants you all to know that he let himself be put in a headlock."

Enada sighs out the window and says, "Worthless words, even from a mute. It's not the first time he's let me put him in a lock." She turns to face the large man. "Scourge Kutz, do you not remember Ambrose Bay?"

Poe never knew that Scourge's eyes could grow so large. Her uncle scratches his head and mumbles, "Ambrose Bay? Why we haven't been there in close to thirty years. Weren't you still competing back then?"

The large man nods slowly and again begins to make signs. "Dark Wind? Impossible ..." Poe translates.

Enada simply laughs. "Did you not learn that thirty years ago? Every single thing about me is impossible. But now is not the time for that. Right now, these kids have their own Ambrose Bay to win."

"You're really the daughter of Lord Hardrime—*the* Lord Hardrime, The Maestro?" Sense asks as they push through the crowds.

Ieiri takes the lead. It's almost as if she enjoys elbowing people out of the way. Enada strides behind them with a look of amusement on her face.

The only time Poe's ever seen this many people in one place before was for one of her father's concerts. She didn't realize that there were this many people in all of the Three Kingdoms.

"Yes, Sense. I told you that already. Now's not the time to be star-struck. I'm still the same old Poe. Nothing's changed." She looks back to see if her uncle and her father's best friend are still keeping up. They're falling further and further behind, but at least, she can still make out the top of Scourge's head in the distance.

"I'm sorry ..." Sense begins.

"You don't have to apologize to me," she says.

"I'm sorry for the loss of your father," Sense tells her. "You must miss him very much. He really was a great man."

"Yeah. Thanks, I do," she says.

He points towards the fine, white-metal chain she wears around her neck. "Is that how you can talk, now?"

"Yes," she says, almost smiling. "I'm so very glad to have it back."

They catch up to Ieiri, who's arguing with the Sitters guarding the entrance to the battlefield.

"Forgive her, she's with me. I'm with *Monsters To Believe In*," is all he has to say to get the guards to allow them to pass. Ieiri grumbles all the way to the sidelines. Poe tries not to laugh.

"Enough. This is where we take our leave," Enada says to her student.

"But ..." Ieiri begins.

"Our fight here is over," Enada says. "We will watch the match from the stands just like everyone else. But first, tell me what you have learned today?"

Ieiri thinks for a moment, before answering in an almost fearful tone, "Matches are won or lost, on and off the battlefield?"

"Good enough," the Master of the Dark Wind tells her. "You may sit in a chair."

"Farewell, children," she says to Sense and Poe. "And may you find Glorious Defeat later rather than sooner."

"Never Fall," Ieiri says before turning to catch up with the outcast Daughter.

Now, it's just Poe and Sense alone on the sidelines. "Uncle and Scourgey finally made it," she says, pointing towards the entrance to the field and waving.

"Good, but who we really need to find is the Head Official," Sense says, scanning the area. "Or maybe someone with even higher authority than that."

They spot the Official's Table on the far end of the field. "Of course it would be all the way over there," he says, hurrying towards the other side.

"Just exactly what do you have in mind?" Poe asks.

"Victory," he replies with a smile.

The officials actually look relieved to hear their request. They must have been more than worried that the most anticipated match in years was about to result in a no-show.

They even seem somewhat receptive to the option of a slight delay. But just as the strategist begins to make headway, the officials grow quiet.

The Princess has arrived.

"Absolutely not. A delay is unacceptable," the Princess says. "If they are not here at the appointed time, they must be disqualified. The rules are more than clear on the matter."

"Your Highness, what of all the people that have come to see the match? This is the largest crowd we've seen in quite some time," the Head Official implores

"We must all abide by the rules. It is your job to make sure that we do," she says. "I for one am unwilling to take part in setting such a precedent, and I am sure my grand-uncle will say the same."

As if summoned, a grandfatherly man clad in amethyst robes approaches, trailed by no less than a dozen retainers. Each and every head present, bows to King Love VI.

He waves them to stand and nods for the Head Official to explain the situation. He listens silently, all the while smiling warmly. Then, finally, he speaks.

"I am truly sorry to disappoint all those gathered here today, but Princess Achylsa is correct. We have more than the honor of our country to consider in this matter. The last thing the Three Kingdoms is in need of is another Tear-related scandal. I will make the announcement myself that the match has been canceled. My people deserve at least that much," the King tells them.

Poe studies the Princess. Words not befitting her upbringing come to mind.

Sense, who just moments ago, almost convinced the Head Official to break the rules, now, looks subdued in the face of the King. He has something to say, but has lost his voice.

"Excuse me, Your Highness, King Love," Poe says. "We have a proposal for you that may be of some help in sorting this situation out." Sense has yet to tell her what he has in mind yet, but she knows he has some sort of plan.

"And just who are you, young lady?" The King of Wysteria gives her a grandfatherly smile. Before Poe can answer, her uncle is there beside her.

"Your Majesty, King Love!"

"Sir Hardrime. It has been far too long." The King greets him warmly. "My deepest condolences on the loss of your brother. The world may never see the likes of him again."

"Thank you, Your Highness. You have always been far too kind to the House of Hardrime. The accommodations you have prepared for us this visit have been particularly impressive," he says before gesturing towards his grandniece. "May I introduce The Maestro's daughter herself, Poesy Hardrime?"

She curtsies and accepts his blessing upon her outstretched hand.

"I am truly sorry for your loss. Your father was a remarkable man. He was always a great friend to the Three Kingdoms and I hope that we, too, will also become good friends." He tilts his head towards her. "Was there some matter you wished to discuss?"

"Yes, Your Highness, but I believe that it may be best for my friend explains." She shoves Sense forward, whispering into his ear, "This better be good."

"Your ... Highness," Sense stutters before spitting it out. "With such a large crowd gathered here today, we have a very unique opportunity ...

"Right at this very moment … for the very first time in the whole world, Poesy Hardrime, The Maestro's only child, is willing to make her debut on the world stage."

King Love's eyebrows actually rise.

"But the window for her to honor us with such a historical performance is very short," Sense says. "It's now or never."

This is his plan? Poe wonders in disbelief. *He wants me to perform here, in front of all these people? Me?*

"She is willing to unveil—for the very first time—a song she has composed herself," he adds.

I don't know if I'm ready for this , but … "Not only that, I started working on it with my father. It is his last song."

The King considers it. The Princess at his side burns holes into the young pair with her blank stare. She tugs at the King's robes as if to remind him that she's still there.

"I would gladly accept such a gracious offer," the King finally replies. "But alas, Wysteria cannot afford to add to our current reputation as rule-breakers. Not with our current status, such as it is. I hope you can understand."

"Your Highness, what if we were to have the postponement approved by one of the highest ranking officials on the World Circuit?" Poe makes her way through the small crowd. She grabs the back of her father's oldest friend as he tries to sneak off. She reaches inside his coat and pulls out a badge—a badge of an International Head Official.

"I am pleased to present before you, the dreaded Scourge Kutz," she announces. Although he no longer serves in official capacity, a Head Official on the International Tournament of Tears holds the title for life. The large man gives a shrugging nod.

"Very well, then. It's settled. Please make your preparations immediately. I will personally present you to the world for your debut," the King tells her with a pat to the head. He leans over to his niece. "I am sorry, Achylsa. You know that you have my full support in all of your endeavors, but this really is a rare opportunity to reintroduce our beloved nation to the world."

She bats not an eyelash before turning and walking away.

Poe and Sense do a little dance of joy. But their celebration is short-lived. Suddenly, she begins to realize just what she's gotten herself into.

"Trust me," Sense tells her, seeing the expression on her face, "This is going to work. The others are on their way. We just need to hold off until then."

Poe watches as Sense plays with a piece of equipment she's never seen before. He explains that it controls every Tear-light in the stadium. There is no soul on the field, but the two of them. Still, the crowd pays them little attention. They are not the ones that the people have come to see.

She sees them, though. Mothers and fathers, brothers and sisters, old and young: all of them, giving off an energy she's never felt before. But here in the middle of the field, it is almost quiet. *Like the eye of some great storm.*

King Love makes his way towards them. Behind him, attendants carry a device that will broadcast his words for all to hear.

He begins his announcement talking of her father. The citizens of Wysteria shout their approval. All she can think of is him. *Father, they still cheer your name.*

The King mentions her name. At first, they do not know what to make of it. But soon they are cheering even louder.

"I'm ready when you are." Sense hands her Desi.

This is all happening too fast. She stares at the instrument that her Father played for so long and all of a sudden it hits her, *this is his. Who am I to think that I could play Desi for a crowd like this?*

"Poe?" Sense says.

"I don't know if I can do this," she whispers. *It took me a year just to finish one song. And he started it for me. If I go out there now, I'll just bring ruin to the Hardrime name.*

"What are you talking about?" He grabs her by the shoulders. "I know how it feels watching from the sidelines—wishing there was something more that you could do. Sometimes, I feel like I'm not really a part of it, but we are. Don't you understand? I learned just how important a part of it we really are these last couple days. They weren't going to even show up without you.

"Don't you understand, Poe? This is a battlefield and this is your battle."

"We've stalled enough; they'll make it back in time," she says, turning away. "I can't do this, I'm sorry."

He just looks at her.

"You don't understand. My father ..." The iciness of her cold-blue eyes has melted and now threatens to flow at the slightest blink. "He was the greatest; the greatest ever. Me? I'm nothing. I'll just end up tarnishing his name. They'll never listen to me." It's all she can picture right now, the disinterested looks on the faces of those going about their business as she tried to play.

"You don't know what it's like," she says, "... to play for people that don't listen—that don't care."

Sense goes quiet for a long moment before speaking again. "You really are brave. It must have been hard, pouring your heart out day in and day out, and no one seeming to care. But not everyone was ignoring you. There were always those who were listening—Captain was listening.

"And because he did, we all got a chance to listen to you, too," Sense says. "We got a chance to know you and become friends with you ... not because of who your father was or how many songs you can play, but because when you play, we can really hear you.

"Things are different now. You have fans—us. We'll always be listening. Even if you play every note wrong, we'll listen the whole way through and be proud of you at the end."

The faceless people going about their business as she plays fades from memory. The shockingly silly smile on the Fate's face that first day replaces them. And when she closes her eyes, she can see them all ...

They're all chasing dreams, willing to face embarrassment or defeat or indifference for some reason or other—for one another. There's no truer example of that than the Fate. He's never said so in so many words. He's never had to. Everyday, he shows them what it takes.

At first, you can't help but laugh, but stick around long enough and you can't help but to start feeling ashamed. And then you choose. *This is my dream,* Poe thinks. *This is my chance. Am I going to fail even before I try just because I'm scared?*

Across the Tear-speakers booms, " ... and now give a heartfelt welcome for the international debut of Poesy Hardrime!"

"If you still want me to tell them you can't, I will."

Poe looks up and laughs. "Even if you did, it wouldn't stop me. I'm going out there and playing *our* song, no matter what."

Poe looks back at Sense with his drum between his legs. His echo-box is on one side and the contraption to control the lights on the other. He gives her a thumbs-up. *I can do this.*

She sticks her hands out wide and the crowd erupts in cheers. She waves them to quiet down and they do. All eyes really are on her. On the near sideline, her friends have already begun to arrive.

"Hello?" she says, a little too close to the amplifier. Her wavering voice echoes throughout the arena. She leans a little away and says again, "Hello, Wysteria!" This time her voice carries loud and powerful for all to hear.

"I'm going to play something I wrote with my father. Some of you may have heard me practicing it, but here's the whole thing. It's called 'Our Song,'" she says softly.

Cheers erupt all over again, but the crowd grows quiet as she steps back and begins to strum.

She closes her eyes and sings:

Wisdom has a price
It costs everything

Until you lost it all
How can you find begin?

Bottom's where it starts
Dreams achieved is the end

And if chasing dreams is wrong
Then we're proud to live in sin

No matter what they tell us
Impossible's not a thing

So try to knock us down
We'll just rise right up again

When it's all just too much, can you show me that smile?
The one that lets me know that it's all really worthwhile.
If I play for you, will you stay and listen for awhile?

How do we do it?
It's cause Fate is our friend

Brute hope is our sister
Our Brother a godsend

Good Sense is always with us
On that you can depend

We laugh in the face of danger
And come shining through in the end

We're legends in the making
In fact, legends we'll transcend

Failure's not an option
Our Wills will never bend

When it's all just too much, can you show me that smile?
The one that lets me know that it's all really worthwhile.
If I play for you, will you stay and listen for awhile?

The final note hangs in the air forever. *How can it be so quiet?* she wonders, too afraid to open her eyes.

When Wysteria shouts out their love, it echoes throughout the whole kingdom for all to hear. She doesn't try to hide her tears.

Her whole life has been about keeping to herself, and for the first time she shared her all. Never has she felt so brave. *Father, this is for you.*

She holds his guitar up high and shouts, "Those things which we yearn for, Desi Derata, Transform: Fiddle!" One of the Tears set in the instrument's side glows and there is a blinding flash. When the light recedes, Poe holds a fiddle and bow.

"Once more! Once more!" they shout and she plays it again. Slow and sweet, Desi cries, each note a memory of Poe's own voice. She finishes, knowing she's given it her all.

The applause reminds her of something her father once said that never made sense until just now. *"I'm so famous now, it scares me. They cheer before I even begin, but as long as they cheer loudest when I'm done ... well, then I know I really did it."*

"Did what?" she had asked him.

"Touched my heart to theirs. And as good as they may feel at having their hearts touched by mine, imagine how my heart feels being touched by all of theirs."

She takes it all in. *Now, I know, Father.*

"Thank you," she whispers. "Thank you, my friends.

"Thank You, Three Kingdoms. I couldn't have done it without you!" she shouts, causing them to roar even louder.

She holds one hand up and grabs Sense's with the other. She lifts their hands high and then bows.

Finally, she motions for them to let her speak and says, "I'd like to thank Sense for accompanying me—and all my friends on *Monsters To Believe In.* Go, Monsters!" she yells.

And there they are, each and every one of her friends. They are the ones cheering loudest of all.

I really am lucky, she thinks before spotting one of their opponents. Before she met them, there was one guy that actually stuck up for her, at least, once in awhile. She won't forget that.

"Also, I'd like to thank Kase Shake, who when no one knew who I was, defended me like he does everybody else," she says before grabbing Sense and running off the field.

She runs up to the Fate and gives him a long, held-in hug. He gently pushes her aside and says, "Excuse me, I am looking for someone."

"It's me, Poe ... Pooh," she tries to tell him.

He tilts his head as if that would make things more clear.

"It's me. I'm fine. I'm sorry I tricked you. I wanted to tell you, tell everybody, but by the time I got to know you and trust you, I just didn't know how."

"You look like him and you even sound like him," he admits. "But where is your scar?"

"It was make-up!" Poe says. "It's really why I was in the bathroom so long in the morning, not because of what you thought. You can stop calling me Pooh, but really, I don't mind."

"Pooh cannot talk in front of other people." he says.

She grabs the white-metal chain around her neck. "My uncle brought this with him. It's that necklace I told you about."

"So you tricked me?" he says.

"Yes, I'm really, really sorry," she says. "Really! You're my best friend, ever. You woke me up—inspired me when I was at my lowest. I never could have done this without you. You're everything. You're my muse."

"How do you know that?"

"I just do."

"I amuse you?"

"Muse! Just being around you, inspired me. I learned so much since meeting you all. You reminded me why, after I forgot. Thank you so much," she says, realizing she has to tell him all this now before it's too late.

"Fate, did you like the song?"

"Yes, of course," he says, grinning widely. "It was the best!"

It's her turn to be quiet. He looks at her and says, "So, you really are Pooh? And you are safe and unharmed?"

"Yes, and yes!" she says.

"You found yourself?"

"Yes!"

"Thank you for being found," he says, turning to the rest of their friends. He smashes his fist into his palm and says, "Monsters, are you ready?"

"Yes!" they shout back.

"Let us do this, then!"

Sense goes over the game plan as they make their way towards the Staging Area. The fact that there is no mention of the Fate in the plan must mean it actually is true. He really won't be stepping onto the battlefield. Poe has so many questions, but decides now is not the time. By the looks on the others' faces, they have just as many for her, too.

"That may just work, Sense," Riser says as the strategist finishes.

Poe looks around: Riser is grinning, Wake's worries dance across his eyes, Monster stays strong and quiet, and Rachel tries to hide the tremble in her hands underneath the hem of her sweater. But still, they look relieved. They've all been so good to me. *Will I ever meet the likes again?* she thinks, grateful for them all.

Riser places a hand upon her shoulder and says, "I should've known you were my sister. You've always been far too talented to be a stinky boy."

"I still can't believe it, the daughter of The Maestro, Lord Hardrime himself," Wake says. "Your performance was beyond amazing."

He's about to face The Royal Team and he doesn't look half as nervous as he did back in Greenwood. They've all changed. Well, except for Fate. He'll always be the same. That's something she can forever count on.

There's no time for any more. The match will wait no longer. She follows them to the Staging Area and watches as they don their gear. *They look so tired. Have they slept? Have they eaten?*

The announcer is saying something over the Tear-speakers. The horn will blare any second, now.

The Fate puts his gauntleted fist forward. They form a ring of sorts, hands touching in the middle.

"Aye, Riser?" Fate says.

"Yes, Oppa?"

"I was just wondering ... if you could be anywhere in the world just now, where would it be?" he asks.

"Why, there's no where I'd rather be than right here, right now."

"Is that so?" he asks. "What about you, Way? Anywhere in the whole wide world, where do you most want to be most, right now?"

"Well, I guess, I really want to be here, too," Wake says.

"How about you, Shine? Monster? Sense? Pooh?" Fate asks.

Each of them smiles and answers in turn. "There's nowhere I'd rather be."

"Not on some beach, basking in the sun? Fate asks.

"No way!" they all answer.

"How about in a nice fluffy bed?"

"No way!"

"Where do you want to be?"

"Right here, right now!" they shout.

"Good," Fate says softly. "Because right here, right now is

where dreams are made true. Right here, right now is where legends begin. And right here, right now, we are together."

"Together!" they all repeat.

"Now, together let us go out there and do it ...

"The impossible—the hard way!" They shout as they throw their hands in the air. The horn blares and they rush out onto the field. The Fate follows as far as the other end of the Staging Area and stops.

He trembles, watching as they go. But at least, Poe's there for him.

"Everything's going to be alright."

CHAPTER 63

PRINCESS

[BATTLEFIELD: RAINBOW FOREST]

When the announcer finishes spewing out all their titles there is no breath left in him. The Princess hears not a word of it. This is her final chance at gaining some measure of Virtue during these games.

How did things end up like this? Even a victory now is failure—a loss unimaginable.

She spares a glance at her champion, Kase Shake. Grim-faced, his eyes quake with the fury of his namesake. She has seen him like this before. It is a good thing.

The horn sounds and so begins the last match of the year. She watches her champion charge forward, followed by the three from the Boryeon Tribe. The three Mud-Men were handpicked to ensure their victory over the Troublemaker. *Why hasn't he been leaving the Staging Area? Is it all part of some sort of trick or could it be something else?*

There is no chancing it, however. The plan will remain unchanged. *The Royal Team* will not be suffering another defeat —not today. Princess Achylsa floats a short ways behind the others, her slippers leaving wisps of violet that disappear into the wind.

She takes her time. There is no hurry. She knows every inch of the Rainbow Forest—every crystalline tree that sparkles reflections of its leaves of many colors.

It's not only where the last match of the Grand Finale is set each year, but also where she learned to play—again.

If her enemies have any sense at all, they'd be waiting at the Alabaster Fields. The large clearing filled with white grass is where every match for as long as she can remember has been decided. The thought gives her pause. *Will they surprise us even in that?*

A steady stream of numbers and letters are whispered over the speakers. They are coded messages from the Royal strategist that let her know all she needs to know. Her enemies await her at the Alabaster Fields and their Captain has yet to enter the battlefield.

Everything is so still. Across the field of white grass, her enemies wait for her. They are split into two groups—each pair, dark blotches against a flood of white.

A single infant's cry breaks the crowds' silence. And then, there is only the wind. The tall ivory grasses begin to dance. *It is time.*

She gives the signal and the trio of Mud-Men begin to circle Esperanza and Brother Monster. Kase Shake draws his short spears and advances towards the Avenoys. She looks over at the brother, a wasted act, unbefitting someone in her position. She wonders why.

The Princess positions herself between the two groups so she may aid whoever may need it most.

A drum begins to beat and her enemies come to life.

Kase makes his move. The Chosen One raises his twin spears high above his head and drives them deep into the ground.

The air fills with strands of fine, white grass that remind her of the whiskers of the late King's beard. His mustache had been short and prickly, but those on his chin were so soft she would nuzzle them out of sheer joy. There, tucked tightly against his neck, was once her favorite spot. After her grandfather died, this field made a poor substitute.

"Earth Craft: Plow Through!" Kase shouts. He charges forward holding the handles of his spears like a wheelbarrow and driving his spearheads deeper into the ground with each step.

The ground before him tears apart. Dirt, rock, and stalks of white fly all about. Wake and his sister move out of the way easily enough.

But the Chosen One's goal is accomplished. "Earth Summon: Rock Armor of the Lion!"

The bits and pieces of earth thrown asunder coalesce around him. In moments, he is armored in rock and stone.

Kase is already tall for a boy, but now, he is almost twice that. Covered from head to toe in thick stone, he is now more behemoth than man. On his chest is the face of a lion, and it roars.

The Princess looks towards the other grouping. The Mud-Men have already turned the area surrounding them into muck.

Esperanza's activated her boots and hovers just above the sinking ground. Their Healer, however, is stuck. *They will not last much longer*, she decides.

On the other side, Kase draws a wide circle around the siblings. When the ring is complete, he shouts, "Ground Seal: Plateau Stage!"

The ground begins to shake, and the ring marked by the Chosen One starts to rise, creating a giant platform of solid stone.

Wake and Rachel stand at the center of the newly-formed plateau, while Kase looms on one end. His spears look small in his current form, nothing but claws.

Everything is going exactly as planned. All that is left is ... "Terraform: World of Muck and Mire." All three of the Boryeon shout it in unison. It is a Unified Tech that requires all three to perform, but with it, the whole battlefield turns to mud.

Even if the Troublemaker decides to leave the Staging Area now, he'll not manage a step through the thick sludge.

Princess Achylsa hovers there, her slippers exuding violet mist. The Mud-Men slide through the sticky muck as if on ice. Esperanza is the only one on the other team that should not be hindered by it. Rachel Avenoy may Trip the Light for a step or two, but eventually she too will be mired. The others will be too slowed to matter or stuck altogether.

She turns her concentration back towards Kase's battle. Wake Avenoy has summoned a globe of water, and the siblings deploy their Dual Stance: Shimmering Ocean.

Kase swipes at the pair, a single slash that sends dust and grass flying. He follows through with a fury of strikes that manage to separate the pair just for a moment.

In a single leap, he clears the sister and stabs directly at the heart of her brother, bringing him to his knees.

"Wake!" she cries, charging forward with her orb. She swings it around wildly, hitting nothing but air. Kase takes a step back before coming at them once more

A low horn blares and the gates to the Staging Area slam shut. *Why isn't he fighting?* the Princess wonders.

On the other side of the field, the Mud-Men have taken some minor damage, but the other team's Healer has paid the price. His one good hand is encased in mud and his feet mired in muck.

She goes over and tosses a heal on the Boryeon before heading back to wrap things up on the other side.

"About time," Kase says.

"I apologize if I kept you waiting," she tells him.

The Chosen One has suffered not a scratch, but neither have their opponents. He wants to change that, though. And to do that, he's going to need her backing. "However, I am here now. Please feel free to begin."

"Rock Armor, Release!" Kase shouts and his stony armor comes crashing down around him. He stretches his arms out wide and shouts out, "Earth Summon: Dust and Grass, Wings of the Falcon."

Tiny curls of dust and thin, white grass swirl around him, ultimately, coming together to form giant wings at his back. He flaps them once and then twice.

And then, he's high above them—so high, he's leapt the moon.

"Violet Summon: Blood Mist," she commands. A thick purple fog begins to cover the plateau.

Kase dives. She concentrates on thickening the mist. Now, neither Avenoy will be able to see. "Talons of the Desert Hawk!" he screams.

Instead of Wake's voice, she hears his sister's. Rachel Avenoy is calling out where their enemy's attacks are coming from.

Kase Shake is deflected. He flies high and dives again.

Rachel is not supposed to be at the level of seeing attacks; at least, not according to the latest reports. *She must have little problem with head-on attacks*, the Princess realizes.

Her suspicions are confirmed as Kase's second dive ends just as the first.

"We're going to have to do this the slow way. Stay up there," she orders. He will only be able to maintain his wings for a short while longer. She has to do this now or he too may get caught in the poison. "Blood Mist Transform: Violet Smog."

The cloud turns a pernicious purple, thick and sweetly smelling afoul. One of the Avenoys is quick enough to escape. Whoever it is, manages to activate their boots and land a short distance away. *But what does it matter, they'll be trapped by the muck wherever they land.*

She turns her concentration onto the one who remains. Whoever it is, they are on their knees, grasping at their throat.

When the Violet poison finally clears, Wake Avenoy stands there with his head stuck in a Globe of Water—the very same one he'd summon in order to see behind him earlier. He pulls his soaking head from the sphere and begins to laugh. "What do you know, that actually came in handy."

The Princess rarely gets angry, but the sight of him laughing strikes a cord deep within her. Kase Shake's wings blow off into the wind and he lands next to her.

The object of her ire doubles over in laughter. "Secret Technique of the Bae: Mul HoHeup!"

"What is he talking about?" Kase asks, not understanding what's going on.

She understands, though. Wake Avenoy stuck his head into the Globe of Water and activated some sort of Water Breath Technique. *Did he plan it, or was he just lucky?* Either way, she's tired of being made a fool of.

"Finish him!" she whispers. Kase is more than strong enough to beat him straight up. With her heals for support, Wake has no chance.

Kase charges in, both spears ready to strike. But Wake Avenoy is more slippery than he looks. *Why won't he stop laughing?*

"This isn't funny. This isn't some game!" she yells. "You have no clue what's at stake!"

"I don't know about all that," Wake admits, barely avoiding another blow. He summons his own weapons. "Water Summon: Dual Falchions."

"Freeze!" He raises his swords to deflect a jab paired with a thrust. "Melt!" he commands, turning one of them back to water, all the while laughing that maddening laugh.

The Water Knight strikes back. Kase blocks easily enough. With each blow, Wake's swords of Water trickle splashes in all directions.

The Princess looks down at her dress, annoyed at the water dripping down its front.

"Why?" she asks. "Why are you doing this? You have enough points for you and your sister by now. You can stop trying so hard. What are you fighting for?" He just laughs some more.

"I'm sorry, no disrespect intended," he says. "Really, the last thing I want is to embarrass anyone."

Wake whirls and slashes both swords before him to meet her champion's attack. Their weapons clash and they are locked in a standstill. Until, Kase throws the boy backwards with a mighty shove. The Princess looks down at her newly sodden sleeve. At this rate, that boy is going to ruin her dress. Not that it really matters. She just hates being wasteful.

"I didn't mean you, by that. I meant, I didn't want to embarrass myself, mostly ... but my teammates, too. Captain would do the same for me."

"You don't even know anything about him," the Princess shouts. She almost says more, but stops herself in time. It's been a long time, since she's thought of such things, but now the memories come flooding back.

The Princess's Earliest Memories

There was once a time that she was the one that was always smiling and he was the one that didn't know how.

There were more children around back then, but they were the closest in age. He couldn't speak a word despite being older, while she could already recite one of her grandfather's speeches by heart.

But what he could do, was listen. There weren't many to take the words of a four-year-old seriously. She even touched him once and he didn't start crying like he did when anyone but his mother tried.

She knew better than to try it often. Instead, they would just play. Hide and seek was of course their favorite. A palace was a wonderful place for such a game.

The last time they played was the last time she played anything, at least, for fun. It was her turn to hide. The spot she picked was ingenious, one she had been saving for a very long time. She knew that it may have been considered cheating—but just a little. It was an unspoken rule that the parts of the castle frequented by adults were off limits, but this room could fall either way.

When she heard the footsteps, she became as still as she could and waited. She didn't mean to spy, but that's exactly what she ended up doing.

The Princess couldn't understand everything the familiar voices whispered, but she could tell that her mother was crying. That's how she learned what befell the King. There, hiding alone in the dark, is where she learned of the death of her grandfather and aunt.

She ended up winning that day. He never came to find her.

The next day, her grand-uncle was anointed the sixth Love to sit upon the throne. Her mother talked to her for a very long time. It was hard to understand most of what she said. She spoke of things that were so big, so far away.

The little Princess tried to tell her mother that Love's shouldn't cry, but her mother just whispered, "My only darling, you have it all wrong. A Love does not laugh. But cry? A Love may weep oceans. This, at least, is allowed."

It didn't sound very fair, so she gave her mother a hug to make her feel better. But that just made her cry all the harder.

She sat there in her mother's arms, sticky in tears, her hair matted and drying into curls that clung to her face, her gown so wet and twisted it had become one with her mother's. She had never seen her mother like this before. She was scared.

When her mother finally spoke, she knew why she had been afraid. "I'm so sorry, my precious little darling. I will be leaving you all alone. I have to go the Temple. It is the only way. It falls upon me to take her place."

The Princess didn't understand any of it at all.

Finally, he came and found her. He burst in screaming, followed by the Old Man. The boy wrapped his arms around her. In her small world, this was what shocked her most.

As he stood there trying not to let her go, he spoke for the first time. He said one word, "No!"

He screamed it over and over. Her mother told the Old Man to take him away before it was too late. But the boy needed only one word to let them know what he thought of that idea: "No!"

She didn't want him to go away. She didn't want to be left all alone, but all she could say was, "Yes." Even then, she knew where her duty lay.

The Old Man did something to make the boy fall asleep and that was the last she saw of him for many years. The one she now thought of as nothing but a Troublemaker.

Present

"He's nothing but a fool. A selfish Troublemaker who thinks of nothing but himself." she screams.

He doesn't know what really matters. How else could he have caused so much trouble? What … What if she had left with him and the Old Man that day?

She shakes the thought from her head. *I've come too far. No one else can do this. I don't want anyone else to have to try.*

At least, Wake Avenoy has stopped laughing. Even Kase stares back at her in surprise. Tears stream down her face. She wipes them away, but her sleeves are already wet with the stupid splashes from Wake's Water.

"I'm sorry, Princess," Wake begins to say.

"Don't be!" she screams, directing the next shout at her only friend. "Why is he still standing?"

"This is taking too long," Kase says, trading blows with the Water Knight. "I'm going to use that ..."

"Whatever, just do it!" the Doll Princess yells, the cracks in her porcelain showing.

Wake Avenoy leaps high into the air while summoning all the Water he can. He comes crashing down between Kase and the Princess. All he manages to do is soak them a little more. She knows that such attacks will add up, but this is the first clean blow that he's landed. *He's desperate and just trying anything,* she thinks.

The Chosen One crosses both spears high above his head and begins to whirl them faster and faster. She begins to chant the words that will heal her. It's a special healing Tech, one that will even restore the Water Knight's unusual damage.

Wake Avenoy slides towards her, both swords aimed at her center. *I know how your Pure Water works,* she thinks. *It'll take a lot more than this to finish me.*

As the sword of Water and Ice pierce her very center, she is surrounded by the Sphere of Protection. *How can this be? An attack like that shouldn't be enough ...*

"I'm sorry, Princess," Wake says. "You didn't account for the Splash Damage."

She finally understands. All those attacks against Kase were really directed at her. Those small splashes of Water were eating away at her all along.

She wants to scream. She wants to cry, but she's not going to do any of those things; not again, not today. She just nods at

Kase to finish what he's started. *This Tech is strong enough to take out a whole team. It should be saved, but that boy needs to be dealt with right now.*

Kase Shake gives his spears a final whirl overhead before bringing them smashing down onto the stone platform. "Earth Splitter!" he cries.

A crevice begins to form, splitting the plateau in half. The force of the blow knocks the center of the platform downwards, thrusting the sides of the plateau up. Kase Shake leaps backwards off the shaking stage, clapping his spears together. "Earth Entomb!"

What had been the top of the platform are now two chunks of stone that float perpendicular to the ground. As his spears slam tight, the slabs of earth come together, crushing the Water Knight.

When it's all over, what's left of the plateau crumbles back to the earth, she sees Wake Avenoy encased in his own Loser's Ball. It bounces and rolls all around, finally, coming to a stop near her own.

His eyes are mad with laughter and his mouth mocking. She decides once and for all she does not like him. Not one bit.

"Don't be so pleased with yourself," she says. "You may have managed to take me out, but your teammates are still outnumbered. Even with Riser's damage, without a Finisher, your team won't manage much more than a scratch."

"That was some ride," he says, clapping his hands together in imitation of what had just happened. "You're right, we won't take another one of you out. But you're the only one we had to; no one else on *The Royal Team* uses a Hand of Fate." He wiggles his gauntleted hand.

What is he talking about? She finds herself snorting in response, "Whatever, I know Kase will finish this for me."

"I believe in my team too," he says. "It's up to them now."

His smug face is the very last thing in the whole wide world she wants to look at right now. She tries to turn away.

"Princess, I'm sorry." he says, suddenly quiet and serious. "Really, I wish things could have been different."

She can tell he speaks the truth. His concern is more frightening than his laugh. When she looks at him, he holds her gaze.

"Why is your Captain still in the Staging Area? What sort of trick do you have planned?"

"There's no trick. He hasn't told us anything, but what we do know is ... is that he met with the Glissade."

Of course! I should have guessed as much. "Is that all? Is that all they asked of him?" *That's not fair at all.* Her Challenge was so much more—is so much more.

"Yes, Princess."

There is no way to win then. Even if Kase and the Boryeon reign victorious, Wysteria will lose.

"Princess," he says. "Everything is going to turn out as it should ... for all of us."

"Be quiet! You don't know anything!"

CHAPTER 64
BROTHER MONSTER
[BATTLEFIELD: RAINBOW FOREST]

"So, what do you make of the Captain's latest antics?" Riser asks, acknowledging him more than the huge mallet being swung at her head.

She manages to just duck out of the way, causing the largest of the Mud-Men to curse. *Why she is doing that—acting like they don't even exist. Doesn't she realize just how rude she's being?*

She asks again, "He's just a big letdown, isn't he?"

"No," Monster says, feeling like he's the one letting them down, right now.

It's bad enough that his feet are stuck tight in the thick sludge, but the first thing that their attackers did was to encase his good hand in mud.

He tried to wipe it clean. Riser tried to cut it free, but none of it did any good—the summoned clay would always flow back together, binding tight back around his one good hand.

Now, he's stuck wearing two casts, one he set himself and another of hardening clay.

He can't move his feet. He can't heal. He can't so much as scratch the itch just under his nose. Which is the least of his worries at the moment.

The female Mud-Man scoops a handful of sludge into her slingshot and sends it flying towards him. As she chants, the muck transforms into a dozen buzzing wasps.

Esperanza slices through them in a single stroke. "But he's a bad influence. Just look at what happened to your arm."

He answers her with a grunt before turning his attention back to his stuck legs. All he's managed so far, is to learn that the more he struggles, the more he sinks. Being still, at least, keeps him from sinking any deeper.

It's only him that's having any trouble, though. Everyone else is moving around just fine. The Boryeon glide effortlessly across the muck, while Riser levitates just above.

"He poisoned your once cowardly mind," Riser says, finally, turning back to face their enemy.

One of them wields a hammer with a stone head the size of a keg. The other brandishes a battle-axe that blots out the moon. Behind them, a girl flings mud that hardens and stings.

Riser launches herself towards the one with the axe. He blocks Ehecthal, but Riser lowers her shoulder and bowls him over. As she is about to finally deliver her first clean blow, his friend with the hammer appears behind her.

She's forced back, once again. No matter what small advantage she's able to gain, it's not for long enough. *Not with me like this.*

And what she's saying is not even right, the Half-Orc thinks. *Really, he's more like,* "Medicine," he mumbles aloud.

"Are you asking me for medicine?" she yells back over her shoulder. "You know that I don't carry anything like that on me."

"No, I'm saying he's not like poison; he's more like medicine," he says. *Is now really to talk about this?*

"That's a new one." She leaps straight up to avoid another batch of stinging bullets. And then, he notices just how annoyed the Mud Men are becoming.

Treating them like they aren't even there is really getting to them, he realizes as he watches the mud flinger cry out in frustration at her latest miss. He knows exactly how she feels.

"With all that's been going on, I never got a chance to

properly thank you," she says, slicing the tip of her sword across the surface of the muck. Mud splashes all over the face of the one with the axe. "Anyway, thank you."

"Sure," he mumbles. "You're welcome."

She grins at him and says, "I'll even let you chose where we eat next."

"Well, about that—This morning, I asked the kitchen to start roasting a pig."

"Daebak! I like your sauce best, by the way."

The talk of food is the final straw—the three from the Boryeon Village retreat and huddle up. They begin to chant in unison, "Unleash Tri-Summon: Three-headed Mud Golem!"

A massive mound of sludge and muck begins to grow. The mud flows upward like a thick dark geyser, eventually, forming a gargantuan, misshapen man.

Twisted and towering, the Golem raises its three heads and screams in anguish. The landscape, at least, begins returning to normal, leaving only scattered puddles of mud here and there.

The Mud Golem rips a crystalline tree right out of the ground and begins stomping its way towards them. Each squelching footstep draws more and more gasps from the crowd.

Meanwhile, Monster watches the Mud-Men continue to chant. *It takes all three of them focusing at once to keep that thing out. At least, they can't attack alongside it. Maybe, we can use that to our advantage.* But Monster's hopes are dashed as soon as he sees the Boryeon start sinking into the mud.

With a final belch of muck, they disappear into the ground altogether.

The three-headed Mud Golem screams, shrieks, and roars, each head agonizing in its own way. It shoves the tip of the tree into the gaping maw of its left head and begins to chew.

The right head opens its own mouth and sends a shower of crystalline splinters flying towards them. There is nothing he can do, but hide behind his own casts. But Riser is there.

"Perfect Defense: Roaring Rose," she shouts out, surrounding them in a protective shell of condensed Air. Countless splinters impale themselves against the invisible barrier.

All three of the Golem's heads don't notice in time and it too meets the same fate. The Golem runs straight into the invisible petals and is sent flying backwards.

It lands with a deafening plop that sends a small tidal wave of earth and mud rushing towards them that coats their barrier with sludge.

Now, that it can see that something is there, it stands and begins to slam its middle head against the Air Petals.

Through the dripping silt, the Half-Orc can see the behemoth's three heads clearly for the first time. The left head is eyeless, with only a gigantic maw where its face should be. The right head has what he thinks is an eye and a hole the size of a child's head for a mouth. The center holds the other eye, which opens and closes as it smashes its hardened, protruding forehead against the Rose of Air.

Skulled like a battering ram, the middle head whips back and forth, raining down blow after blow. With each thrust, its neck grows longer and more snakelike. Soon, it is cracking like a whip of boulders, but somehow the Roaring Rose holds out.

Frustrated, the Golem tries something new and reaches low, wrapping its thick, sludgy arms around the base of the Rose. It grunts, groans, and cries as it tries to lift them. But Riser's creation doesn't budge.

The heads stop screaming, but the quiet that replaces it sounds just as awful. All that can be heard are the squishes and squelches that the Mud Golem makes while it feels for an opening. It finds just that at the tip of the closed blossom and begins trying to pry it open.

Riser is by his side preparing herself for when it breaks through.

All of sudden, the Golem begins making a new awful sound—a sound so horrible that it makes Monster not even want to look. But he has to. Instantly, he regrets it.

Outside of the Roaring Rose, a scene from an abomination's nightmare unfolds. The left head has begun eating the right. It chomps down hungrily, while the right can do nothing but wail. As one head cannibalizes the other, the neck of the once-middle head grows longer and longer.

All the while, its hands pull and pry at the tip of the Roaring Rose. Finally, it works the opening wide enough to let its middle head pass through. *It's almost long enough to reach us ...*

The Golem begins to raise its battering ram-like head, straightening its long and winding neck, until it is staring at them from far above. The head whips out of sight for an instant, only to return crashing down directly at them.

Riser has no choice ... before the blow lands, she releases the Roaring Rose. For a moment the Petals of Air twist ever so slowly inward before unfurling in a burst of Air that sends all of them sprawling.

The now two-headed Golem picks itself up, lays its one remaining eye on Monster and begins to charge.

Brother Monster braces himself. But it's a blow, not from the front, but from the side that ends up knocking him over.

He lands so hard that he's counting a new broken rib with each struggling breath. But the force of that collision pales in comparison to the one that comes next.

Ehecthal and the charging Golem collide, and for a moment the world is torn in two, and in the next, it's exploding all around them.

When he regains his senses, the first thing he sees is Riser laying at his feet.

She moans, but her eyes remain closed. Her glowing armor is nearly gone. *She took the blow in my place ...*

From the forest's edge, he hears the Mud Golem screaming. *She managed to knock him clear over to the other side, but at what cost?*

"Esperanza! Please, wake up!"

A trickle of blood flows down the side of her mouth. She coughs so hard that her whole body trembles.

She won't last long like this. He looks down at the hand he should be able to use. The new mud cast has dried and is now as hard as his other.

It's gotten so dry and stiff that a good smash, against something hard enough, may just do it ... But there is nothing solid enough nearby. *Ehecthal!* he thinks, only to see that the katana has landed far out of reach.

The ground shakes and then he can hear it. Heavy, squelching footsteps, stomping their way towards them.

He wipes away at the blood around her mouth. *Her fangs are so tiny,* he can't help but think.

Fangs ..., he considers for the first time. Could he?

He lifts his mud-coated fist up to his mouth and opens wide. With everything he has, he bites down into the summoned clay.

It feels as if his fangs may just splinter, but it's the clay that cracks, instead.

It tastes awful, but still better than just about any other dish he's ever tasted—ever. He does it again and again, until he can see a finger and then two. When he's cleared enough of the foul muck to see his palm, he presses it against the girl in his arms.

"Lay Hands!"

The Golem is almost upon them, but Riser glows so bright that it has to stop and shield its one remaining eye.

Before she's even fully up, Monster is yelling at her to, "Roaring Rose! Now!"

The Daughter begins to spin.

The Mud Golem smashes against the Roaring Rose once and then twice before blinking its giant eye and remembering just what to do.

"I'm sorry, that's all I could think of," Monster says. "Now, we're just trapped, again."

"Trapped, huh?" Her eyes flash, her mind races. She crouches low and whispers, "Don't heal me anymore."

The behemoth of sludgy earth begins to pry the tip of the blossom open and once again, it whips its neck back. As it thrusts its head downwards towards them, Riser launches herself straight at it.

He notices her empty sheath, too late. "Wait! You don't have ..."

Above him, Riser and the petrified skull meet. The conclusion is undeniable. Her Sphere of Protection starts to form. But even as it starts to close tight, she continues to push upwards, rising ever so slightly higher, pinning her Loser's Ball against the serpentine head and the opening of her Roaring Rose.

Outside, the other head screams.

The Golem tugs and pulls, but can't remove its head. It pounds and pounds against the barrier and then finally, it goes quiet. The eye above Monster blinks at him and then fills with tears as it begins to whimper. He almost feels sorry for it.

It's trapped! And since we didn't have to actually destroy it, its masters should remain stuck underground, too.

"I hate this thing. But I have to admit, it makes a fine cork." She gives her Loser's Ball a punch. "What, you didn't think I could do it? If you had, that would have been ... "

"Unforgivable," he finishes for her.

Riser laughs and says, "Now, it's all up to Unnie."

CHAPTER 65
RACHEL
[BATTLEFIELD: RAINBOW FOREST]

Rachel smashes into another branch. It hits her square in the stomach, leaving her gasping for air. It takes a couple of tries, but the words finally come out, "Spikey, wait!"

Leaping clear of the plateau to where the chipmunk was waiting had been easy enough. After that, all she needed to do was wait. Wake did his part by taking out the Princess—the only one with the ability to track Rachel.

And soon after, the ground turned back to normal, meaning that Monster and Riser were also able to accomplish their mission . Everything is going exactly as Sense told them it would. Now, she just has to do is her part. *"Unlike everybody else, their strategist won't be able to see through your eyes. We are going to use this to our advantage. At some point after you and Wake engage the enemy, find a way to slip away and hide."*

Which is just what she did. All that's left is for her is to go as fast as she can. Unfortunately for her, it's not as easy as it first sounded. Even with Spikey to guide her through the Rainbow Forest, she can't seem to get very far without tripping over a root or running into some stray branch.

It hurts everywhere.

"Squeak, Squeak?"

"I can't keep up, you're going too fast. I keep running into things." Her palms are already a ragged mess and her skirt is beginning to stain red where it brushes against her knees.

The chipmunk scurries back and forth and then begins squeaking. *He's performing some sort of ritual*, she realizes.

Spikey finishes and continues down the path. But now, he's leaving behind giant marks that she can somehow see. *They must be tear-made*, she thinks. One such mark hangs in mid-air

When she reaches it, she finds a large rock. He's marking the obstacles in the way. "Oh, thank you, Spikey. You never cease to amaze me!"

She follows the bouncing aura, careful of obstructions that the chipmunk marks. *If we keep this up, I may just be able to make it back without having to fight anyone. All I have to do, is get their Flag and return it to our side without them noticing. And since their strategist can't see through my eyes and the Princess can't tell them where I am through her gauntlet, we may just have chance*

She tries not to think about how much her knees hurt or how sore her right hip is. Instead, she focuses on each step. *Win the moment, that's all. Don't think too far ahead. Just concentrate on reaching one mark and then the next. Spikey's little legs must be getting tired too and he's still going.*

The Chipmunk is circling something. Is that it?

She reaches out and finds it, a cold hard shaft with a silky cloth tied to its tip. Rachel pulls it free and Spikey leaps up and seizes it in his mouth. She marvels at the properties of the flag. *Only a Crier can pull it free, but even a Tear Companion like Spikey is allowed to hold it. It even changes size to match whomever carries it.*

We're halfway there. All that's left, is to get it back without them figuring it out.

CHAPTER 66
KASE
[BATTLEFIELD: RAINBOW FOREST]

The Chosen One curses loudly. *So, that's what they've been planning all along. A desperate ploy,* he thinks, hastening his steps. *I'll reach her long before she can capture it.*

One hundred yards in front of his enemies' base, he finds a spot to end it all. *She'll have to pass this way. The leftover mud on each side will funnel her right to me.*

Even with victory assured, he cannot get the Troublemaker off of his mind. Especially, after what the Princess told him earlier ...

They say Kase's father was once a jovial man—that Senzen Shake even treated his first son, Anga, lovingly. Sometimes, when Kase tries hard enough, he can almost remember the face of his dead brother, but always, the image seems to just slip away.

What couldn't be forgotten was that Anga was a caring brother and a mighty Crier. No one ever talks of him or the day of his death. All that's left of his memory are a few choice curses by their always-angry father.

Just the smallest reminder of Anga brings out the fury that is Senzen Shake ... and half the curses were always directed at a certain pair of names. Today, he found out those names belonged to the Fate's parents.

The approach of his targets snaps him out of it. The girl and the chipmunk come to a stop before the bottleneck. "Rachel Avenoy, it's over. Please hand over the flag."

Her reply is, "Grab the Sun."

She looks down at the chipmunk and says, "Go, Spikey!" The chipmunk heads for his right, just as she activates her 128's and charges straight for him.

"Do you really think something like that would work against me?" he grumbles to himself. He knows how just how powerful the Sun Orb is—that it may even stop an average Unleash. But his is far from average.

He surges forward and begins to ... hum.

It's something he picked up not too long ago. After last year's defeat in the scrimmage against the Slate, the Chosen One became prone to cursing—outbursts here and there when he thought no one else was around. Soon, it became more.

Whenever the memory of the loss came upon him, he would find himself cursing. At some point, it ending up becoming a problem, he tried his best to control it. Even though he managed to suppress it somewhat, the thoughts still jabbed at him.

He found himself uttering half-curses in the middle of conversations. People began to look at him strangely and the whispers began.

The loss haunted him and soon other little things did, too. And when those thoughts popped unbidden into his head, he needed to make some sound to let it all out. So he began to hum. With the humming he found some control over his outbursts.

The humming came from deep within, a shaking from his very core. And with it came his first Unleash.

Kase hums and inside he trembles, a shivering that begins at his very core and spreads throughout his whole body, culminating in fists that shake so fast that they seem still.

In each hand, he grips the spears once wielded by his father—Claw of the Desert Falcon and Fang of the Sand Lion.

He thrusts one towards the scampering chipmunk and commands, "Unleash! Falcon's Claw: Thousand Years of Pain, Shred Millennium!"

The second spear he aims at the desperate girl. "Unleash! Lion's Fang: One Thousand Deaths, Chiliad's Devouring!"

The dual Unleashes were meant for *him*, but this will have to do.

His spears are a blur, thrusting back and forth a thousand times with each passing instant. One of his blows can take out half a Crier's Spectral Armor. Each of these attacks are equal to a thousand of those.

The blind girl's Orb of Sunlight cracks like an egg and she is sent flying backwards. He's surprised that she doesn't let go even as she bounces and slides to a halt. She lands waist-deep in a patch of muck.

Nothing remains where the chipmunk once was. *But, the flag didn't return*, he realizes. *That means...*

He looks down at the struggling, blind girl, watching as she fails even to stand. She finally lifts her muck-covered face and spits out a mouthful of sludge.

She's done, he thinks, surveying the field for the tiny creature that somehow slipped by.

He finds the chipmunk struggling in the other pit of muck. The tiny chipmunk manages to almost swim through the clinging silt, but it is not fast enough.

The fact that both of his opponents have survived, angers him far more than it should. He stomps his way slowly towards the chipmunk. He raises his spear for the finishing blow. *Finally, victory is ours.*

CHAPTER 67
SHINE
[BATTLEFIELD: RAINBOW FOREST]

I *failed. I couldn't do it*, she thinks. *This is all I could manage in the end.*

She looks down at the cracked Sun Orb still in her grasp, wanting nothing more than to lay there and weep. *I'm sorry*, is all she can think. *He's just too strong.*

A blow like that would've surely finished nearly anyone else on Tour, but she's still there. Couldn't she just be satisfied with that?

After all, what could she really expect to do? She can barely lift her face out of the sludge to catch a breath.

When she does finally manage to raise her head, she catches a glimpse of the little chipmunk still struggling towards their goal. And Kase Shake striding towards his slow-moving, tiny aura.

One more time, she tries to get up, pushing with everything she has. All she manages to do is pull a muscle she never even knew she had.

She cries out in pain, only to be silenced by another face-full of mud.

Even if I free myself, what could I do? The answer's obvious. *Nothing.*

No! I can't give up—not now. Not after everything we've gone through. Wake, Esperanza, Monster, Sense, Poe … Fate. Not after everything he's gone through—it can't end like this. Rachel reaches forward once more, struggling, splashing—making it nowhere. *I must look like a fool; a dumb, blind, foolish girl, struggling in the mud—too stupid to know it's over.*

But she keeps trying. *Where there's a will, there's a way.* Why that old saying popped into her head, she doesn't know. *That's what he calls my brother, Way. He started calling him that after he learned his Unleash. He said that just listening to Wake speak had shown him what to do. I've listened to my brother all my life and that's never happened for me!*

When she tries to remember some hidden wisdom in the words of her brother, all she can recall is a joke—of the one time she asked him why he likes Water so much.

Her brother didn't say anything, but instead, he summoned some of his Aspect and drank deeply of it. *Because whenever I'm thirsty, it really hits the spot,* was his answer.

She looks down at her useless, cracked Sun Orb. There's nothing left but a shell of its former self, slowly leaking sunlight back into the world. *Could I do that, too? Is that even possible?*

She pulls the leaking Orb close to her mouth and drinks of the Sunlight.

What once was Rachel Avenoy whispers ...

"Consume the Sun: Celestial Being, Shining Fate!"

The world shatters around her. She feels the warmth of the Sun flow through her. It feels just like the touch of a perfect day upon her skin, but surging inside her.

She is up, her arms outstretched, her feet where no ground can touch them. The nasty, filthy mud is gone. Everything is gone; there is only her. No longer does she feel tied to the Earth; the world is now tied to her—it revolves around her.

Renewed and cleansed by the Light, Shine takes a step towards the brave, struggling chipmunk. But it is not like any step she has ever taken before. It is more like she Tripped the Light without even falling.

And suddenly, she's there, scooping her tiniest friend out of the mud. She sets him down somewhere solid.

For a moment, he doesn't move, but just stares up at her.

"It's okay, Spikey," she tells him. "It's just me. Now, go."

He bolts for the goal. Behind her, she hears a terrible rumbling.

Kase Shake brings his two spears together above his head. He releases his grip and they begin to float high above him. The ground beneath him strains and groans. Piece by piece, the Earth gathers over his head.

A shaft thicker than a wagon begins to form. The hardest stones come together to create the form of a spearhead.

Above Kase Shake floats a spear so large that even Titan Blue wouldn't attempt grasping it.

But the Chosen One does. "DEFY! Immortal Creation: GodSpear!"

The spectator's hoarse voices scream louder than ever. A Defy Tech is a Power Move even above an Unleash. To see one at this level is unheard of.

Kase starts to hum and the GodSpear begins to shake. His feet sink deep into what remains of the ground. The land quakes, the Coliseum trembles; even the air between them quivers. The whole world shudders and becomes a blur.

Slowly at first, and then faster and faster with each step, he charges straight for her.

She can see him—for once she can really see someone's face, in the here and now. It's a handsome face, full of determination, but twisted with fury.

The promise of obliteration comes for her, a hundred ton spear that will strike her one thousand times with a single blow.

And she has no weapon of her own. *But that does not matter, Shine*, a voice tells her. Not, if what he told her is true.

"Do you know why I made you a Shield?" the Fate once asked her.

"Because I can't hit or heal," she answered.

"Anyone can learn how to hit or even heal," he said "But only a very special person can become a truly splendid Shield.

"You may not have learned this, yet. But the Life of one's Spectral Armor is not based on how tough you are or how many hits you can physically take, as many believe. It is a representation of one's Will.

"And your Will is truly magnificent, Shine. You wish to inspire others—people that you have not even met or will ever meet. It is a precious Will, one that is sincere in its unselfishness. Your Will is greater than your own.

"That is why it was so difficult for you to embrace. Your Will is not something you feel for yourself, but one you take upon for everyone—everywhere. You may feel that you are unworthy of such a Will, but you are the only one worthy of it. Once you accept this, no force, how great—will be able to stand against you. So embrace your fate with your own two hands and protect it as if it was everything. That is what it means to be a Shield."

She didn't entirely understand what he meant, so she asked, "But, your Will is so much greater than mine? I've never met someone so determined as you—that works as hard as you do."

"You are mistaken, Shine. I work hard to make up for my Will. You see, my Will is not even my own—I borrowed it and it is selfish.

His answer confused her, but even more, it made her sad ... because a part of her knew it was true.

And right now, a part of her knows that if they ever lost, that he may just disappear forever, never to be seen again.

He's selfish like that; coming into their lives, giving them something to believe in—something to care about.

And giving them so much to lose. She isn't going to let that happen, though.

With her own two hands, she won't let that happen. Because who would be inspired by that?

But why are her hands trembling ... *No, it's the world that trembles and it's been shaking for so long now that it almost feels normal.*

The Chosen One is almost upon her.

But even if he makes the whole world shake, she's not going to let him pass.

"Kase Shake, it's over. Please put down your spear," she offers, just as he had offered her.

The Shining Fate holds her hand outstretched before her, giving him a chance to take it. But he just keeps coming.

So she curls it into a fist and brings it smashing down onto his GodSpear.

The world begins to dim as her light fades away. But she doesn't need it anymore. At some point, the horn had blown. *Spikey made it!*

But why is it so cold all of a sudden?

It doesn't last but a second, though. She feels two strong arms wrap something warm and soft around her. *Towels!*

"What ..." Shine begins to say.

"It is my duty to uphold your honor," the familiar voice of her Captain says.

She should've known it was him just from the way his arms shuddered at first, but slowly, the trembling goes away.

"Um ..." she begins, but can't finish.

Her thoughts are fuzzy and she feels her legs giving way. There's nothing left of her.

Something else really just doesn't feel right, but she's too tired to figure it out.

But no matter how tired she is, there's something she has to ask.

"Fate?"

"Yes, Shine."

"Why do you want to captain a team to 100 in a row?"

"Because I was told it would make all of us happy."

She's heard him say that before, but she just wanted to hear it again. "See, you're not selfish," she whispers to herself.

Now, he's carrying her in his arms. There's no reason to protest too much, he's warm and the day is cold. His heart beats steady and strong, helping hers slow down. Everything is going to be alright.

But … "You better put me down," she says. "Wake might get the wrong idea."

Just as she thought, he's the next to arrive, but to her surprise, he begins to thank the Captain profusely. *What in the world is going on?*

As loud as the world is, she begins to get that sleepy feeling. She tries to make out what is happening, but it's all just so confusing. The Fate is begging Wake to take her, and her brother is refusing adamantly. All she can do is just try to stay awake.

She wants to remember it all; the voices of her friends, the cheers, and the announcer screaming that they won. *Is it really over?*

"We won, right?" she asks with the last of her. "I did what I was supposed to?"

"Yes, you inspired the world. You can rest now."

And she does just that.

Rachel Avenoy wakes up surrounded by the sounds of revelry. It's so loud that she wonders just how she slept through any of it all. *How long have I been asleep? Are we back at the inn?*

"So the hero of the hour is finally awake, huh?" says the familiar voice of her favorite Daughter of Enyo.

"What happened?"

"We won, is what happened," Riser answers her.

"It wasn't all a dream? It's really over?"

"If you mean are we done competing in Wysteria ... then, yes."

Rachel still can't believe it.

"Don't worry, I dressed you," the Daughter says.

"What?"

"Well, when you got all Celestial Being on us, you blew away everything around you ... including your clothes."

Her face suddenly feels very warm.

"It's alright, though. You looked great."

The Daughter wraps her arm around her and stops teasing. "No one could see anything when you were all shining. And he had you covered up by the time you came down."

The bits and pieces of her last waking memories begin to make more sense. "Is Spikey okay?"

"He's fine. He's resting inside favorite hood."

"Where's the Captain? I want to thank him."

"Last I saw, he was eating dirt."

"What? Why?"

"Something about trying to be like you ..." Riser giggles. "He wanted to see if he could turn into an Earth Elemental or something."

"Oh no ... someone has to stop him," Rachel worries.

"Don't worry, the others were trying to do just that when I left them," Riser tells her, "It looks like they succeeded. Here they come now ..."

And then, they're all really there, all of the ones she wants to see most in the world. She feels their hands patting her on the back. One ruffles her hair and another grabs her hand.

Her friends surround her ...

Riser—the sister she's never had.

Her brother—who never stops looking out for her.

Monster—always gentle, always strong.

Poe—who paints her world with sounds so beautiful.

Sense—who always has the answer.

And the Fate—the one she believes in so much, that she was able to believe in herself.

Spikey, too!

Why am I crying? But she can't help it, she's just so happy. And then, she smells the food and realizes just how many meals she's skipped in recent days.

But before she can eat, she has to ask, "So we can keep on being a Team?"

"Of course," he says, "Is that not what we fought so hard for?"

"The Triple Threat Feat, we got it? We're all going to School next year?"

"Hmm ... something like that. But let us discuss that later," her Captain says. "Right now, it is time to celebrate."

SIR HARDRIME
[COURTYARD, SEVEN CORNER'S INN, SARANGHAE]

"Uncle ..."

"Just a moment, Poesy," Sir Hardrime says. "Can't you see that I'm talking to Miss Enada right now?"

"Pardon us, Master Enada. He'll be back in just moment." Poe grabs her uncle's hand and drags him away.

Once they're far enough, he asks, "What is it, girl? You're pushing my patience, especially for being as naughty as you've been."

"Uncle, have I told you how much I've missed you?"

He doesn't like the sound of this. "No, actually you haven't."

"Well, I did and very much so." She tries to smile sweetly at him, but all he sees is wickedness. "I know I haven't been the best of nieces ..."

"I lost the little of the hair I had left," he says, lifting his hat to show her. "Thanks to you ... not being the best of nieces."

"I'm sorry, Uncle. Truly, I am. But I really learned a lot these past months. So much; not just about music or life, but of the importance of honor and hard work, too."

He stares at her flatly.

"And you know how I promised to go to school and never run away again ..."

"Of course, I do," He reaches into his coat and pulls out the Promise Tome. "I hope you aren't having a change of heart."

"No, nothing like that. In fact, I've taken the first step towards applying to one of the most prestigious schools in the world ..."

Now, he's really confused. "And just which prestigious school might this be?"

"You know, the one the great genius Wolak teaches at ..."

"No, you did not!" *That would mean* ... "Scourge! Where are you? We're leaving right this instant!"

The large fellow lumbers over. Poe gives him a preemptive hug. "I just declared my Wysterian citizenship." The Scourge makes his clacking sound.

Sir Hardrime looks at her closely. "Poesy, do you really plan on staying here and going on Tour next year?"

She nods.

"You'll be under his care?" He points at the young clown.

She nods, smiling.

He looks at Scourge Kutz, who just shrugs. "Very well, then. But if you do not get in, I will send you straight back to your last academy."

"But, Uncle ..." she begins, before realizing just what he's said. "Really?"

He sighs and finally nods. She begins to bounce and doesn't stop even as she hugs them both. In fact, she bounces all the way back to her friends.

The dreaded Scourge Kutz gives him a questioning look.

"I'm actually rather fond of that boy. And for as much as we worried over Poesy ... she's been doing just fine. She's really matured."

He smiles. "Besides, did you see the way he reacted when she tried to hug him back at the Coliseum? I can sleep well at nights, knowing she'll be under the care of someone like that.

"And did you know his other student is internationally ranked? I'm sure with a girl like that on her team she won't have too many issues getting into Wysteria's Criers College."

MONSTERS
To
BELIEVE IN

The FATE

AGE: 17
HAIR: BLACK
EYES: BROWN
HEIGHT:
5' 10" 178CM

TEARED EQUIPMENT:
STICK,
HAND OF EARTH,
TERRA BOOTS

FAVORITE FOODS:
SEAFOOD,
LETTUCE WRAPS

LIKES:
CAPTAINING A
TEAM TO WIN
100 IN A ROW

DISLIKES:
NOT CAPTAINING
A TEAM TO WIN
100 IN A ROW

RISER

Esperanza
ENYO

AGE: 16
HAIR: BROWN
EYES: GREEN
HEIGHT:
5' 8" 173CM

TEARED EQUIPMENT:
EHECTHAL, HAND OF AIR, GUST BOOTS

FAVORITE FOODS:
PORK BELLY, BEEF RIBS, OX TAIL

LIKES:
FIGHTING, STRONG PEOPLE, HER MOTHER

DISLIKES:
COWARDS, STUDYING, NUTS & BERRIES, LOSER'S BALL

Wake
AVENOY

WAY

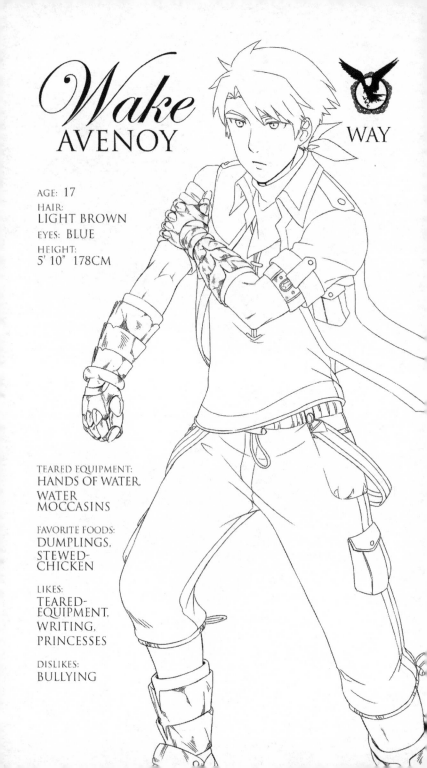

AGE: 17
HAIR:
LIGHT BROWN
EYES: BLUE
HEIGHT:
5' 10" 178CM

TEARED EQUIPMENT:
HANDS OF WATER.
WATER
MOCCASINS

FAVORITE FOODS:
DUMPLINGS.
STEWED-
CHICKEN

LIKES:
TEARED-
EQUIPMENT,
WRITING,
PRINCESSES

DISLIKES:
BULLYING

Shine

RACHEL
AVENOY

AGE: 23
HAIR: BLONDE
EYES: BLUE
HEIGHT: 5' 8" 172CM

TEARED EQUIPMENT:
HAND OF THE SUN,
SLIPPERS OF THE SUN

FAVORITE FOODS:
SWEETS,
CREAMS,
DESSERTS,

LIKES:
TEAR MEMORIES,
ANIMALS,
KIDS,
PAINTING,
NAPTIME

DISLIKES:
CRUELTY

SENSE

Arthur
BANNISTER JR.

AGE: 16
HAIR: BROWN
EYES: LIGHT BROWN
HEIGHT: 5' 5" 165CM

TEARED EQUIPMENT:
GREEN HANDS OF FATE,
GREEN BOOTS

FAVORITE FOODS:
APPLES

LIKES:
LEARNING THINGS,
DISCOVERING THINGS,
KNOWING THINGS,
SHARING THINGS

DISLIKES:
BEING LAST,
PEOPLE WHO BLAME OTHERS

Brother
MONSTER

BRUN

AGE: 17
HAIR: DARK RED
EYES: BLUE
HEIGHT: 6' 5" 195CM

TEARED EQUIPMENT:
HANDS OF FLAME

FAVORITE FOODS:
NOODLES,
PICKLED
PEPPERS,
SPICY SAUCES

LIKES:
HEALING,
COOKING,
PRAYING,
READING

DISLIKES:
VIOLENCE,
ARROGANCE,
IGNORANCE

Poe

AGE: 16
HAIR: PLATINUM BLUE
EYES: PALE BLUE
HEIGHT: 5' 4" 163CM

TEARED EQUIPMENT:
BATON,
ICE BOOTS

FAVORITE FOODS:
HOT
CHOCOLATE
CHICKEN SOUP

LIKES:
MUSIC,
TALKING

DISLIKES:
AUTHORITY,
PAINFUL-
MEMORIES

IEIRI
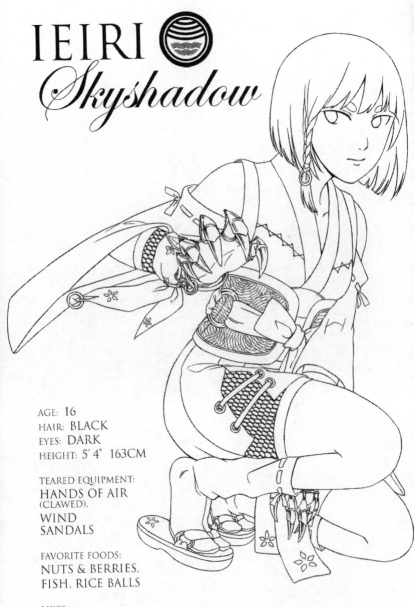
Skyshadow

AGE: 16
HAIR: BLACK
EYES: DARK
HEIGHT: 5' 4" 163CM

TEARED EQUIPMENT:
HANDS OF AIR
(CLAWED),
WIND
SANDALS

FAVORITE FOODS:
NUTS & BERRIES,
FISH, RICE BALLS

LIKES:
THOSE WHO DREAM UNDENIABLY

DISLIKES:
INCOMPETENCE, LIARS

If you are reading this right here, right now — it proves with beyond a doubt that dreams really do come true.

Thank You!

Made in the USA
Middletown, DE
11 October 2016